Nakobee

A Mirror Gate Chronicle
By
TJ Boyer and
Elizabeth Ajamie-Boyer

Nakobee

(A Mirror Gate Chronicle)

Copyright © 2017 by Timothy Boyer & Elizabeth Ajamie-Boyer

Authors: TJ Boyer & Elizabeth Ajamie-Boyer

Website: https://mirrorgatechronicles.wordpress.com
Email: tjboyer.author@gmail.com

Cover art:

First paperback printing, 2018

ISBN: # 9781980452867

Rev: 1

Other books in the Mirror Gate Chronicles

The Quest
The Journey
The Rescue
The War

The Reluctant King
Invasion

Vanished

Nakobee

The World Rednog and the Thorns
Nogar the Golden Dragon

Atrell

Books by Elizabeth Ajamie-Boyer

Memories of War
Freedom to the Prisoners
My Soul Awaits

All books are available on Kindle and Amazon

Email: storiesbytjboyer@yahoo.com
Web page: www.mirrorgatechronicles.wordpress.com

Prologue

As Shaméd appeared in the room, the people screamed. When Téral saw him, he ran over and wrapped his arms around Shaméd's waist.

"It is ok Téral. Go back to your mother." He turned to Nakobee and said, "Nakobee, I have seen the events. Do you want to explain what you were thinking?"

"Lord Shaméd, as you asked I have been watching the woman and her child. I saw her two days ago with a bruise on the side of her face. Today, I was witness to it happening. Her brother has been beating her. He was hitting her out behind the house today. I stepped in to stop him. I thought if I am here to watch her, then you would not want any harm to befall her or the child. He tried to hit me, but I pushed his hand away. Then he drew a knife and attacked me. I did not want to hurt him, so I grabbed him by the wrist and neck. I took the knife and tossed him aside. I thought he would stop after that so I turned to see if the woman was ok, and to tell her who I was. That was when he shot me with a crossbow. My reflexes just took over, and I threw the knife. I am sorry, Lord Shaméd, for killing him."

Shaméd saw the small bolt in Nakobee's back was not bleeding. Since it was still there, it meant Nakobee was unable to reach it.

"Why did you block yourself inside? Why not just return?"

"You told me to stay and watch over the woman and boy. I could not leave. They might be harmed by the city guards."

"Then here is what I want all of you to do. Nakobee, take them to the world room. Terrine, I want you all to go with him. You will be safe. You and Téral will come and live with me. The others can stay if they want. If they do not want to stay, we will help them return to their own families, or find a safe place for them. Nakobee, when

4

Reklan is ready, take them through. I am going out there now."

Shaméd disappeared.

Entering the infirmary, Shaméd saw Nakobee sitting on a table. The arrow had been removed and he had a bandage wrapped around his chest. Shaméd walked over.

"Nakobee, I want to thank you for what you did."

Nakobee tried to stand, but the nurse who was working on him poked him with a needle.

"Sit down. I'm not through with you. Shaméd does not care if you jump up when he is talking to you. He is not like those stupid bureaucrats."

"That is correct. Let her finish caring for you. I have something to do right now, but I will be back to see you later."

Shaméd looked at the nurse and asked, "Did the arrow do much damage?"

The nurse said, "He will be fine. The bolt was mostly in his jerkin. Only half the tip was in his back. No real damage was done. If he wasn't so big it might have been worse. He will be a little sore, but no real damage was done."

Turning, he walked over to Téral who was being looked at by Doctor T.

"How is he?" asked Shaméd.

"The boy is fine. He could use a good meal, but otherwise he is fine. The women, like the boy, just need some rest and food. Where were they?"

Shaméd nodded toward Nakobee, "You will have to get that information from Nakobee. If you are done with the boy, I would like to take him and his mother to meet with Nogar."

"Like, I said he is fine. After the meeting you need to feed him."

"We all will eat as soon as the others are released."

Reaching over Shaméd picked the boy up and stood him on the floor.

"Let's go for a walk. I want both of you to meet someone."

Shaméd came into the infirmary. Nakobee was still sitting on the bed. He walked over to him.

"Nakobee, I would like to talk with you now, if you have a minute."

"I'm ready to leave. Do you want to talk in the hallway?"

"That will be fine. Doctor T, Nogar has asked to be informed on the health of the guests. He asked me to contact Jane and Elizabeth to set up rooms for them."

Looking around the room at the women, he said, "All of you will be guests of King Nogar. You can stay here until we find your families or you decide where you want to go."

"We will contact Jane and Elizabeth, and make sure they are settled in," Doctor T said as he motioned to one of his nurses.

Shaméd and Nakobee left the room. In the hallway they walked a few feet from the door and stopped.

"Tell me how that man was able to shoot you in the back."

Looking around, Nakobee did his best to stand straighter.

"As I said, I stopped him from hitting Terrine, and was in the process of leading her and the boy to safety. I didn't see the crossbow. He must have had it hidden. I had the gate to the alley open and was about telling her to leave, when he shot me. I am sorry that I killed him."

"I don't care that he is dead. I'm just not happy you got shot. Why were you not wearing your armor?"

"I don't like the feel of metal on my skin. I'm bigger than most men and there is no armor available in my size."

Shaméd looked at Nakobee. He could see he was correct. Nakobee was twice as wide as he was. Only armor made for an ogre would fit him, and it was hard to come by.

"Until we get you armor, you will wear my cloak whenever you are off-world."

Taking off his cloak, Shaméd handed it to him.

"I cannot take this. It is yours and only one of the Thirty-Six can wear it."

"I do not need it, but you do. I have my dragon armor and if you are going off-world with me, you will need the protection. Keep it, and again thank you for protecting Terrine and Téral. I have to get back. Could you do me one more favor?"

"What do you need me to do?"

"Talk with Elizabeth for me. Let her know Terrine and Téral will be staying here longer than the others, and they are to have their own room. Now I really must go. I will try and come back tomorrow."

Nakobee stood watching Shaméd walk away. He remembered what his sister had said to him, and his words to her.

"I'm sure Lord Shaméd will live. I don't think there is anything on this world that could kill him. He has lived for almost two thousand years. I will remind him that he is to protect you."

"I don't need protecting."

Nakobee stood there and grinned as Shaméd started walking.

Nakobee said, "He is still trying to protect me. Kaila would be happy."

Chapter One

Balls of fire hurtled down upon the village, lighting the sky like the mid-day sun. The deafening screams and the eruptions of the fire balls crashing into buildings, lurched those sleeping out of their beds.

More explosions came quickly after the first fire ball. Buildings burst into flames and people staggered out into the road, confused in the darkness. The old ones tried to catch and calm the children who were running and screaming. The village warriors, men and women, were grabbing their weapons and running toward the attackers.

Keely ran to Nakobee. She grabbed his hand as he reached for his spear.

"No, my son you will not fight. You will take the children to safety."

He looked into his mother's eyes.

"I want to fight beside my father."

Keely smiled at her son. She was so proud of him. She again saw he was almost as tall as his father. Soon he would be a mighty warrior.

"Your father and I know what is in your heart, but your first obligation is to protect the young. Gather as many of the children as you can. Take them to the caves and go through to the river. Once there, get into the boats, and go down the river to the village Ondo. Find your grandparents. You must protect the children, but most of all, you must protect your sister."

He looked at his sister. She was standing there in front of the other children. She was young, only thirteen years old, but she showed no fear. He knew that one day she would be a great leader like their mother.

"Yes, Mother, I will protect them."

Turning, he raised his spear and called out, "Come, out the back and head to the cave."

Kaila turned and led the other children out the back of the building.

Keely stood, and with her sword in hand, headed out the front to fight beside her husband.

As Nakobee led the children to the cave, he felt he would never see his parents again. But single-mindedly, he gathered more children as they went toward the cave. They left the village and entered the trees. As they went by, he counted how many were with him. There were only thirty in the group. He saw that most were ten to twelve years old, and two were maybe five. There were five boys and one girl he knew to be the same age as his sister. They were part of the ten children all born in the same month. The ten were born one day after the other. Kaila was the first, the twins, Lea and Leo were last.

The Shaman said it was an omen that there were five boys and five girls born in the same month. He said it would bring great power to the land. Nakobee realized there were only seven of them there two were females. He hoped the others and more of the children would find their way to the cave.

None of the children were as old as Nakobee. Nakobee's mind was filled with anger.

"Only thirty out of a couple of hundred. I should have searched more."

He stopped and looked back at the village. He saw the fires. Every building was an inferno. He could hear screaming. The fighting continued throughout the village. He knew there was no safe way for him to go back and search. He turned back toward the caves and continued to run.

Nakobee stopped when they reached the cave. Once more he looked back in the direction of the village. Kaila stood at the front of the cave. He heard her yelling at the children.

"Keep going all the way to the river. We must reach the boats."

There was a shriek. Nakobee turned and saw five enemy warriors. They came running out from behind boulders near the cave and they were heading for the children. Kaila stood there with her small sword. The twins, Lea and Leo, and another boy stood with her. Each was holding his sword, ready to protect their future Queen.

Nakobee ran at the men heading for his sister. His spear entered the back of one. As the man fell, Nakobee jumped over the body pulling the spear out. He hit the next one with the end of the spear, knocking him to the ground. One of the boys moved in and stabbed the enemy as he rolled on the ground.

As Nakobee continued his forward momentum, he reached out and grabbed the arm of the third man. Twisting him around, he smashed his fist into the man's face. He saw teeth and blood spew out as the man's head twisted around. The man went limp, fell back, his head smashing onto a rock when he hit the ground.

The last two men drew closer to Kaila and the boys. The first man swung his spear hitting Kaila in the arm. The shaft hit her, pushing her back. Leo caught her as she fell. He was dragging her out of the way when one of the men stabbed him. As Leo fell, Lea and Kaila drove their swords into their foe. As the man died, the last man moved in.

Nakobee let out his tribe's war cry. The man stopped and turned to face Nakobee. Nakobee slowly circled, moving his weapon at the ready, so he was between the man and his sister. He stood there looking at him. The man glared at them.

Nakobee saw that he was not a big man, none of the enemy were. Nakobee looked at him and glanced at the dead men. He thought except for their beards they could pass as children. The one in front of him was very skinny. If he stood straight, he might come to Nakobee's chest.

The man screamed and ran at the boy standing to Nakobee's right. The boy ducked under the man's sword and drove his own into the man's chest.

They stood there looking at the five dead men. They had stopped them. Kaila bent down and was helping Leo with his wound. Nakobee looked at them.

"You were all very brave. Each one of you fought like true warriors."

He looked at each of the older boys.

"Keep Kaila and the other children safe. I will meet you at the boats. If I'm not there when the sun rises, take them south to Ondo."

He started to turn, but Kaila reached out taking hold of his arm.

"You cannot go back. Mother said you were to protect us and take us to grandmother."

He looked down at his sister's face. *How could one so young, be so wise?*

"You are already showing you will one day be a great leader like our mother. I will do as she and you say. For now, that is. When you and the others are safe, I will make those that did this pay."

Chapter Two

Sword Master Zale stood with Queen Kailee and First Sword Kouly. They were watching the children playing in the river as it flowed unhurried by the village. There were men out in the deeper part of the river fishing. A group of men to the left were mending nets.

Sword Master Zale gestured toward the children.

"Who is the young man watching the children? I have never seen him before. Is he the new recruit?"

Kouly answered, "Yes. He is the one I contacted you about. His name is Nakobee. He is our grandson. His family lived in the High River Province."

Sword Master Zale looked at him, then back at Kouly.

"He is a large lad. How old is he?"

Kouly smiled as he stood staring at the children.

"He takes after his father. His father's people are very large and they are great warriors. He is only fifteen."

"Do you want to send him in for training?" asked Sword Master Zale.

Queen Kailee spoke, "Yes. But I also would like help in a small matter."

"What can I do for you?"

"My daughter and her husband, as well as the people from their village, are missing. Their village was destroyed last month. Nakobee, along with those children, are the only ones who survived, that we know of. The village was completely burned to the ground.

We searched the ruins and found many bodies, some women, but mostly men. I did not find my daughter. We found Natook, her husband. He was dead, along with many of his warriors. It looks like those they did not kill, they took captive."

"What would you like from me?" asked Sword Master Zale.

"First, I would like Nakobee and the rest of the children to be taken to Rednog. I want them to be taught how to fight like your warriors. That way they will be able to defend their land against this new enemy.

I would also like Kaila to be trained, not only how to fight, but also how be a leader. All the children must be returned in five of our years."

Sword Master Zale looked at the children. The one called Nakobee stood there like a statue guarding them.

"Do you know who attacked them?"

"We have no idea. We found none of the enemy's bodies. The last request is this: we would like one of your people to come and help us find out who did this."

"I have told you we do not interfere with the worlds we visit. If your counsel would consider joining our coalition, then we would be able to help. Until they will, our laws don't allow it."

Queen Kailee turned to look at Sword Master Zale.

She said, "I met with the Counsel of the Queens after the attack. I asked them to let you and your people come here. They reminded me that King Nogar and you have been asking us to join this coalition for the last eight generations.

When King Nogar came here so many years ago, he told our ancestors he would help us if we joined him. They told him no. They did agree to permit our orphans to go to your world to be trained.

When my mother became Queen, I saw you come here to take our orphans away. You asked the same question again. She said no. Every time you come, you ask us to join you.

When I became Queen, you came again. I, and the other Queens, were amazed because you had not aged at all. You asked your question, and we said no, again. To answer your question, they said this, 'Why should we join people not willing to help those in need without first getting something from them besides their orphans?'"

Sword Master Zale looked at her and smiled.

"We have been helping you, by caring for, and educating your unwanted children. Then we return them to you with advanced skills. Have you not benefitted from this? Have you not allowed them to strengthen your armies and teach your warriors new skills?"

"My people have. But most of the other villages still treat them as orphans," Queen Kailee said.

Sword Master Zale pursed his lips and nodded his head and then said, "I will talk with Nogar to see if we can send people. I'm not sure if the council will approve. However, I'm sure Nogar will.

Now that we have settled the matter of the children, what happened to their village?"

Queen Kailee looked at Kouly. Kouly faced him and said, "That is what has the counsel worried. Natook's warriors were fearsome and some of the bravest I have ever seen. Their village was over two thousand strong."

"The force that attacked must have been formidable. How were they attacked?" asked Sword Master Zale.

"We do not know. We asked the dwarfs, elves, trolls, and the other tribes if they knew anything. They all said they didn't. We have searched for clues and have also found nothing. We only found ashes; everything was burned to the ground.

The attack came at night. When it started, Nakobee said Keely, his mother, told him to take as many of the children as he could gather and leave.

14

Out of a village of two-thousand men, women, and children, he could only gather thirty children. He took the children through the cave to the river. They took some of the boats and escaped."

Sword Master Zale looked at the children and felt a twinge in his chest.

"I can take them today. I will send word to you as soon as I know about someone coming to help."

Kouly looked at him and nodded his head in agreement.

Queen Kailee spoke, "Please take him and the rest of the children. Train them all to be soldiers. As I said, we would like all of them returned within five of our years so they can join us again. Kaila is a princess and will be a leader one day. Treat her as one of the others. She knows her destiny, as do they all."

"I understand what you are saying. I will talk with Nogar. I'm sure he will send someone to help. As for the lad and the children, have you told them where they are going?"

"Yes, they all know."

"Then we should go over so you can introduce them to me."

They walked over, Nakobee turned and bowed to Queen Kailee and greeted Kouly.

"Grandfather. Is this the man?"

Nakobee looked at the stranger standing by his grandfather. Nakobee noted he was not a tall man. He stood only a little taller than his grandfather. What surprised Nakobee the most was the color of his skin. He was not dark like Nakobee's people. He had never seen a man with such fair skin. He heard that most of the elves were fair skinned, but this man did not have the look of an elf. His hair was long and straight, its color was a brown and white.

He wore leather that looked like the Crocodes that lived in the rivers, with their scales and rough skin. He had a metal sword on one side of his hip and a long knife on the other. Whoever this man was, he must be rich to have such metal.

As Sword Master Zale looked into the eyes of the young man, he thought, *"This boy is even bigger up close."*

Kouly looked at him and the others as they gathered closer. His expression showed deep affection for them.

"Yes. You and the others will go with him to train. Learn all you can. Your sister will be taught as well so she may grow to be as great a leader as your mother."

Sword Master Zale looked down and saw a young girl standing beside the young man. He looked at her, then up at the boy. Both had deep blue eyes. It was a striking contrast to the brown and green that the rest of their people had. Their skin was as dark. Nakobee had tribal scars and tattoos on his chest and arms. Most were from the trials he would have gone through as he matured.

The children of this world went through many trials as they grew to adulthood. The young girl had only two scars on her left arm. Both looked as if they happened only a few days ago.

"Hello. I'm Sword Master Zale. You are Nakobee, and who is this beautiful young lady with you?"

She did not move, but stood her ground behind Nakobee. She looked up at him with curiosity.

"She is my sister and her name is Kaila."

"I see. May I ask how you hurt yourself, young lady?"

"She was cut during our escape. Most of the children were hurt. I fought off those that came after us. I'm only sorry that I could not have stayed and fought with my father."

Sword Master Zale looked at the young man.

16

"My lad, I'm sure you would have been a great help to him. I also believe he is more proud that you were able to save your sister and these children.

From what I was told, you and the little ones would be dead or taken if you had not done what your mother had told you to do."

Sword Master Zale turned and looked at Kouly.

"You said you did not find any enemy bodies."

"We did not. We found blood where Nakobee said he had slain those that followed him. But the only bodies were of our people."

He looked back at Nakobee.

"You said you fought off the attackers. Can you tell me what they looked like?"

"They were scrawny, ugly, weak things. They were not tall or very strong. They used clubs and spears and were hairy. They were human, but they looked more animal than man. I do not understand how they could have beaten my father and his warriors."

"Did you see or hear anything that was not normal?"

Kouly stepped in front of his grandson.

"Why are you asking him these questions? He was fighting to save the lives of the children. He did not have time to look around."

Sword Master Zale looked at Kouly then back at the children.

"This is something he will have to learn to do. Whenever you are in battle, you must look and listen for anything that is not normal. Now lad, I want you to close your eyes. Relax and think about that night. Did you see or hear anything as you were leaving?"

Nakobee closed his eyes and tilted his head up. Kaila did the same, as well as the rest of the children.

After a minute he opened them.

"I heard whistling. Like a screaming sound. When I looked up I saw balls of flames coming down from the sky."

Leo opened his eyes and spoke, "Yes, I saw them as well. There was one that hit near our home before you came to get us."

Nakobee looked at the young boy who stood near him. Kaila looked up at Sword Master Zale. Several of the other children said they also saw the balls of fire as well as heard the whistling.

"Was the enemy tossing stars down at us?" asked Kaila.

Sword Master Zale knelt down. Kouly had said she was thirteen and Nakobee was fifteen. She looked to be only ten years old. He saw in her face neither fear nor worry. She was indeed one of these warriors.

"All of you remembered well. As for their tossing stars at you? I do not think so. I do think they found a way to toss fireballs."

He looked at Kouly and said, "It would appear that someone on this world has invented catapults."

"There was also loud chanting. I heard the voices as we went into the cave." said Nakobee.

The expression on Sword Master Zale's face went somber.

"Lad, if you heard chanting then we need to tell Nogar right away."

He looked at Kouly, "I need to return. If they are ready, I will take them now."

"They are ready."

Kouly looked at his grandchildren. His mind raced. He knew he might never see them again. He could only hope they would return in the five years as he asked. The children who had left his world before this always returned after twenty years. Most who knew them were very old or dead when they came back.

"Both of you learn and be brave. I hope to see you soon."

Sword Master Zale reached out and Kouly took hold of his forearm. Sword Master Zale smiled.

"Do not worry Kouly, they will be returned in five years as you asked. Come children, we are leaving."

Sword Master Zale started walking and Nakobee stepped beside him and asked. "How will we travel?"

Sword Master Zale stopped and looked at the children.

"What you are about to see may frighten you. Do not be afraid. Be the brave warriors that I know all of you are. Nakobee, you go first, then Kaila you follow. Take two steps this way. You will feel a slight tingle, then you will see a friend of mine."

They took their steps slowly and disappeared. One at a time the rest of the children came forward, not one of them showing any fear. When the last one was gone, Sword Master looked at Kouly, "I will return."

Chapter Three

When Sword Master Zale arrived, he saw there were two young men and one young woman standing there with the children, as well as Reklan who was working the Mirror.

"I see that everyone has arrived. We will now take you to your rooms where you will be staying. Please follow me."

He, the two young men, and the young woman led them out of the room and down the hallway. After a few minutes of walking they arrived at a door. It was the door to the room where they would live. One of the young men opened it, stepped in, and held the door open. Sword Master Zale walked forward and stood by the door.

"All of you will stay here. Your training begins tomorrow. I know this is all very strange. You just have to remember why you are here. You are here to learn how to fight. You will return home to avenge your people and to fight those who attacked your home. It will take time. Time and hard work. The hard work I know all of you can handle. I have seen your people. They are mighty warriors. The length of time it takes will be difficult. You will learn how to be patient. You will learn how to fight better than any warrior on your world. You will also learn what battles to fight. Learning when to fight is the hardest lesson for a warrior. You will learn how to make that choice."

Sword Master Zale pointed to the man next to him.

"This man is Allen, the other is Ted. They will be with you until you leave. They are the group leaders and teachers for the boys. The young woman's name is Clara. She will be the group leader and teacher for the girls. If any of you have questions or needs anything, ask them. If they cannot help you, send word for me. I will come as soon as I can and try to answer your questions. They will provide you with clothes and other necessities. They will show you where everything is and how to use everything here. Remember, if you have any questions or concerns, speak with them."

Nakobee looked at Allen, Ted and Clara. They were not as old as Sword Master Zale, but they were older than he. Sword Master Zale was the first white skinned human he had ever seen. He thought it strange that these people who could do such wonders never got out in the sun.

Sword Master Zale turned and left. Allen stood there and smiled at the children.

"Hello children. I will get all of your names as the day progresses. If you would all follow me, I will show you where the washrooms are, and how to use them."

He stepped forward and they moved back making an opening. As he walked through they all turned and followed. In the room, they walked by beds and cabinets on either side of the room. As he stepped through another doorway, he stopped. He stood in a small room. It was ten feet by twenty feet. There were three other doors, one straight across form the one they just came through. And two others on the other wall.

"These walls are for privacy. As you can see, unlike the main walls, these are wood. The castle where we are is carved into the mountain. Most of the rooms are inside the mountain. There will be many rooms where there will be wooden walls. As you can see most of the wood walls have carvings. Please be careful with them. If you ever get the desire to carve on a wall, please ask before doing so. We encourage those who like to carve, but we do not want to undo any carvings that are already here."

He raised his arm and pointed to the right.

"The room on the right is the same as the one we just left. The boys can take one side, the girls the other. You decide. The washrooms are through those doors. The boys get one, the girls get the other. They are the same, so it does not matter which you choose. I will let you decide who get which one.

Outside of these rooms, there are washrooms that are marked for males and females. I will show all of you the marks. Please do not enter the wrong room.

Now follow me and I will show you how everything works."

Leading the way, he entered the door on the left. The two doors were five feet apart. As the children stepped in, they all stopped and looked at their reflections on the walls.

Allen stood there and smiled as he pointed.

"This is a mirror. I know on your world you have them. I do not believe you have any this large. Each washroom has one. There are also showers. This way and I will show you the rest of the room."

Allen led them to each location in the room, showing them how each device worked. The handle with the blue mark for cold water and the handle with the red mark for hot. The little children were the most impressed. They kept pressing the buttons making the water disappear down the drains.

A man called out from the door, "Allen, their belongings and bedding are here."

Allen turned and held up his hand.

"If all of you will now follow me, we can return to the other room. There you will pick out your clothing, personal hygiene supplies, and bedding."

When they reached the room, they saw carts with stacks of bedding, clothes and other items. The children stood there looking at everything and at the five people standing nearby.

Nakobee looked at them, then over at Allen.

"We know what most of these are. But why is there so much of everything?"

"We did not have your sizes. You can pick and choose whatever you like. Later as each of you grow, you will be able to get larger clothing. I will show you what the other items are for. Now all of you go pick out what you would like."

The children moved slowly at first. As they touched the items the five people moved among them to help. The two females, as well as Clara, gathered the twelve girls together and took them to one side. The three men moved toward the boys to help them.

As they picked out what they wanted, the door opened and four more people came in. Two were elves, the other two were ogres. The children stopped and watched as they entered the room.

The children were staring. Kaila walked closer to the ogres. She saw one was a female the other was a male. Kaila stood in front of the male. He was tall, but not as tall as the female. His skin was a darker green than hers, and his tusks were longer.

"What are you?"

The male ogre looked down at her.

"If you are asking me my name, it is Lau. If you are asking me what race I am, I'm an ogre."

Allen moved close to Kaila and touched her shoulder.

"We know you do not have ogres on your world. This is your first introduction to one of many races that live here."

She looked up at Lau.

"May I touch your skin?"

Nakobee called out, "Kaila, do not be rude."

Lau gave a soft laugh.

"It is not rude. The child wants to see if my color comes off. Go ahead and touch. It does not come off."

Kaila reached out as Lau held out his arm. She ran her hand across his arm.

"Your skin is soft. I love the color and the different shades. Where are your scars? Are you not a warrior?"

The female ogre grunted and Lau glared at her. Then he looked down at Kaila, and said, "I have been trained as a warrior, I am, however in training to be an engineer."

"That is because he is so small. Look at his hands. They are like a young female's."

Lau stood straight, his eyes squinted as he gave a low growl.

Kaila looked at the female ogre and smiled.

"What is your name?"

"I'm called Gala"

Kaila nodded her head at Lau.

"You like him. Are you going to be his mate?"

Nakobee yelled, "Kaila that is enough. Leave them alone. Come back here and pick out the things you need. They do not have time for your games."

The female ogre shook her head and looked surprised, and asked, "Do you read minds? It is forbidden to read minds without permission."

Kaila looked up at her and said, "I do not read minds. I can tell by the way you look at him that you like him. Why have you not told him?"

The humans that were in the room were smiling. Allen stepped between Lau and Kaila.

"You should return and finish picking out what you need."

Turning, Allen spoke to the others, "Please set the food and drinks on the table. I will have them removed when the children are finished."

They set everything down and headed to the door. As Lau stepped passed Gala, he grunted, she grunted back.

Chapter Four

Kaila jerked awake, the dream still vivid in her mind. As she sat there in her bed, cold chills raced through her body, and sweat ran down her face. She looked around the room. She remembered where she was. She and the other children were on the world Rednog. They were safe. The demons from her dreams could not get her here. At least, she hoped that was true.

Shameka and Pamilla came over. They sat on the edge of her bed. Shameka moved closer and slowly reached over, putting her arms around Kaila and held her tight. She was afraid she would be yelled at for touching the future Queen. Kaila closed her eyes and relaxed from the touch.

Shameka asked, "Kaila, are you all right? We heard you scream."

"I'm fine. It was just a nightmare."

The two girls looked at each other. Shameka looked at Kaila and said, "Was the nightmare about the attack on our village?"

Kaila looked at her, lowering her eyes said, "Yes."

"We both have had the same dream."

Kaila looked at them and said, "Do not tell Nakobee that I had this dream."

"Do not worry, everyone here has had bad dreams about what happened. The little ones more than the rest of us. I think the boys have had them as well. They just won't admit it."

Kaila looked at them and smiled. She moved and Shameka let her go.

"Thank you both. I'm sorry I woke you. Did I wake any others?"

"No, we only heard you because we are in the beds next to you."

"I will be fine now. Go back to sleep. Again, thank you for being with me."

They moved back to their beds, Kaila laid down. It took some time, but she finally fell back to sleep.

Normally when children came to Rednog for training they were split up. Nakobee and the children were kept together, because they were there to be trained in combat and then returned.

Kaila would train alongside the children, with the exception of four hours a day when she would go to a classroom and learn diplomacy.

Rednog does not have a true night, so a time table was created for them. The world where the children came from had a twenty five hour day, eight day week and an eleven month year. Their training was set up for ten hours. Then they were taken to the rooms so they could prep for their night.

Weapons training started at an early age in their village. When a child turned five they would begin training on how to use the sling. When they turned ten, they would start training with the spear, and progress to other weapons such as the sword.

The first morning after they arrived, Allen stood in the doorway and called out.

"Good morning, everyone. Wake up and let's get started. Gather your things and wash your faces. When you are all dressed, we will go get breakfast."

It did not take long for them to be ready. Clara had entered the door to the girl's side and was doing the same routine. When they were all dressed and ready, Clara and Allen led them out into the hallway and down to the dining hall.

As they entered, the children let out a small gasping sound. The room was large. It was full of tables and chairs. They saw humans, elves, dwarfs, and other races they did not know. Some were walking with trays of food and others were sitting and eating. None of them looked at them as the children entered.

When they were all in the room Allen stopped them. He raised his hand.

"This is the dining hall. This is where you will eat most of your meals."

Nakobee stepped closer and asked, "I have a question. The children that are not of age, where will they be kept?"

"During the day, they will be with other human children of the same age. They will learn to read and write. Every night they will return to your rooms. When they turn five they will join in the training. Is that what you were asking?"

"Yes, thank you. Why will they learn how to read and write?"

"Allen smiled, "All of you will be taught how to read and write."

"That will not be necessary, only Kaila needs to learn how to read and write."

"Everyone will learn. It is our way and you will learn the benefit as time goes on. Kaila is to be trained in diplomacy and leadership. I understand she is going to be one of your leaders, correct?"

"My sister will take our mother's place if we do not find her. Two of the girls will be trained with Kaila."

"That will not be a problem. Do you know who they will be?"

"They are Shameka and Pamilla."

Allen smiled and said, "Then tell them to be ready to go with her. Now let me show all of you how to get food."

He raised his voice, "Everyone please follow me."

They followed and he showed them where to get trays and where the food line started. They had many choices. Most of what the children saw turned their heads and they made nasty sounds. After getting what they wanted, they all found tables and sat.

When they were finished eating they were shown where to put the empty trays. As they stood in the hallway, Allen looked over the children.

"Your meals will be here. Remember how you got here. If you forget, just ask someone or if at any time you get lost, go to one of these and press this button, and ask for help."

Allen had moved over to the wall and stood next to a small mirror. He pressed the button and a voice spoke.

"How may I help you?"

"I'm showing the children how to use you."

"Very good, if you need anything just ask."

"Once it answers, you can ask for help."

Of course we will try to always eat together, but there may be times when some of you will come here alone. Now we will head to the training hall."

Chapter Five

The first couple of weeks went by quickly. The younger children were taught basic fighting forms on how to handle a spear. The older children who already had some training, were observed and shown how to improve on what they knew.

The older children were given swords. Every day for two weeks they trained with their spears and swords. On the third week, they began hand to hand combat training.

They were all standing in the training hall lined up waiting for the morning instructions.

Allen stood there looking at the children. Lau came in, walked over, and stood with him.

"Nakobee, please come here."

When he stood in front of Allen, he looked into his eyes.

"Nakobee, since you are the biggest male, I have asked Lau to come and help teach you how to fight. I was told by your grandfather that you are very strong. Lau will make sure you do not lose any strength during training."

"How would I lose my strength?"

"Someone your size will always pull their punches with those they know. You would not want to hurt one of your friends. That is why Lau is here to show you that no matter how hard you hit him, you cannot cause him harm."

"Is this a goal? You want me to learn how to hit so hard that I could hurt someone as big as him?"

"You are here to learn how to hit someone, so that after you hit them they do not want to face you again. That is what you will learn."

Nakobee looked at him and at Lau who stood there staring straight. Nakobee nodded his head and returned to the others.

Allen looked at the group and said, "Now I want all of you to pair up and we will begin."

The rest of the day they learned how to stand and throw punches. The next day they spent two hours with sword, two hours with spear, and three hours learning how to fight hand-to-hand. This went on for the next six months.

On the seventh month, those who showed skills with the sword changed to three hours in training. Nakobee was one of them.

After one year Nakobee was the best swordsman of all the children. Leo and Lea were the runner's up. In hand-to-hand combat, no one could take Nakobee down except Lau, but by the middle of the second year, Lau was hard pressed to succeed in doing so.

The second year, each of them were given bows and arrows. They spent four hours a day for the next year learning how to shoot them. By the third year, they started learning how to make bows and arrows.

The training went on for five years. Each year they got stronger and others would be brought in to fight and train with them.

Midway through the fifth year, Allen met with Sword Master Zale.

"I do not know what more these children can learn. Even when they are not on the field they practice. After the first week, they would sleep six hours and then practice in their room. How much longer are we going to keep them here? Nakobee is asking every day when they will return home."

"I have heard his request. I'm going to send Shaméd to work with him. He has not lost a fight in a year. Even Lau is hard-pressed when fighting him."

"What can Shaméd do?"

Sword Master Zale smiled.

"You know what Shaméd can do."

The next day they were standing in the training room, getting ready to break for the mid-day meal.

Allen stood in front of them and spoke, "You all have come a long way from the children you were when you started. I have never been as proud of any warriors as I am of all of you.

As you know, many of those who have come here to practice with you, have said the same thing. Nakobee, you have proven you are the greatest warrior among your people."

They all cheered and those close to him slapped him on the shoulder and back.

"Now, I would like you to meet a friend of mine."

He turned as Shaméd walked in, stopping near the rack of swords.

"Everyone, this is Shaméd. He came here many years ago after his family was killed. Shaméd, I would like you to sword fight Nakobee. Pick a sword and meet me in the middle of the room.

Nakobee, please get a sword and join us. Everyone please make a circle."

Nakobee walked over and picked out a two handed sword. After checking the balance, he turned and entered the circle the others made.

Allen stood in the center with Shaméd. Nakobee walked over and stood in front of Shaméd, looking him straight in the eyes.

Nakobee was now twenty years old. He had grown several inches taller. During his training, he had become one of the best swordsmen, winning 90% of his matches.

Allen looked at them.

"The rules are simple, the first to score three points wins."

Stepping back, he raised his hand.

"Begin."

Nakobee slashed forward. Shaméd blocked. Nakobee went after him with a back slash and a jab. Both were blocked. Then he slashed and jabbed as he twisted around trying to get behind Shaméd.

As he stepped around, Shaméd blocked Nakobee's blade and tapped him on the head.

Allen yelled out, "Point."

They both stepped back and Nakobee stared at Shaméd. He shook his head. They raised their swords and Nakobee attacked. After three blocks Shaméd tapped his blade on Nakobee's chest.

"Point."

After calling out, Allen stepped forward.

"Nakobee, you do not have to go easy on him. Fight him, like you would Lau."

Allen stepped back. Nakobee looked at Shaméd and smiled. He rushed toward him, his sword swinging in every direction. Shaméd's blade blocked each blow. Shaméd took each strike with a smooth and precise step. After fifteen blocks, his blade slipped past and tapped Nakobee on the chest.

"Point and game. Shaméd wins."

Nakobee stepped back and looked at Shaméd.

"How did you do that? You never attacked. You just defended yourself, yet you were able to win. I do not understand."

Walking over to the sword rack, Shaméd put his blade away. Turning, he looked at Nakobee and grinned.

"Attacking is not always the best idea. Defense is sometimes a better offence. I, however, cheated."

"You cheated? How could you cheat?"

"I was reading your mind. Of course, I stopped after the first point. I learned how to read your moves. You broadcast every move before you make it. I can teach you how not to do that, if you would like."

"You can read my mind? I thought no one was allowed to do that here?"

"You are correct. Those that can, are encouraged to not read other's minds without the person's consent. That is why I said I told you."

Nakobee stood there looking at him.

"You can teach me how not to show my moves?"

Shaméd smiled and patted his shoulder.

"Yes, I can. I can do that and more. It is time to eat. We should go and get some food. You and I can talk about me training you as we eat."

They started walking out. As they reached the door, one of the swords fell off a hook. Shaméd raised his hand and without looking, the sword lifted from the floor, and floated back to the hook. After it was in place, those who saw what he did stood there staring. He stopped and looked at them.

"It is ok. You know magic is practiced on this world. I have been in training for a few years."

"How long does it take to learn how to do that?" Nakobee asked.

"At least two hundred years."

Shaméd stepped through the door and headed for the dining hall. The others slowly followed.

After that, Shaméd worked with Nakobee four hours a day for two weeks. At the end, no one could read his attacks. Nakobee, as well as Shaméd, was pleased.

During the five years the children were on Rednog, they learned everything about warfare. The lessons they learned would make them better warriors on their home world. Only those that were trained here would be a match.

They were taught as many forms of fighting as there were races on Rednog. The children under ten were trained to the level permitted on their home world. The older children would continue their training once they were home and of age.

Each child craved to learn everything they could. No one had ever seen children so dedicated to learning how to be warriors.

The last year, the older children were each given a tree to be carved into their own canoe. It took each one three weeks to complete their canoe. When they were finished, each canoe was marked with their names and their new village name. There were twenty five canoes completed and ready to be shipped home.

The name for their new village was decided the week the last canoe was finished. They needed a new name since their original village had been destroyed. Two names were suggested, but only one received the majority vote, so they all agreed. Their new village name would be Keele. It was in honor of their former queen, and mother to Nakobee and Kaila, Queen Keely.

Three months before they were to leave and go home, Nakobee and a few of the older boys were put on guard duty. It was to teach them discipline and to show them more of Rednog.

Nakobee was on his last week when he was called to be the guard to three new recruits. He was to walk each one, one at a time to the council room where they would be interviewed.

His duty stopped the day he lost his temper with one of the young boys. He was about to hit him for what Nakobee said was his rudeness. He was dismissed from duty. It was fine with Nakobee because in three days he was going home. He had grown tired of doing this guard duty. It was boring.

Finally, the day came for them to return home. Five years had passed on their home world. Nakobee was now twenty years old and Kaila was eighteen. She would be able to be leader of her village, as soon as they had the people. The youngest of the thirty children were or would be ten that year. They would continue their training on their home world, along with the other children Nakobee would be gathering once they were back.

Allen and Sword Master Zale stood in the gate room with Nakobee and Kaila. The other children had all returned to their world through the Mirror.

Kaila smiled at them.

"It has been a wonderful experience being here. I, as well as the others, have learned so much. You have shown us many wonders. I know it will not be too long in our future when our world will join with yours."

Sword Master Zale smiled at her.

"We are glad to have been of help. We have given your leaders the reports on what we have found regarding those who attacked your village. I'm afraid it is not much. I'm not supposed to tell you, however, since you will soon be a leader of your own village, I will say this: they used magic. A strong and dark magic. Also, they have disappeared. There was no trace of them a mile from your village. We kept our people on your world searching, but in these past five years they have found nothing.

Also, we will send people to your village. They are rebuilding it according to the plans you drew up. If needed, more people will come and help. Lord Nogar, like you, wants your village built and completed as soon as possible. It looks like the two of you are the last, so I will bid you farewell. I will see you again soon."

They said their goodbyes and stepped through the mirror.

Chapter Six

The thirty children had through the mirror first. When the villagers saw them, they gathered around. The villagers saw how they were dressed. Each young warrior was dressed in leather armor. They each carried a spear, shield, and a metal sword. They made a circle and waited.

Nakobee arrived he stepped to the side. Kaila came through a minute after him. When she appeared, they all stood straight and called out her name.

"Kaila, Kaila, Kaila."

She raised her hand and they stopped. By doing what they had done, it showed the villagers that their future Queen had arrived. She walked forward with Nakobee by her side. Queen Kailee and her husband Kouly, Nakobee's and Kaila's grandfather and grandmother, met them.

Kailee stepped forward and looked down at Kaila. She saw Kaila wore the same armor and weapons as her warriors, only her armor was more ornate. She raised her hand in greeting.

"Welcome, future Queen Kaila. We welcome you and your tribe to our village. We offer you a place to rest until you are ready to return to your own home."

Kaila raised her hand in greeting.

"We thank you Queen Kailee, and we appreciate your offer of hospitality. We will only stay one day. Our boats will be here tomorrow morning, then we will head home as soon as we are loaded."

Kailee looked at her granddaughter and with sadness in her eyes nodded her head.

"Then we will celebrate your return tonight."

Turning she called out to a man nearby, "Taoke, start the preparation for a great feast. The children of my daughter have returned with her people. Tonight, we celebrate."

The people cheered and everyone ran to get things started. Of course, Queen Kailee and Kouly knew the day before that Nakobee, Kaila, and the others were returning. They had to make a show of the return for the people.

Taoke returned after stepping away for less than two minutes.

"My queen, things are being prepared. Would you like me to show the warriors where they will stay?"

"Yes, and make sure they are well taken care of."

As Taoke led the children, now warriors, away. Queen Kailee looked at her grandchildren and waved.

They followed her to her home. When they were inside, Queen Kailee turned and grabbed Kaila up into her arms hugging her and crying.

Nakobee and Kouly stood there waiting. They understood that they had to wait for the Queen's emotions to settle. Kailee may be a great queen, feared by many tribes, but she still was a grandmother who had lost her only child and now she was holding the only female child of her blood.

When she let her granddaughter go, she stood there looking at her.

"You have grown strong. I see in your eyes wisdom. It was a good thing sending you to the far land to learn their ways. Do you believe it will help us? Should we think about joining them?"

Kaila looked at her and asked, "If I may be so bold, may I speak freely?"

"Of course, Kaila. Speak freely and openly. I want to hear and know your true feeling about this other world and those who live there."

"I will speak to you as a future Queen then. Sending our children there is a great service to our people. I believe we should not only send the orphans, but the ones who want to learn to become warriors and even engineers.

We should also teach everyone how to read and write. What we learned there is far better than what we teach here. I have watched those in training to be engineers.

They learn how to make great bridges and machines that move water to wherever they want it. It is something we need to learn. You have seen how those who return are treated. They have no family, they are kept alone, and they never get promoted in our armies. They are lost soldiers who should have been teaching our soldiers from the first day of their return.

I may have over spoken, but this is what I feel must be said. And since you asked, I needed to tell you."

Queen Kailee looked at her granddaughter and at the two men who had heard her words.

"I did ask you the question, and I should have been prepared to have an answer that I might not have liked, or wanted to hear. I was hoping you would have said we should break all ties with them. Since your words are not what I was hoping, I will wait to see how your village and land does with this new way of thinking.

For tonight, you will be my granddaughter and everyone will celebrate. Now both of you go refresh yourselves and get ready for the feast."

That was their dismissal. Nakobee and Kaila turned and left the hut. A man was waiting for them, he led them to a large hut that held their people.

Inside she looked at them and called them together. When they were all there, she had them sit.

"When we get back to our village, people from Rednog will be will be there. They were sent to help rebuild our home. I was told they will send more, later. When it is completed they will leave. They do this because they want us to succeed. They help us in secret, because of the law.

No one must learn of their help. When our village is complete, we will send word out to all the villages. We will ask those that were taught on Rednog, that if they want to come live with us, they may do so; they will become part of our family. We will also send word out that all orphans and misfits that any village does not want, they may come to us to live.

We will teach and train every one of them. We will grow to be the biggest, largest army and people in the land. We will expand our land all the way around the great lake. One day we will learn who came and killed our parents. When we do, we will make them pay.

Their blood will soak the ground and their bodies will be burned and tossed in one grave. It shall be marked so as never to be touched.

Nakobee, when our boats arrive tomorrow make sure they are loaded and ready to leave. I want to go as soon as the last one is in the water."

The feast was indeed a real feast. There were three animals killed and roasted. Breads, fruits, and drink were served. The celebration lasted well into the night. It was late when they all went back to their hut to sleep.

Sunrise found Nakobee and Kaila and the thirty children standing down near the river waiting. As the sun rose to the second hour, the canoes began arriving.

One by one they appeared from nowhere and slid out on the shore of the river, gliding down into the water. The villagers who were there saw and wondered at the great feat.

When the last one arrived, packages also began arriving. Soon nothing more came, and Sword Master Zale stepped through. He walked toward Nakobee and Kaila.

"Good morning. I suppose you had a great time last night and are ready to head home."

Kaila smiled.

"Yes, we are in a hurry to see what is left of our home. We are also thankful for the offer from King Nogar. We will be in his debt for what he is giving us."

"King Nogar told me everything he has given was given without any obligation. It is a gift from a friend to a friend. He has hopes that what you will be doing will make your land grow and become strong."

"It will. We learned much from you and your people. We have made plans and are confident that we will succeed."

Sword Master Zale looked at both of them.

"Before I leave, I should tell you those that were to be sent to help, arrived a month ago. They have cleaned the village areas and started building your new homes. By the time you arrive to your home, Kaila, the main barracks will be completed. The walls and the rest of the buildings you drew, should be completed within a month.

Also, the council has agreed that Allen, Clara, Lau, and Gala can come and live with you to help rebuild your home and teach those you recruit. They were told they can stay as long as you wish and have a need for them."

"Thank you, and please thank the council for us. It looks like the boats are ready and Queen Kailee and Kouly are coming to wish us good-bye. We hope to see you soon."

Sword Master Zale gave a slight bow to Kaila, then he turned giving Queen Kailee the same bow.

"Good morning, Queen Kailee. I'm sorry I cannot stay longer, I do wish you and your village a great year."

"We are glad to see you. We thank you for all you have done for our children."

Sword Master Zale stepped back and disappeared. Queen Kailee gave a slight shiver as that happened. She looked at Kaila and smiled.

"I see you are all loaded and ready to leave. You have a long trip up the river. I wish you well and hope your rebuilding goes as well as you expect. Is there anything I can do before you leave?"

Kaila looked at her Grandmother. She was hoping she would ask this question.

"Yes, there is one thing. I would like to ask if you could send messages to all the villages for me."

"What message would you like me to send?"

Kaila looked at both of her grandparents.

"It is a simple request. We are asking that any and all orphans they have, be sent to us. We also ask that any misfits that they do not want, be sent as well.

The last request is also if they do not want the warriors who were trained off-world, could they send them to us? We, of course, ask this in friendship and will pay the normal price of one coin for all orphans, but not anything for their misfits. We might be willing to pay for the warriors. It will depend on how they were treated. We will not pay more than one coin each."

Queen Kailee looked at her granddaughter. She had listened to her words and if they had come from a grown woman she would have been angered and slightly impressed. Instead, she was proud of the words coming from her granddaughter. She spoke straight and blunt. She was determined to grow a village and if she had to do it with orphans and outcasts, she was going to.

"If you are willing to take orphans, we have five here in our village. I can send for them now, so you may take them with you. I will even wave the price for them."

"I will hold two boats for them. Please send for them and I will tell those in the two boats to wait. And I thank you for not selling them to me. I will in turn send a small portion of our harvest next year, as a token of kinship."

"Do so only if it will not harm your growth. I would ask one question of you."

Kaila looked at her grandmother.

"What is your question?"

"Where are you getting the coins?"

"We have earned many coins during our stay on Rednog. Enough coins to rebuild our home bigger and stronger than it ever was."

Queen Kailee looked at her granddaughter and smiled.

"I'm glad to know you will not have trouble hiring the men you will need to help rebuild."

Queen Kailee turned and whispered in the ear of a young man near her. He ran to do her bidding.

Kaila gave a bow and walked toward the river, Nakobee right beside her. He had not talked because it was only the women who were allowed to talk when doing business or unless a man was invited to speak.

When they reached the river, Nakobee pulled two warriors aside. He explained that five orphans of unknown age were coming. Once they arrived, they would need to find room for them in the boats.

When he was finished speaking, the young man that had gone to get the orphans returned with them. Nakobee looked at them. Three were about two years old, the other two looked to be about five years old. He gave the younger ones to the boats with the older girls. The two boys he placed in his own boat. Since he was the only one in that boat, he knew it could handle the extra weight.

Once loaded, the boats were pushed out. They entered the river, and the young warriors began paddling, working their way to the center. As they disappeared around the bend in the river, Queen Kailee and Kouly turned and headed back to her hut.

Chapter Seven

The fifty miles up the river would take longer than it did when they came from their village. The current in the river ran strong near the shoreline, but out near the center, the current was slower and that was where they would be during their trip up. Most of the year it was not deep and that was why the current was fast.

The river was wide in most places. In some parts it was a mile wide, with dark green water and the smallest section was only three hundred feet wide. Trees grew along most of the bank all the way to their village. There were water birds and fish leaping. When they were going slowly, they could hear amphibians croaking. It would take three days to reach their landing.

The first night they pulled over to the bank two hours before sundown. They found a sandy beach and docked their boats. At the edges of the beach the same bushes grew thickly, like a hedge of safety around them.

The children, now considered to be warriors by their own people, landed, spread out, and set up camp in record time. As the sun set they were sitting by fires and eating, with five young men posted as guards. They would be replaced every three hours.

In the morning, they repeated their trip up river. They dropped fishing lines from each boat as they rowed along. Catching fresh fish would make their trip and stomachs feel better.

The trip was uneventful yet it was good training for them. It showed each of them how much they had learned and that they would be able to handle whatever came at them.

They landed at their old port three days later at noon. They unloaded the boats and began the trip through the cave to their home. It would take four trips to bring all their belongings. They knew this and even argued with Sword Master Zale. He had wanted to drop all their things at their village. Kaila said no, it would look strange if they did not have all their belongings with them when they left their grandmother's village.

The trip through the mountain cave took an hour. When they stepped out, everyone stood there looking down at their village. What they saw now was very different from what should have been. They saw buildings and a great wall. There were people moving all around the village working. They knew it was the men from Rednog.

They moved out with their packs, heading for the village. Nakobee continued standing there looking out at the land. The mountains went north and south reaching high into the sky. Spread out in front of him, he saw the great savanna. From this vantage he could see for miles.

The trees were sparse and the great plain looked vast. Off in the distance he saw great beasts roaming about in herds. Shifting the weight of his pack, he moved off down the path.

An hour hike brought them to the edge of the village. They entered what soon would be a gate, they could see the three buildings that the people from Rednog had built. Two were completed, the third had its walls completed and men were working on the roof.

Off in the distance, there were men working on the walls that were to be built around the village. On the east side the wall was already five feet high.

They saw off to the left where they grew their crops, there was a full field. Then Kaila saw the trees planted near the inside walls. They were the fruit trees their people grew, which bore their favorite fruit.

The fruit started out green, but as it ripened, it turned a deep purple. After they picked the fruit, they would take the branches and grind them up. They would place the pulpy mixture in big pots with water. When it was boiling, they would place their cloth in it.

The longer the fabric stayed in, the darker purple it would be. This was how their mother chose the color for their land. It was a purple banner with a drawing of the fruit in the middle.

Allen and Clara met them as they entered the village.

Allen spoke when they were close, "Hello, as you can see we have made great progress."

Kaila pointed out at the field and said, "I see that. I would like to ask how you grew the crops so quickly. I also see the trees along the inside walls. They are our fruit trees and what we use to color our clothes. Where did you get so many?"

Allen and Clara smiled.

Clara turned to look at the field and answered her, "The field was not our doing. Months ago people came and planted the field. Lord Nogar wanted to make sure you would have food during your rebuilding. As for the trees, Kinn found them and did what he calls *cloned* them. He said you would need the fruit and the trees to color all of the uniforms you will be making."

Kaila smiled as she looked at the trees. What she could see were maybe a thousand of them all along the inside of the wall.

"I will need to thank him again for thinking so far ahead."

Allen smiled at Kaila.

"I have one more surprise for you. When we arrived we found some children out in the field. They fled when they saw us. So we put food out and they returned. A boy named Kal came in, and we talked. They are from a village fifty miles west of here. Their village was attacked. From his description it sounds just like what happened to yours. There were fifty children left who survived the attack. There are only forty now. Some died from wounds and five of the babies died from hunger. We bandaged those who were hurt and gave them food and milk for the young ones.

We told them the new Queen of this village was coming and they would be welcomed. Would you like to go meet with them now or after you get settled?"

Kaila looked at him, then at Nakobee. He nodded his head. Kaila looked at Allen

"Now would be a good time. Did you send word to Sword Master Zale about the children?"

"Yes, he sent people there to check for survivors. I'm sure he will come as soon as he knows anything."

"Then please lead the way so I may meet them."

Allen and Clara led the way, Nakobee and Kaila followed. They left their things on the ground. They knew someone would take them to where they belonged.

They walked over where the children were sitting. When they were near, two children broke away and met them. Allen pointed at the young boy.

"Kal, this is Queen Kaila and her brother, Nakobee. I do not know the young woman's name."

Kal bowed to Queen Kaila and stood next to the young woman.

"This is our queen, Queen Serena."

The young girl frowned at Kal, then bowed toward Kaila and spoke.

"I'm not the queen. I'm just the leader."

Kaila looked at her and spoke, "Just as I'm not yet the queen of this land. Soon I will be, but not yet.
So please Serena, tell us your story. What happened, and how did you find your way here."

"Our village was attacked in the night. Our warriors fought bravely, but they were no match for the fire and the magic of the enemy. I'm not of the royal family. Dane, the mate to our leader found me. He told me to gather as many of the children as I could and lead them here. I did as he asked and gathered all that I could find. We went north out of the village, running through the forests and savannas. Three days after leaving the village, we saw that no one was following us.

I believed we were safe. We began working our way back to the great lake. Once there, we headed along the shore making our way here. We lost some of the younger ones from hunger and a few from their wounds. We did not have very much food or medicine, only what we could grab as we ran out.

When we saw the fields, we looked around to see if anyone was here. There was no one, so we took some of the food. The next day, these people showed up. We were worried that they would attack us, so we hid. They must have known we were here. They left food and water out for us and called out saying they would not harm us.

I was scared when I saw the two green creatures. None of us have ever seen anyone like them."

Nakobee interrupted her, "They are Ogres and are our friends. Their names are Lau and Gala."

"We have met them. This one named Allen told us their names and who they were. He also said we would be welcomed here until we find out when we could go home."

Kaila smiled at her. She knew this girl had been given a great burden and a great honor. She appeared to be eighteen, the same age as herself. Serena was tall, Kal stood only to her shoulder.

"What are the ages and gender of those that are with you?"

"I'm eighteen, the oldest. There are ten who are fifteen years, Kal and nine others, five boys and five girls. There are ten boys and five girls that are ten years and fifteen girls between the ages of five and ten. There are forty-one of us all together. If you let us stay here until we hear from our village, we will work and help to rebuild your village."

"I welcome your help. All of you may stay as long as you want. Allen has told me he sent people to your village to see if they needed help. When we hear from them, I will inform you of their findings.

For now I must return and see what needs to be done. Allen will let you know if and when you may help."

Serena and Kal bowed to Kaila, then turned and headed back to where the other children were waiting.

Kaila, Nakobee, Allen and Clara headed back to the village. As they walked Allen gave them an update.

"As you can see, we have built your home, Kaila, and two of the barracks. Each will hold a hundred warriors. Per your plans, there will be a total of ten barracks built. The building for homes and the families will begin in a day or two. The walls will go from the lake to the mountain on either side of the village. It will completely enclose the village. The dirt to build everything is coming from outside the wall. This will give you a ten foot wide and ten foot deep trench. Once the wall and trench is completed, we will open the wall near the lake and let the water in. We are also rerouting the small river from the mountain to the village. This way you will have fresh water to all the buildings.

We estimate to be completely finished with all the buildings and the wall within two months.

The main fields for your food will be outside the wall. There are small gardens in and around the inside wall."

"Only two months? How can you do this so fast?" asked Kaila.

"We have the work force and we also have a wizard helping us. It would normally take a week to dry the bricks, but he is doing it in an hour. It makes it a lot faster."

"Is Shaméd here?" asked Nakobee.

"No, it is not Shaméd, it is Kinn. Remember I told you he was here cloning the plants? After he is finished here, he is heading to the Elves on this world to talk with them. We are hoping they will build a closer friendship with your group and later help get this world to join the Coalition."

Kaila looked at Allen and Clara.

"We will do all that we can to make that happen. For now, let us finish our home. Then, we will worry about getting the others to join. Do you agree, brother?"

Nakobee nodded his head, "Yes, I agree."

Chapter Eight

The next morning as the sun rose across the great savanna, it found Serena standing in front of Kaila's home. The guard stood near the door. He had told Serena that when Queen Kaila awoke, he would let her know she was there.

Kaila woke like always, just before the sun rose. It had been hard to do when she was on Rednog but she had set a routine and stuck to it. Since they had lived on the timeline of their world it was easy to keep to a time for the sunrise. Now with the sun rising, she found she was early.

She had heard Serena talking to the guard and hurried to get ready. As she stepped through the door, the guard stepped aside.

"Serena, is there something I can do for you?"

"I wanted to make sure that you knew what I said yesterday was true. We are willing to work until we can return to our home."

Kaila smiled and stepped closer. She was about to speak when she saw a movement to her right. Her instinct took over as did the guard's. Both turned, drawing their weapons. Sword Master Zale smiled as he appeared.

"Good morning, Queen Kaila, Leo. It is Leo and not Lea, right? I'm sorry for not letting you know I was coming. That is something I will remedy today."

Leo smiled and nodded his head. He stepped back beside the door. Sword Master Zale looked over at Serena.

"This must be Serena. Good morning to you. I hope you and the other children are doing better."

Serena looked at him as he walked forward. She had seen him appear out of thin air and stepped back, a little afraid at what might happen. When she saw both Kaila and the guard react, and then they both relaxed and greeted the man, she was even more confused. She looked at Kaila.

"Are you not concerned about a man appearing from thin air?"

Kaila smiled and answered, "Not when he is a friend and a mentor. Serena, meet Sword Master Zale. He took the children that survived the attack of this village to his home many years ago. There we were trained and taught how to fight and survive. We have now returned to reclaim our home. I suppose he is here to tell us what has happened with your village. Is that not correct Sword Master Zale?"

"As always Queen Kaila, you get straight to the point. Yes, I'm here to tell you about the village. Serena, do you want the other children to hear what happened or just you?"

"I think from your expression, I should be the one that hears what has happened to our people."

"Very well, let us go somewhere to sit."

Kaila pointed toward her home and said, "Please come inside. We can sit and have a drink."

Kaila led the way in, Leo moved back in front of the door.

Inside Serena looked around. The place was large. She saw that at least thirty people could live there. There was not much furniture. Over in the corner there was a bed and two packs near the wall. In the center of the room was a table and six chairs. Other than that, the place was empty.

Kaila walked over and pointed to the table.

"Please sit. I'm sorry to say all I have to offer to drink is water. May I pour you both a cup?"

Zale stood near the chair as he waited for Serena to answer. After looking around, she looked at them and realized they were waiting on her. She moved forward reaching for the jug of water.

"Sorry, Queen Kaila. Let me serve you."

"No, you both sit. This is my home and I serve my guests."

Zale sat after Serena, while Kaila poured the water into three cups and handed them out, then she also sat.

"Now, Sword Master Zale, please tell us what you found at Serena's village."

He took a sip and placed the cup down.

"We found pretty much the same thing we found when we came here five years ago. Every building was burned to the ground. There was no one alive. The only bodies were those from the village. I would like to know if Serena could give us a description of those that attacked the village. It might help us figure out who is behind all of this."

Serena looked at them. Hearing that there was nothing left of her village made her feel empty inside. She was not sure what she was expecting, but she never thought that her people would be dead. But what did she really expect? If this village, one of the mightiest in the land fell so many years ago, how could she have hoped hers would be able to hold out?

"I only saw a few of them. There was fire coming from the sky, and loud noises everywhere. My people came out of their homes ready to fight only to be cut down as they exited.

The enemy were of normal height. They wore very little clothing. Most were covered in shredded cloth wrapped around their bodies. They moved and fought like demons. They growled like animals. I saw one with many arrows in its body and yet it kept moving.

I had heard stories about demons, but I have never seen one. When I saw those that attacked my village that is what I believed they were. I changed my mind when I saw Dane kill one of them. They are men, just deformed. Maybe they were men possessed by demons. I have heard demons can do that."

"You say those who attacked you were men, but their bodies were deformed. Can you describe how they were deformed?"

Serena looked at Zale, then Kaila.

"They were big, like your brother. Their faces did not look human either. They were twisted like they were in pain."

"You say they were big like Nakobee. Do you mean his height or the brawn?" asked Queen Kaila

"I do not know this word brawn."

Kaila nodded her head, and explained. "His muscles, my brother Nakobee takes after our father. He is a very big man, his strength is almost twice that of a normal man."

"Then yes, his brawn. They had large arms and chest but they were not tall like Nakobee."

Sword Master Zale leaned back in his chair, closed his eyes and seemed to be talking to himself. He stopped and looked at Kaila and Serena.

"Sorry, I was talking with Reklan. He believes as I do, that these men may be created by demons from humans they have taken. Those who attacked your village were smaller; but these sound much larger. We need to bring someone here to search out these demons. We will contact Queen Kailee to get permission to come here to do this."

Kaila leaned forward on the table, and spoke. "We do not need her permission. This happened on our side of the mountain. I can give you permission."

Kaila stared at Sword Master Zale waiting for him to answer.

"I'm sorry Kaila, you are not officially Queen yet. You have to have a village with over two hundred people. You only have thirty."

Serena leaned forward and looked at each of them. Then said, "She has more than thirty. Count all those out there working. There must be at least a hundred people."

Sword Master Zale looked at Serena.

"Serena, those people building this village are people from my home. They do not count. Kaila cannot even count the four that I'm leaving here to help her."

"That is right. That is why I told Queen Kailee that I would take all the orphans from every village. I need to grow this village before they will accept me as a Queen."

Serena turned to Kaila, in a clear voice said, "Then you have forty more. My village is gone. We will join yours. All we have to do is gather a little over a hundred more."

Kaila smiled at her.

"Thank you. We will accept you and the others as our own. I'm hoping within a month others will come. Hopefully they will arrive before the Queens realize why I'm asking for them.

Sword Master Zale, go ask Queen Kailee's permission. I just ask that you please wait a month. Give me time to get our home built."

"I can do that. I will also let Lord Nogar know what you are doing. I'm sure he will try to figure out more ways to help."

"Thank you. Is there anything more you need to tell us? I have to eat and get working on the walls."

Sword Master Zale smiled and stood.

"There is only one more thing."

Reaching into his pocket he pulled out two gold chains with stones attached.

"These are for you and Nakobee. The green one is yours and the blue one is for him. They are…"

Kaila interrupted him.

"I know what they are. You give these to those who are servants of King Nogar. We are not servants."

Sword Master Zale stood looking at her.

"No, you are not servants. And we do not give them to servants. We give them to those who work with us. They will record everything around you. We will in turn have said information. This way we can help you if there's a problem. It is a way for you to call us. It is also a way for us to let you know when one of us is coming here.

To speak to us, all you have to do is take hold of the stone and speak. You can speak out loud, or think it in your mind. Ask for me, Shaméd, or Reklan. One of us will come as soon as we can. Do not wear the stone when you want to have privacy. We will be able to see everything you are doing.

As I said before, the blue is for Nakobee, the green is yours."

Kaila took the stones and looked at them. The stones looked clear, she could almost see through them. She looked at the gold metal chains. Once more the people on Rednog were showing how advanced they were. She placed the green one around her neck.

"We both thank you. You agree to give me a month before speaking to Queen Kailee?"

"Yes, I will wait one of your months. Thank you for your hospitality. Next time, I will bring something to share with you."

Smiling, he stepped away and disappeared. Serena jumped making a gasping sound, almost falling out of her chair.

Kaila grinned at her, as she took a sip of water.

"They do that, I think to show us just how much power they have."

Serena looked at Kaila and in a shaky voice said, "You know some powerful people."

"You have no idea how powerful. Come, let us find Nakobee to give him his present, and to let everyone know that you and your people are now part of our tribe."

They walked out and headed for the wall, Leo following behind. As they walked the smell of the food cooking had them turning toward it. There were people already there getting food and sitting at the tables eating. Kaila looked at Serena.

"You should go get the others. Come back here and eat. We will put all of you in the other building. Since you are now family, you should have your own house and be inside the walls, even if they are not yet completed."

Serena nodded her head and walked away.

Kaila walked over, picked up a plate, and loaded it with food. She found Nakobee sitting at a table with Allen, Clara, Lau, and Gala. They all greeted her as she sat down.

She slid the stone over to Nakobee. The others saw it and smiled.

Nakobee picked it up, looked at it then asked, "What is this for?"

"Sword Master Zale gave us both one. When you need to talk to him, hold it in your hand and talk."

"That will be good when I have a question for him."

Nakobee placed it around his neck and went back to eating. Kaila looked down at her food, then up at the others.

"He told me the village Serena came from was destroyed. Those who did it were not like the ones that attacked our home. They were bigger. He thinks demons might be involved. Serena said she thought they were demons. He is giving us one month before speaking with Queen Kailee."

Nakobee looked at her as he swallowed his food.

"Is it so we can gather more people? Do you think the other villages will give us their orphans and those that were trained on Rednog?"

"They will until they realize why we want them. Then they will hold onto them and fight us. They will not want us to rebuild our village, let alone to let me become queen of our land."

They sat and ate in silence. Nakobee knew their plan would only work until the other villages realized their true plan. That was why Kaila said they would pay one coin for each child. She knew they would do it for the money. Even if they could gather the couple hundred needed to make a village, they would not be a true village until there were at least two hundred over the age of eighteen.

Chapter Nine

The next few weeks were busy. Two hundred more people came from Rednog to help with the construction. The place was going to be the largest human village on this world. The wall began at the lake, going straight toward the mountain for three miles. A tower was built every mile. Each tower could hold five men, with living quarters for ten warriors at the base.

When it reached the mountain, they built the wall using the mountain. They attached it to the mountain when and where it was secure to do so. The wall ran along the mountain for five miles, with towers like the outside walls, then it turned and headed back toward the lake. Over all, the wall was three miles by five miles by four miles.

Inside the wall, there would be ten barracks for the warriors. Each one could hold a hundred people. In the middle, there was a building that could hold two hundred people. It was for meetings and gatherings. Kaila's home was nearby.

There would be at least two hundred homes, stores, and other buildings built inside the compound. Queen Kaila took her learning from other worlds to heart when she designed her new home. She wanted one safe from invaders. The walls were all made from earth. They were four feet thick and the walls of the buildings were two feet thick.

The homes humans lived in on her world were all made from mud. They were sticks and wood frame with mud packed in and around the walls. Most villages did not have walls around them. Hers would have one that any invader would have trouble getting through.

Kaila knew it might be difficult to place warriors on the walls, since most villages did not have more than two hundred warriors living in them. She was planning to have at least seven hundred. She was also going to make sure there was enough food and money for all of them. This was her most important concern.

They had moved twenty of the boats through the caves to the lake. Ten more boats arrived from Rednog. They were much larger. Five boats were able to hold ten men with room to carry loads of fish or cargo. The other five were four times the size of their canoes.

Chapter Ten

Forty five days after arriving at their village, a group of people landed at the river. They were met by the guards and word was sent to Kaila that they were coming with children. Nakobee went to meet them and arrived as the boats docked. He stepped out of the mouth of the cave as a group of men walked forward.

Nakobee called out. "I bid you greetings from Queen Kaila. She asks what she can do for you."

One of the men walked forward.

"I'm Kroni. Word was sent to Queen Krooni saying you would buy our orphans. I have brought ten from our village. Their ages are five to ten years. Are you still buying them?"

"Yes, we are. We will give you one coin for each after inspecting them."

"Why do you need to inspect them?"

Nakobee grinned and answered him, "Because we do not want children who cannot do any work. If you do not want us to inspect them, then you are free to leave and take them back with you."

Kroni looked at Nakobee. He was not sure what to think. Kroni had to look up at Nakobee. He stood there thinking this man was big, and he was at least a foot taller than any of Kroni's men. He had heard that the men from this side of the mountain were large. This was the first one he had ever seen.

"You can inspect them."

Nakobee waved at Lea. Lea moved over and checked out the children. When he was finished, he nodded his heads.

Nakobee looked at Kroni, and said. "They are acceptable, here are your ten coins. You and your men can leave."

Nakobee stood there holding out his hand with the coins.

Kroni took the coins, and looked at Nakobee.

"I was hoping to meet Queen Kaila."

"We call her Queen, but she has not been officially proclaimed queen by the other leaders."

"I understand that, but it does not stop the fact that I want to meet her."

Nakobee looked at the man. He now understood the real reason he wanted to meet his sister.

"If you are thinking of courting her, come back next year. She has made it very clear that she will not be looking for a mate until she is nineteen."

The man shifted his stance. His hand brushed the sword by his side. He was not accustomed to being treated this way.

"Perhaps I should fully introduce myself. I'm Kroni, eldest son of Queen Krooni. We deal in wool and exotic fruit. Our village and land is very wealthy."

Nakobee had seen him brush the sword handle. The sword looked similar to the ones he and his men had. The sheath was different though. It was wooden. Nakobee's village used metal.

"I know who you are. I recognized your colors. That still does not mean I will disregard my Queen's orders. We have bought the children. If you are interested in seeing Queen Kaila, return next mid-year."

Kroni started to move closer. Lea and the other guards moved forward. Nakobee held out his hand.

Nakobee glared at Kroni and in a low voice said, "Are you challenging me?"

Kroni looked around. He saw the smiles on the men behind this big man. His own men had moved back in a defensive position. He still was unsure of this man. He had fought many men and won, some almost as large as this one. This one looked and felt different, though. He acted like no one he had ever faced before.

"No, I was not challenging you. I'm just not used to being treated this way."

"You should get used to it. A warrior that has only fought in staged battles should pick his fights carefully."

This made Kroni stand straighter. He felt slighted and now he wanted to challenge this man. He chose his words carefully.

"Who are you to insult me this way?"

"I'm Nakobee, brother and First Sword to Queen Kaila."

Kroni had heard of a Nakobee, the grandson of Queen Kailee. When he was fourteen, he fought three men in the ring, and won. No one at that age had ever done that. Even if he fought him now and won, he would give up any chance of winning the hand of Kaila. It would be smarter if he left and returned next year.

He bowed his head toward Nakobee and said, "I'm honored to meet the brother and the First Sword of Queen Kaila. Please give her my regards and I hope to see her next year."

Kroni turned and headed to his boats, his men close behind. Lea led the children to the caves and Nakobee stood watching Kroni and his men paddle up river. When they were out of sight he headed back. The three guards stood there smiling. They were hoping to see Nakobee fight and beat this Kroni.

Chapter Eleven

Two days later, five men showed up. Once again Nakobee came.

When he came out of the cave he saw the men sitting near the water. They stood when Nakobee walked toward them. They were a little over five feet tall. That meant they came from the northeast tribes. Their gray hair and scars, showed them to be seasoned warriors, even if the way they were dressed did not show it. They each carried a staff and a bedroll and were dressed in rags.

"Greetings, what can Queen Kaila and her people do for you?"

"We were told she was taking in any warrior who was trained on Rednog. We trained there and the village that we come from said we were free to leave."

"They did not want you?" asked Nakobee.

"They never wanted us. Queen Krooni paid Queen Kailee five coins for us when we returned from Rednog. To her, that meant we were honor bound to stay as well as being treated like slaves. We have always been outcasts and kept on the outskirts of the village and fed scraps. We have lived that way for the last ten years. A month ago, we were told to come here and see if Queen Kaila would buy us. If she does, we are to send the money to Queen Krooni."

Nakobee looked closer at them. They looked hungry.

"Can you tell me who took you to Rednog?"

"Sword Master Zale."

"Who is the King of Rednog?"

"King Nogar."

"What race of being is he?"

The man looked at Nakobee and said, "Why are you asking us these questions?"

"Because we do not want to let just anyone into our village. Besides, once in, and you go through training and you do not have the skills you say, it would be a shame to kill you for spies."

The man nodded his head and began to speak, "King Nogar is a dragon. He can shape shift to any form. When he takes human form, he takes a form that resembles Lord Shaméd, the human boy he rescued."

Nakobee smiled at him and then asked, "How long were you there?"

"We were there for thirty of this world's years. We were told that we had to stay that long to make sure the ones who knew us, were old or dead."

"Kroni, son of Queen Krooni, was just here to sell us their orphans. Why did you not come with them?"

The man stood straighter, his expression showed he was not happy to hear this news.

"As I said, a month ago a messenger brought word to our village that Queen Kaila was buying children and those that were trained on Rednog. Kroni, Queen Krooni's son, told us to come here to see if Queen Kaila would buy us. He told us that if she did we were to send him the money. We did not know he was coming here with children. We also did not know there were orphans in any of the villages."

Nakobee looked at the man, then at the others. When he returned he was going to speak to the children and ask them if they were indeed orphans.

"You are welcome to our home and family. My name is Nakobee, brother and First Sword to Queen Kaila. Tell me your names"

Each one introduced themselves. The one who talked was named Karl, then Nuka, Flan, and Naate, when the last one stepped forward Karl spoke for him.

"This is Janae. He lost his tongue when he talked back to Kroni."

"That seems a harsh punishment. Why did he talk back?"

"Janae told Kroni he was tired of his calling us overpriced trash. Janae told him if they did not like us, then they should release us so we could leave. Kroni took offense to his words and had his tongue cut out. That was last year. Our lives there were worse since then."

Nakobee shook each man's hand.

"As I said, you are all welcome to our home and family. We will accept all of you. As for paying Queen Krooni, or her son Kroni, I think they will wait a long time for any coins. We will not send her anything. Instead each of you will receive the coin.

Follow me to your new home. We will get you cleaned up and some food and new clothing."

As they walked through the cave, Nakobee asked another question, "Since you were on Rednog, you should have left with weapons. What happened to them?"

"Kroni took them from us. He said they were too good for us to have."

Nakobee disliked this Kroni even more. These men were walking for over a month. It was no wonder they were so thin. That was also why the sword Kroni carried looked familiar, it did not come from this world. It was a good thing they had not fought. If he had seen the blade, he would have asked him how and where he had come by it. He did not think this Kroni would have spoken the truth.

When Nakobee returned to the village he tracked down the children. They were, as he suspected, not true orphans. They were children from families with too many children and no way to support them. This was something many families did. He did not like it, but he understood why it was done. To the village and families they were orphans.

Over the next five months there were six more groups that showed up. The groups ranged from ten to thirty. The population of the village grew with the influx of over one hundred children.

On the sixth month, Lea and Lou again were on river duty. They saw fifteen boats coming down river. Word was sent to Nakobee.

When the boats arrived, the first three docked and the men in them climbed out. They all stayed near the boats except ten. Those ten warriors were dressed in dull leather. They walked up the shore and stood off to the side, not saying a word. All of the other warriors were dressed in colorful cloth and leather armor. The rest of the boats docked, and one man, obviously the leader, stepped out and walked forward.

Each boat had ten men in them. The leader was dressed in bright clothing and metal armor. On his head was a feather headdress. Only four men were with him, and they were the rowers.

Lea pointed and whispered, "Look at the peacock."

The man walked up to Lea and Lou who were standing in front of the cave. He stopped when they did not move. Thirty men stood behind him waiting.

"Step aside. We are going to see Queen Kaila."

Lea looked at him, and in a stern voice said, "You will wait here. Word has been sent that you arrived. Someone will be here soon."

"You do not tell me to wait. I wait for no man. Now step aside or you will be forced away."

Lea placed his hand on his sword, and took a step away from Lou.

Lea glared at the man, and said, "You will need more men to do that."

The man stepped back and yelled out, "Kill them."

Before any of them could move, Lea drew his sword, reached out grabbing the man's chest plate, and put his sword tip at the man's throat.

"Are you sure you want to do that? You might get your fancy clothes bloody."

The man's face turned darker. The ten men who were standing off to the side grinned, then their faces went blank. They had not moved during the incident. They did move when the fancy man snapped his fingers.

The man showed very little fear. He spoke loud so all could hear.

"If they do not release me, kill them and destroy their village. Do you hear me?"

One of the men in dull leather spoke, "Yes."

As they started to move closer, Nakobee stepped out from the cave.

"I see there is a problem here. Maybe, I can help. Leo, what's going on?"

Lea was about to speak, when the fancy man spoke first, "This man grabbed me and threatened my life. Tell him to release me at once. Or I will have my men kill him."

Nakobee moved closer, looked at the man and then at his warriors.

"You will need more men to carry out that order."

The man looked up at Nakobee, his face showed his anger.

In a loud voice he said, "Do you know who I am?"

"No, and I do not care. You came here and threatened my men. No one does that and survives."

The man still looking at Nakobee, said in a loud and clear voice, "I am Quoin, First Sword to Queen Liseran."

Nakobee had heard of this tribe. His father had called them arrogant and blowhards. He moved closer and looked into the man's eyes.

"I do not care. I heard you threaten my men. That alone gives me reason to kill you and your men. Tell me why you are here before I follow through with what I have said."

The man glared at Nakobee, and seeing that it was just four of them, against his thirty, he straightened his shoulders.

"I will tell you again to release me or I will order my men to kill all of you, then we will march in and destroy your village."

Nakobee reached out. Lea, seeing Nakobee moving forward, released Quoin and stepped back. Nakobee put his hand around Quoin's neck and pulled his face within an inch of his. Quoin's toes were just touching the ground.

"Ok, he has released you. Now I have you. Do you think you will live if your men so much as lift a finger?"

Nakobee saw the ten men off to the side spread out. The other men stood back waiting.

Nakobee looked at the ten men. He saw how they were standing.

He spoke at them, "You were trained on Rednog?"

The leader said, "Yes, we were."

"Then you know of Lord Shaméd."

"Yes, we know Lord Shaméd."

"You should know I trained with him. All of us learned how to fight from him. Are you here to fight, or was there another reason for this visit?"

"We are here because Queen Liseran, or rather Quoin, wishes to sell us to Queen Kaila."

Nakobee, still looking at the man said, "Then we should talk. How much does he want for you?"

"You should ask him."

Nakobee, still not looking at Quoin, asked, "How much do you think I should pay him for you?"

The man glanced at Quoin, then looked at Nakobee. His expression never changed. He moved his hand away from his sword, as did his men.

"You should challenge him to a fight. If you win you get us for free. If he wins, you pay ten coins for each of us, instead of the one coin each."

"That sounds fair."

Nakobee looked down at Quoin.

"Do you agree to the challenge?"

Quoin tried to speak. Nakobee realized he could not because his grip had tightened. He let the man go.

"Well do you agree or not?"

Quoin's hands went to his throat to rub it. After catching his breath, he straightened his clothes. Getting himself in order, he looked at Nakobee. He had fought all the men that were trained in this placed called Rednog. They were not hard to beat. This one may be bigger, but he knew he could take him.

"I agree, with one change. When I beat you, you will pay twenty coins for each man."

Nakobee smiled at him.

"You will inform your men that when I beat you, all of you will leave and never return."

"Agreed." Quoin said.

His men moved further away. Quoin stepped back handing his headdress and cloak to a soldier. He drew his sword and did a couple of swipes and lunges. Then he turned and looked at Nakobee.

"Whenever you are ready."

The ten men moved, placing themselves so they were between Quoin's soldiers and the fighters.

Nakobee drew his blade and held it up.

"You may take the first swing."

Quoin lunged at Nakobee. Nakobee brushed it aside and slapped Quoin in the head.

Quoin stepped back glaring at Nakobee. He raised his blade and came forward swinging and lunged at Nakobee.

Nakobee blocked each attack then he knocked the blade to the ground and put his sword to Quoins throat.

"You lose. Now you and your men leave."

His men started to move forward, but stopped when the ten men drew their weapons, turned and faced them. They stopped and stepped back.

Quoin picked up his sword and after putting it away, stood there and glared at Nakobee.

"This is not over. One day we will meet and I will not be so forgiving."

"Please feel free to return any time for another sword lesson. Just leave your men in your village. If ever you and your men return and act like you have, I will be forced to take it as a threat and kill all of you."

Quoin turned and headed for his boat. Once in, his men pushed it out and the rest climbed into their boats and headed back up the river. After a few minutes, Nakobee looked at the ten men who had moved off to the side and waited.

"You seemed sure I could take him."

The man smiled as he said, "You did say you fought with Lord Shaméd. If you could hold your own with him, you could beat Quoin. Besides, all these years we had to let him win. It was that or death."

Nakobee burst out laughing, and as he did, everyone there did. When they were done, Nakobee looked at the man.

"What is your name?"

"Tao, I'm the leader of these men. We are very glad to at last be among real men. The last fifteen years have been hell.

Chapter Twelve

The unknown attackers still had them worried. Sword Master Zale had waited the month and talked with Queen Kailee. She had denied the request to allow them send people to look for the unknown enemy.

A year later they still did not know who the enemy was. They had tried to go back in time to see the attacks, but for some reason they could not focus in on the events. So far the only known attacks they knew about were the ones in Kaila's land. And those were five years in between.

The wall was completed, and Kinn was now getting ready to make his way to the elves of this planet. His mission was to help build an alliance between them and Queen Kaila's people. This would start what they hoped would be all the people of this world uniting, and perhaps then they would agree to join the union with King Nogar.
Kinn and Queen Kaila were in the meeting hall waiting for Nakobee. Shameka and Pamilla, her companions, were serving them wine.

Kinn raised his cup and tasted the wine.

"This has a sweet taste. Where does it come from?"

"Reklan sent three casks, along with some other items Sword Master Zale asked for. He thinks we might need help in the next year, if I'm not voted queen. I told him we will work something out."

Kinn took a sip, and looked over the rim of his cup.

"I was thinking about that. What if you send a group to the Dwarfs? You could see if you could buy some swords from them?"

"I do not have the money to buy swords for all my warriors."

"That is true, but you do have enough to buy some. The point of going there would be two fold."

Kaila looked at him and asked, "Besides buying weapons what would the other reason be?"

"That my dear is the best one. I have surveyed the mountains around you. They are rich in minerals, rich enough that you could tempt a group of dwarfs to come and live here."

"Why would we do that?"

Kinn smiled as he answered, "Because if they come, they will mine the mountain and they will give you a percentage of what they get. They will also be able to make weapons for you. They will also help protect your land, since in part it will also be theirs. This in turn would mean you can claim them as your subjects."

Kaila sat there staring at Kinn. What he said made a lot of sense.

"It seems kind of hard to believe they would do that. I have heard they are very difficult to deal with."

"They are. I do know of a person that can talk a dwarf out of his eye teeth. And I think he would be willing to come here to help you."

"Who is this man and how much would he charge for his service?"

"He is not a man, he is a dwarf and he is the nephew of Reklan. As for charging you, he would do it for free."

"Why would he do it for free?"

"Because he is trapped on Rednog and wants to go home. If he comes here and helps you, then Reklan might let him go."

"Why won't Reklan let him go home?"

"Because he owes him money. Doing you a favor just might be enough to pay off his loan."

"That makes no sense. If he owes Reklan money and he does this for me would that mean I owe Reklan?"

"Of course not. Everyone on Rednog wants this world to join the coalition. This would help that occur."

She looked at him and said, "I agree if the Dwarfs came here it would benefit both our people. Can you talk with this man and see if he will come here to help?"

"I will talk with Reklan and have him talk with Karlen to see if he would help us."

Nakobee walked in and sat at the table across from Kinn. Leaning forward he asked, "When will you be leaving, Master Kinn?"

"I was just going to tell your sister that I will be leaving in the morning. I should be back within a month to let you know the result of my talks."

"We will miss you but I do understand the need for you to meet with the elves. You have done a lot of the work that would have taken us years to complete."

Kinn gazed at them as he answered, "We all want you to create a home here that will grow. Any help we give you now, will be helping us in the future. You will have a village that will be comparable to a small city. One day this place will be able to hold a couple thousand people within its walls and maybe five thousand outside. You will have a small fleet of ships to sail the great lake and out to the ocean. We all have great hopes for you."

"We are glad to know you have such faith in our dream. My sister is the one who believes someday our world will join with the others and we will be able to send our children to Rednog to learn. I just want us to live in peace and not have to worry about war."

Kinn stood and smiled.

"That is what we all want. Now if you will excuse me, Reklan wants to talk with me. I will see you both soon."

He took two steps from the table and disappeared.

Chapter Thirteen

One year after Nakobee and Kaila returned from Rednog, they had over four hundred people living in the village of Keele. One hundred and fifty were trained warriors from the age of fifteen to thirty. There were one hundred additional warriors, females and males, in training. They were mainly children between the ages of ten to fifteen.

When word was heard they were accepting people willing to help rebuild, people began coming. Fifty more adults came to live with them. These were mostly the outcasts from other villages. But they were willing to work and live in a place that would accept them and not treat them as slaves or outcasts. People who refused to work were sent away.

There might be enough adults and warriors to force the other Queens to accept Kaila as a true queen, then Kaila could take claim to her mother's land. All she had to do was call a meeting of the others who would have to come to her. That would cause the biggest uproar. When they saw Kaila's home and what she had built, they might not call her Queen, but they would be forced to acknowledge what she had done. However, some might want to take it away from her. If that happened, then she would have to fight to protect it from anyone who thought they could. That would mean more trouble for her and her people.

Kaila and Nakobee were sitting in her home talking about the progress of the village. Kaila looked at Nakobee.

"I would like for you to take some men and sail along the lake and check on the villages that were part of our mother's land. We have not heard from any of the other villages and I'm worried. They are small and no one would know if anything happened to them.

It has been six years since our village was destroyed. We need to find out if they are still willing to be part of our clan. We also need to make sure no more villages have been raided. We must let them know we are here to help them, and let them know we will check on their villages twice a year."

"I can leave tomorrow and be back in a couple of months. When are you going to send word to ask for the meeting?"

"I will send word when you return. I'm not in any hurry. Our crops are coming in and the fishing is going well. We only need the meeting to please grandmother. We both know she wants me labeled a Queen so I can reclaim mother's land."

"It is not wrong for us to lay claim, no one has come and challenged us. And if they did, I believe we would win."

"I believe you are right. We have a strong army. They may be young, but they are a formidable force. Go gather your men and supplies. I will see you later to finish our talk."

Nakobee stood and went in search of Tao. He would take his men and leave him in charge of the village while he was gone.

He would take one of the larger ships. It could hold fifteen men and supplies. He would take that ship, ten men, and supplies for two weeks. He would also take Kal, the fifteen year old who had arrived here before them. Kal was going to show Nakobee his home and assist with meetings with other villages.

The next day Nakobee met with Kaila. Word had been sent from the cave that another fifty men, women and children were coming through.

Kaila asked, "Why don't you take more food?"

"You will need the food here. Every day people are showing up, and you will need it for them. Tao knows how to handle things while I'm gone. He is older and has more training than I. He knows what needs to be done."

They were standing on the dock that went from the shore out fifty feet into the lake. It was built for the ships. One day it would hold twenty. Now it held twenty small boats, mostly for fishing.

The fishing boats were already moving out. Nakobee looked at his sister and then at the small ship. He was taking ten men and would be gone for a month maybe more. He did not feel right about leaving, but he knew Kaila would be safe.

Getting on board, he waved and the ship moved out. They rowed the boat out and let the sail loose. Once it filled, the small ship took off.

Kaila stood there and watched for almost an hour before turning back to her home.

The ship stayed within eyesight of land. They had a routine: the men would fish when they weren't rowing. An hour before sundown they would head for shore and make camp.

The first night Kal watched when the boat landed and three men moved out to check the area. The rest cleared a space and began setting up camp.

He was confused when he saw the men placing poles into the ground with their sharp points sticking up around the camp.

Walking over he spoke with Nakobee, "Why are they putting poles in the ground?"

Nakobee stopped cutting the pole he was working on.

"We are a small group. The poles will keep out anyone trying to enter without our knowing."

"They will do this every night?" asked Kal

"Yes, we will do it every night. You will help tomorrow. Tonight, you go help the cook."

Nakobee went back to cutting his pole. Kal walked over to the cook and helped set up the table and started the fire.

The sun was setting and the food was being prepared. Their first night they ate fresh fish from that day's catch.

Watch was set for one man awake for two hours. They drew straws to see who got which watch. Nakobee was set to take the last one. This was the way they would work until they returned.

The next morning they were moving out as the sun rose above the mountains. At the rate they were traveling they would reach Kal's village at noon. The wind was strong and the sky clear as they arrived. As they beached their boat, the men slowly walked toward what was left of it.

Most everything was gone; grass was growing where once stood homes. There was little left, only some wood on the beach where the boats had been.

Kal stood looking at what once was his village. He slowly walked to where his hut used to be. Standing in front of a pile of ash, he held his breath and fought back tears. Nakobee stood next to him.

"I know how you are feeling. Six years ago this happened to my village. We will find out who is doing this and make them pay."

Kal pointed out at the mounds.

"The village had twenty huts. The three in the middle were the biggest. They were where we had meetings and our leader lived."

The men walked through the village searching for clues. Two hours later they were back at the boat. Kal had found the graves of those who were killed. Sword Master Zale's people had buried them.

Nakobee looked at each man. He saw in their faces they had found nothing. They still had no clue who was doing this and what their motives were.

"We have a couple more hours of travel time. We will camp further along the lake. Tomorrow we will continue our search to see if the other villages are still there."

"We should camp here so we can go through the rubble. We can pull out anything of value. It will help in the rebuilding of Keele."

They all looked at Kal who had spoken. He stood there looking at the ruins and waited to hear their answer.

Nakobee nodded his head toward Kuok.

"We will stay here tonight, then. Kuok, set up the cook camp. The rest of you keep searching. An hour before sundown we will set up the barrier."

Nakobee watched as his men moved out to comply with his orders.

It amazed him how they obeyed. He was at least ten to fifteen years younger than them. They had years more of training on Rednog than he, yet each man looked at him and did his bidding without even a slight hint of disrespect. He admired their training and wanted everyone who came to his village to have that same kind of loyalty. He would make sure his sister would have the greatest realm on this world. Never again would his family have to flee then fight to regain their land.

As the sun set the men gathered around the fire. What little items they found were of minor wealth. There were several spears, five were broken, two swords made from bronze. There were five shields and a pile of pots and other cooking utensils.

"We will leave these here and pick them up on the way back. Kal, these will be given to your group. It will help in building your homes. Let us eat and get a good night's sleep."

During dinner, Nakobee spread out a map and pointed to it.

"We are here. The next village is two days away at the river junction. Then after that, we have to head up the river for another two days. The village there is at the base of the mountain. It is a large village, and it is supposed to have three hundred people. If both of these villages are still there, we will head back down the lake to the sea. There is a fishing village where the lake meets the sea. Once we reach it, we will continue across the lake to the other side. Then we will go back along the lake to the last three villages. Once we return to Keele, we will take a group of men and search the mountains for the other five villages.

We need to get an accurate count of those living in each village and find out if they will swear allegiance to my sister."

Kuok, was standing nearby and spoke, "I think they will swear allegiance. Your family and village have been the place where the Queen sat for generations. I see no reason for them to not stay loyal."

Nakobee looked at him and smiled.

"I'm glad you feel this way. We will know the answer when we reach each place. For now, let us clean up and get some rest. We have a long trip ahead of us."

Nakobee stood, folded the map, and placed it in his pack. Then he walked over to his bedroll and lay down. Each man did the same. The one on watch moved out and took his place.

In the morning, they left after eating. The small pile of things that had been collected lay near a rock pile. A skin was laid over them to protect them until they returned.

The next two days were easy. The fish caught during the day were eaten at the night meal. The wind kept them on course and at a steady speed. When the wind died down in the afternoon, they would row.

A few hours past noon of the third day after leaving, they saw the village at the mouth of the river. As they rowed near they saw warriors standing on the shore, ready with spear and shield. There were about fifty of them.

Nakobee called out to them, "Greetings, I'm Nakobee, son of Queen Keely. We come here to speak with the elders and leader of your village."

There was only one dock with five boats tied to it. Several smaller boats were spread out and pulled up along the shore. Nakobee could tell that earlier there had been people sitting mending nets. Some boats were on racks, while others lay on the ground.

A man called out as he pointed to a clearing near the dock, "You may put your boat there."

They rowed to the shore. When the boat hit dirt, two men jumped out and held it steady so Nakobee and the others could get out. Drawing the boat up on the shore, they turned and looked at the warriors.

Nakobee approached the men there.

"As I said, I'm Nakobee, son of Queen Keely. We are here to see if this village is well and still holds its allegiance to the Queen and her people."

The man that waved at them stepped forward.

"Queen Keely was killed and her village destroyed over six years ago."

"That is true. My sister, I, and thirty of the village children escaped. My sister, Kaila, will be named Queen by year's end."

"How could that be? If you say only thirty children escaped, you do not have the warriors for her to become queen."

"We returned here one year ago. We now have over one hundred warriors. There are four hundred people living in the village we have rebuilt. The village between yours and ours was attacked and destroyed last year. Their survivors are now living with us. I'm traveling to all the villages loyal to my mother. We are hoping they will still swear allegiance to my sister, Queen Kaila."

An old woman stepped forward. When she got to the old man, they talked. When they stopped, she turned and spoke, "If you are the son of Queen Keely come close to me so I may look at you."

Nakobee walked over and looked down at her. The old woman moved close putting her hands out.

"Lean down so I can touch you and look into your eyes."

Nakobee knelt down on one knee. The old woman looked at him and ran her hand over his face and around his neck, and then across his chest. She smiled as her hand came away.

"You are who you say. There are not many men as tall or big as young Nakobee. The scar on your neck tells me you are him. I was there visiting Queen Keely when you were hurt and received that scar. Your mother was not pleased that you were careless with your spear."

"I was not careless, the other boy was just lucky."

She laughed.

"Yes, he was. Now I know you are Nakobee, son of our Queen Keely. Walk with me to my home. We will talk on the way. Your men may stay here or come with you."

Nakobee looked at his men. "Move the boat away from here and make camp. We will leave tomorrow at sunrise."

As they walked she spoke, "Tell me Nakobee, how is it you have grown your village so fast?'

Her warriors moved away, most went to the nets and began working on them. Five warriors stayed with Nakobee and the old woman.

"We sent word to the villages letting them know we would pay for their orphans and outcasts. That included any orphans who were sent off-world."

The woman stopped walking and looked up at him. Her face showed a surprised expression.

She said, "And they sent you these orphans and warriors?"

"Yes, these men who are with me are part of a group sent from Queen Liseran."

She laughed, shook her head and started walking.

"How many children and misfits have you bought?"

"We have bought many children and warriors. Those with me, I won in a fight. The rest that are there just came and asked to be part of our village. They were dissatisfied with their prior living arrangements."

They arrived at a hut and she sat on a log that lay in front of it.

"Sit. Ki, bring us something to drink."

Nakobee sat on the log across from her. One of her warriors went to get drinks.

She looked at Nakobee.

"I never thought a queen or anyone, would be so dumb or hard up for money that they would sell their people to another village. Did they not think by doing that, your village would grow and someday be a threat?"

"That is what I told my sister, Kaila. She told me that none of them would think that far in advance. They would take the money and hope none of the other villages would do it. As for the misfits, she said once word was out that there was a village that would accept them as an equal, many would come just for that chance of freedom. She was right and the day I left, word was sent to her that fifty men, women and children were coming through the cave to see her."

"Your sister is as smart as your mother. Where were you and the other children for all these years?"

"We went off-world to learn how to fight and grow our village."

"I have never heard of children leaving and returning so soon. How is it you did?"

"It was so we could rebuild our home. Queen Kailee made the arrangements for it, and said that was the only way we could leave."

Ki returned with drinks. He handed one each to the old lady and Nakobee. Nakobee took the drink. He nodded his head to Ki in thanks. He took a sip; it was the fermented drink made from the milk of their beasts added to water. He had never liked the taste, but he knew if he didn't drink it would be rude. He took another sip and placed the cup down on the ground near his foot.

"I do not want to sound rude, but I do not know your name. The map I have, shows the villages' locations, but not their names or those that rule them."

"Forgive me. I'm Larea. We are and always will be part of the clan Zolotov. The name of our village is Zotov. We took that name when we swore an alliance with your ancestors.

Lore has it that many years ago, your ancestors saved mine when our village was being attacked by trolls. Twenty of your warriors were on a hunting trip when they saw the attack. They came and fought killing the fifty trolls, and saving our village. My ancestors swore their allegiance and they were brought here. Your ancestors told them it would be their home as long as they wanted it to be."

Nakobee looked around at the people, the tallest of them stood five feet. From afar they would look like children.

"When I return I will let my sister know you and your people are still with us. Is there anything we can do to help you?" Nakobee asked

"We are just glad that you are back. I will send word by runner to Queen Kaila tomorrow. If you have anything you would like to say to her give it to me and my runner will take it."

"If you will just let her know we are safe and heading up river, that will be all I could ask."

She looked at him and said, "Are you going to see if the village is still there? If so I would suggest going by land. The river is running strong this time of the year. It would take you five days or longer to go that way. That is if you rowed every foot of the way."

"How long will it take by land?"

"Three days if you have a wagon, but if you and your men carry what you need, it will only take two days."

Nakobee sat there thinking it would be good for his men to do some walking.

"Then we will leave our boat here and start out at first light tomorrow."

Larea slapped her hands on her legs and stood.

"Then tonight we will celebrate the return of our Queen."

She turned and looked at Ki.

"Ki, tell the others we are celebrating. A feast will be held in honor of our new Queen Kaila. Nakobee, let me take you to the spare hut. You and your men can sleep there and leave at sunrise."

"Thank you, but we will move our boat out of your way and sleep on the beach. We will be gone before your first fishing boats leave."

"As you wish. Then I will let you return to your men. I'm old and need to rest. The feast will begin at sunset."

Nakobee stood and walked toward the beach. Larea went inside the hut. When he reached the beach, he saw his men and called out to Tourna. Tourna walked over and stopped when he reached Nakobee.

"Tourna, tonight they are throwing a party in honor of Queen Kaila. We will attend it for a couple of hours. They told me the river is running too fast for us to travel on, so in the morning we will leave the boat here and will walk up the river."

"I will have the men pack for the trip. Will we be leaving what we cannot carry here?"

"I do not think anyone will take it. Leave it in the boat and put the sail over it."

They headed toward the others.

Chapter Fourteen

A barrage of flames came crashing down onto the village. The night sky lit up, buildings exploded bursting into flames. Within seconds the night filled with the smell of acrid smoke and the sounds of people screaming as they ran from the burning buildings.

Soldiers on strange looking beasts, rode through the streets tossing torches on the buildings still standing. Other soldiers on foot ran between the buildings attacking and killing with clubs and spears as the people ran out of their homes. The village was completely destroyed within an hour.

As the sun rose and the night faded, six animals with dark shapes on their backs moved slowly into the destruction. When they reached the center of the now destroyed village, they stopped. Those sitting on the animals were all dressed in black.

The soldiers on foot were collecting those not dead, and dragging them into the center of the village. The survivors huddled there on the ground in front of the strangers.

As the dark figures on their large beasts towered over them, they looked down at those still alive. One of the dark figures moved forward and spoke, "This is what happens to those who will not bow to our King. We are taking your children. The rest of you will be allowed to leave and spread the word that we are coming. Tell them to be ready to lay down their weapons and surrender. We will be coming soon to the other villages. Tell them to be ready to pledge their allegiance to us. If they do not do this, then what happened here will happen to them. Those who resist us will be killed. Those still alive will be taken to serve our King."

Twisting his beast's head around, he and the others rode out of the village. The foot soldiers followed leading the young men, women, and children, now tied together. Only the old, wounded, and crippled were left. They sat there huddled, watching their young being dragged away. Not able to do anything, they hung their heads in shame, and the women were wailing and weeping.

Soon they stood and gathered what supplies they could find and headed out to spread the word.

Chapter Fifteen

The party lasted late into the night. Nakobee and his men left early, going back to their camp three hours after sundown. They had some trouble getting to sleep as the villagers were still partying.

As the sun rose, they were up and packed, and heading north. There were a few villagers, mostly young children working in the fields. They waved as the group went by on the trail.

Since the land was flat and open with tall grass, and some scattered trees, they made good time. At noon they stopped for a rest and food.

Nakobee looked at his map and saw that they had traveled eighteen miles in six hours. He looked over at his men.

"Tourna, if we travel fifteen more miles, we should reach the bend in the river. It looks as if there is a large rock outcropping. I think it will make a good camp. To make the fifteen miles before sundown, we will have to run half the time. Are the men up for it?"

"I believe we are. When we were with Queen Liseran, Quoin would have us run ten miles a day."

"Why would he do such a thing?"

"He said since we were trained off-world, we would do all the running. This was so his men could do all the real fighting."

Nakobee shook his head.

"I should have cut off his hand. The more I hear about that man the more I dislike him."

Tourna smiled.

"He is a hard man. Most of his own people, besides his soldiers, do not like him. The people do not leave because there is no place for them to go and his warriors won't leave for the same reason."

Nakobee sat there, thinking about what he just heard. After a few minutes he looked at Tourna.

"If you or one of your men went back there and told the people that we would accept them as equals, do you think they would come?"

Tourna sat there looking at Nakobee and then at his men who had heard Nakobee's words.

"I believe some would come. Others would wait to see if those who left were indeed treated as equals."

"What about the soldiers? Would any of them leave?"

"Those without families would. Those with families might, if they could bring their families with them. We could go and see? Do you want to send someone as soon as we return?"

"I was thinking of talking it over with Queen Kaila first. If she agrees then we can send three of you there. We can make up some reason for sending you."

Nakobee glanced up at the sun, then at the men.

"Let's get moving, we have a long way to go before sundown."

Everyone stood. After putting their packs on, they followed Nakobee down the trail.

Nakobee walked for an hour then ran for an hour. They did this until they saw the rock outcropping in the distance. They walked the last mile.

Reaching the rocks, Kal began building a fire so the cook could prepare their meal. The rest set up camp, making sure the area was secured.

Nakobee placed his pack down and saw that the men were setting up camp without his saying or doing anything. He stood there watching and he thought, *"These are good men, well trained. Queen Liseran was unwise in letting such men go."*

He walked to the river and removed his clothing. He walked into the water and relaxed letting the water remove the dirt from the long trip. When he was finished he stood and dried off, then put his clothes on.

When he returned he called out, "Anyone who wishes to go down to the river and get clean, I would say to do it before the sun sets. I still want guards placed during the night."

They talked among themselves and half went down to the river to bathe once the camp was secured. When the last of the men returned from the river, dinner was ready.

They ate and as the sun set, they sat around the fire and sang songs. Nakobee sat there watching. He was one who did not like singing. He told those who wanted him to sing that he sounded like an animal dying. Kaila had told everyone that he had a great voice; he was just shy.

Two hours after sundown the men went to sleep. The guard went and stood on top of the rocks. Nakobee, like before, was taking the last watch.

In the morning they woke, ate, and were on the road as the sun broke over the distant mountains. As they walked, they noticed the trail was beginning to grow steeper. The mountains were looming higher and as they approached, they could see more trees. The village that they were heading to was at the base of the mountains.

As the sun reached high in the sky they stopped for lunch.

A few minutes after sitting down one of the men called out, "People are coming toward us."

Nakobee stood and moved out on the trail and waited for the people. As they approached, he saw that they were walking slowly and some seemed injured.

"Tourna, send some men to them and see if they need our help."

Tourna pointed to two men who picked up their spears.

Nakobee called to them, "Leave your weapons. We don't want to scare them."

The men put their spears down and started running toward the group. Nakobee stood watching. As his men came closer the people fell to the ground. Nakobee could hear the cries. He began running to them, also. When he reached them he saw they were huddled together in fear. His men stood off to the side not sure what to do. One looked at Nakobee.

"Sir, we told them we were not here to harm them. They all just collapsed and the women started crying."

Nakobee walked over and looked down at the men who moved in front of the women. He saw that the men were old, and some were deformed. All of the women were old. None of these people were younger than fifty years.

"I'm Nakobee, brother to Queen Kaila. We have returned and are visiting all the villages to see if they still are loyal to our clan. Where do you come from? And why are you in such fear?"

One man looked up, his shame clear in his eyes. He had only one arm and a long scar on the right side of his face.

"I'm Kuku. We are all that is left of the village Sukuma."

"What has happened?" asked Nakobee.

"We were attacked by demons in the middle of the night. They burned our village and killed our warriors. They took our young, and those you see here are all that were left. We were told to spread the word that they are coming. Those that will not bow down to them will be killed."

Nakobee stood there looking at them. There were five men and ten women. This was all that was left of their village. He was dismayed.

"Can you tell me how they attacked you?"

"They were like demons, and fire came down from the sky. Those on beasts rode around setting our homes on fire. Others on foot ran among our huts killing anyone who fought back. I stabbed three before being hit from behind. When I woke, I stood and was walking around. I was grabbed, taken and tossed like a sack onto the ground with those you see here.

Then one of them, on his beast, told us they were taking our young and we were to go to all the villages and tell them that they are coming."

Nakobee reached down taking hold of the man by the shoulders. He raised him up to his feet. His head came to Nakobee's shoulder.

"You fought well. You killed three of them before falling. You should be proud."

The man looked at him.

"That is the problem. The men I stabbed did not fall, they kept on fighting. They went by me as if I was not even there. They did not even react when I stabbed them. That is why I say they were demons. Men would have died from the wounds I gave them."

Nakobee looked at him. He saw the fear in the man's eyes. The females had stopped crying, all staring up at him.

"Come with us. We will feed you and tend to your wounds. Then we will return to Zotov. There we will take our boat and return to Keele, the new home of Queen Kaila."

They slowly stood and followed Nakobee. When they reached the others, his men began helping the wounded. The cook built a fire and made a stew. An hour later, they started back down the trail toward the lake.

They reached the rock outcrop where they made camp just as the sun was setting. Nakobee walked away from camp out on to the savanna. When he was a couple hundred feet away, he took hold of his amulet.

"This is Nakobee. I need to talk with Sword Master Zale. I have a problem that he needs to hear about."

He repeated it three times before heading back to camp. As he approached, there was a movement to his right and Sword Master Zale appeared.

"What is the problem?"

This time Nakobee did not flinch when he appeared. After Sword Master Zale spoke, he headed back away from camp. He stopped after a few steps.

"There has been another attack on one of our villages. That makes two, besides mine, that I know about. The attacks were all the same. Only this time they left fifteen people alive."

"There are survivors? What did they say?"

Sword Master sounded surprise.

"They said demons attacked them. They were told to inform all the other villages that they are coming and they must surrender to them or die."

Sword Master Zale stood there thinking. After a few seconds he looked around.

"Give me the location of this village. I will go there and check it out. Are you continuing on to the other villages or returning home?"

"I'm taking these people home and then going to the other villages. They must be warned."

"Then return home, by the time you get there I will have an answer about this last attack."

Sword Master Zale turned and disappeared, Nakobee headed back to camp.

The camp was subdued that night. Nakobee knew it would take one more night to reach the lake. They would have to travel slower with these people.

In the morning they headed out as the sun rose, and set out at a slow walk. Two hours before sundown they made camp. The next morning they were up and walking after the sun broke over the mountain. Nakobee thought if they kept this pace they would reach the village by sundown. He walked up to Tourna.

"Tourna, take a man and run ahead to the village. Let Leader Larea know we are returning. We will stay the night and leave early in the morning."

Tourna nodded his head and went and tapped a man on the shoulder. They were both running within a minute of talking.

As Nakobee predicted, they reached Zotov as the sun was setting. As they entered the village, people came out to greet them. Leader Larea was in front.

She stopped as Nakobee walked up to her.

"Greetings, friend Nakobee. I'm sorry to hear about the village Sukuma. We have prepared food and drink for all of you. I know you will want to leave in the morning, so I sent bedding down to your boats for the others."

"I thank you, as do the people from Sukuma. Did Tourna tell you what happened to the village?"

"Yes, he did. I was going to ask if we should stay, or head to your village for safety."

Nakobee looked at her and smiled.

"That is why you are the leader. I think you should pack everything you can and come to Keele."

"We will start packing in the morning. Will there be room for all of us?"

Now Nakobee smiled even bigger.

"You will be amazed at how large our new home is. We have a walls built all the way around it. There is room for thousands of people to live within them."

They walked on without talking. Later, after everyone ate, Nakobee led the fifteen people and his men to where his boat was drawn up on shore.

"We will sleep here tonight and leave at first light. We will be in Keele in a few days. You will be welcomed as one of our clan. There will be a place set up for you. Each of you will let us know what you are best at doing."

Kuku stepped forward with his head bowed and asked, "Will we be slaves?"

"No, you will not be slaves. We do not believe in slavery. You will be free men and women. You will have the same rights as do all of who live there."

He walked back to his people where they were preparing to sleep. It was three hours after sundown, and guards were in place before Nakobee rested.

In the morning they loaded the boat and headed to Keele. The men took turns rowing. And like the trip down, some fished as they traveled.

Two hours before sundown they rowed to shore and made camp. They made a fire, ate, and set up sentries. In the morning they repeated the day before.

As the sun was setting on the fourth day, they drew up to the docks of Keele.

Waiting at the end of the dock were Sword Master Zale, Kaila, and twenty soldiers.

When the boat was made secure, Nakobee climbed out, as did his men. Then they helped the old ones out, and his men unloaded the boat.

Nakobee walked over to his sister.

"Greetings Kaila, I presume Sword Master Zale told you about the raid on the northern village."

"Yes, he has. He also told me there is nothing left of the place."

She turned and looked at Sword Master Zale.

"It might be better if you told him what you found."

Nakobee looked at them both.

"If you have information on those that raided the place, let me call over Kuku. He is their leader."

Nakobee called out to the group of people standing off to the side.

"Kuku, come over here please."

The man stopped talking to the woman he was near and walked over.

"What may I do for you?"

"There is nothing you can do for me. I want to introduce you to Queen Kaila and our friend Sword Master Zale. He has visited your village and has news about those that raided it."

94

Kuku turned and looked at Kaila and when he saw the metal on her head he dropped to his knees and bowed.

"My Queen, I'm honored to meet you. I and my people are sorry to be a burden to you and we will do whatever you want us to do."

He was still bent over when Kaila stepped closer and touched his shoulder.

"You and your people are not a burden. I'm sorry to hear about your home. We will do whatever we can to help rebuild it. Now stand before me so we may listen to what Sword Master Zale has to say."

Standing, he looked at the man to her left. He had not looked at him at first. Now he did, and he was surprised at how white his skin was. He had heard of strange men that had fair skin, but had never seen them. He nodded his head.

"Nakobee said you have been to my village. How is it you have been there and back so fast?"

"I have ways to travel quickly. I went to your village yesterday and came back this morning. I have already told Queen Kaila what I found. But, Nakobee wants me to tell you and him.

I arrived there with two others. We searched through the rubble and found many bodies, all of them belonging to your village. Before you say anything, we buried them according to your ways.

The good news is we found one body that belonged to those that attacked you. It was a Troll. Its body was badly deformed. The deformation happened before it was killed.

After examining the body, we found it had been dead for a long time. We believe it was possessed by a demon. We came to a better conclusion about that after we brought a wizard there. He discovered the remnants of the demon. We now believe that the demons on this world are attacking your people to take over the bodies.

I have sent for a Troll Ambassador so they can contact the troll communities. We need to find out if they knew about their people being attacked, and if they did, when it happened. Ambassadors have already met with the elves and the dwarfs. We need to find out if any of them have been attacked. We think they are taking your people to enslave, as well as the trolls, and perhaps the others."

Nakobee, his face showed his confusion, asked, "Why would they do this?"

"To start a war. If they use trolls to fight humans and humans to fight dwarfs, it will cause more hatred and discord between all of you. And there is nothing more demons like better than to cause hatred and start wars."

"What can we do?" asked Nakobee.

"I have asked King Nogar to send a couple of wizards here. He told me we had to get the approval of Queen Kailee and possibly all the other leaders as well. He wants me to go and talk with her first."

Nakobee was about to speak, when Queen Kaila smiled at him.

"I have already told him that since this has happened on my land I'm the only one they have to get permission from. Sword Master Zale agrees and has told King Nogar, but King Nogar still wants to let Queen Kailee and the other leaders know what is happening. I said Sword Master Zale could go, but not until we have a plan to fight these demons."

Nakobee looked at Sword Master Zale.

"When you find out anything from the trolls, I would like to know. If they have been attacked, I would like to send out word to all the clans and see if any will come and help fight the demons."

"That is a good idea. If none come however, King Nogar has informed me he will send more men here to help you fight."

Sword Master Zale looked at each of them.

"I must leave now. I will return as soon as I have more news."

Taking a step back, he disappeared. Kuku jerked back.

"What wizardly magic is this?"

"It is good magic. Do not worry. Living here, you will see many people come and go that way. Now let me see if we can find a place for you and your people to live."

Nakobee led him back to his people.

Chapter Sixteen

Three days after Sword Master Zale left, he returned with Shaméd. They walked toward Nakobee and Queen Kaila.

"Greetings, Queen Kaila and First Sword Nakobee. We have good news and some that might not be so good."

They turned and waited as they came closer.

"Greetings to you, Sword Master Zale and Lord Shaméd. We are always glad to see you, even if you bring us bad news." Queen Kaila smiled, as she said the last part.

Sword Master Zale and Shaméd gave her a slight bow then turned and shook hands with Nakobee.

"What news do you have for us?"

"The council has met with King Nogar and they have agreed to help you. They are sending Lord Shaméd and one hundred men. That is all they will send until you can prove that your world is willing to resist the attackers. What that means is you must gather one thousand soldiers before they will send any more of our people here to help you. Do you think you will be able to accomplish that?"

Nakobee looked at his sister as she turned toward him. They stood there staring at each other before they turned back.

"We have five hundred soldiers of our own. If we ask the other tribes for help, we might get a couple hundred more. What about the Trolls, Elves, and Dwarfs? Have you heard from them? Would they help us?"

"We have heard from all of them. They all have had several villages raided. Each of them was burned to the ground. The Trolls found evidence that Elves did the raids. The Elves found evidence of Trolls, and the Dwarfs say they found evidence of humans. Each is blaming the other. We believe that Dwarfs were used in the attack of your village. We have told them everything we know about what happened with your people, and theirs. They all agree that the demons have been working on their distrust of each other. King Halafarin Bryyra of the Forest Elves was the first to agree to help. They will send one hundred. We have not heard from the other Elves or the Trolls and Dwarfs."

Nakobee looked at the ground, walked a few steps away, and then came back.

"When will your people come? Will we have time to build more buildings for them?"

Shaméd answered before Sword Master Zale could.

"We will be camping outside the walls up the river, near the mountains. The Elves will be staying there with us. If any of the other races come they will stay there as well."

"Why so far? We have room here for over five thousand warriors."

Shaméd answered, "You have the space, but not the buildings. There will be a lot of coming and going by way of the Mirror. We do not want to make your people more upset. Believe me it will be better this way.

What you need to do is send messages to all the human tribes asking for warriors. Once we get them all here, we can develop a plan of attack. In the meantime, I will have my men searching your world for the demons. They can't be too far away.

From what I have found out so far, the demons first attacked a Dwarf village. It happened a year before the attack on yours. Then they used the Dwarfs, possessed by demons, to attack your village. Like we have said, each time they raid, they use the ones captured to attack the next race. From what we have found in the last two villages, it looks like they are now ready to speed things up. The recent attacks on the human villages were within a few months of each other. During the last year a total of six villages were raided: two human, two Dwarfs, one Troll, and one Elf.

They may have enough bodies to carry out a larger attack, now. That is why I'm sending out patrols to gather more information."

"When will you begin?" Queen Kaila asked.

"The men began arriving as I left camp. As soon as they all arrive and set up their camp, I will begin sending them out. If you will excuse me, I will take my leave and go there."

"May I go with you?" asked Nakobee.

"I believe for now, your place is here with your sister and your people. We will come to get you and your men when the time is right."

Shaméd took a step back and disappeared.

"I think we should help. What can we do from here?" asked Nakobee.

"You can keep training your men. The next most important thing you can do is send messengers to the other villages. The more help you have, the better the outcome will be. For now I will leave and check on the others to see when the elves will be arriving." said Zale.

He bowed, stepped back, and disappeared.

"I really do not like it when they do that. You would think they would at least take a few more steps before just disappearing."

Kaila looked at her brother and smiled. He smiled back and they walked toward the men training.

One week later, Shaméd came riding up to the gate. There were three men with him.

At the gate he called out, "Greetings, I'm Shaméd. We are here to meet with Queen Kaila and Nakobee."

The two guards talked to each other, one turned and climbed down the ladder. On the ground, he climbed onto a steed and raced toward the buildings.

The other guard called down, "Open the gate."

He looked at the men on steeds.

"Lord Shaméd, we were told you would be coming. Please enter. The Queen is expecting you."

The gate swung open, and Shaméd and the three men rode in. They reached the building where Queen Kaila lived. Two guards were standing near the door, and a steed was tied off to the side. The two guards came to attention when Shaméd rode up. The man who rode off from the gate came out of door. He went straight to his steed, mounted, and rode away.

Nakobee followed a moment later.

"Greetings, Lord Shaméd. Do you come with good news?"

"Greetings, Nakobee. Yes, I come with good news. Can we have a meeting with Queen Kaila and yourself?"

"Yes, tie your animals there and come in."

Nakobee waited as Shaméd and the three men tied their animals and walked over to the door.

Nakobee recognized the three from his guard duty on Rednog. He glared at one of the young men, who grinned a toothy grin at him. Nakobee turned and entered the building. Shaméd and the three men followed.

Inside, they walked to the long table in the center of the room. The table was twenty feet long with chairs on each side, and a larger chair was at one end. Queen Kaila was sitting there waiting.

Shaméd and the others stopped and bowed.

Shaméd spoke, "Greetings Queen Kaila. I bring you news of the other races and what we have found so far."

"Welcome, Lord Shaméd, please sit and tell us this news."

"First, let me introduce these men."

He turned and pointed to each one as he spoke their names, "This is Jym, that is Jon, and standing back there is Rae. They are friends of mine. I met them on their home world many years ago. They are on Rednog learning so that one day they can return to their own world in the hope that their world can join the coalition."

"Greetings, friends of Lord Shaméd. Please sit and I will have refreshments brought for you."

Kaila looked over at a young woman and nodded her head. The woman turned and left the room. Lord Shaméd sat in the chair closer to her and across from Nakobee. Jym, Jon, and Rae sat at the other end of the table.

Queen Kaila saw this and spoke. "You do not have to sit so far. Please come closer."

Rae spoke, "Your Majesty, we are fine here. You three need to talk. We are only here to watch and learn."

"Then that is why you should sit closer. It will be difficult to hear us from down there."

They stood and moved closer. When they were all sitting again, the first woman returned with another young woman. They were carrying trays. They walked around the table and placed drinks and a small plate with bread and cheese in front of each of them, then moved away.

"Now, Lord Shaméd, please tell us what news have you to share?"

"First the good news: the Trolls, Elves, and Dwarfs have each sent one hundred warriors. They are all at our camp at the base of the mountain. The other news is we think we have found the enemy's camp."

"That is good news. Do we have a time for our attack?"

Shaméd took a sip of his drink, then looked at Nakobee, and then Queen Kaila.

"That is the first problem. We found a large camp of demons on the other side of the mountain deep within Queen Liseran's land. We know of the little trouble Nakobee had with Quoin. So there might be a problem if an army shows up.

We are thinking that I, or another, might go there to let them know about the Demon army that is on their land."

Queen Kaila looked at her brother and smiled, and then she looked at Shaméd.

"I think that might be a good idea. We have not heard from any of the other lands. It might be due to the fact that I'm a new Queen, and they just do not want to help me. Or they might not want to leave their land without any warriors to deal with an invading army."

Shaméd nodded his head in agreement.

"That is another point. We have used the mirror to look across the land belonging to the humans. Your land is not the only one with villages destroyed. We have found four on the outskirts of Queen Liseran's land and three in Queen Kailee's land. I'm not sure if they know about them, or if they do, they are not telling anyone.

From what we found, those villages were completely destroyed. There was nothing left of the buildings or animals."

Nakobee looked at his sister.

"I would think Queen Kailee would have said something if she knew about the raids. Maybe you or Sword Master Zale could talk with her?"

"Master Zale thought the same thing, which is why he went there to talk with Queen Kailee and Kouly."

"Is there anything more you need to tell us?" asked Kaila.

"I have informed you about the location of the Demon horde, and that I will be going to talk with Queen Liseran. If things work out we should be able to march against them within the month.

We do have patrols out searching the countryside to make sure no more of your land has been attacked."

"I thank you for that. May I ask how the Trolls, Elves, and Dwarfs are handling the information? From everything I have heard, they have never been sympathetic to what happens to the other races."

"They each have been told. We have people from my world working with them. I do not think there will be any trouble."

"That is good to hear. I would not want to cause trouble among our people and the other races. If there is nothing more, I need to get back to my studies and Nakobee needs to see how the work is going."

"I have nothing more to report."

Queen Kaila stood. Shaméd, Jym, Jon, and Rae, as well as Nakobee, also stood. Queen Kaila left the room and Nakobee led the others to the door.

Once outside Shaméd spoke, "You have done a great job rebuilding your home. The walls and buildings are coming along very nicely. I noticed that you have increased your crops. There are even some gardens near the buildings."

"Yes, we think there might be a lot of people coming so we wanted to make sure we had plenty of food, if and when that happens. We have also increased the size of our livestock. Master Elfaren said *It is better to be over prepared than to be without.*" That is something I took to heart. I use it in everything we do. It is better to have more food and better protection than we need. That is why our walls are so high. Most walls built around villages are only three feet high. Ours are twenty feet high and four feet thick. They will withstand anything that is on this world."

Shaméd grinned.

"You might want to remember, anything that can keep others out, can also keep you in. Making sure you are safe within your walls is one thing. Making sure you are safe and can live within them is another."

Nakobee stared at Shaméd, contemplating his words.

"I will have to think about what you have said."

Shaméd and the others mounted their steeds. He nodded his head.

"Until we meet again, Nakobee."

Shaméd turned his animal toward the gate and the four of them rode away.

Nakobee stood there watching for a few seconds, then he headed to where his men were working on another building.

As they drew closer to the gate Jon looked at Shaméd.

"What was that all about?"

"I wanted him to think about what he is doing. I know why he is building the walls so high. I just don't want him and his people to be trapped inside them."

They rode on in silence. At the gate, the guards opened it and they rode out toward the mountains.

Chapter Seventeen

The trip back to their camp would take four days. Shaméd and his group rode to the village that had been attacked. After looking it over, they headed north to their camp.

The land was open with scattered trees and tall grass everywhere. The wild life was mixed in with the herd animals from the village.

"Why do you suppose they didn't take the herd animals? It makes no sense." said Jon.

Shaméd answered without looking at him, "That is a good question. If it is demons doing this, you would think they would have taken them. More important, if it is any of the other races, you would think they would have taken the animals to add to their fortune."

They rode on in silence.

"The only reason I can think of is because they knew they were returning. Why take something if you know you will need it later," Rae said.

They looked at Rae, none of them saying anything. They just kept riding. They rode through the small herds without them reacting. It was as if they had nothing to fear.

When they returned to camp they were met by Sword Master Zale. They rode up to where he stood.

"Did you find anything of importance on your little adventure?"

They got down off the animals, tied them, and stood in front of Sword Master Zale.

"Nothing we did not already know. Have you found out anything more?"

"Come inside. We found another place where demons are hiding."

Master Zale turned and led the way inside his tent. He walked over to the table in the center and sat in one of the eight chairs. Shaméd, Jon, Jym, and Rae took chairs across from him.

"We have confirmation that the demon army in Queen Liseran's land has been there a long time. They may be there with her permission. Until we find out, we will have to wait. We do have scouts watching their camp. We found another camp located at the edge of Queen Liseran's land near the Troll's kingdom."

"Have we talked with the Trolls?"

"Yes. After giving King Tragi proof of demons using his people to attack other races, he was not happy. He knew about the raids on a couple of his villages and the people missing. He did not know who was responsible until now."

"Will he help us?"

"Yes, he gave us fifty of his warriors. He and the rest of his army will only fight on his land, though. He will not break any of the ancient laws. His warriors are patrolling the land in search of the demons."

"Have we heard from the elves and the dwarfs?"

"We have heard from both. Karlen met with King Deleon inside his mountain. He has agreed to send fifty of his dwarf warriors to help with the war. Like King Tragi, he has his men searching.

King Laquan of the Elves, will send fifty of his archers. He has locked his borders to all traffic. There will be no trade until this is taken care of."

Shaméd sat there writing down some notes. He looked up.

"With those one hundred and fifty warriors and our twenty five and the men that Nakobee has. That gives us only six hundred and seventy five warriors. Can we get more from the council?"

"I do not believe any more help will be coming from Rednog. Catera will be arriving soon. He is one of two elves coming to help in case magic is needed. I do not know the name of the other who is coming.

I was informed by the council that under no circumstance are you to use any magic. Only Catera and the other elf are to use magic."

"That is sort of stupid. Why can't Shaméd use magic? He is a wizard, after all."

Jon sat there looking around at the others. Sword Master Zale glared at him.

"Because they said he could not. I did not ask them for their reason. I was told and I follow orders, as will Shaméd."

"To me, that is a very stupid order to follow."

Everyone looked at Rae, he had not spoken since arriving and Shaméd was surprised at his comment.

"We are to follow orders from the council. We may not understand them, but they are wise and know what they are doing," Shaméd said.

"They are not here. You are a great swordsman and one of the best fighters I have ever seen. I, however, would feel more comfortable knowing if we were in real trouble, you could use magic to get us out of it."

"Let us hope we don't get into such a situation," Shaméd said as he looked around the table.

Two days later, Shaméd was called to Zale's tent. When he arrived, Berko, the man who was sent to speak with Queen Liseran, was there. He was chosen because he could pass as a human of that world. He was of medium height with dark skin.

Berko was not in a good mood. He was dressed in the blue-green robes of the tribe belonging to Queen Kailee. He stood at the end of the table looking at Sword Master Zale and Shaméd.

"I have never been treated so badly. That man of hers, Quoin, is a pompous backend of a steed. He stood there glaring at me. He would not let Queen Liseran speak. Every time I asked her a question, he would answer. He said they have never had any trouble with the demons. He told me, if we are having trouble with them, we should go and talk to their leader.

He said their treaty with the demons has benefited them very well. He and Queen Liseran would never do anything to damage it. As far as they are concerned, if we have any grievances with the demons, we should stop trying to drag them into it.

When I was there, demons walked freely around the village. I saw that people were afraid of them but could do nothing when they were abused by them."

"Do you think Queen Liseran and Quoin are offering humans to the demons?"

Shaméd sat there waiting for the answer.

"They have way too much wealth for the size of their kingdom. There were very few people working the fields and the animals just roamed the land. For that matter, I saw more warriors than workers.

I found a servant who said the demons give Queen Liseran her weight in gold every full moon. They have been doing it for the last five years. In the last year they have been spending more time in the village, and he heard there is a camp on their land. The servant told me the people are frightened. The agreement was that the demons do no harm to the Queen's people and she allows them to stay there. The humans are afraid of the demons. Those who complain about the demons, come up missing, and no one says anything for fear of their being taken next."

Shaméd was angry. He looked at Sword Master Zale and said, "We need to tell Nogar and the council. If there are humans on this world working with demons to kill all the races, they need to hear about it."

Berko looked at Shaméd and Sword Master Zale.

"I can leave now and give King Nogar and the council my report."

Sword Master Zale was visibly upset with the news. He looked at Berko.

"Do that. Please return when you are finished. We may need your help talking with the other humans."

Berko faced Sword Master Zale, saluted, turned, and took two steps and was gone.

Shaméd looked at Sword Master Zale and said, "This is not good. How do we fight demons who are working with humans? We cannot attack one without attacking the other. And we cannot do either without more proof."

Sword Master Zale nodded his head and answered, "That is true. I will go and talk with Queen Kailee and First

Sword Kouly. They need to know what Queen Liseran and Quoin have done. Maybe they can talk with Queen Liseran. They might figure out that their daughter was killed because of this pact between Queen Liseran and the demons."

Master Zale pushed his chair back and stood and so did Shaméd.

"Since you are going to Queen Kailee, I will return to Nakobee and Queen Kaila and inform them of what we have found out." said Shaméd.

Master Zale took a step and disappeared. Shaméd left the tent and went searching for Rae, Jon, and Jym. They gathered supplies to last them a week, packed their animals, and rode out three hours after sunrise.

Chapter Eighteen

When Shaméd rode up to the gate, the same guards were there and they recognized him. They waved the group through as the gate was opened. The four rode straight to where Nakobee lived. Nakobee was just walking out as they arrived.

"Greetings, Shaméd. What brings you back so soon?"

"Greetings, Nakobee. We have more news about the demon horde. Can we meet with you and Queen Kaila?"

"I will send word to her that you wish to see her."

Nakobee turned and spoke to a man standing nearby. The man nodded his head and ran towards the Queen's home.

"Come inside and have a drink as we wait."

The group climbed down from their steeds. Two men came over and took the reins of the animals and led them to water. Shaméd and the others followed Nakobee inside. They walked over to the table and sat. As they were sitting down, a man servant came in carrying a tray. He set a cup in front of each of them and poured wine in each cup.

"When do you think we will attack the demon army?" asked Nakobee.

"That is what we need to talk about."

Shaméd was about to say more but the door opened and Kaila entered. They all stood.

She waved at them and spoke, as she walked over to the table, "Please sit. Shaméd, it is good to see you. I hope since you have returned so soon, it is because you bring good news."

"I'm afraid I do not bring good news."

Queen Kaila sat next to her brother and looked at Shaméd. She waved him on to speak more.

"We found where the main body of the demons is holed up. Like we thought, they are camped on Queen Liseran's land."

"Does she know this?"

"Yes, she does. We were informed by First Sword Quoin that they, or as he pointed out, Queen Liseran has made a pact with them. The demons can stay there with her blessing and protection. As long as they do not harm any of her people, and they tithe her weight in gold every full moon, they can stay."

Queen Kaila looked at him in disbelief.

"They would condemn all the other races for gold? Don't they know when the demons are finished with us, they will turn on them next?"

"I do not believe they have thought that far ahead. They are only interested in the gold. After finding out how robust Queen Liseran is and how much gold that is, I think they are just too greedy to care."

Nakobee slammed his fist down on the table and yelled, "We will attack them anyway. They do not have the army to fight us."

"I'm afraid they do. You only have maybe five hundred warriors, most of whom are young and untried. We brought twenty five warriors. Add that to how many the trolls, dwarfs, and elves are sending. That means at best we have six hundred and seventy-five warriors. The demon army is over five thousand strong, and if Queen Liseran does send her men to fight, that would be another thousand. We would lose.

We need to train and build up your army. All we can do for now is hope they do not attack anymore villages. You need to send word out to the others under your rule. Let them know that they need to be ready to fight or flee if the demons come at them.

You might have to bring all of them here to be safe. That would help build up your army and keep more of your people alive."

Nakobee looked at his sister. Her head was down and her eyes closed, she was deep in thought. No one spoke as she sat there thinking.

Finally, she raised her head and opened her eyes.

"Nakobee, you will send word to all the villages. Inform them of the danger we are facing. Tell them it will be their choice if they want to come here or stay, and hope the demons do not attack them.

I want more people working on the walls. They must be finished by the next full moon. We will also need to stock up food supplies. If the other villages come we will have to have plenty of supplies."

She stood and the others stood as well. She looked around the table.

"I hope, Shaméd, we can count on you and your men."

"You can. We will have them pack up and come here as fast as they can."

"Good. I will leave and get started on the things I can do. Nakobee, if you would do as I asked?"

She looked at her brother, then nodded at each man, and then left.

Jon, Rae, and Jym headed to the door. Shaméd and Nakobee were right behind them.

Outside Jon spoke, "Well, that was straight and to the point. Looks like we have a long ride to camp and then back here. Just what I like to do, ride and have my back side bruised."

Shaméd looked at him and the others.

"All of you will stay here. I will return to camp and bring the others back."

Jon stood by his steed looking at Shaméd and said, "I still have belongings there. There is no way I will want any of those ruffians packing my things."

Rae looked at Jon, and in a questioning voice spoke, "You just said you did not want to ride there and back."

"No, what I said was, looks like we have a long ride to camp and then back here. It's just what I like to do, ride and have my backside bruised. I did not say I did not want to do the riding."

Jon leaned closer to Rae and whispered. "Besides, you know the history I have with him." Jon shrugged towards Nakobee. "He just might decide now that I'm here, he can do what he almost did in the council room."

Rae was going to argue but Jym put his hand on his arm and shook his head.

"Don't. It is not worth it."

Jym looked at Shaméd.

"Rae and I can stay and help Nakobee."

Shaméd looked at Jon, "Then mount up. We leave now."

Shaméd and Jon mounted their animals and rode toward the gate. Rae and Jym stood there with Nakobee.

"What do we do now?" asked Jym

Nakobee looked at them and said, "I want to ride to the mountains. Do you want to go with me?"

"That is why we are here. We go wherever you need us to go," Rae answered.

"Then come on."

Rae and Jym took the reins of their animals and followed Nakobee to the stables. On the way, Nakobee found Lea and told him to send men to all the other villages. Lea said he would take care of it.

Once they arrived at the stables, Nakobee asked one of the men there to pack an animal with two days of supplies. Then he picked out one for himself, and saddled it. When everything was prepared, they mounted and rode away.

They headed for the north gate. As the gate closed behind them, Nakobee took the road going along the base of the mountain. As they rode, Nakobee looked at Rae and Jym. He had done that several times.

The last time he did, Jym spoke. "Why do you keep looking at us?"

"I was trying to think of the reason they would send you three here?"

Jym looked at Rae who just shrugged his shoulders. Jym answered, "It is part of our training?"

Nakobee looked at Rae with a puzzled expression.

"Training? You have been on Rednog for maybe a year, and you are already being sent out for training? I could believe the both of you were chosen to stay on

Rednog, but not the other one. He is annoying and he could bring out the anger in a priest."

Rae grinned, "We know. We have known Jon a long time. We are used to him. As far as the time thing, five years have passed since you left Rednog."

"Five years? It has only been a little over a year since we returned here."

"Yeah, we know about the time thing. Time on Rednog is different than on your world, and even on our own world."

They rode on in silence. Five hours later, they stopped and Nakobee sat there looking up at the mountain.

"What are you looking for?" Asked Jym

"These mountains are filled with caves. I have been thinking it must be how they have been coming to our land. In all the years my people have lived here, we have only found two caves that go through the mountain. One is just north of our village. The other is somewhere around here. We have not used it in many years because it is so far and the path through is long and difficult.

As for going over the mountains, there are only a few places you can cross over. None are within a month's ride of our city."

"When you find this cave, what are we going to do?"

Rae leaned forward in his saddle.

"I plan on entering to see if anyone has used it, recently."

They dismounted and after tying the animals to a tree, Nakobee turned to them.

"We should make camp here, then start looking for the cave opening. It should be somewhere around here."

"How do you know it is here if no one has been to it in a long time?"

"Because when we are children we are taught where the caves are in case of an attack and we need to retreat. Everyone knows the location of the main cave. It is just up the mountain from our village. This one is over there."

Nakobee pointed up at the mountain toward a group of tall trees. Those five large trees were planted many years ago to mark the location. I remember hearing that many years ago, when my father was with a group of warriors, lightning from the sky came and set the land on fire. The fire swept fast across the dry land, burning everything. They had to hide in this cave for five days.

When they emerged, the land was completely destroyed. All the animals that could not escape, were dead. It took years for the trees and animals to return."

"That must have been hard for your father to have seen. Was he the son of the chief?"

"My father was a young warrior. He had come across the mountain and joined our clan. The leader at that time was a cousin to Queen Kailee. If you are going to ask how my father met and married my mother I will tell you. He saved her life years after the great fire. His reward was getting a beating for touching her.

Queen Kailee was not impressed that one of her warriors, let alone one from another land, would dare touch the daughter of the Queen, even if it meant saving her life. She told him she was glad he saved her, but he should have taken his own life after doing so."

Jym was shocked at what Nakobee said.

"That is a little extreme, don't you think? He saved the Queen's daughter and for doing that, he got a beating? You are saying they were supposed to just stand there and watch her die."

Jym looked at Rae and asked, "Would you have saved her if you knew you would get a beating?"

Rae looked at Nakobee and grinned.

"If I loved someone as much as Nakobee's father did, yes, I would take a beating to save the one I loved."

Jym stared at Nakobee, a grin slowly spread across his face.

"Oh, that was why he did it. Did they get married soon after that?"

"No, Queen Kailee would not let them get married. Not for two years. There was an attack on our village by Trolls. Queen Kailee's cousin was killed. My father and ten other warriors fought off the Trolls, killing those that did not flee. Only my father, ten warriors, and a handful of people survived. My mother said she would come here and rebuild the land. Queen Kailee agreed, and she sent a hundred warriors with her. A week after my mother was here, she named my father First Sword. A year later she married him."

"Was Queen Kailee mad?"

"She was furious, but she could do nothing. My mother had not only rebuilt this land, she had brought in five tribes to help protect it. Our village grew from just over a hundred to over two thousand. Our holdings grew from a couple thousand acres to all of the land from the mountain down to the sea, and around the great lake. My mother had increased her territory a hundred fold."

Rae spoke, "Your mother sounds like she was a great leader."

"She was. The people loved her. Each tribe increased their territory each year. Three years after she became queen, they expanded to the other side of the great lake. Her kingdom became the third largest in the land of humans."

After they set up camp, they headed up the mountain. As they went, the trees grew thicker. They stopped when Nakobee raised his hand.

Nakobee bent down and touched the ground, and after looking around, he stood and looked at them.

"We are a few hundred feet from the cave. People have been here. Someone tried to cover their tracks, but they did a bad job."

"Do we go closer?" asked Jym

"Yes, but slowly. I do not want to have to fight our way back."

They spread out and made their way closer to the cave. They stopped when they reached the edge of a clearing. They were twenty feet from the cave opening. They observed the cave and saw five men and what they could only think of as two large beasts.

Nakobee looked over at Rae and Jym. He motioned for them to retreat. They met back in the trees, about three hundred feet from the cave.

Nakobee in a soft voice asked, "Did you see the two beasts? Could either of you make out what they were?"

They both said yes they saw them, but they had no idea what they were.

Nakobee said, "They could be demons, or humans possessed by them."

Jym and Rae nodded their heads in agreement.

"We need to let Shaméd know what we have found. If we go cross country it will take two days to reach his camp. We might be there the same time he arrives."

Nakobee stared up in the direction of the cave.

Rae whispered, "Then we should head back to camp and move it. We are too close to stay there."

Nakobee looked at Rae, nodding his head. "I agree. We need to leave before we are caught."

They stood and headed back down.

Suddenly, ten men came screaming out of the rocks and trees, their weapons whipping through the air. Rae blocked one man's sword as he stabbed another.

Jym blocked a sword and moved back when two came at him with spears.

Nakobee grabbed the spear that was thrust at him with his left hand, and slammed his right hand into the man's jaw. The sound of bone crunching was loud, at least it sounded loud to Nakobee. The man fell to the ground and Nakobee drew his sword. As he turned, he blocked the blades of two men coming at him. With the spear in one hand and his sword in the other, he attacked. Ducking and turning, he drove the spear into the chest of one soldier and blocked the other man's downward swing.

Bringing his sword up, then back down, he sliced through the warrior's uniform, opening up his stomach. The man fell back, dying as he fell.

Turning, he saw Rae and Jym back to back fighting warriors. Nakobee moved in to help. He hit one in the head with his fist. The man fell, rolling down the hill, stopping only when he crashed against a tree. Two men turned to face him with their spears. He blocked and jabbed the one on his right, killing him. As he killed this last man, he saw that Rae and Jym had taken care of the last three soldiers.

Nakobee spoke as he looked around, "We need to leave fast, before they are missed and others come looking for them."

As they turned to leave, they heard movement. The warrior Nakobee had hit and had fallen against the tree, stirred. Jym went over and turned him face up.

Jym looked at Nakobee and said, "He is alive, just dizzy. Do you want to take him so you can ask him some questions?"

Nakobee looked at Rae then back at Jym and answered. "Yes."

The man opened his eyes and started to scream. Jym hit him with the hilt of his sword, knocking him out. He checked his pulse, then nodded his head.

"He is still alive."

Jym tied the man's hands. Looking at his feet, he looked back at Nakobee.

"We will have to wake him and make him walk. Unless I tie his feet and we carry him."

Nakobee knew neither of them could carry the man down the hill.

"Tie his feet. I will carry him."

Jym tied the man's feet. Nakobee put his sword away, bent down and with one hand grabbed the front of the man's uniform. With the ease of one so big, he raised and tossed the man over his shoulder. They headed down to where they left the animals. Within an hour, they reached camp, and were soon on their way with the man on the back of Nakobee's beast.

Chapter Nineteen

As night fell, they found a grove of trees and made camp. They did not make a fire. They hobbled their animals and ate cold rations.

As they sat and ate, the soldier they had captured glared at them, his expression showing hate, but his eyes showed what he really felt: fear. He did not know if he would be tortured or what would happen to him. All he knew was he hoped they would not take him back to Queen Liseran. He knew if Queen Liseran got him back, Quoin would have his skin slowly peeled off, and then he would be fed to a demon.

Nakobee stood and walked over to the soldier. Standing over him and looking down, he spoke, "Will you speak for food? Or will you go hungry, and we just beat you until you talk?"

The soldier looked up at Nakobee. The man standing in front of him was twice his size. He was not fat, he was all muscle, and the man's arms were bigger than his own legs. He looked as if he had been in many battles from the scars on his body.

The only clothing he wore was an animal skin around his waist and leather boots, and the large stone on a metal chain that hung around his neck. There was a sword and large knife on the belt hanging around his waist. He had never seen a human as large as this. He had heard of men who were giants living north of the Snow Mountains, but he had never seen them or heard of any this far south. He decided to just sit there.

Nakobee bent down, grabbed the front of his uniform, and raised the man into the air. With their faces just inches apart, Nakobee glared at him.

"I asked you a question. Will you speak for food, or go hungry, and we just beat you until you talk?"

The soldier wet himself and in a weak, shaky voice, said, "I will talk for food."

Nakobee lowered the man back to the ground. He walked back to the packs, reached in, and pulled out some dried meat. He looked at Rae and Jym who were sitting there with their eyes wide, and a shocked expression on their faces. Nakobee winked at them and walked back to the soldier.

He handed the dried meat to the soldier, and then squatted down in front of him. As the soldier took a bite of the meat, he looked at Nakobee staring at him.

Nakobee asked, "I can see from the color of your uniform you are one of Queen Liseran's men. What are you doing in Queen Kaila's land? And do not lie; I hate liars."

The soldier swallowed, his hands were shaking. He tried to speak, nothing came out. He tried again, but still nothing. His eyes rolled back into his head and he passed out.

Nakobee stood and walked back to Rae and Jym.

"If all of Queen Liseran's men are like that, we have nothing to fear."

Rae looked at Nakobee then over at the soldier on the ground.

"Nakobee, you do understand how scary you look, don't you?"

Nakobee looked at Rae and then at Jym who nodded his head.

"I don't understand. Why do you think I'm scary to look at? I don't think I'm ugly. Do you?"

"You are not ugly. I suppose some would say you are an attractive man. You are, however, very large and intimidating. When you look at people, you scare them. Did you not ever wonder why the humans on Rednog moved out of your way when you walked down the hallway?"

"I thought it was because of Lau. Most humans move out of the way when ogres are coming at them."

"Yes, they do, but most humans on Rednog have never seen a human as large as you. That and the fact every one there heard about the fights between you and Lau. No student has ever stood up to him or any ogre, until you did. They thought you were crazy when they heard about it. Then when they found out you did not die, they were both impressed and terrified."

"Why would they be terrified?"

"Because they had never heard of a human who was not a wizard, holding their own with an ogre."

Nakobee looked at them and gave a little laugh. "It is easy once you know their weaknesses."

Jym leaned forward.

"Ogres have a weakness? What is it?"

Nakobee was not sure if they were messing with him.

He asked, "Neither of you know their weakness?"

They shook their head, no. Their eyes were wide. Nakobee leaned forward and said. "Their shins, hit them in the shins and they go down. That is the only place I found that they feel pain."

Rae looked at Jym. They both smiled.

"Now, what are we going to do with this soldier over there?" Nakobee said as he pointed at the man.

"When he wakes, I will talk with him. He might not be so afraid talking to me. I will point at you to give him the impression I will give him to you if he doesn't speak."

Rae smiled at Nakobee, who just sat there not fully understanding the meaning of his words.

A few minutes later the soldier woke and Rae walked over.

"Hello. Did you have a nice nap? Do you think you can speak now?"

The man looked from Rae to where Jym and Nakobee sat. Nakobee was sitting there staring at him.

The man's body shook. As he turned to look at Rae he thought, this man was different, he has fair skin, not dark like his or his people.

He looked at the man's ears to see if maybe he was an elf. They were normal. He took a closer look. Besides Rae's skin color being different, he had long blond hair. The man wore a brown shirt with a leather vest. The vest had four metal knives in sheaths attached to the front. On his forearms he had leather gauntlets with four more metal knives. On each of his boots were knives, the handles were made of bone.

The sword on his hip he knew was a metal sword. The hilt looked like the ones the old warriors had. He also had a long knife across from his sword. This man must be rich to have so much metal. He felt safer talking to him.

"Yes, I will tell you whatever you want to know."

"Good. Just to be sure, you are one of Queen Liseran's men, correct?"

"Yes. I'm Lieutenant Lepton of the third regiment."

"Good, now Lieutenant Lepton why are you in Queen Kaila's kingdom?"

"We are here under the orders of First Sword Quoin."

"Ok, why did this Quoin order you here?"

"We are to help the demons gather bodies and guard the cave from anyone entering it."

"Why do the demons need bodies? And why is Quoin helping them? And why does the cave need guarding?"

"The demons need bodies to overrun the humans. They mark some so they can be controlled from far away. Some demons enter the bodies, then control them as their own. They use these bodies to fight other tribes. Then the demons are not suspected.

As for the reason First Sword Quoin is helping, I would assume it is because of the gold they give him."

"You mean the gold they give to Queen Liseran?"

The man looked even more nervous, he spoke in a low voice, "I do not think Queen Liseran knows what First Sword Quoin is doing. She does whatever he says. Every full moon when it comes time to weigh her, she just sits on the scale and smiles at the people."

Rae looked over at Nakobee and Jym, then back at Lieutenant Lepton.

"You are saying Queen Liseran knows nothing about the raids and the killings going on around her kingdom? You want us to believe she is that stupid?"

The man lowered his eyes. Again in a low voice, he answered, "My Queen is a child."

"Your Queen is almost twenty years old."

"What I mean is, she has a child's brain. Her mother died giving her birth. She should not have lived, but her father did everything to keep her alive. When she was ten years old, he knew that her mind would never grow. She would always be a child. In his despair, he killed himself. That was when Quoin took over. He was the personal guard to the young Liseran, and he knew what was happening. He grabbed the title First Sword saying the young Queen gave it to him. When people asked her, she of course said yes. He has been in control ever since."

"How is it you know so much? I would think anyone who knew the truth would have been killed by this Quoin. Why is it you are still alive?"

With his eyes still down he shook his head.

"It is because I'm his brother."

Nakobee and Jym both sat straighter when they heard him. Rae thought about his next few words before speaking them.

"You are his brother. What do your parents and the rest of your family think about what he is doing?"

"They are all dead. When he was fifteen and I was ten, our parents and sister, as well as most of those in our village died in a plague. All those left alive were taken and made soldiers. Because we had no family, we were assigned to the royal house. My brother was given the chore of being the personal guard to the then, Princess Liseran. He, as you now know, made good use of the position. I, being his little brother, was given the rank of Lieutenant and assigned to the north lands.

When the demons came six years ago, I was reassigned with a small group of warriors who would work with them. I knew what he was doing, but there was nothing I could do. He disbanded the elders and he is in complete control. Anyone who speaks out against him is given to the demons."

Rae stood and walked over to Nakobee. Sitting down across from him, he just looked at him.

After a few seconds, Nakobee spoke, "When I first met this Quoin, I thought he was worthless. Now after hearing what he has done, I think he is a worm."

Jym looked at Nakobee and asked, "You met this Quoin? When?"

"When word was spread that we would pay for any soldiers or people other kingdoms did not want, he came to our village with men trained on Rednog. We had some words, we fought, I won. He left without being paid."

"You fought him and did not kill him?"

"The fight was not to the death. It was about how much money I would pay for the men he brought. Now, of course, I wish I had killed him."

"That might have been a bad thing."

Nakobee looked at Rae, and asked, "Why do you say that?"

"If Queen Liseran really has a child's mind, and you had killed Quoin, a demon would have taken over her body and her people would be suffering even more."

Nakobee nodded his head in agreement.

"We need to tell the other lands about Quoin. They might all unite against him."

"From what Sword Master Zale has said about the humans on this world and what I know about humans, I don't think it will change their minds. They will want to protect their own kingdoms first."

Nakobee stood and walked over to Lieutenant Lepton. The man shook visibly when he approached.

"I'm not going to hurt you. I want your word you will not try to escape, otherwise we will tie you to that tree. I believe you would sleep better if you could spread out."

"You would take my word?"

"Why not? You are a Lieutenant, an officer in your Queen's army. We are not officially at war. So until you lie to me, I will treat you as you should be treated, as an honorable man. Now do I have your word?"

Lieutenant Lepton looked up at Nakobee.

"Yes, you have my word. You also have my apology for all the wrong I have done you and your Queen."

Nakobee nodded his head. He reached down and cut the bindings, then turned away, but stopped. He looked back.

"One last question. Why are you guarding the cave?"

"We are guarding it so no one will know about the gold."

"Gold? What gold?"

There was the sound of confusion in Nakobee's words.

Lepton wiggled, he was now even more frightened. He was unsure how this Nakobee would react to what he was about to say.

"The demons said there was gold in these mountains. They have humans and dwarfs working there bringing it out. That is where they are getting the gold they give Quoin."

Nakobee looked down at him. He was trying to grasp the words of what he just heard.

"They are using humans and dwarfs as slaves, forcing them to dig gold from *our* mountain. Then they are giving our gold to your brother? This is how they are paying for their war? I will rip your brother's arms off if I ever see him again."

Lepton looked at him and knew that his brother would indeed lose his arms if Nakobee ever met him again. Nakobee's face contorted from the anger he was feeling. He turned and headed back to his bedding.

Rae and Jym watched as he walked away. They hoped he would not take out his anger for Quoin on Lepton.

Nakobee looked at them before sitting down.

"If we are doing a night watch, I will take the last one."

He stretched out on the ground, closed his eyes, and went to sleep.

Rae looked at Jym. They looked at Lepton. They saw the man was scared for his life.

Rae said, "I will take the first watch. I will wake you in four hours."

Jym started to speak, but just shook his head and moved to his bedding and closed his eyes.

Chapter Twenty

In the morning, Rae and Jym woke to a small fire that Nakobee was sitting near. A pot was on the fire and three bowls were laid out. Nakobee seemed to be in a better mood.

"I have made gruel. Come and get some before we head out."

Rae looked at Jym. Neither had any idea what gruel was and were not looking forward to finding out. They came and sat on rocks by the fire and looked into the pot. Inside, they saw what looked like a white paste.

Nakobee scooped up a spoonful and put it in a bowl and handed it to Rae. Then he did the same to the next bowl. Rae and Jym sat there looking at their bowls.

Rae bent and took a sniff. He took hold of the spoon and took a bite.

After he swallowed, he looked at Nakobee.

"This is not bad. It could use something to make it a little sweeter, but it does not taste bad."

Nakobee picked up a gourd and tossed it to him.

"Add some of this; it is a sweet paste."

Rae pulled the cork out and tipped the gourd. After a few seconds, a thick yellow paste slowly came out. Rae mixed it in, put the cork back, and then took a bite.

"That does make it better."

Jym looked at Rae. He was trying to see if Rae was tricking him. He knew Rae had a difficult time eating food that others made. He only ate the food he made, or if he knew the person who was cooking.

Jym took a small bite. As he swallowed he looked at Rae.

"You're right, it is good."

Reaching for the gourd, he poured some of the sweet stuff over his food. He stirred it and took another bite.

"I think I could get use to this. What is it made from?"

Rae spoke before Nakobee could answer, "Do not tell us. I do not want to know until after I have eaten. Maybe not even then."

Nakobee smiled and kept eating. When he was done, he stood and walked over to Lepton.

"Would you like some gruel?"

He looked up at Nakobee and in a low voice answered, "Yes, thank you, I would like some."

Nakobee handed him a bowl full. Then went back to the fire and put it out. He started cleaning the pot and putting things away.

Jym watched as Nakobee worked. Looking at Rae he grinned.

"I think Nakobee is a lot like you. He likes to cook and clean. It might be fun watching you two fight over who does things when we are out in the field."

Rae looked at Jym and grunted as he took another bite. When they were done, Rae cleaned his bowl as well as Jym's. They loaded the animals and when they were finished they turned and looked at Lieutenant Lepton.

He sat there waiting, not sure what was going to happen. He did not have long to wait.

Rae looked at Lepton and spoke, "Well, who is going to kill him?"

Lepton almost wet himself again.

Nakobee looked at Rae and frowned.

"No one is going to kill him."

Rae looked at Nakobee and said, "We cannot take him with us. No one is to know we were even here. And if we are still going to meet Shaméd, we will have to take him back to Keele, first."

"Rae is right," Jym said.

Nakobee looked at both of them.

130

"We are taking him to Shaméd. When we get there Shaméd can clear his mind. He will never remember anything."

"Shaméd can do that? I did not know he could do that, did you?" Jym said as he looked at Rae.

"No. How do you know he can do that? We have known Shaméd longer than you. And we did not know he could do that."

Nakobee stood there staring at them.

"He is a wizard. All wizards can do that."

Turning he stepped closer to Lepton.

"If you give me your word you will try not to escape or attack us, you can ride behind me. Otherwise you will ride tied up on the pack animal like baggage."

"Even if I escaped, there is no where I could go. I give you my word I will do nothing to hinder your mission."

"Why do you say there is nowhere to go? You could return to your people."

Lepton looked at Nakobee and said, "By now they have found my squad. They are dead and I'm missing. My brother would kill me as soon as I returned. He does not believe anyone could escape if ever caught. He also knows I would break if captured and questioned. Besides we are trained to kill ourselves the first chance we have if we are ever captured."

"That is a little extreme, but useful. If you are dead the enemy cannot get anything out of you. So why did you not kill yourself?" asked Rae.

The man looked down at his feet.

"Because I had nothing to kill myself with."

"You could have refused to talk, and Nakobee would have snapped your neck. Then, you would be dead and we would never have learned about your brother."

Rae stood there waiting for his answer. Nakobee glanced at him. Jym never stopped looking at Lepton. He knew what Rae was doing.

Lepton looked at his feet then answered, "The other reason is because I did not want to die. I have never wanted to be a soldier. I lasted this long and was only made Lieutenant because of my brother."

"What did you want to be?" asked Rae.

Lepton looked at him, not sure how to answer the question. He stood there thinking. Should he be honest or just stop talking?

"I wanted to be like my father."

"What did your father do?"

"He was a farmer and a rancher. We had a large spread near Fendal."

Rae looked at Nakobee and said, "He can ride behind me. Your animal can hardly handle your weight."

Jym burst out laughing. He stopped when Nakobee turned and glared at him. Then Nakobee leaned his head back and laughed at Jym and Rae.

"You are right, I do scare people. I will have to be more careful."

They mounted and headed out. They rode until noon. The sky was clear and a slight breeze made the air feel cool. They stopped near a stream and tied their animals under a group of trees. Rae handed out dried meat and bread.

Jym was looking around at the landscape. The grass was tall, almost waist deep. The trees that were around were thirty feet apart and in small groups of five, as if they had been planted that way. He was just about to ask Nakobee about the trees, when he noticed a movement. It was on the other side of the stream. The grass was moving in the opposite direction of the wind.

Using his left foot, he tapped Rae's right boot. Rae looked at him and was about to speak when he saw Jym move his head. Rae looked in the direction and saw the grass moving.

Standing, he walked over to his steed. He laid his cloak over the saddle and checked his knives on his chest and arms. Then he untied his bow and arrows, and took them off the back of the saddle.

Turning he called out to Nakobee, "I heard you were not bad with a bow. Care to make a small wager on who is better?"

Nakobee looked at Rae. Taking another bite of meat, he stood and walked over to him.

"Why are you challenging me?"

"I'm just trying to pass the time. Are you afraid I might beat you?"

"I do not care if you can shoot a bow better than I."

"Come on, how about you try and hit that tree on the other side of the stream, that one a little to the right?"

Rae pointed and Nakobee looked. As he did, the grass stopped moving, but not before he noticed. Nakobee walked to his mount and removed his bow along with his quiver of arrows.

Looking at Jym he spoke, "Do you want to take part in the bet, Jym?"

Jym stood, walked over to his mount, and after removing his bow and quiver, he walked over and stood next to them.

"Who is going over to retrieve the arrows?"

"The loser, of course," Rae said as he drew an arrow.

Lepton sat there watching. His face said it all, he was confused. His mind raced with what they were getting ready to do. It made no sense to him.

As Rae let loose his arrow it missed the tree, landing in the tall grass. A man jumped up screaming.

Nakobee called out, "Stop, do not run. We will not harm you. Walk over here, or we will be forced to fire another arrow, one that will not miss."

The man stood there shaking. He was covered in dirt and what little clothing he wore was in shreds. Slowly he walked toward them. As he reached the middle of the stream, something came leaping out of the grass. It bounded toward the man. They all looked up to see what it was. What they saw was a large beast.

Nakobee let his arrow fly; Rae drew and let his go at the same time as Jym. All three hit the beast in the chest as it flew over the man. The impact from the three arrows drove it back and it crashed headlong into the tall grass. The man screamed and ran.

Nakobee and Rae ran toward the beast. When they arrived where the beast had fallen, there was nothing there except their three arrows. They stood looking around trying to see the blood trail.

"I do not see any blood, do you?" asked Nakobee

Rae looked toward the shoreline. There was nothing, no trail that showed where the beast could have gone. No tracks, no blood.

After looking through the tall grass, Rae picked up the arrows and looked back at Nakobee.

"It just vanished. There is no trail or blood, as if it was never here."

They heard yelling and turned to see Lepton holding the man who had tried to run away. Nakobee looked at Rae.

"I did not expect him to help capture the man, did you?"

Rae shook his head no. They walked over to where Lepton stood. He had a firm hold of the man. One arm was twisted behind his back, and Lepton's other arm was around the man's neck.

Jym was already there. He looked at them as they came up and said, "I saw him running, but he got to him before I could."

Nakobee reached over and took hold of the prisoner. Looking at him, he saw the man was even dirtier than he first thought. He was also covered in blood, and there were scars on his chest and arms. He thought this man had seen many battles.

"What was that thing chasing you?"

The man looked at Nakobee. Nakobee let go, and the man dropped down on his knees at Nakobee's feet.

Rae saw the man's face twitch, he thought he saw him grin before he fell to the ground. He was about to say something but the man started talking.

"You are First Sword to Queen Kaila. I did not recognize you. I'm sorry for bringing the beast to you. You are not harmed are you?"

"No, we are not harmed. Now tell me about this beast."

"It and many others attacked our village two nights ago. I was out in the field guarding the flocks. When the attack started, I saw men walking in. They were herding these creatures. When it was over, only a few people were alive. Those that could walk were placed in chains. Anyone too injured had their heads cut off and fed to the beasts."

"You survived because you were with your animals in the field? Why did they not kill the flock?"

"I do not know. All I know is the ones herding the beasts had trouble keeping them from coming out there."

"Then why was this one after you?"

"As they were leaving, I crept into the village to see if anyone survived. There was no one alive. I packed what supplies I could find and headed out to warn the other villages. Yesterday, I thought something was following me. I lost my things last night when I ran from my camp. I crouched in the grass hoping to stay hidden. I was heading for the water when I saw you. I did not know if you were with the others. So I was crawling away. I did not know the beast was so close."

Nakobee nodded his head and patted the man on his shoulder.

"Come, sit with us and share our food. You can go with us to…"

"Back to Keele, we are heading for Keele. We were out checking the land. Queen Kaila is thinking of increasing her herds. We are making sure the land can handle the increase."

Nakobee looked at Rae. He wondered why Rae was lying and was about to speak when the man looked at Lieutenant Lepton.

"Where did you find him? His uniform is that of a Lieutenant belonging to Queen Liseran."

Nakobee looked at the man, then Lepton. His stomach tightened, and now he felt uneasy and he began to understand what Rae was doing.

"Yes he is. Queen Liseran is willing to sell us some of her livestock. The Lieutenant is here as a representative for her Majesty. Now come with us to our camp."

Nakobee turned his back and started to walk away. The man took a step to follow him. As he did a knife appeared in his hand and he jumped at Nakobee.

Lieutenant Lepton grabbed the man before Rae or Jym could do anything. They fell to the ground rolling and Lepton tried to take the knife away.

The man was on top of Lepton, when Rae kicked him in the head knocking him off. As he started to stand,

Nakobee reached down with his left hand and grabbed the man by the neck and held him in the air. With his right, he took hold of the hand with the knife and twisted. There was a snapping sound and the knife fell. The man never let out a sound, he just glared at Nakobee.

"Now what is your name and why did you try to kill me?"

The man moved his mouth but only gurgling came out. Nakobee shook him. The man gurgled again.

Rae spoke, "You might want to loosen your grip. I think you are choking him."

Nakobee looked at Rae and then back at the man. He dropped him to the ground. As he landed he jumped up and started to run. Jym tripped him with his bow. The man landed face down. Nakobee walked over, flipped him on his back, and put his foot on his chest.

"Where did you think you were going? You cannot get away. We could shoot you with an arrow before you went more than a few feet."

The man glared up at him his mouth opened and a strange sound came out. There was movement off to their right. The beast they had seen before appeared a few feet away. It jumped in the air hitting Nakobee in the side, its claws raking his arm.

Nakobee and the beast rolled through the grass. Nakobee's right hand was wrapped around the beast's throat. His left hand was holding off more attacks from the front claws. He managed to get the beast on its back. His left hand came down and was hammering its head.

His hand was slipping from around the beast's neck. The beast snapped at him. With the beast's mouth open, Nakobee reached in with his left hand, grabbed its tongue, and he pulled. The beast choked and started pulling away.

Rae and Jym drew their bows trying to get a clean shot. Nakobee pushed away, and as he did Rae and Jym let loose their arrows. The creature disappeared and their arrows hit the ground.

Nakobee slowly stood. He turned to Rae and Jym who were standing there with confused looks. They all looked around trying to see where the beast had gone. They looked back at the man to ask him. What they saw was Lepton sitting on the man, his hands wrapped around the knife he had driven deep into the man's chest.

He spoke before any of them could, "I was not sure who he was until he attacked you. I have seen men like him. They control the beast, or I should say they are part of the beast. See the marking on his forehead? The only way to kill the beast is to kill the man."

"Looks like there will be a lot more we have to tell Shaméd."

They looked at Jym. Nakobee nodded his head.

Nakobee walked over to his animal and started gathering his things. Rae was behind him and tapped his shoulder.

"What are you doing?"

"I'm packing up so we can leave."

"Not until we dress your wounds. Your back is all cut up, and so is your arm."

"They will heal."

Rae looked at Jym who just stood there and shrugged his shoulders.

Lepton walked over to Rae and stepped between him and Nakobee. He looked at Nakobee.

"Nakobee, we need to clean the wounds to make sure they do not get infected. Also the smell of the blood will draw other animals to us."

Nakobee looked at Lepton, then Rae.

"He is right; please clean the blood off my back."

Rae started to say something but Lepton shook his head. Nakobee sat on a rock. Rae removed the first aid pack from his saddle and walked over to him.

He cleaned the cuts on Nakobee's back. There were six long abrasions. Two were deep, so using his needle and thread, Rae stitched them up. Cleaning the blood off, and applying ointment, he wrapped Nakobee's back with bandages to keep them clean.

Nakobee's arm had three cuts, but none were very deep. Rae cleaned them, put ointment on the wounds, and then wrapped his arm with bandages.

"There, all done. I'm afraid you will have some scars on your back and arm, but they won't be too bad."

"Scars are good. They are proof of a warrior's battles."

Rae started to speak, again, but Lepton cut him off.

"These will prove how brave you were and show everyone how you fought the beast and won."

Nakobee looked up at him.

"You won the battle, I only held him off so you could do it."

Nakobee grinned as he stood. He walked to his animal and said, "We should get moving. It is another day of riding to Shaméd's camp."

The rest of them gathered their things and headed to their animals. They mounted and rode away without talking.

Chapter Twenty-One

They reached Shaméd's camp at sundown two days later. As they rode in, Nakobee looked at the layout. There were stakes driven into the ground all around the camp, their points sticking outward. Inside the stakes were twenty small tents. Eight tents were ten feet by ten feet and two were six feet by six feet.

Rae rode up to one of the six by six tents. The tent was a light blue-green color. All the others were a dark green. As they dismounted, Shaméd came out.

"Hello, I see you made good time. Come inside and we can eat."

They entered and Lepton stopped. A small gasping sound escaped his throat. Nakobee looked at him and smiled.

"I reacted the same way my first time seeing this. You get used to it."

"What is this place? Does he work with demons as well?"

Shaméd answered, "Lieutenant Lepton, please come and sit, and as you eat, I will explain everything."

"How did you know my name? And, I'm no longer a lieutenant. You can just call me Lepton."

Shaméd nodded his head. They all walked over and sat at the long table where food was already laid out. Rae and Jym started right in. As they were eating the tent door opened and Jon walked in.

"Well, I see no one is waiting for me."

He hurried over, gathered some food, and took a seat. Jym looked at him as he sat.

"We were hungry. If we had waited there might not have been anything left."

Nakobee and Lepton started eating. Shaméd took a drink from the cup he was holding, then set it down.

"I received the update from your crystal. I saw what happened on your trip here. You were very lucky with that beast. Most people do not understand they are controlled by a human host."

Rae looked at Shaméd and asked, "How does that work? Lepton had to kill the human to kill the beast. I have never heard of that. Was it a true demon or just some sort of mystical beast? I thought demons could not be killed by normal means?"

"Some demons enter the host and take over the body. It makes it easier to walk among their enemies. They project a beast outside of the body in order to kill their enemy. Doing that makes the demon hard to kill. Lepton however, handled it very well."

Shaméd pointed at Lepton and everyone turned and looked at him.

"Rae, as for your last question, killing demons is possible. It is just difficult. Once demons take on a physical form, they are vulnerable. The demon's life force will return to its own realm when it dies."

Nakobee looked from Lepton to Shaméd.

"If you have the updates, then you know his story. I believe he can be trusted."

"I agree. His mind is confused on who we are and why we are here, but he has lost faith in his brother. And most important, he is willing to help us stop him. That is, as long as we do not kill him. He hopes we kill as many of the demons as we can, though."

Lepton sat there looking at Shaméd as he talked. His mind was racing as he heard the words. He had no idea how this man knew what was in his mind.

Shaméd looked over at Lepton.

"It is because I can read your thoughts. Do not worry, I will not read your mind again. I did it this time to make sure you were being truthful. Since you are, I'm sure Queen Kaila will reward you when the war is over. I believe she would welcome someone who likes to farm and raise animals."

Lepton sat there looking at Shaméd, and then he looked at Nakobee.

Before he could say anything, Nakobee spoke, "Shaméd is a wizard. A very powerful wizard, as you can see by his tent, and he can read your mind. He is here with his men to help us fight the demons.

Of course, when we asked for his help, we had no idea what we were fighting. Now that we know, I'm glad to have him and his people here to help us."

Lepton spoke in a low tone, "I can understand why you would want a wizard. He looks young to be a wizard. Is he still in training?"

Everyone laughed. Lepton sat there looking around, not sure why.

"I'm a lot older than I look. At least a couple hundred years."

Lepton sat staring at them, even more confused.

Shaméd started talking again, "Do not worry about it. We need to concentrate on finding out what the demon's main goal is."

Lepton got control of himself. He looked around, then said, "They told Quoin they wanted to remove everyone that would not submit to Queen Liseran's rule. They told him they were helping him so he and Queen Liseran can rule the world."

"Your brother has no idea that when everyone is gone, he, as well as those that are left will be killed?"

"I do not believe he is thinking beyond the gold they give him. He has changed since becoming First Sword."

Shaméd gazed at him.

"We will see if we can change his mind. Until then, we will have to figure out a way to stop the demons."

Just then there was a slight breeze in the air and Sword Master Zale appeared. Lepton jumped, falling out of his chair, and landed on his back with his feet in the air.

"Sorry lad, I did not mean to scare you. Let me help you up."

Sword Master Zale walked over with his hand out. Lepton scuttled away like a crab on all fours. Sword Master Zale stopped walking. Lepton sat there staring at the pale man who had appeared from thin air. His mind raced. All he could think was, *"Do all these pale humans have such power?"*

Zale dropped his hand.

"Ok then, stay there on the floor. I am going to sit in a chair."

He turned and walked to the table. Before sitting, he gathered some food. Everyone looked at Lepton and then at Sword Master Zale.

"What did the council have to say about the news that demons are involved?" asked Shaméd.

"They said, unless all the people of this world ask us for help, then no more than those who are already here, will come."

Shaméd shook his head.

"We can only hope the other tribes will ask for help. Until that time, we will have to make do with what we have."

"Shaméd, we will break camp and move to Keele. Nakobee, are there any more villages between here and Keele"

"No. Those that have not been destroyed have already packed and moved to Keele."

"And you have sent word to the villages across the lake?"

Nakobee looked at Sword Master Zale, and answered. "Yes, word has been sent. Hopefully they will be there by the time we arrive."

"Good."

Sword Master Zale pushed his chair back and stood. Patting his stomach, he looked over at where Lepton still crouched on the floor.

"You might want to explain about the Mirror to this young man. We cannot have him reacting that way every time we arrive. Well, my stomach is full, I'm tired and I'm going to bed. It has been a long day. Shaméd, let everyone know we will break camp first thing in the morning."

Sword Master Zale walked to the door. He stopped and looked at Lepton, shook his head and left.

Nakobee stood, walked over and helped Lepton to his feet.

"Shaméd and Sword Master Zale are from another world. They travel here by way of a giant mirror. The mirror is a gateway. Maybe we can show you one day. Until then, just believe me when I say it is very powerful magic. It might even be more powerful than anything the demons have."

Shaméd stood and took a step back. Rae, Jym and Jon looked at him. They stood and Jon grabbed food before moving away from the table. Shaméd waved his hand, all the food but the plates for Nakobee and Lepton disappeared.

Lepton saw that and his legs went out from under him, again. Nakobee caught him before he hit the ground.

"I think we will have a long night explaining all this to him," Rae shook his head after speaking.

Nakobee took Lepton to the table.

"Pick up your plate, you will need to eat."

He picked it up and stood there looking at Nakobee, who had picked up his own plate.

Nakobee spoke to Shaméd, "We will sleep next to your tent if that is all right with you."

"That will be fine. Outside you will find a pack for Lepton. He may keep it as long as he needs it."

Everyone left and Shaméd went and sat in his chair by his bed. Picking up a book he opened it and began reading.

Outside, the four removed their belongings from the animals and went behind Shaméd's tent. They set their camp up, then they sat down.

Jon had disappeared as they began this. He returned later with all of his belongings. Lepton sat eating, and when he was done, Rae and Nakobee looked at him.

Nakobee spoke, "We will explain to you about the mirror and those that are here."

The next two hours they talked. Lepton asked questions and they answered them. When they were done Lepton looked at them.

"Why don't our Queens want to join with these people? It would seem to be a benefit if we did."

"I do not know. My sister wants to join them, as I do. As soon as we have the people, we will begin dealing with the other tribes. We think they will join when we explain all the benefits."

Lepton looked down at his hands, then up at Nakobee.

"This war with the demons might be the turning point. I saw trolls, as well as dwarfs, here. I assume they are here from their own tribes."

"Yes, there will also be elves joining us soon. We can talk more on the trip to Keele. Now try to get some sleep."

Chapter Twenty-Two

In the morning everyone was busy breaking camp. Within three hours they were packed and ready to leave. Lepton was amazed at how efficient the men were in breaking everything down. They even packed the stakes from around their camp.

As they were getting ready to leave, Nakobee talked with Sword Master Zale and Shaméd about the trip to Keele.

"Your plan of taking the road to Lake Zolotov, then to Keele, will take ten days, maybe longer because of the wagons. The large animals can only travel so fast. We do have three more, the ones that came with me. We can add them to the harnesses, also. If we travel diagonal to the trail, we should make it in seven days."

"Is there a road that travels at this angle?" asked Sword Master Zale.

Nakobee answered, "Not really. There is a hunting trail. It is not as wide, or as well used as the main road. But it should cut the time by three to four days."

"This trail? Are you sure the wagons can make it? Are there any ravines that will cause us any trouble?"

"I took the trail when I was younger. There are no ravines. There is some sand, but mostly we will be traveling through tall grass. The grass will help feed the animals. I only suggest this because you said time was important."

"Yes, time is important. But getting us trapped out in the savanna would cause us more harm than it would in helping us."

Sword Master Zale walked around in a circle and thought a few minutes. Then he looked at them.

"Where is this trail?"

"I believe it is a half day from here."

"Good. Shaméd get everyone going. I will meet you at the trail."

Sword Master Zale closed his eyes, then opening them he took a step back and disappeared."

"Where is he going?" Nakobee asked.

"He is going to check your route. He will use the Mirror. This way he will be able to see which way is faster and easier."

Shaméd got everyone moving. The dwarfs led the way, followed by the humans. Then the wagons followed with the trolls at the end, because that was where they said they wanted to be.

Just before noon, Sword Master Zale appeared in the road ahead of them. He walked to Nakobee and Shaméd.

"The trail looks good. There are no great obstacles and the ones that might be will be taken care of by the time we reach them."

"How will they be taken care of?"

"Kinn is going to smooth them out. He will make the road wider and more passable."

Nakobee asked, "I thought he was with the elves trying to get them to come and help?"

"He was, he did, and they are helping him with the road."

Nakobee was about to ask another question when Sword Master Zale turned and disappeared.

"Now where did he go?"

"Probably to Keele. He is not one for walking."

An hour later, they turned off onto the hunting trail. It was easy to find as there were rocks piled up on either side of the now wider trail. Just before nightfall they stopped at a clearing, one that had been made for them.

Nakobee shook his head and Lepton stood there with a confused expression.

The stakes were put in place around the camp. Guards were picked and fires started. All this was done within two hours after stopping.

Lepton, who sat with Nakobee, looked around.

"Nakobee, would it be wrong for me to ask what I must do to be one of your clan?"

"Law says you would have to ask your Queen to be set free. If she will let you, then you can come to us. However, since we are not in a position to ask her, I would say you should wait to see what happens."

Lepton looked down and went back to eating his food. Later they went to sleep. In the morning they broke camp and headed out again. Each night they stopped at a clearing that had been made for them. The fourth day as they started to make camp, they saw Kinn and a large group of elves walking toward them.

Kinn called out as he approached, "Greetings. I hope you found the road better to travel on."

"Yes, you did a fine job. Are you here to travel with us or are you going to be leaving?"

"We are finished with the road. The rest of it will cause no problems for your wagons. We will continue with you."

"Good. We will soon be fighting alongside each other so we might as well get to know one another."

Kinn and the others began to set up camp. As the sun started to set, they were sitting around a fire eating. Rae kept looking at Kinn. When he would look up, Rae would look away.

Kinn spoke, "Is there something bothering you?"

Everyone looked at Rae.

"I was wondering why you are here?"

"I'm eating."

"I mean, why are you here on this world?"

"I'm here like you, to help the people of this world."

"I'm here for training. You are done with training. Do you always go to worlds in trouble?"

"I see what you are asking. I'm here because like Sword Master Zale, I'm one of the Thirty-Six. As you have learned, the Thirty-Six are a chosen group that can go off-world whenever a world is in need of help.

We are also the ones that go in search of artifacts relating to the One, or what you call the Creator. We are the ones who help build relations with Rednog and the worlds we are trying to recruit."

"I see. That is why you were on my world. You were there searching for artifacts and trying to get my world to join yours."

"I was there to help you and Shaméd. Your world has already been searched for artifacts relating to the Creator. As for recruiting your world, that is up to your leaders. So far, they want nothing to do with Rednog. That is why we just watch and wait. One day, you may have a leader more open and willing to join."

Nakobee nodded his head.

"When Kaila is made the official Queen of the tribe Zolotov, we will campaign to the other tribes to join Rednog. We will show them the benefit to having an alliance with someone as powerful as King Nogar."

The rest of the conversations were about what the elves and Kinn did to the road.

In the morning Sword Master Zale was there. He called a meeting with the leaders of the groups. When they had all gathered, he turned to them.

"First, I want to say how glad I'm your leaders let you come and help Nakobee and Queen Kaila. We all know that what is happening here, is also happening in your own countries. That is one reason we are glad for your help. We are also positive that when the war is over here, the enemy will increase their attacks in your lands. They are attacking one country at a time, dividing each race so the others will not help.

This is a tactic we have seen on many worlds, and is a tactic common to demons.

I would like to officially introduce each of the leaders. When we reach Keele, I will make a formal introduction to Queen Kaila. So as not to make one less important than the other, I will introduce you as you came here."

Sword Master Zale looked at the five dwarfs standing in front of him, all in full armor. Sword Master Zale pointed toward a dwarf. He was in very ornate armor and stood four feet five inches tall. His long red hair hung out from under his helmet. His green eyes were hard to see, hidden under his long eyebrows.

"First let me introduce Commander Sewegar Ferdra. He is the commander of King Seweryn Daral's Dwarfs 4th Brigade. His second in command is Goisch Yorald. I believe your title is Major Goisch Yorald."

Goisch nodded his head yes. He was a matched set to Ferdra. They could pass as brothers, they looked so much alike.

Sword Master Zale turned toward the five trolls standing to his left. They were dressed in skins, their swords on their hips, and spears in their hands.

Sword Master Zale pointed at the one who stood just under seven feet tall. Most trolls were a light brown color. This one was much darker. His skin was a blue black, his eyes were black, and his hair was shades of black, blond and red.

"King Jojin of the trolls sent Commander Kazkoo. Beside him is Sub-Commander Kuroji."

Turning, he faced the four elves standing next to Kinn. He looked at the tall elf standing beside Kinn. He was a little taller than Kinn. His long black hair was pulled back, not a hair out of place. His deep blue eyes looked as if they could see through you. Like the other elves, he was wearing full elfin armor. The high polished silver metal would reflect any light, making those facing it look away.

"King Halafarin Bryyra of the forest elves, sent Commander Braern Carphyra."

The tall elf bowed his head at Master Zale.

"I believe the gentleman to your right, is Sub-Commander Zhoron Daephine"

The elf nodded his head. He was the opposite of Carphyra. Daephine had green eyes and long blond hair that was tied just like all the elves.

"As for our names, you all know me. That man there wearing dragon leather is Shaméd. The big man next to him, with the purple sash is Nakobee. He is First Sword and the brother of Queen Kaila.

Now that we all know each other, let us hope the trip to Keele is a quick and safe one. Let's break camp and get on the road."

Within an hour they were moving down the road. This time the elves were in front. Their pace was faster, so within a few minutes they were well ahead of the group. The next few days went by quickly.

The morning of the last day they were getting ready when Sword Master Zale found Nakobee.

"We should be at the walls of Keele by noon. Do you want to use the Mirror and talk with Kaila before the group gets there?"

"I see no reason. They will see us long before we reach the walls. The guards will let her know we are coming."

"I just wanted to ask."

Sword Master Zale turned and walked away. Nakobee headed to where Shaméd and the others were.

Just before noon, an elf came running back to the group. When he reached Sword Master Zale he bowed his head.

"Commander Braern Carphyra has sent word that you need to stop the wagons. There is an army at the walls of Keele. He says if you and your men spread out to the right, we could box them in."

Sword Master Zale called Shaméd and Nakobee over.

"Lads, it looks like we are going into battle. There is an army attacking Keele. Commander Braern Carphyra wants us to move to the right and try to box them in."

Nakobee looked at the elf that had brought the news.

"Could you see how many there were?"

"When we saw the dust in the air Commander Braern Carphyra sent a scout to see what it was. He returned telling us there was at least ten thousand men. He could not get a good description of them. The Commander moved us into a gully and he sent me back to let you know."

Sword Master Zale looked at Nakobee. He could see the fear in his eyes.

"Do not be afraid for your sister's life. Your walls are tall and strong. Remember she has an amulet. There are people keeping an eye on her. Right now we need to see what we are up against."

He looked at Shaméd.

"Lad, can you pull up a map of the surrounding land so we can get a look at the enemy?"

Shaméd knelt down to the ground. Taking out a couple of stones he placed them at arm's reach. Then he whispered some words. The dirt began to swirl, spreading out five feet. Everyone stepped back. It kept growing upwards, until it was above their heads, then it just dropped away.

What was left was a picture of the landscape around Keele. They saw the army, spread out facing the wall from the lake to the mountain. They were just out of distance of the archers on the walls. Shaméd and the others could see that when the first attack happened the enemy lost a lot of men to those arrows.

That was one of the things Nakobee brought back from Rednog, the long bow and arrows. The bows on their world were a smaller version, but the ones he and his men trained on were larger. They had longer arrows and the bow was two feet longer.

The army's dead bodies lay stretched out on the ground. Sword Master Zale looked at the landscape.

"If we move our men this way, we can drive them towards the lake. If these are demons, they will be trapped. Demons cannot cross water. We attack first with bows then move in with lances and swords."

Commander Kazkoo looked at Sword Master Zale and spoke, "I agree with your plan. If we leave the wagons here, who will stay and guard them?"

Sword Master Zale nodded toward Jon.

"Jon and a few of my men will stay here."

"Why do I have to stay?" asked Jon.

"Do you want to go where the fighting will be?" Jym asked.

Jon looked at him, and said, "No I do not. I just don't like being told I have to stay behind."

Sword Master Zale rolled his eyes, looked at Jon and asked, "Jon, would you stay here with a small group of men and guard the wagons?"

Jon perked up and grinned at Sword Master Zale.

"I would love to stay here and help guard the wagons."

"Good, then the rest of us will gather what we will need and move out. Jon, get the wagons off to the side of the road. Try and cover them so if any demons fly over, they will not see you."

Jon looked at Sword Master Zale wide-eyed as he walked away. His voice was shaking when he said, "There are demons that can fly?"

Jym laughed as he patted Jon on the back. Leaning close he whispered. "Don't worry, they will not come here."

Chapter Twenty-Three

They were a mile behind the enemy. They could see the warriors on the walls were holding their own. The long bows were doing their job. There was nothing on this world like them. Those going against them were confused about how they were being hit from so far away.

They could see that the enemy only had spears and a few swords. They were attacking a village unlike any they had ever seen. The walls were pressed mud and rocks that were twenty feet high and four feet thick. The people on the walls were shooting arrows at them and striking every time.

Sword Master saw the first fireball hit the gate. It burst into flames spreading out across the walls. Only the gate was burning, and it went out a few seconds after being hit. Three more fireballs went flying toward the walls. He called Shaméd over.

"Lad, do you think you can stop that demon?"

Shaméd looked at the demon standing off to the side of its army. It was not very large, black in color, with what looked like red lava veins flowing around its body.

"I can stop it but once I do, they will know we are here."

"Don't worry. We will attack the same time as you."

Shaméd moved away from the others. Raising his hands a small blue light began to appear between them. As it grew, it floated further up into the air. When it was twice as large as Shaméd, he threw it. The ball of blue light went hurling toward the demon.

Sword Master Zale spread his men out so when they advanced they would drive the enemy toward the lake. When Shaméd let the blue fireball go, Zale gave the command. Arrows went up into the air. When they hit the enemy army it caused a panic. The demon was struck by Shaméd's fireball at the same time. When the flames cleared, the demon was gone.

A group of the beasts and a couple of small demons ran toward the lake. The rest of the demon army dropped their weapons and followed.

When they began running, Sword Master Zale gave the next command and his men started forward, chasing after them.

Sword Master Zale saw a large group far in the rear who turned and retreated. They were on some sort of large animals and it looked like there were a couple hundred of them. He was unsure why they were leaving. After seeing them, he knew if they had attacked, they would have over powered his small group.

As the group fled on their beasts, the other demons running on the ground began disappearing. By the time he and his group caught up to those fleeing toward the lake, there were no demons, only about a hundred deformed creatures.

Sword Master Zale and his men surrounded them and dragged those that had wandered into the lake back out. The group was a mixture of the four races on that world, trolls, dwarfs, elves, and humans. All of them were deformed in one way or the other.

They were tied and bound so they could not run. When that was done, they saw a group emerging from the city Keele. When the group arrived they saw that Kaila was in the lead.

Nakobee called out, "What are you doing outside the walls? Leo, take her back at once."

Leo looked at him, then Kaila, and he shrugged his shoulders. Before he could say anything, Kaila did.

"I will not go back. I'm out here to get a look at who has attacked us."

Nakobee took hold of the reigns of the animal she rode. He looked at Leo, then at her.

"The enemy may have retreated just to draw you out. They might return and attack us even now. You must be kept safe. Return to the city. We will bring the prisoners in so you can see them."

She looked at him, then saw Sword Master Zale looking at her. His expression said even more than what Nakobee's had. She nodded her head and turned around. Leo and the five men followed.

Nakobee turned and saw Sword Master Zale watching. Shaking his head, Nakobee walked over and began looking at the prisoners. He saw that their bodies were cut and deformed, as if they had been tortured. Taking a closer look, what he thought were cuts from being tortured, he realized were symbols. Symbols were carved all over their bodies. All the symbols were the same, except the ones on their heads. He noticed all the symbols on their foreheads were the same. The trolls had different markings than the humans.

Walking over he looked at the elves. They also had different markings on their foreheads. As did the dwarfs.

Kinn walked up and looked at the man Nakobee was staring at.

"The symbols on their heads is the name of the demon controlling them. That is why it looked like there were so many. They were using an illusion spell. Each one was made to look like ten, or even more, than what was really there. Look back at the walls. You will see half the bodies are gone. When an arrow killed the real one, the illusion failed, and the counterfeits disappeared. It is a very good trick to use. It causes fear and confusion. You should be proud of your men. They did not give into their fear. They held their ground and fought bravely."

Nakobee was proud to hear such words from someone like Kinn. It made him feel proud of his men and all the work they had gone through.

Nakobee gave orders to take the prisoners to the city. Once inside the wall, they were put into the stockades and guards were assigned. The stockade was built a mile from the gate. It was a long narrow building built against the city's outer wall. It was twenty feet wide and one hundred feet long.

Sword Master Zale informed the leaders when everyone was settled, to come to the large building with the flags. It was the only three story building at the center of the city. It was in the middle of twenty, two story buildings.

The leaders and their groups were impressed with this city. None of them had ever seen walls or buildings like the ones they saw there. The dwarfs were impressed because they had never seen humans make anything larger than mud shelters. Dwarfs made their homes in caves, usually, with few buildings above ground. The inside of their dwellings were very ornate. As for trolls, they lived in shallow caves. The elves, however, had impressive homes built high in trees. There were long bridges leading from one to the other.

As they were heading for the meeting, Commander Ferdra looked up at the tall elf walking near him.

"Commander Carphyra, are you as impressed at what these humans have created as I am?"

"Yes. I find what they have done very impressive to say the least."

Commander Ferdra grinned behind his long beard. He knew, like the elf, what these humans had done here was beyond their ability. Never in the history of this world had any human created anything close this.

"How do you think these humans built all this in just over the year they have been back?"

"I would assume it is because they had help from King Nogar. He wants us to join this world group he has."

"Yes, I was told about that. I would like to know how the walls were made and how they built them so fast."

"You should ask Nakobee. I'm sure he would tell you."

They walked the rest of the way in silence.

158

Chapter Twenty-Four

Jon was sitting by one of the wagons getting ready to eat when the attack happened. A spear hit the ground next to him. He rolled under the wagon to get away. As he rolled, he kept trying to hold his food. He dropped it and his body rolled over it, smashing it into the dirt. When he came up from under the wagon, he had his sword out. Looking down, his saw his food was beyond even what he would eat.

The sword shook in his hand. He had never learned how to use one. He was always in counseling when it was time to train with weapons.

As he stood and looked around. He heard a noise, when he turned to see what it was, his feet went out from under him. He started falling, but moved his hands just in time to keep his face from hitting a large rock. Bouncing off the rock, he rolled away. When he tried to get up, he felt searing pain. Then everything went dark.

Jon woke sitting in a chair. As his eyes focused he saw a body off to the right. He saw what looked like a deformed elf. The exposed skin looked as if was burned and scarred. Its back was twisted and there was a hump. What clothes it was wearing were dirty and torn. Its hair was long, gray, and a mess. He turned and saw that Jon was awake. Jon saw his eyes. They were red; bright red.

In a squeaky voice, the elf looked at him and spoke, "Good, you are finally awake. It has been three days since your capture. We could not be sure if you were dead or just faking it. I told them you were not faking it. No one could fake being asleep after being cut and stabbed as many times as you were.

Now, you will answer my questions, or I will be forced to read your mind and take what I want. That will of course cause you a great deal of pain. That is why it would be better for you to just answer my questions. Then your death will be painless. If you do not cooperate, then you will have to be tortured. Like I said, I will have to use my mind reading ability. This will cause you a great deal of pain and at the end you will still be dead. Do you understand what I'm saying to you?"

Jon looked around. He was in a large tent. There were several tables with bottles and other glass containers. Some had little fires under them. It looked like a laboratory. Jon looked at the elf and smiled.

"I have never heard an elf talk so much. You must be bored or in dire need to hear your own voice. Do you have anything to eat? I'm hungry. My lunch was interrupted by a group of... Well I am not sure who or what they were. I never got a clear look at them when they attacked us. I suppose they were friends of yours, since I'm here with you. Anyway, I dropped my food and I'm hungry. So when do we eat around here?"

The elf blinked at him. He stood there not sure of the words he heard spoken by this human.

"You are a prisoner. You do not ask for anything. You will answer my questions, or you will be tortured. Do you understand?"

"Yeah, I heard you the first time. But really, when do we eat? I'm so hungry I could almost eat anything."

The elf was about to speak when the flap of the tent opened and a large creature walked in.

Jon looked at it. His mind was trying to figure out what it was. It was not a troll, ogre, or anything he had ever seen on Rednog. It was tall and very large. It had large horns that were curved on its head. They reminded him of the ram back on the farm.

It was not wearing any clothing. Its body was shimmering red. Jon saw what looked like scales, not like the ones on dragons or even the Lizarians, these looked different. They looked like they were not really there, almost as if they were in a state of flux, trying to become whole but couldn't.

The creature spoke, "Have you found out anything from him?"

The elf bowed, almost to the ground. When he stood, he kept his face down not looking at the creature.

"My Lord, he just now awoke. I tried to probe his mind when he was out, but there was nothing there, only vague memories that had nothing to do with this world. Now that he is awake, I will be able to get the information you desire."

The elf bowed again, he moved back when the creature moved closer.

"See that you do. If you cannot get anything of value, kill him. We will capture others that you can get information from."

The creature turned and walked out. After the flap of the tent closed, Jon looked at the elf.

"He is something to look at. Or I should say something you don't want to look at. What is he?"

The elf looked at Jon. His voice was low, but still squeaky as he answered, "You do not know Lord Lug? He is the Sub-commander of Lord Pluug, the leader of the demons."

Jon grinned and tried not to laugh at their names. He got control of himself and looked at the old elf.

"That is what a demon looks like? They are really ugly. Why did you call him lord? You are an elf. Are you his slave or something?"

"Lord Pluug found me when I was two hundred years old. Elves on this world are taught that any elf who can read minds is taken to the temple. There they are raised to become part of the inner-circle. When my family discovered I could read minds, guards came. I saw in their minds it was all a lie. They were not going to take me to live and be part of the inner circle. They were going to take me and kill me. Each elf tribe can only have five mind readers at a time. Anymore and the other tribes will go to war with them. Only when a mind reader is about to die, they bring in a new one. Since elves live three to five thousand years, you can see that during that time there will be many mind readers that are killed. I did not want to die, so I ran. I survived for a few years alone. I was hiding in a valley when Lord Pluug found me. He offered me riches and a life that would be fulfilling."

"Well I can see from your looks he lied. Why don't you just leave?"

The Elf looked at Jon. Fear spread across his face and showed in his eyes. He paced around the room.

"I cannot leave Lord Pluug. He has marked me. There is no where I could hide from him. If I did leave, the pain I would suffer when he captured me would be unbearable. No one, once marked by a demon, can ever leave. No, no, I can never leave."

The elf was walking around the tent shaking his head. He stopped and glared at Jon.

"How did you do that? Are you a mind reader? I should not be telling you these things."

He grabbed his head with both hands, his eyes closed and he stood there mumbling to himself. A few minutes later he looked at Jon.

"I do not know what kind of human you are, but I will find out. I have never seen or heard of a human with white skin. I will keep you alive until I learn everything about you."

Jon grinned at him then asked, "Great. When do we eat? If we eat, I will tell you whatever you want to know."

The elf looked at him and slowly walked over to a table where there was food. He picked up some bread and meat, walked over, and laid it on Jon's lap. Then he untied his hands.

Jon grabbed the food before it could fall to the floor. After he ate it all, he leaned back in the chair and looked at the elf.

"What is your name?"

He had his back to Jon and was working on a glass beaker that was over a small flame.

"My name is Seiveril Jomaer."

After saying his name, he jerked straight. He spun around and glared at Jon. Raising his hand, a bolt of energy shot out. It hit Jon in the chest knocking him back. He was unconscious before he hit the floor.

Chapter Twenty-Five

Kaila was sitting at the table holding her drink. Leo walked in and saw her downcast expression.

Walking over he asked, "Another nightmare?"

"Yes, but this one was different. I saw our new homes on fire. Nakobee, you, and the other men were standing in front of me. There were these large creatures that came at you. They killed you all. Then one came slowly to me and said, there is nothing you can do to stop us. All of you will die.

I woke and came out here. Should I tell Sword Master Zale about the dream?"

Leo with his arm around her, knelt closer, and said, "Does he know about the other dreams you have had?"

"Of course not. Only you and Shameka know about them."

"Would it help if you told him? If not, then don't. I'm here if you need to talk. If you want, I can stay outside your door at night if you think it would help you sleep?"

Kaila smiled up at him, squeezed his hand, and said, "That would be awkward. I will be fine. Now what do we have planned for today?"

Everyone was gathered in the meeting hall. They were waiting for Nakobee and Queen Kaila. Nakobee was meeting with Kaila. He had told her what transpired on his journey. She, like him, was upset about what the demons were doing. She took a few steps with her head down. Nakobee could see she was deep in thought. She stopped and looked at him. Her expression changed from that of anger to grinning. Nakobee was unsure of what to make of the change.

Standing there grinning, she spoke, "I think I have a way this news will benefit us. It just might even build an alliance between us and the dwarfs."

When they came into the room and sat, Kinn looked at everyone gathered around the table.

"Queen Kaila, I will explain why the prisoners are unable to talk. When demons take control of someone, they wipe their minds. They leave only the very basic needs, like hunger. The markings on each of the captive's foreheads are the names of demons controlling them. The body is alive, but the mind is not. They can never return to the lives they once had. It is better if we kill them."

"Is there is nothing we can do?" Nakobee asked.

"Nothing. They are just empty shells and the longer they are alive the more the demon that controls them will learn. You should have killed them by the lake. By bringing them inside, you showed the demons what is here."

"They are locked inside a building. The demons can learn nothing."

"Have you not seen some of the captives looking out the windows? They are being controlled and being told what to look for. It is in all of our best interests to kill them now, before they learn more."

"I agree," said many voices around the table.

Sword Master Zale stood and looked at Queen Kaila.

"Queen Kaila, if I might interject my own thoughts on this matter?"

"Sword Master Zale, we all bow to your wisdom. Please tell us what we should do with the prisoners."

"I agree with Kinn. The prisoners should all die. It would be the honorable thing to do. Kinn and I will destroy the bodies. This way none of you will be burdened with the task."

Sub-Commander Kuroji spoke, "I will help. It will take a long time to kill all of them with a sword if just the two of you do the killing."

Kinn answered, "Thank you, but we were not going to kill them by way of the sword."

The troll looked at him and asked, "How were you going to kill them?"

Everyone looked at Kinn who looked around at each of them.

"I was going to shut down their bodies, sort of like putting them to sleep. It is painless, even though they are already dead and do not feel any pain."

"What will we do with the bodies? Will we have to burn them?" Sub Commander Kuroji asked.

"Yes, they will have to be burnt. We will build a large pyre outside, far from the walls. I have a transport spell that will take the dead there."

Heads nodded around the room as everyone agreed to let Kinn and Sword Master Zale take care of the prisoners.

Nakobee stood and spoke, "I would like to take a group of warriors to the cave to see if we can root out the enemy there. Queen Kaila, may I take some warriors to do this?"

Queen Kaila looked at Sword Master Zale. He nodded his head yes.

"Sword Master Zale, you think this is a good idea?"

"I do. I would also like some dwarfs to go along to look inside the caves. The demons are getting their gold somewhere. It might just be from your mountain."

The dwarfs perked up when they heard about the possibility of gold being in the mountains. Commander Sewegar Ferdra and Major Goisch Yorald looked at each other. Commander Ferdra sat up and looked toward Queen Kaila.

"Queen Kaila, we would be honored to help search your mountains for gold or anything that might bring your land more wealth."

Queen Kaila smiled at him. She understood what he was saying and this was what Sword Master Zale had told her to be ready for.

"Commander Ferdra, if you and your people find gold or any other desirable metal, maybe even some gem stones anywhere in my mountains, I would be delighted at the discovery. In fact, so delighted that I would offer you and your people the rights to mine said material for a sixty/forty split."

Commander Ferdra perked up at the offer, smiling back, he nodded his head.

"If we did all the work, we would of course accept the sixty percent."

166

Everyone around the table looked at him and Queen Kaila. They were waiting for her response.

"Commander Ferdra, let us not debate over something as meager as who will make more. How about we just split it fifty-fifty. This way we both make money and we can say we are equal partners. How does that sound? Besides, you will also find metal that will make fine swords and spears. You could even make armor for my warriors as well as your own. That metal I will let you keep, as long as you sell the weapons and armor to us at a large discounted price."

Queen Kaila smiled at him. Commander Ferdra grinned from ear to ear. It was hard to see it beneath his beard, but she could tell he was very happy.

He bowed and said, "My Queen, you are a shrewd negotiator. I accept your offer. I presume you will have papers drawn up stating these facts? Or would you like me to have them drawn up?"

"I thank you for the offer, however, that will not be necessary. I will have the documents drawn up just as soon as you and your people discover what is in my mountains.

Now if you will please excuse me, I have other things to attend to. Sword Master Zale, please carry on with the plans for the war."

Queen Kaila stood and so did all the others. When she was gone they all sat again to discuss their plans. In three hours they knew what they would do.

Kinn and Sword Master Zale headed for the building holding the prisoners. Shaméd, Rae, and Jym went to build the pyre. Nakobee took a few men back to where they had left the Jon and the wagons.

Commander Ferdra had his men make camp near the south wall. Commander Kazkoo had his men make camp near the east wall. Commander Braern Carphyra was the only one who agreed to use one of the buildings for himself and his men.

Kinn and Sword Master Zale arrived at the door of the stockade. Once inside, it took very little time to shut the prisoner's bodies down. They laid on the ground and Sword Master Zale walked around looking at their faces.

"It is a shame we cannot bring them back with their souls lost to the demons. One day the Creator will come and make peace with them."

Kinn touched his amulet and said, "Shaméd are you ready for the bodies?"

"I'm ready."

Shaméd raised his hand and bodies began appearing. Presently, Kinn and Sword Master Zale appeared beside Jym and Rae. They stood there with their heads down. Kinn said a prayer and when he was finished he raised his hands. The pyre burst into flames.

The fire burned all day and night and the smoke blew out across the lake. In the morning there was nothing on the ground, not a single ash. No evidence of a fire was anywhere. Kinn had disposed of everything.

Nakobee returned with news that the wagons were mostly destroyed. Ten men were found alive, six were dead, and five including Jon, were missing. They buried the dead in the graveyard near the city. They found Jon's sword and backpack near a wagon. There was no blood, so the conclusion was he was taken alive with the others that were missing. For what purpose these men were taken was anyone's guess.

Everyone including Queen Kaila was back in the meeting hall. They were all standing around talking about the wagons and missing men.

"They were taken to help replace those that were killed." said several people there.

"Nonsense, they were taken to be tortured. To see what they know." Commander Ferdra replied.

"Then why not take all the men?" Commander Kazkoo said looking at Ferdra.

"You heard what the men said; there were only twenty demons that attacked. Once the fighting started, those that captured our men left, leaving the rest to fight. Our men killed five demons. The only thing that saved them was the spells on their weapons. Everyone knows how hard it is to kill a demon."

Queen Kaila pounded on the table and everyone turned to face her.

"We can all speculate on why our men were taken. For now, we can hope they do not suffer.

Tomorrow, Nakobee will leave with Commander Ferdra and his men. They will go to the caves. If there are guards, they will be dispensed with, and the caves reclaimed. We will establish a base camp on each side of the mountain at the openings of both caves. They will then search the caves and inside of the mountain.

The rest of us will begin stocking our food banks. We do not know how long this war will last and we do not know how many people will evacuate to here.

For now we have a lot to do. I expect everyone to do their part."

She turned and left. The others did as well. At sundown a group of people showed up at the gates. There were two hundred men, women and children. They brought everything from their village, all their animals and even the materials to build their homes. Queen Kaila arrived at the gate to welcome them. They were led to a location inside the walls where they could set up their homes and let their animals loose.

Over the next three weeks, Kaila stood at the gate as more people came. She greeted each group and their leaders as well as their clans-folk. Each group brought everything they owned. The city of Keele was growing. Soon there would be several thousand people.

Kaila knew there was no way the other Queens would not vote her Queen of her territory. Nakobee had sent word about his victory at the cave. She was growing anxious about what the future held for her and her people.

Chapter Twenty-Six

Around noon, three days after leaving Keele, Nakobee, Tourna, Commander Ferdra, and fifty dwarf warriors, arrived at the trail leading to the cave. They slowly moved up the mountainside. When they were almost there, Tourna waved everyone to stop. He pointed off to the left and right. They saw two human guards standing beside trees. Commander Ferdra sent two of his men out. A few minutes later, the guards were gone.

When they arrived at the cave opening, they saw five men sitting around a fire. Nakobee could not see any of the large beasts he had seen before. The dwarfs were getting ready to charge. Nakobee stopped them. Tapping Tourna on the shoulder, Nakobee signaled that they would use their arrows. Tourna nodded his head, they pulled arrows out of quivers and each put three, tip down, into the ground. They each put an arrow in their bow, drew back, and let fly. As the arrows flew through the air they quickly pulled an arrow from the ground and fired again. They did this two more times. Each arrow struck their target. Nakobee's last arrow went into the blackness of the cave. As the soldiers fell to the ground, the dwarfs ran in. As they approached the cave, a soldier came staggering out, an arrow in his chest. He hit the ground as they arrived at the opening.

Commander Ferdra called out to his men, "Check the inside. Make sure it is safe."

Nakobee and Tourna retrieved their arrows and began to drag the dead soldiers off into the trees. When they were done, the dwarfs that went into the cave were back. One walked up and stood in front of Ferdra.

"Sir, there is no trace of the enemy in the cave. We searched a hundred yards in to make sure. Inside, we did find bedding for nine men."

"Nine men? We only saw eight. Take some men and search the area. And send a man deep inside to keep watch. The last man may be in there somewhere."

"Yes sir."

The dwarf turned and sent men out searching the land around the cave, and then sent two men inside to keep watch.

"If we keep men here we need to keep them inside. If any of the enemy shows up on this side and sees our men, they will do the same to us that we did to them."

Nakobee looked at Commander Ferdra nodding his head. He bent down and took the meat that was cooking off the fire.

"I agree. It is a two day hike through the mountain from this location. We will camp here tonight and leave first thing in the morning for the other side.

We will have to keep a diligent watch out for the enemy. As you said, we do not want them to do to us, what we did to them. We should also bury the dead."

Those still there began to clean things up so it would not look as if there was a fight. Ten dwarfs moved deep into the woods to dig graves. By nightfall the area looked as if nothing had happened.

A small fire burned in the pit and Tourna was dressed in the uniform of a dead guard. Nakobee sat just inside the cave. There were four dwarfs out in the trees as lookouts. All the other dwarfs were inside the cave. Some had moved deeper in to look at the rocks.

The night went by without incident. In the morning they ate cold meat, cheese, and bread. They left ten men inside the cave to guard it. Nakobee led the way to the exit on the other side of the mountain.

The cave was huge with old stalagmites and stalactites. There was a green light shining from the ceiling. The dwarfs carried small poles that gave off a low yellow light.

Three hours in, they found water flowing from the wall. The water fell down into what looked like a carved out rock bowl. It overflowed creating a small stream that ran along the path. Since they could not tell time by the sun, Nakobee stopped them when he found markings on the wall.

"This is where we turn off. There is an open area where we can make camp."

He moved on and the others followed. Commander Ferdra was glad about the camp area. He and the other dwarfs were tired. When they reached the site, they made camp, ate, and placed guards out. In the morning they were up and moving along. After a few hours of walking, they heard noises. They spread out to see what they could find.

They found a wide fork in the path and off to the right one path branched off down a side tunnel. There were metal rails on the floor and large wooden carts being pushed by humans and dwarfs chained to the carts. A large creature was walking behind each cart. It used a whip whenever it thought those pushing the cart were too slow.

Commander Ferdra fidgeted and was ready to attack when Nakobee grabbed his arm.

"We need to see how many there are. Send some of your men out to look."

Commander Ferdra sent men out and the rest moved further back down the cavern. An hour later the men returned. They crouched down and whispered what they found.

"There are maybe a hundred humans and twice that many dwarfs. We saw only five of those large creatures. Two of them have spears and one has a club. The ones following the carts only have whips.

We could not go out toward the other end. The way is too narrow. We did go down where the carts are coming from. They are mining a large deposit of gold. The walls are thick with it and there is also a vein of silver."

Nakobee looked at Ferdra.

"We should move in and kill the creatures guarding the prisoners. Do you think we can do it without making too much noise?"

"I will send men in to signal the dwarfs that are there. When the fighting starts, we will not have anything to worry about."

Nakobee nodded his head and said, "Tourna and I will be at the junction waiting for those that return. When they do, we will handle them."

They moved out, forty dwarfs moving swiftly and silently. Nakobee was amazed at how quietly they moved with all their armor.

He and Tourna headed for the junction. It was not long before a cart returned. Two humans were pushing it, there was no sign of a guard. A couple of seconds later, two more carts with humans and three dwarfs appeared. Behind them was a large creature. Nakobee and Tourna drew arrows, and when the creature was in plain view, they let them fly. One hit the beast in the neck, the other in the chest. It fell and Nakobee ran out with his sword and cut its head off.

Those pushing the carts had ducked behind them so as not to get hurt. When they saw Nakobee and Tourna they began to cheer. Nakobee waved them to be silent.

"Be quiet. We do not want to sound an alarm. How many are outside?"

A dwarf spoke up, "There are ten more like that one, and three demons. I do not think your arrows will kill the demons."

"We have special arrows for demons. They can kill some or cause so much pain they will flee. How many more carts are behind you?'

"Six more will be coming soon. If they see the body they will sound an alarm."

"We will hide it. Tourna, set them free and take them to the others. I will remove the body. Commander Ferdra should have taken care of the rest by now."

Tourna used his knife to break the locks. When they were all free they loaded the chains in the carts and moved down the tunnel. Nakobee picked up the body and was reaching for the head when a human male came over, grabbed it and stood there holding it.

"I will take this."

Nakobee nodded his head and went back down the way they had come. He found a deep fissure and tossed the body in. The man tossed the head in.

Turning, Nakobee looked at the man. He was about five feet tall and skin and bones. Around his waist was a piece of leather.

"My name is Nakobee. I'm First Sword to Queen Kaila."

"I'm Kar. I lived in the village Kappa. It was raided last year. I think it was last year. I have been down here so long I lost track of time."

"I have not heard of any raids in Queen Krooni's lands. I will send word to her that you and those with you are free. How many were taken?"

"Those not killed were brought here. When we started walking, there were five hundred. When we arrived, only two hundred were left."

"You and the others are free now. We will rid this land of demons and these other creatures. Come, we must get back to the others."

Nakobee led the way and soon they were with Commander Ferdra and the others. Everyone was crowding around, trying to meet those that saved them. Food and water was passed around.

Nakobee looked at Ferdra.

"We need to get ready for the next group coming back in. I will take Tourna and a few of your men to take care of them. Wait for us here."

Nakobee left and ten dwarf warriors followed. When they reached the junction they heard carts coming. They moved to the side and waited.

Four carts with two humans and two dwarfs pushing each one went by. Then two large creatures appeared. Nakobee and his men attacked. It was not a fight, the creatures were dead before they knew what happened.

Commander Ferdra came with his men and the ex-prisoners. Nakobee looked at the men they had just freed.

"Are there anymore down there?"

A man spoke, "No, we were the last ones."

"Then we need to go."

They followed him to the cave opening. They caught the ones there by surprise. The fighting was over quickly. The eight creatures died easily.

They moved slowly and seemed to only know how to use the whip but not how to fight. The hard part was killing the two demons. They stood their ground and fought, killing five dwarfs.

Nakobee had hit a demon with two arrows and it was screaming as it fought, the last arrow sank into its throat. It fell to the ground dead.

Tourna had done the same to the other. His last arrow hit the demon in the chest. It fell a few seconds later. Now that they were both dead, the prisoners that were in chains off to the side were released. They ran over and attacked the dead bodies.

Nakobee walked away a few feet. Once alone he took hold of the amulet.

"This is Nakobee. I need to get in touch with Sword Master Zale. Can you tell him to come to me?"

Letting go of the amulet, he returned to the others. He stood watching the humans and dwarfs dancing and singing. There was movement beside him and Sword Master Zale appeared. Those that saw him appear jumped back.

Sword Master Zale moved closer to Nakobee and as he did another man appeared carrying sacks. Then three more men with sacks came through.

"I brought food and clothing. More will be coming. This was all I could get on such short notice."

Nakobee smiled as the men began passing out food and clothes.

"How did you know we need food?"

Sword Master Zale pointed at Nakobee's chest.

"Remember, it records what you see and hear. I sent word to Queen Krooni that her people are free and will return soon. Your sister is very happy about the gold. She is looking forward to building and improving your land."

"I'm sure she is. Do you know she wants to teach our people how to read and write? She wants to bring the words we learned on Rednog to this world so all the people can learn."

Sword Master Zale nodded his head.

"That is a bold move. When people know how to read and write, they grow less reliant on their leaders and want to learn more. What she is doing will be a new beginning for all the people of this world."

Chapter Twenty-Seven

It was early morning and Kaila was with a group of men and women going over reports. She was concerned about the progress of the walls, the new buildings, and the food supply. The outer wall was almost complete, but the north wall near the mountain still needed to be finished.

The buildings were another thing. With all the people showing up, they were falling behind in making places for them to live.

The material for the buildings was becoming difficult to find. The walls were easy. They used the dirt and rocks from around the outside. But they had to search further and further for wood to be used in the interior and for the roofs.

The same for the food. She did not want to be short on food with so many people coming.

Leo stepped into the room, walked over, and leaned close to her ear.

"A messenger from Queen Kailee is here. He says it is important."

Standing straight, she looked over at the door where the man stood waiting. He was dirty and looked as if he had not slept in days.

Queen Kaila looked out at those around the table and said, "If you all will excuse me for a minute, a messenger from Queen Kailee is here. Keep talking about how we can get things completed faster and improve the crops."

She walked away with Leo beside her. When she was standing in front of the man, he bowed, then stood straight.

"Queen Kaila, I'm sorry for my appearance. Queen Kailee said I had to give you this message as soon as I arrived."

"Do not worry about how you look. I'm sure she would not have sent you if it were not important. Is the Queen alright?"

"Queen Kailee and First Sword Kouly are in good health. The message is this:

He closed his eyes and began to speak. "Kaila, two of my villages have been attacked. In the first village we found no survivors. In the second one, only the old were left to give us this warning. The attackers said their army is coming and anyone who does not bow down to them will be killed.

I now believe what you and Sword Master Zale were saying is true. We are at war. I have sent word to the other villages to come here. They are to bring everything they can carry. My army will begin to patrol the roads and bring in as many people as they can find. Let me know what more we can do."

The man opened his eyes, bowed and asked, "Do you have anything to send back to her?"

"Yes, but first you must rest and eat. I will call for you when I'm ready. Leo, have a man take care of him, please?"

The man bowed and left with Leo. Leo returned before Kaila had taken two steps.

"We can have boats ready to leave by morning. They can go there and bring Queen Kailee and her people here."

She smiled at him, and taking his arm, she walked to the other side of the room.

"She would never agree to that. She believes our home is like before. She does not know about the walls or everything we have done. No, I will go and talk with her, myself. I will bring her and my grandfather here and show them. Maybe that will convince them to come."

They stopped walking. Leo turned and looked at her.

"It will take three days to get there. Even if she agrees it will take four more to return. You cannot be gone that long."

"I know. That is why I will ask to use the Mirror. There and back in three hours. Even Queen Kailee cannot say no to that."

He smiled and bowed. Stepping back, he turned and left the room to resume his duties. Kaila walked over to the table where a small argument was going on.

An hour later the room was empty. Everything was settled. People would be moved around where they were needed. The good news was, those that came were bringing their animals and what food they had. If nothing happened to the crops, there would be no food shortage.

Kaila took hold of the amulet. She had never done this. She had been told how it worked but she was hoping she would never have to use it.

"This is Queen Kaila. I need to speak with Sword Master Zale."

She was about to say the words again when he appeared.

"Queen Kaila, I was just coming here to let you know Nakobee has freed those that were working in the gold mine. He will be leaving Commander Ferdra and his men there to build a stronghold. He will return with the humans as soon as they are well enough to travel."

"I'm glad to hear all is well with their mission. I called you because Queen Kailee sent word that two of her villages were attacked. I would like to use the Mirror to go there. I would like to have her see how it would be safer for her and her people to come here."

"I can arrange that. Are you sure she will come?"

"No, I think it will be difficult to convince her. I hope she won't be stubborn and stay."

"When do you wish to go?"

"As soon as you can make the arrangements. Can we take her messenger with us?"

"Let me check to make sure no one on Rednog will be upset. I will return in a few minutes."

Sword Master Zale disappeared and Kaila walked over and sat. Not even two minutes later, Sword Master Zale returned.

He looked at her and said, "As long as we stay in the Mirror Gate room there will be no problem with bringing him."

"Thank you. I will send for him and we can leave as soon as he is here, if that is ok with you?"

"It is fine with me."

Kaila walked to the door, opened it, and spoke to the guard standing there. She returned and sat in her chair. Sword Master Zale stood off to the side. She saw him standing and waved at him.

"You do not have to stand."

"It would not look good when the others arrive, besides I'm not that old."

He winked at her. She was going to say something about his age when the door opened and Leo came in with the messenger.

"My Queen, you sent for us." Leo spoke as he entered the room.

"Come, both of you. We are going to talk with Queen Kailee."

Leo moved closer to her.

The messenger glanced at her and spoke, "Queen Kaila, I do not mean any disrespect, but I just arrived. It is a long way to Ondo."

Kaila smiled at him.

"Do not worry, it will only take a few minutes to get there. Now come over here so we can tell you how we are going to do it."

He came closer and stood next to Leo. Sword Master Zale looked at Leo.

"Leo, take hold of his arm and step to your right. Hold him steady."

Leo took hold of the man's arm, looked at him and said, "Follow me."

They both took two steps and disappeared.

Kaila went next, then Sword Master Zale. When he arrived he saw the man on the floor. Leo shrugged at him.

"He just collapsed and I could not hold him."

Leo bent down and picked the man up and tossed him over his shoulder.

Reklan called out, "It is ready."

As before, Leo went first, then Kaila, and finally, Sword Master Zale. They arrived a few feet from the house of Queen Kailee. The guards were standing there holding their spears on Leo who had unceremoniously dropped the messenger on the ground. They were unsure of how he and Kaila had arrived. When Sword Master Zale appeared, they relaxed. They were used to seeing him appear and disappear.

Kaila looked at them and spoke, "We are here to speak with Queen Kailee."

One man turned and went to the door and entered. A few minutes later First Sword Kouly came out. When he saw Kaila, he smiled, walked over, and gave her a hug.

"Granddaughter, I'm glad to see you."

After he released her, he stood straight and in a deep and proper voice, spoke, "Queen Kaila we are honored by your visit, please come in, and take refreshments with Queen Kailee."

They followed him in, Leo picked up the messenger. When they were inside, Kouly saw Leo and shook his head.

"Which one are you? Never mind, put the man down over there."

Leo did as he was told, then went and stood next to Kaila.

Queen Kailee looked at her granddaughter and smiled as she walked over to her.

"It is good to see you. I see from my man over there, you received my news. Is that why you are here?"

Kaila smiled as she said, "I came to ask if you and your people would like to come to my city for protection. We have done amazing things. There are twenty foot tall walls all around our city. We have buildings to house over

182

a thousand people. More are being built. You and your people are welcome to come and share what we have."

Queen Kailee hugged Kaila. Then she walked to her chair and sat.

"I cannot do as you ask. It would be a sign of weakness to my people and the other Queens. If I leave, they would come here and take my land. Then I would have to fight to take it back. No, I will stay. I will let you take the women and children, as well as the old. My warriors and I will stay and fight for my land."

Queen Kaila bowed her head.

"I knew you would not come. If you want to send the women and children, send them. We will be waiting for them."

Sword Master Zale spoke, "Queen Kailee, will you be sending them by boat or will they walk?"

She looked at her husband, who looked at Sword Master Zale.

"The old ones and the very young children will travel by boat. The women and older children will walk. They will be bringing the herds with them. We do not want them to scatter. Besides, you will need them to feed those who are coming to you."

"I will send warriors to aid them."

Then Kaila turned to Sword Master Zale and Leo.

"If both of you would leave us, I would like to speak with them alone."

They both bowed and turned. As they did the messenger was waking. When he saw where he was, he jumped up and bowed to Queen Kailee.

"My Queen, please forgive me. I did not mean to be so rude."

He was about to say more, when Queen Kailee waved him to be silent.

"It is all right. You have done a great service for your Queen. You may return to your family."

He bowed and walking quickly, left.

Sword Master Zale and Leo followed. They waited outside for Kaila. Two hours later, she came out. Her eyes were red rimmed and swollen. Leo did not say a word. His eyes grew soft and sad. He stepped close to her and waited. Kaila looked at Sword Master Zale and nodded her head.

"I'm ready to return home."

Sword Master Zale moved his arm to the right.

"Leo, please step forward. We will be right behind you."

Leo took a step and disappeared. Sword Master Zale moved his hand, and Kaila took a step, also disappearing. Sword Master Zale followed. They arrived in the Mirror Gate room and without speaking, stepped back through the mirror to the meeting room. As they arrived there was a knock and a man entered.

He looked at them and bowed.

"My Queen, are you ready for lunch?"

She looked at the old man, then Sword Master Zale. She was about to speak, but Sword Master Zale held up his hand.

"Remember, time means very little to us. We were only gone a few minutes."

Kaila looked back at the old man and said, "Yes, please bring the three of us food and drink."

He turned and left and she looked at Leo and Sword Master Zale.

"You both will share a meal with me. We can talk about how we are going to help those people get here safely."

Leo said, "I will take care of sending men to meet Queen Kailee's people. If you would like, I will personally go to make sure they arrive safely."

She looked at Leo and said, "No, you stay here with me. I feel safe with you near me."

The food arrived, Kaila looked down at her food and everyone began eating. No words were spoken for a few minutes. Then Kaila looked up.

"We should begin with, how we are going to build more buildings? We are already a month behind."

"Kinn and the elves that came with him can use their magic. They should be able to have the walls up in a week. We will just have to find a faster way of getting the lumber here to finish the buildings." said Zale.

"I will leave that in your capable hands."

They talked about the food supply and how to start training the new warriors in the ways of Rednog.

There was a knock on the door. Kaila called out, "Enter."

Nakobee, Rae, and Jym came in, and stopped at the end of the table.

Nakobee spoke, "Jon is still missing. We three are thinking of going searching for him. We would like your permission to do so."

Kaila looked at her brother then at the other two.

"Just the three of you?"

Nakobee was about to speak, when Rae cut him off.

"We would like to take five others."

"You are asking me to let eight men go searching for one man. Is this one man so important I should send men out searching for him?"

Rae looked at her, then Sword Master Zale.

"He is my friend, and Jym's. We come from the same world. If it were one of us that was missing, we think he would do the same. We told Nakobee what we were going to do, and he insisted on coming with us. Five others were taken at the same time. That makes eight men searching for six men."

Kaila looked at Sword Master Zale. He lowered his head and closed his eyes. When he opened them, he nodded his head.

Kaila looked at her brother and said, "Pick your five men. I expect you all to return in two months' time with or without your friend or the others."

Rae and Jym both said, "Thank you."

Nakobee looked at them and without speaking, turned to the door. Once outside he grinned at them.

"I told you my sister would let us go."

"I just hope we will find him in the time she has given us," Rae said.

"Do not worry. Karl and his men are great trackers. We will find Jon and kill those that took him."

Rae and Jym looked at Nakobee. They both thought it strange that he was willing to help Jon.

Chapter Twenty-Eight

Nakobee went searching for Karl. He headed to where he and his men were training the new recruits. Rae and Jym followed him. There were three hundred men and women who wanted to be trained as warriors for Queen Kaila. Rae and Jym came up beside Nakobee.

"The men I'm picking were trained on Rednog. They learned a great deal there, more than those who were with me. Those men were on Rednog so many more years than we. They're much more skillful. Their tracking ability is beyond anything I have ever seen. They have become a great asset to us."

They continued toward the warriors who were training the youth in the art of war. They were split up into groups where they learned how to use the sword, spear, and the new long bow and arrows. Nakobee pointed at them as they walked.

"You know that every child at the age of five learns how to use the spear. Now they are being taught better tactics using these same weapons. They will learn how to fight side by side to lock their shields to make a wall to hold back the enemy. Then they will learn how to fight with a sword and shield. After that, they will be taught the long bow. Those who show promise and skill will be placed in our archery squad where they will spend more time until their skills are superior."

Nakobee, Rae, and Jym reached a small group using spears and shields. They walked up to the man teaching them. He stopped and called everyone to halt. Then he turned and faced Nakobee without speaking.

Nakobee looked at him and spoke, "Karl, I need you, Nuka, Flan, Naate, and Janae to go with us on a mission. Get them and pack your weapons and prepare food for a week. We will be gone about a month. We leave first thing in the morning."

Karl nodded his head. Nakobee turned and walked away. Rae and Jym looked at each other and followed. As they walked away, Jym looked at Rae.

"He did not ask any questions or even speak. What kind of training are we in for back on Rednog? I don't think I would just follow orders without first asking questions."

As they left, they heard Karl call out. "Kenya, come and take over. You will be in charge until I return."

Karl left, heading out to gather the others. Rae stepped closer to Nakobee.

"We should see if Shaméd can go with us. He would be a lot of help."

"We do not need a wizard. We need stealth. If you are worried about being killed, you can stay here. I assure you we will find Jon and do what must be done to bring him back."

"Yeah, about that. I thought you did not like Jon. So why all the fuss with helping us get him back?"

Nakobee stopped and looked at Rae, then Jym.

"It is true I do not like Jon. He is, however, here to help my people and that makes him a friend, a friend who was taken by the enemy. I will do whatever it takes to bring him back or avenge his death."

Nakobee started walking. Jym looked at Rae.

"Let us just hope we do not have to avenge his death."

Rae smiled and they both followed Nakobee. The next morning as they stepped out of the building where they slept, Karl, Nuka, Flan, Naate, and Janae were already there. They were wearing packs like theirs, packs from Rednog.

"You got to keep the packs from Rednog?"

Karl looked at Rae in puzzlement.

"Of course we kept them. They are tuned to our bodies. Just like yours. No one else can wear one after it's been tuned to the one to whom it is given."

"What do you mean tuned to your bodies? No one told us the packs are tuned to our bodies."

"How long have you been in training? We were taught the use and function of the packs the first day they were given to us. Did you not pay attention when yours were given to you?"

"We were handed them as we walked through the gate. No one told us anything about them. As for how long we have been in training, the three of us have only been on Rednog five years."

The others looked at each other, their faces showed puzzlement.

"You three must be important or expendable to be sent out before being completely trained."

Rae was about to speak, but Nakobee cut him off. "You will have plenty of time to learn more about each other in the next few days."

Nakobee walked away and the others followed. Jym looked at Rae.

"If it is true about the packs it explains why mine fits better. The first day I put it on I thought it would kill me, it was so uncomfortable."

Rae walked alongside Jym. He looked around before speaking. "I know what you mean. It sort of reminds me of the one I got from Train Master. This is bigger and now it fits and does not hurt when wearing it. What do you think about what Karl said? You know, about our being important or expendable. Why do you think we are here?"

Jym answered, "I asked Sword Master Zale the day he came for me. He said it was because Shaméd asked for the three of us."

"He asked for us?" Rae said in a puzzled voice. Rae continued walking, his mind racing trying to figure out what was going on. They reached the north gate and went through.

Once they were outside, Karl and Nuka ran off. They were heading to where Jon and the wagons were attacked. They would reach the site before the others and search for clues on the directions the enemy went.

Once they found it, they would follow the trail. Nakobee had explained that if they lost it or could not find a trail, they would head for the other cave, then travel through and look for the demon's main location. He believed that was where they would take Jon if he were still alive.

When they arrived, Karl and Nuka were sitting near a large bush.

As they approached, Nuka spoke, "There is a trail. It is faint, but we should be able to follow it. It seems like they were trying to hide the direction they were headed. A mile out the trail is clearer. They are heading for the mountains."

"They might be heading for the cave. Let us hope Commander Ferdra and his men can hold them off."

Nakobee waved his hand and Nuka and Karl led the way. They went at a slow jog. Rae and Jym were not pleased at the pace they set.

Just before sundown, they made camp and ate cold food. Nakobee set up a two hour rotating guard watch. Rae and Jym would start theirs the next night.

They arrived at the cave three days after leaving Keele. They could see the remnants of a battle. Dead trees and burnt landscape showed it was not an easy fight. They approached slowly, not sure what or who they would find.

When they were close, five dwarfs stepped out of hiding. Everyone jumped. When Nakobee saw who they were he called out, "Stand down."

One of the dwarfs stepped closer.

"You are Nakobee. Do you wish to speak with Commander Ferdra?"

"Yes. I see there was a battle. Did you lose any men?"

The Dwarf smirked up at him.

"We lost no one. Those that attacked however lost many. The demons fled over the mountain carrying those they could. We just finished burying their dead."

He turned and they followed him to the cave. When they arrived they saw a large wooden door with large metal hinges. Nakobee stopped and looked at it.

"When and how could you have built this in such a short time?"

"We can do a lot when we have the material to work with. It took us a day to build this and the one on the other side. Give us a month and we will have homes inside."

They entered the door. As they did, he could see the openings where those inside could fire arrows. Nakobee worried that it might not be easy to take this back from them if they decided not to honor their bargain.

They found Commander Ferdra inside watching men working the rock walls. They were carving them out making rooms. He turned as Nakobee walked up.

"Nakobee, good to see you. I suppose you are here to make sure we are all right. And as you can see the demon horde was no match for my men. This is a strong mountain. It will make a fine home. We thank you and Queen Kaila for offering it to us."

"I'm glad you and your men survived the horde of demons and that you are happy with your new home. We are on our way through to see if we can find where they are heading."

"I might be able to help with that. Word has come to us that a large force of demons with a mixture of the four races, are fifteen days march north of Queen Liseran's land. They are where her lands meet up with the demon's homeland. Word is it is a very large army. I would not be surprised if they are not getting ready to invade the humans, and then the trolls. They will need more bodies to fight the elves and my people. It is not that easy to attack people living underground."

"Let us hope we can stop them before they kill all humans and the trolls. Can you send word to King Tragi to let him know of the possible invasion?"

"Yes, of course. Now I suppose you will want to move on, so I will let you continue, and I will get back to work."

He turned and walked away yelling out orders. Nakobee walked back to his men and they headed for the other side of the mountain.

Two days later they reached the far side and stopped at the tunnel and the new large door. Like the other side, the dwarfs had made a lot of changes. There were now eating areas, rooms with beds, and even functional latrines. Nakobee was impressed with how hard these dwarfs worked.

As they exited, they saw a group of humans talking to a dwarf. The human leader looked at them, then walked over to Nakobee.

"The dwarf over there said you are the one called Nakobee, First Sword to Queen Kaila?"

Nakobee looked at the old man. He was tall, as tall and as large as Nakobee.

There was a long scar on the man's right arm. He was dressed in a bright blue robe. Those with him were also dressed in blue. His people were also tall and large in stature. They all carried spears, and the women and children carried packs on their backs. Further away there was a group guarding their livestock.

The man's face was old and wrinkled, yet somehow he looked familiar. These people might be from his father's homeland or even his father's tribe.

"Yes, I'm Nakobee. Who may I ask are you?"

"I'm Gonta, leader of what is left of the tribe Atoka. There are only what you see here left of a once great nation. Only two hundred men and three hundred women and children are left. We are coming to ask you and Queen Kaila for sanctuary. We will work hard for you and help protect and feed your people."

Nakobee stood there looking at the old man. He realized his eyes were blue. The name of the tribe he was from was the same as his father's.

"The name, Atoka. You say that is the name of your tribe?"

"Yes, you have heard of my people?"

The old man tried to stand taller.

"My father's name was Natook. It is said he came from the land of the Atoka. Could it be possible he came from your land?"

The old man looked deep into Nakobee's eyes. He saw that they were blue.

"How long ago did your father come here? And is he still alive?"

"My father arrived almost thirty years ago. He was killed over six years ago by what we now know to be the demons' doing."

The old man looked down, after a few seconds, he looked up.

"Natook was my brother. I should have known you were part Atoka with your blue eyes. I'm sorry to hear he is dead. Our mother was also killed just over seven years ago by a horde of demons. For the last seven years, we have been fighting them. Our sister, the last queen told me to take what was left of our people and search for our brother. We heard about you and your sister building a force to fight the demons. We thought we would come and join you and then continue our search for him. It looks as though my search is over. We have found his people. We had hoped to find a place to rebuild our home."

Nakobee took hold of Gonta's shoulders.

"You and your people have a home with us as long as you want. Come sit with me so I can prepare a message for you to take to my sister. It will explain to her your situation."

They moved over to where some logs were placed for people to sit. Nakobee reached in his pack, taking out paper and a writing stick. He wrote a note to Kaila letting her know that this man was their uncle and they could possibly be all that is left of their father's people. When he was finished he handed it to Gonta.

"This will get you into the walls of Keele. Once inside, have them take you to see Queen Kaila. Give her this paper. She will welcome you."

He sat looking at the paper, then up at Nakobee.

"You can write?"

"Yes, many of our people can read and write. Soon everyone who wishes to can learn."

He reached out his hand and said, "Thank you, son of Natook."

"Come, I will explain to the guards who you are and they will let you pass."

Nakobee led them to the door where he told the guards there who they were. Nakobee said goodbye and Gonta led his people into the mountain.

Nakobee turned away as the last one passed through herding the flock of animals.

Rae looked at Jym, then Karl.

"Do all the people on this world travel with their animals?"

Karl stood there watching the people entering the mountain.

"These people lost everything. What they have with them is all that is left of a once proud people. The Atoka tribe is what myths are made of. Their warriors are legendary. Our history says that one of their warriors could fight and kill ten warriors from any other tribe. They are the biggest and strongest of the people on this world. Some say they are as strong as a troll. Now look at them, reduced to just over a few hundred."

"If those people are anything like Nakobee, they can fight and hold their own with an Ogre," Rae said

Karl looked at Rae and asked, "What is an Ogre?"

"You know the big green guy named Lau?"

"Yes, I met him once. Is he an ogre?"

"Yes, and he is a small one. Nakobee and Lau did a lot of training together. Nakobee not only held his own, but he beat him a few times. Ever since Nakobee did that, the humans on Rednog are fearful of him."

Karl looked at Nakobee as he stood near the gate watching the people entering the tunnel.

"I can understand their fear. His people are great warriors. It is sad to see a tribe as great as theirs reduced to so few."

Karl lowered his head and walked back to the others who were waiting.

Nakobee returned and without speaking, walked by as he headed down the trail.

Chapter Twenty-Nine

The team was on the road for five days when they saw smoke. They entered a large orchard and carefully approached. When they were close they saw six buildings on fire. They spread out and moved slowly to see what had happened. As they moved in, they saw people trying to put the fires out. They were all elderly and some were wounded.

They could see no others around, so Nakobee waved his arm and they all moved in.

When the people saw them they stopped and huddled together. The old men grabbed what weapons they had and stood in front of the others.

Nakobee raised his hands and called out, "Do not be afraid, we mean you no harm. We are here to help."

Nakobee and the others came closer, and as they did they saw the dead. They removed their packs and Rae began moving the bodies off to one side. Jym, Nuka, and Flan did the same. Karl, Naate, and Janae went with Nakobee to help put out the fires.

Janae filled buckets with water from the well, the others took them and tossed the water on the fires. The old people saw them and came to help. It did not take long and the fires were out. Only one building was still standing. It was made with mud and grass. The others that burned were all made with grass-thatched roofs and wood walls.

Nakobee looked at the people. There were about twenty of them. The ones who were wounded did not have life threatening injuries, but left untreated, they could still die.

"Let us help you with your wounds. We have medicine."

Nakobee went to his pack and removed the bundle of medicine. The old people came over and Karl and the others brought their packs of medicine, as well.

Nakobee opened his pack as an old woman stood in front of him. She was maybe five feet ten inches tall. They were all tall. Even the old men, bent over as they were, standing straight would be over six feet. Their clothing was dirty, but he could see the red and yellow patterns in the cloth. They were Queen Liseran's people. He wondered why they were attacked since there was an agreement between her and the demons.

Karl brought a bucket of water and set it next to Nakobee. He took a cloth and dipped it into the water. He looked into the old woman's eyes.

"Little mother, this may hurt."

She looked up at him and in a shaky yet stern voice said, "I'm not unfamiliar with pain."

Nakobee smiled and wiped the dirt away. When he was finished, her wound was wrapped and she looked back up into his eyes.

"For someone so big you are very gentle. Do you have a mate?"

Nakobee looked at her not sure what to make of her words. Karl stood there grinning.

"Little mother, are you asking me for yourself?"

She laughed, her sad face crinkling, and looked at her friends who laughed, also.

"No, I'm asking for my granddaughter. She is very beautiful. She would give you many strong children. I would be happy to see her with someone like you."

Nakobee sat there astounded. He looked at Karl for help.

Karl's grin grew bigger as he said, "Do not look at me! I cannot help you. But maybe you should not say anything until you meet her granddaughter?"

Nakobee frowned at him, then he looked back at the old woman.

"I'm not free to take a woman. I'm First Sword to Queen Kaila."

"Oh, you are spoken for and bound to a queen. Please forgive me. I should have known one like you would be a mate to a queen."

"No, Queen Kaila is my sister. We are rebuilding our land. When the time is right, I will pass the title to the one she chooses."

She smiled and looked at the old man next to her. She winked at him, then looked back at Nakobee.

"Then there is still hope for my granddaughter. Good. When you see her, you will believe my words. She is indeed very beautiful."

"Yes, well maybe we can talk about this some other time. Let me help the others."

Karl moved away as he could no longer keep from laughing. Rae came over and looked at Karl.

Rae asked, "What is so funny?"

Karl was about to speak, but Nakobee called out, "Never mind. I could use some help with these people."

"We were going to bury the dead, but wanted to ask them if there are any rules we need to follow."

The old woman stood and walked over to Rae. She looked up at him then over at Jym who had followed Rae.

"You two need to get out in the sun more. Come, I will help you with our dead." She looked back at Nakobee and said, "You can continue with the others."

The old woman took Rae by the hand and led him away. Jym and Janae followed. The others stayed to help the wounded.

The old man who sat grinning at Nakobee said, "My woman is pushy. Our granddaughter is a lot like her. She has turned down every man who has come asking to be her mate. I think she would not say no if you asked."

Nakobee shook his head, looked at him and spoke, "Your village has been attacked and many of your people have died. Your homes are burnt to the ground, and you two are asking me to take your granddaughter as my mate? What is wrong with you?"

198

"Nothing is wrong with us. Our granddaughter lost her parents years ago. We took her in and raised her. We have been searching for a mate. She needs a strong man. You seem to be one that would take care of her. As you said, we have lost everything. It will take years to rebuild, and we may not be able to do it. There are very few young people left.

When our granddaughter returns with the others, she will want to stay and rebuild. But what happens if the demons return? There are not enough men to fight them. The demons are too many and too strong. There are only fifteen youth with Hasina."

"Your granddaughter is away? Where is she?"

"She and fifteen other young people took the animals to the river for fresh grass. They take them twice a week. I'm glad it was her turn. If she had been here she would have been killed. Or even worse, she could have been taken with the other young people."

Nakobee sat there thinking as he cleaned the man's wounds. He finished and looked at him.

"Who was the elder here? Is she or her mate still alive?"

The old man looked at Nakobee, then at Karl who had stopped to hear the response.

"I'm sorry, we have done you a disservice. You come here and help us and we have never given you our names. I'm Onex. The woman you met is my mate, Leader Nectar. Our village is called Orchard. We make fine wine and dried fruit."

Nakobee grinned. Now he understood why the old woman was so pushy, she was a leader and as such, used to having her way.

"Tell Leader Nectar I meant no disrespect to her or her granddaughter. When we are finished here we will leave to continue our journey. We might be able to stay a day or two."

"We would welcome you. Now I must get busy. I need to check what is left of our supplies."

Onex stood and walked away. It did not take long to clean and bandage the rest of the wounded. By sundown there was a large fire a couple hundred feet from the village. Leader Nectar told Rae that they burned their dead. A large pyre was built and the bodies placed on top. As it burned the rest of the villagers came and prayed.

Rae stood next to Nakobee. Leaning close to him he asked, "Are we staying because you want to meet Leader Nectar's granddaughter?"

Nakobee looked at him, frowning. Rae did not flinch; he just stood there looking into Nakobee's eyes.

"No, we are staying to make sure they will be alright. We might leave in the morning. It looks like they have everything they need. When their young return with the animals, maybe they will leave and go to a safer place."

"Where is this safer place? Queen Liseran rules this land. She is working with the demons. Her people have nowhere to go, unless you are thinking of sending them to Keele, as well?"

Nakobee looked at Rae and he knew he was right. He just could not keep sending people to his land, especially when these people lived under another queen. If Quoin found out that he had given refuge to them, he could openly declare war.

He would have to let them make up their own minds. As the fire died down, the old ones moved back to the village. They had found wraps and laid down next to the mud building. Nakobee led his men into the trees where they made camp.

The morning found Nakobee looking off towards a group of people heading for the village. He watched as the old ones came out to meet them. They were herding animals. The animals were small, rather thick, and almost as round as they were long. Most were white, but a few were black and white.

Nakobee looked at a small group of people coming his way. As they came closer, he saw that it was Leader Nectar and Onex, and a young female was with them. She carried a spear in her left hand, her cloak pulled back over her right shoulder. Her clothing was loose so her steps would not be impeded. She took slow steady steps, as someone who was proud and sure of her abilities. She stood tall and straight. Nakobee could tell by the way she carried her spear, she knew how to use it.

He stepped out calling a greeting, "Good morning, Leader Nectar and Onex. I see your young have returned. That is good. We do not want to be a burden to you, so we will be leaving soon."

"See, I told you he has manners."

The old woman patted the young one's arm.

"Nakobee, you do not need to leave so fast. Meet our granddaughter, Hasina. She is the one I told you about."

The young woman looked sideways at her grandmother, then back at Nakobee.

"I thank you for your help. I'm sure more would have been lost if you had not arrived. I hope it was not too much of a bother for you and your friends?"

"We were passing and saw the fire and stopped. It was no bother. We were glad to help. Now if there is nothing more, I will get my friends and we will depart."

"No, please stay a little longer. We do not get many people coming here. We normally take our wares to Quill to sell. It looks like this year we will have nothing to take. But, that is of no concern to you. We wish to show you our hospitality and have a feast in honor of your help."

"Like I said, you do not have to do that. We are on a tight schedule and must keep to it."

"Then we will not bother you any longer. Thank you again, for your help."

Hasina turned and started walking away. Leader Nectar and Onex stood there looking at Nakobee.

He took a deep breath, let it out slowly, and spoke, "I meant no disrespect. I just thought since you have very little left, giving us a feast would be a burden on your people. I do appreciate the offer, and under any other circumstances I would be glad to stay."

The young woman stopped, turned, and stood there looking at him. She didn't say a word. Nakobee was about to speak when she finally did.

"Your words are accepted. Maybe when you return you and your men will give us the pleasure of providing you with a meal and a better place to lay your heads."

"Thank you, I look forward to that."

She started to turn again, but stopped. She stood there and looked him up and down. Then she moved her head and her body giving him a more profile view.

"My name is Hasina. You are called Nakobee, First Sword to Queen Kaila? And, Queen Kaila is your sister, not your mate?"

Nakobee looked at her, then at Leader Nectar. He saw the smile play across the old one's lips.

"Yes, that is my title, and yes, Queen Kaila is my sister and not my mate."

She dipped her head, turned, and walked away. Leader Nectar and Onex, both grinning, followed her.

Nakobee turned and as he headed back, he saw the others standing near the trees. They were smirking.

He said nothing, just walked over, and packed his things. With the pack on his back, he started walking.

The others caught up with him, and Rae stepped by his side still grinning.

"It looks like you just might have a mate after all. Can you take one before your sister does?"

Nakobee took a swing at him. Rae saw it coming and ducked, laughing as he moved away. They walked in silence until noon. When they stopped to eat and rest, Nakobee looked around at the landscape.

"We are not far from the demon's land. Once there we will have to be more careful. I do not know of anyone who has ever been there and returned. We should try to make maps, so when we return home others will know what we have learned."

They moved on and by nightfall they were tired and ready to rest.

Once again they had no fire, ate cold rations, and slept with guards posted.

Two days later as the sun reached its zenith, they reached a small mountain range. They were not real mountains, more like large sand dunes.

The grassland they had been walking on fell away leaving pretty much nothing. There were no more trees and even less grass. As they climbed a hill they heard noise. Nakobee stopped them and looked at Karl.

"You and Nuka go and see what the noise is. We will move over to that small group of trees and wait."

The two moved off and Nakobee and the others headed back to the trees.

Three hours later Karl and Nuka returned. They were sweaty and covered in dirt.

"What did you find?"

Karl looked at Nuka, and they both took a long drink from their canteens. Then they looked at Nakobee.

Karl spoke, "We found the demons' camp. There are maybe a few thousand, humans, dwarfs, elves, and trolls and they are in a big pen. There are even a couple hundred of those large beasts; big, scary, and not very bright.

There are also some tents near the hill. If it had not been for the spyglass you gave me, I would not have seen the elf standing by the door of one of the tents. He was talking to a creature. The creature was holding a human. The elf grabbed the human by the arm and tossed him inside, then the creature left.

It looks like besides humans, there are some elves working with the demons. It also looks like they are getting ready to leave. Nakobee, we do not have the men needed to fight that many."

Nakobee looked at them, then up at the hill. His mind was racing in thought.

Rae looked at Karl and asked, "This human, what did he look like? Was he wearing similar clothing to what Jym and I have on?"

Karl looked at him and said, "It was not easy to see faces, I thought he was wearing a white shirt, until I saw his back. There were scars, then I knew it was his skin. So, I would say he is your friend."

Rae and Jym looked at each other.

"Was there anything else?"

"Yes, the man stood there staring up at the elf and was laughing at him. The elf went crazy and started screaming. We were too far away to hear their words. Whatever the elf said made the human laugh even more."

Rae and Jym both laughed.

Karl asked, "This is your friend, Jon?" He was confused.

"I would bet a lot of money it was Jon. He is the only human I know that can make an elf mad."

Nakobee asked, "How can he still be alive after all this time?"

"If that was Jon, and they have not killed him by now, believe me, they won't. He must have given them a reason to think he is more useful alive than dead. He will figure out a way to escape."

Nakobee looked at Rae and said, "Are you saying your friend has betrayed us?"

Rae shook his head and said, "No, I'm saying he has confused them into thinking they need him alive."

Nakobee looked at the others.

"We need to head back and let Sword Master Zale know about this."

Rae reached over and tapped Nakobee's chest.

"I think he already knows. If not now, he will soon. Remember what they said about the medallions. They record everything around those that wear them."

Nakobee looked down and nodded his head.

"You are right, I keep forgetting about this. Why don't you and the others from Rednog have them?"

Rae looked at him and said, "I was told those are given to those that live off-world. When we return to our world we will be given ours."

Nakobee looked at him and smiled.

"Let's return to Keele. How do you feel about some running?"

They picked up their packs, put them on, and began running. Rae and Jym both let out a low groan as they followed, hoping they were not going to run all the way.

Chapter Thirty

Running and walking, they reached the village of Leader Nectar by noon the third day. When they arrived, Nakobee left his men at the trees where they had made camp before, and went looking for her.

As he walked up, the old woman smiled and held her hands out to him.

"I see you have returned. Could it be that my granddaughter's beauty brought you back so soon?"

Nakobee, taken back by her words, looked at her. He was not sure what to say. She laughed and grabbed his hands.

"I'm having fun with you, Nakobee. You had such a serious look on your face, so I was trying to make you smile. From your expression, I would say I just confused you. Come sit, and then you can tell me why you are back?"

Nakobee followed her to some rocks and they sat. He looked at her and was about to speak when a young girl came up with wooden mugs. She handed one to him and the other to Leader Nectar.

"Thank you."

Turning, he faced Leader Nectar.

"I'm here to let you know there is a large army of demons a good nine days march from here. You and your people need to leave. If they come this way they will leave nothing standing."

She took a sip of her drink and looked around at what was left of her village and her people. She looked up at Nakobee, her eyes wide and bright for someone so old.

"Where do you think we could go? Our Queen has a treaty with these demons and it did not stop them. I know if they return they will destroy everything. But, we have nowhere to go. We could pack up and head to Queen Liseran. When we arrive, there is no way of knowing what she would do to us. She could make us slaves. I'm afraid we must stay here. We die here, or out there somewhere. I'm old and would rather die in my home."

Nakobee looked at her. He knew how she felt; he felt the same way when his home was invaded.

He took hold of her hands and looked at her.

"You do have a place to go. You can come with me. You and your people will be welcomed in my land as free people. We will give you a place to rebuild what you have lost here. I give you my word this will be done."

"How do you hope to stop this demon army? We have watched it grow for the last eight years, from a few hundred to a few thousand. Once they begin their war, there will be no safe place for any of us."

"We have help. We have united with the other races. The trolls, elves, and dwarfs have all sent warriors to help us fight. We even have wizards who can do amazing things. Trust me, we will not lose."

"You have wizards? You would use black arts to fight evil?"

"The magic these wizards use is not evil. They are followers of the "One." It is their name for the Creator. You would not believe the sights I have seen. Dragons, people who live in the oceans, and people who can fly in the sky, all of them believe in the Creator. These are the ones who are willing to help us fight the demons."

She looked at him, then closed her eyes. When she opened them, she looked up at him.

"I will ask my people. If they agree, we will go with you. Now leave and I will gather them."

Nakobee stood and walked back to his men. Rae and Jym were hoping they were going to camp. They had never run with a full pack for as long as they had just done. They both were impressed with the men of this world.

Rae told Jym at one of their breaks, "I did not do this much running on Rednog, and what running I did, was not with a full pack. These guys are not even breathing hard."

They did not even stop at night. They took three hour breaks after five hours of running and walking all the way back to the village. Rae and Jym ached all over.

Nakobee walked up and stood in front of them.

"Make camp. I told them it was not safe here and they could come with us to Keele."

"You are not going to make them run the whole way, are you?"

Nakobee looked at Rae and grinned.

"I could tell you and Jym were having trouble keeping up. Did they not train you to run on Rednog?"

Rae looked at him not sure why he was grinning.

"We ran but not with a full pack or for so long."

"I understand. The area where Reklan had us run was only a few miles distant. He had us run around it the first day. I asked what kind of running he was teaching and I told him we started teaching our young to run five miles at a time. By the time they are fifteen years old, they should be able to run twenty miles without breaking a sweat. Reklan said that was good, but can you do it with a full pack? We showed him it was not that much harder. Reklan said he was going to start having the new recruits do the same."

"Well, I'm glad they did not start with us. Or maybe I wish they had. We might be in better shape."

Nakobee and the others laughed. They made camp and were setting up a fire pit when two young girls showed up. They were carrying baskets.

Nakobee stood and greeted them, "Greetings to you both. What do you have there?"

"Hasina told us to bring some fruit and bread."

They placed the two baskets on the ground and without saying another word, looked up at Nakobee, giggled and ran away.

"Yes, I do believe you have found a mate."

Nakobee turned and glared at Rae. Rae just stood there grinning

"She is just being hospitable."

"Yes, she is. She is showing her future mate just how good of a host she can be. We, of course, thank her for it."

Rae walked over and looked at the fruit. There was fresh and dried fruit. He took some of each and went back to his bedroll. He sat and handed some to Jym. They both started eating.

Nakobee took some, as did the others. As night fell, Leader Nectar and Onex came to their camp.

"Greetings to all of you. We hope you enjoyed the fruit and had a nice relaxing day."

Nakobee stood.

"Greetings to you, Leader Nectar and Onex. We did enjoy the fruit. Are you here to give me an answer?"

"Yes, we are. I talked with my people and they have all agreed that going with you to your land is better than staying here and dying. We require two days to get ready to leave. Will that be a problem?"

"Why two days?"

"We will have to take clippings of our trees. It will take another day to gather the animals and bring in the ones to carry our supplies."

"Your little animals are going to carry your supplies?"

They both smiled and Onex said, "No, the Leels will just follow us. They are very tame. We have Armels to carry our things. Have you ever seen an Armel? They are very strong and can travel a long time without water."

"I have heard of them, but have never seen one."

"Then you will tomorrow. We have fifty of them, or at least we did a few days ago. We will know how many are left when the children return."

"Return? You sent children out tonight to bring them back?"

"Of course. Once the decision was made, we sent ten out to gather and bring them in. They have done it before."

"There could be demons out there."

"They know how to be careful. Do you not teach your young how to hunt and prepare for adulthood?"

"Yes, we do. I was just worried about them."

"That is nice to hear. You need not worry. As I said, they have done this many times. Now good night, and we will see you tomorrow."

Nakobee watched as they walked away. Returning to his bed roll, he stretched out. As he laid his head down he called out, "Do not forget I have last watch."

In the morning as the sun broke over the horizon, they awoke to noise coming from the village. As the men woke from the sounds, they saw Nakobee staring out at the village. The men got out of their bedrolls, walked over, and stood alongside him.

They looked at the village. What they were watching was unbelievable. There were children leading large animals. Some of the animals were down on their knees, as bundles were being brought over and stacked near them.

"When did these people wake up?" asked Rae.

Nakobee stood there watching the animals arriving. He never looked away as he answered, "The children arrived just after I took over watch. One child was leading three of those large animals into the village. I think they are what Leader Nectar called Armels. Then a little over an hour ago, the others woke up and they all began packing."

Rae looked at the large animals and the villagers running around.

"They do not waste any time do they? What did you say to them yesterday?"

"I told them they needed to leave and that they could come with us. You heard Leader Nectar. She said it would take two days for them to be ready. I did not think they would move this fast."

"They understand staying here is not a good idea and that you are in a hurry to get back home."

Nakobee nodded his head as he spoke, "It would appear that way. These people are very organized. See how each one is working? It is like one person is telling them what to do without us hearing them. Leader Nectar said they would be ready in two days. At the rate they are packing, they might be ready to leave today. I will go after we eat and talk with her."

Nakobee turned and headed to the fire pit. The others followed. Rae stood there watching the village. Nakobee was right, it did seem as if each one knew what to do without being told. A few minutes later he went to the fire and ate.

Nakobee waited three hours before heading over. Everyone had loaded their packs and sat waiting. Even if they stayed another night, having their packs ready to go was always a good idea.

Nakobee was almost there when Hasina came walking out to meet him.

When she was close, she spoke, "As you can see we are packing. We did most of it last night and we will be done by nightfall. The children will have all the animals ready to leave tomorrow at first light. By then we will have our tree cuttings complete, if that is alright with you."

Nakobee could tell by her voice she was not happy about leaving.

"I did not mean for your people to work through the night. We would have stayed as long as you needed."

"If you stay as long as I needed, you would be here until you were old. I do not want to leave our land. My people have been here and worked this place for over ten generations. They built it from nothing to what you see here now. I know you said we would be given land, but do you know how long it takes for our trees to grow? It takes at least five years, sometimes ten, before they produce edible fruit."

"Maybe after the war you can return to see what is left and your people can start over."

Hasina looked at him, then turned to look at her village. When she turned back she pointed toward the trees.

"You know as well as I do, when the demons come through here, they will burn everything. That is what evil does. It destroys. I have lived my whole life close to the demons. I have seen how they treat this world. They care nothing for anything that is alive. It is only by the Creator's grace that we have lived this long before they created an army able to kill us."

Nakobee was unsure how to respond. He was about to speak when Rae and the others came up.

"We do not mean to interrupt, but is there anything we can do to help? We are getting a little restless just sitting over there."

Nakobee looked at them, then back at Hasina.

"If there is anything we can do to help, please let us know."

"You can go help the children. Find Keia. She can show you what needs to be done. I'm going to help with the cuttings."

She turned and walked away. Rae watched her. He patted Nakobee on the shoulder, then moved back.

"She is as hard-headed as you are. She will make you a great mate."

Nakobee turned, but Rae was already too far away for Nakobee to punch him.

Rae grinned as he said, "Just stating a fact. One day you will need to marry and have children. She is a good choice. You have to admit, she is as beautiful as Leader Nectar said she was."

Nakobee turned back and watched her as she met up with a group of people. As they headed into the trees, his mind thought about what Rae said. He was right. Someday he would have to find a mate. He did not know this woman, yet, but that did not mean that given time, they couldn't become close. Maybe she would make a good mate. For now he had to keep his mind on the upcoming war. He turned toward his men.

"Come, let us find these children and help them."

They found the children near the small animals. There was a young girl standing off to the side giving orders. They walked over to her.

"Are you Keia?"

She turned and looked at Nakobee and the others. She stood straighter.

"Yes, I'm Keia. How may I help you?"

"Hasina sent us. She said you could use some help with these animals."

She turned her back to Nakobee as she answered, "Yes, we can use the help. We have to pack grass so we can feed the Leels on the trip."

"You will not need much. The route we are taking has plenty of grass."

She looked back at Nakobee and smiled.

"Leels eat a lot. That is one reason we move them around. If they stay too long in one place, they eat everything."

"Then show us what to do."

She called out, "Ki, come here."

A young man came running over. He stopped in front of her and stood straight.

"Yes, Keia, what can I do for you?"

Like most of the children, he was tall and thin. His hair was cut close to his scalp, he only wore sandals and a loin cloth, and carried a spear in his left hand.

"Ki, take these men and show them how to wrap grass for the Leels."

He looked at Nakobee and his eyes grew wide, then he looked at the others. When he saw Rae and Jym his eyes grew even wider. He had never seen anyone with such fair skin. Then he saw their weapons.

Nakobee and the others could tell by his expression he was not used to giving orders to older men.

Ki leaned toward Keia and said, "These men are going to bundle grass?"

"Hasina sent them to help us. So let them help."

He nodded his head, looked at Nakobee, waved his hand and said, "Follow me."

He started running without waiting. Nakobee and the others ran after him. Rae looked at Jym.

"Does everyone on this world like running?"

Jym laughed and they followed the others.

214

By nightfall the village was packed and ready to leave. Leader Nectar called to everyone as they stood around the fire eating their meal.

"Tomorrow begins a new day for all of us. Tonight we eat and spend one last night in our home. We embark on a journey that will take us and our young to a new place. We can only hope it will be as prosperous as this one was to our ancestors.

We have lived here a long time and are sad to go. However, we know we must leave. We lost many to the demons when they came through here. They took many of our young and the men. They left behind what they thought were just a few old ones. They were wrong. We are not all who were left. We still have young people. Now we will take the few the Creator has blessed to spare, and we will go build a new home for them. We will give them a chance for a new and safer life."

The people cheered. Nakobee and the others cheered with them. Leader Nectar raised her hands.

"Now all of you get some rest. We leave at sunrise."

Chapter Thirty-One

In the morning as the sun's rays broke the horizon, they were ready to leave. Nakobee sent Karl and Nuka out ahead of the group to scout and make sure the way was safe. The others would be spread throughout the small caravan.

The Armels were leading. They were loaded with supplies, and a few were carrying people who could not walk. Those walking helped the children with the animals.

The Leels came last since they walked the slowest, and they followed two children carrying poles with bells.

Nakobee observed the fifteen children who had returned with the animals. Their ages ranged from ten to eighteen. All of them carried spears, even the ones working with the animals.

The first four days went smoothly. They found plenty for the animals to eat and drink. They crossed small ravines and wide gullies, none too hard for the animals or those walking. The land was full of tall grass and trees, some of which bore fruit. The fruit and fresh water kept their food supply replenished.

Karl and Nuka would return at night with a wild animal they had killed, giving them fresh meat. The people were glad they did not have to kill any from their herds.

Nakobee calculated it would take five more days to reach the mountain cave than it did for them to reach the village. He was not worried; they had not seen any signs of the enemy. He hoped it would continue like this.

On days five and six the grass became more difficult to find. They began to cross dry stream beds. Onex said it was because it was summer and it did not rain much in the summer.

On day seven the group stopped for their noon break, when Karl and Nuka came running. Nakobee called to the other men to come to the front so they could hear why they had come back so early.

Karl spoke when everyone was there, "There is a small group coming this way. We counted two demons and three large beasts. They have about twenty people walking between the beasts. They might be humans, we are not sure. We did not get that close."

Nakobee surveyed the landscape to see if there was anywhere the people could hide.

"How far away are they? And can we move out of their way?"

Karl answered, "About four hours. They are not walking very fast. They only slow down when one of the people in the group falls down."

"That sounds like they are prisoners," Jym said

"That is what we were thinking. We saw a couple stumble and fall. A beast came running over, and the humans did not move fast enough to help one of them. The beast grabbed him and dragged him away.

As for hiding, I'm not sure. They are not coming straight this way. But the land is getting flatter."

Onex and Leader Nectar came walking up. Leader Nectar asked, "Is there a problem?"

"We have demons coming our way. Do you know if there is a gully or a ravine anywhere near by?

Onex looked at Leader Nectar, then back at Nakobee.

"It has been many years since I have been this far. I do remember a deep gully that always had water even in the hottest times. It is off in that direction."

Nakobee looked in the direction he was pointing. He stood there thinking. He opened his mouth to speak. Karl spoke first, "If you are thinking of going that way, don't. I think that is where they are heading. As I said, they were not coming straight toward you. They were going off in that direction. I was just worried they might see you if you kept going."

Nakobee looked at him, then at Leader Nectar.

"We are going to have to stay here for a while. Can you have the Leels taken off that way? And how low can the Armels get?"

"They can get very low and they blend into the ground very well. As for the Leels, we can have the children take them as far as you want."

"Flan, Naate, you go with the children and lead them. Go off that way until nightfall, then circle back toward the mountain. We will meet up with you there, if not before."

Onex looked at them and said, "You should take one of the Armels with some supplies."

"Go with him and help him get what they need. The rest should begin camouflaging the others," Nakobee said.

Leader Nectar and Onex looked at Nakobee as he said the last words. They had no idea what the word camouflaging meant. They found out, when he started digging and putting people and the Armels in the holes.

Then he used the dirt as a wall for them to hide behind. They used brown colored cloth to make low tents over the Armels and the people to hide them.

In two hours everyone was hidden. Karl and Nuka left their packs with Nakobee and once again went to make sure the demons were heading away from them. They returned four hours later.

They were all squatted down as Karl spoke, "They reached the gully and it looks like they are going to stay there awhile."

"What makes you think that?"

"One of the beasts ate another captive, and the demons did not even try and stop it. They just moved off and sat near the wall."

Nakobee's face changed when he heard Karl's words. His face got darker and he frowned in anger.

"You said there are only two demons and three beasts?"

They both answered, "Yes."

"How deep is this gully? Could we get close enough to ambush them?"

Everyone looked at Nakobee. Rae and Jym both spoke at the same time.

"What are you thinking?"

"I'm thinking we could kill the beasts, and kill the demons, or at least chase them away. Then we could free those people."

Rae looked at Nakobee and said, "Nakobee, we don't even know if those people are really prisoners."

"Then when we get there, we can see if they are prisoners, or people that have been turned. Either way, I think killing three beasts and two demons and people that may have been changed, is a good idea."

"You are not worried about the demons?"

Nakobee patted his quiver of arrows.

"No, we still have some arrows that Sword Master Zale gave us. And I get to use them again."

Rae shook his head as he said, "If this does not work, we will all die."

"Dying for what you believe in is a noble thing."

Rae looked at him, his eyes showed defiance.

"That may be true, but dying before you get these children to safety, I believe is a foolish thing. I will do as you want because Sword Master said we were to follow your orders. But I won't be happy about it."

Rae walked away. Jym stood and followed. Nakobee looked at the others. He could see they were unsure of his plan. He was about to speak, when Hasina came closer. She looked at him, then the others.

"I will go with you. Your plan is a noble one. Helping those in trouble is always a good thing to do."

"You are not coming with us. You will take your people to the mountains and to Keele."

"Why should I let you go alone to help people that might be of my clan? It would not be right for me to do that."

Nakobee looked at her and in a stern voice said, "It is not right for you to get yourself killed."

"Then you do not think your plan will work?"

The others looked at him. He knew her words rang true. He had to either let her go with them or not go at all.

"If Leader Nectar says you can go with us, then you can come."

As soon as his last word was out of his mouth, she turned and left. He was glad she was gone. She made him uncomfortable. He looked at Karl and Nuka.

"Now to my question: is the gully deep enough for us to sneak up and ambush them?"

"Yes. It became deeper the further they went, changing the gully into a small ravine. The place they stopped is maybe fifty feet down and about thirty feet to the other side. It continues like that for a long time. There is water coming out of the wall. It flows into a small rock pool, then along the side of the gully in the direction they are heading."

"Then we will gather our things and leave in two hours. It will be another four hours before the moon rises, but we should make good time."

Hasina came back with her spear and shield and a water bottle hanging over her shoulder. She looked at Nakobee.

"I'm ready to leave whenever you are."

He looked at her and in a low voice said, "You are telling me your grandmother said you could go, even knowing there is a chance you might be killed?"

"My grandmother told me she would not give me leave. Leader Nectar said it was a noble mission, and I was free to make up my own mind. I have made my mind up and if you and your men are going, then I'm going with you."

Nakobee sat there staring at her. Finally he looked away as he said, "We leave in two hours. You will obey every word I say, understood?"

"I will obey only your words that pertain to the upcoming fight."

Nakobee looked back at her, not understanding why she answered that way. He just shrugged.

"Do you have everything you need?"

"Yes," she answered.

"Then sit, while they go to gather our things."

Nakobee looked at the others, he waved and they left to get their packs. He looked at her as she sat across from him. She sat there staring at him.

He could take her looking at him no longer.

"Why are you staring at me?"

"I have never seen a man as large as you. I was wondering how you became so big. Do you eat a lot?"

He never had anyone mention his size in the manner she just had. He was trying to figure out how to answer her when Rae and Jym showed up. They both sat down next to her.

Rae spoke, "He does eat a lot, but that is not why he is so large. The people in the clan his father comes from are big. They are also very strong. I would say as strong as ten men from this world."

She turned to Rae with a look of interest.

"What do you mean of this world?"

Jym and Nakobee looked at Rae. He sat straight, and looked at them then back at her.

"How was I supposed to know she did not know about other worlds?"

"You did not know about them before Shaméd came to ours and told us," Jym said.

"It does not matter, she heard you, and like you and anyone who can think, would want to know more."

"Yes, I would like to know more. Are you two from another world? I have never heard of humans with skin the color of yours. Only elves and dwarfs have different colored skin."

Nakobee looked at Rae and grinned, he waved at him. He was glad the attention had turned away from himself and to Rae.

"Go ahead, tell her."

"Jym and I are both from another world. Well, to be accurate, two worlds. Our home world and the world we have lived on for the last five years."

He was going to say more but the others showed up. He stood and looked at Nakobee.

"Good, everyone is here. Can we leave now?"

Nakobee smiled as he stood.

"It is dark so we can leave. Karl, you are staying here. If we do not return you are to take these people to Keele. Tell my sister, I mean Queen Kaila, what I have done. She will understand."

Karl was about to argue. Nakobee held up his hand.

"I want your word that you will take these people to Keele."

Karl stood straight and answered, "You have my word."

"Thank you."

Nakobee reached out and took hold of Karl's arm. They shook and Nakobee turned and pointed to Nuka.

"Lead the way."

Two hours later they were stretched flat their stomachs looking into the gully. They saw two demons, but

222

it was too dark to see them clearly. The beasts looked like a cross between a dragon and a large hairy animal.

Rae leaned over to Jym and whispered, "What do you make of those? Have you ever seen anything so ugly?"

"None of the pictures they showed us of demons, and what they have for pets, could have prepared me for what I see below. Look at how big those beasts are."

"Yeah, they could have been bred with dragons. I wonder if they know about this on Rednog."

"If we live through this you can tell Sword Master Zale and he can let them know."

Nakobee waved them back from the edge. When they were far enough back he crouched on the ground.

"We will spread out and Nuka and I will aim for the demons. After we shoot, the rest of you shoot the beasts. It might take a couple of arrows to kill them. Do not stop until they are dead. Nuka and I will do the same with the demons. Let's get back and get this over with."

Nakobee looked at Hasina.

"You will stand near me in case I need help."

She was going to say something but stopped when he glared at her.

They headed back and when they were all in place, Nakobee and Nuka stood. They placed their packs next to their legs and took aim. Hasina stood off to the left of Nakobee, her spear and shield at the ready.

Nakobee let fly his first arrow and Nuka did the same. As the arrows were heading toward the demons, they fired again. The first arrows hit, then two more arrows followed seconds later.

Both demons screamed as they jumped up. One demon, all three arrows in the back of its neck, took three steps and burst into flames. The other ripped the arrows out, but as his body started to burn he disappeared.

The three beasts were hit six times before they stopped moving. When the beasts and demons began screaming, the people ran to the cliff walls and pressed their bodies tight against it.

Nakobee and the others stood there looking down at what they had done. Both demons were gone, and the beasts were dead. Now all they had to do was get below and see about freeing the people. Nakobee turned and was about to speak, when there was movement nearby.

Hasina reacted, her spear thrusting toward the dark shape. She was pushed back a couple of feet. She changed her stance to attack again.

Nakobee called out, "Stop, he is a friend."

Hasina was still in a crouched position, her shield up and spear pointing at the dark shape. The dark form moved closer. She looked at the strange man standing in front of her. He was dressed in leather, the sword in his hand was pointing up. Then he nodded his head at her and slowly sheathed his blade.

His posture told her he was a warrior of high caliber. She relaxed and stood up, then took a step back.

Nakobee spoke as he came forward, "Sword Master Zale, why are you here?"

"I saw the report that you were about to engage in a fight with demons, so I came to help. It would seem you did not need me."

"The arrows you gave me worked. One demon was killed, the other fled as it was burning."

"I'm glad to hear that. Now would you like to go below to check on the people?"

"Yes. Nuka says there's a place we can work our way down."

"I know a faster way. Step this way."

He pointed and without saying anything, Rae, Jym then Nuka and the others stepped where Sword Master Zale pointed. As they each disappeared, Hasina made a gasping sound.

Sword Master Zale looked at Nakobee and said, "Rae already told her about the other worlds, so she might as well see one. Even if it is only one room."

Nakobee moved close to Hasina, put his hand on her shoulder and spoke, "The worlds Rae told you about? You are going to one now. Do not be afraid, it is safe. I have done this many times. Take my hand and we can go there together."

Taking her hand, they stepped forward. Her vision blurred, but when her eyes refocused, she saw the others standing by a wall. Nakobee moved her to them. She turned and saw a very large mirror. The man Nakobee called Sword Master Zale was standing inside the mirror in the place where they were just standing.

He took a step and was instantly standing in the room with them. He looked to his right at a young man behind a large rock table.

"Move it to the other location."

The image in the mirror changed and then she saw the people up against the wall. Sword Master Zale waved his hand toward Nakobee.

"It might be better if you go first. As our young lady said, not many of you have seen people who look like me."

Nakobee, still holding Hasina's hand, stepped forward, they appeared in the ravine. They were back away from the people in the dark. Rae and the others followed.

Hasina took her hand from Nakobee's hand. She and Nakobee slowly stepped out of the dark toward the people. When the people saw them, they fell back against the wall. They were scared of these people who just appeared out of thin air.

Hasina rammed her spear into the ground and laid her shield against it. She moved toward them with her hands out.

"It is all right, you are safe now. We killed the demons and beasts. You are all free now."

They relaxed but were still frightened of what they had just seen. Nakobee stepped forward.

In a low voice he spoke, "We have set you free. You can return to your village and let them know that demons and their beasts can be killed. If you are hungry we have food to share."

Hasina looked at him not sure how they were going to feed these people. Sword Master Zale came and stood next to Nakobee.

He placed a sack by his leg, and whispered to Nakobee, "It looks as if you have everything under control. I will return and let Queen Kaila know you are safe, and will be home soon."

He walked away and disappeared into the dark. Hasina watched as he left. She looked back as Nakobee was opening the sack taking out bread and meat.

The people slowly came closer. They took what he offered them and moved back against the wall. After handing food to all of them, Nakobee saw there was a lot of food left. He had handed food to eighteen who were mostly children. Their ages ranged from ten to twenty. They were dressed in rags that scarcely covered them.

Hasina spoke, "You are indeed a great warrior. You were right when you said you had powerful friends. I believe you just might win this war with the demons. I look forward to be standing by your side when you do."

She walked away heading for the group of people. Taking her knife, she began to cut the ropes that bound them. When they were all free, they sat there watching her. She walked among them talking to each one.

Rae had started several large fires. He was standing by the last one, when Nakobee came up to him.

"We cannot stay here. The demons might return."

"I agree. Most of these here are children. Are they coming with us, or will they return to their own homes?"

"I do not know. Maybe Hasina can answer that when she is finished talking with them. Why did you build these fires?"

Rae said, "If the demons do come back, they will return up there. They will look down, see the fires, and I hope they think everyone is sleeping, then come down and attack. When they find no one here, they will search for tracks. I will take Jym and we will create a path that way, upstream. You take the people back the way they came. Once you get to a point where you can turn off, do so. Make sure you cover your tracks. You do not want them to follow you. Jym and I will meet up with you in a day or so."

A half hour later, Hasina came walking over.

"I talked with the children. The four older ones spoke for everyone. They want to come with us. There is nothing left of their village. They said there was no one left alive, only the dead scattered on the ground."

"They can come with us. But we need to leave now. We cannot stay here. The demon that disappeared might not have died. He could have made it back and told others what happened. The longer we stay, the more danger we are in. Tell them we know they are tired, but explain why we need to leave. We need to go now, with or without them."

She walked back to the children to get them ready to leave. As she left, Nakobee looked at Rae and nodded his head. Nakobee went to the others and told them the plan. They left three minutes later.

Rae walked over to Jym. Jym was holding a large branch in his hand, shaking his head back and forth.

He asked, "We are doing this because we think it will save us, or them?"

Rae picked up his branch and moved upstream.

"Both."

They moved their branches back and forth on the ground. It was not to clear their foot prints, but to make it look like they were clearing away many foot prints.

They did this until they reached a location where they could climb up to the top. They put the branches on one side and climbed up the other.

When they reached the top, Jym spoke, "Do you think demons are really this stupid?"

"We can only hope they are."

Rae looked out across the landscape. What few trees they saw, were scattered. It was a good place for him and Jym to climb out. It would be easy to find their way to the mountains. They headed off. By mid-morning, they found a group of trees and climbed under them to sleep.

Nakobee and the others headed back the way the demons had come. When the walls dropped away, Nakobee led the group toward the mountains. Nuka had run ahead when they began their trek. He was heading back to the main group. He was going to have them move out, and if things worked as planned, they would all meet up in a day or so.

Chapter Thirty- Two

Two days after Nakobee rescued the children, they came to a small stream. They had not met up with the other group, but he knew they were not far away.

The children were sitting by the water. Nakobee and his men stood back watching out for any trouble. Hasina came up to him. She was holding the sack of food Sword Master Zale had left them. She looked at the children then at Nakobee.

"We do not have much food left. The trees here are all bare of fruit. We will have to hunt or pick up our pace, so we can reach the others. We can move off to the right to those trees. They might still have some fruit on them."

"I was going to send Flan and Naate out to hunt. They should be able to find something. We can go closer and check on the first group of trees, and if we find nothing, we will head back toward the mountains. I do not want to veer too far. The faster we reach the mountains the better."

They filled their water bags and moved toward the trees. A couple of hours later they reached them. They scared away the animals there eating the fallen fruit. When the children saw the food they ran and started eating it. Hasina ran after them.

She was yelling, "Be careful. I know you are hungry, but it might be bad."

The children did not stop. They grabbed the fruit and stuffed it in their mouths. Nakobee notched an arrow and shot a small animal as it ran away. Picking it up, he moved off and started cleaning it. Janae built a fire and when Nakobee was done they placed it over the fire.

"You stay here. I will go out and keep an eye out to make sure no one sees the fire."

Nakobee stood and headed away from the group. He had walked a few feet when he saw movement coming toward him. Crouching down, he notched an arrow and waited. As he drew the arrow back he heard his name.

"Nakobee, I know that is you. You are the only one I know who makes such a large silhouette. Please do not shoot us. We are tired."

Nakobee stood as Rae and Jym came walking toward him. When they were close, he held out his arm. Rae took it and Nakobee brought him in and gave him a hug. They parted and Nakobee stood there grinning at Jym. He reached out, taking his arm, pulled him close and hugged him also. Letting go, he looked at them. They were dusty and looked tired.

"It is good to see you both. I'm glad you are back. I was not looking forward to explaining to Sword Master Zale how I lost you."

Jym looked at Rae then at Nakobee.

"I'm not sure if you are being serious or just kidding?"

Nakobee laughed as he once more wrapped his arms around them.

"I'm not kidding. I'm very glad to have you back."

When they were let go, Rae took two extra steps back. Jym saw what he had done and grinned.

Rae said, "We are glad to be back. It is not easy to get any sleep with only two of us taking turns watching."

Nakobee looked in the direction they had come, and asked, "I take it there is no one following you?"

Jym answered, "As far as we could see there was no one. There were plenty of animals, but too far away for us to catch. We only came this way because Rae saw the birds flying. He was thinking there might be water."

"There is water, a small stream back in those trees. It is deep and clean. We also have fresh meat cooking. Come, you can tell us all about how you like traveling alone."

They followed him back to camp. The others greeted them and when the food was finished cooking, they ate. They decided to rest there until the next day.

As the sun broke over the horizon, they were on their way. The children were in a better mood and their pace showed it.

It was taking longer because of the direction they had to travel. Four days later, they were within reach of the mountain. They were heading for the trail that led up to the cave.

As they were walking, they saw a dust cloud in front of them. Unsure, they stopped.

Nakobee called Naate over.

"You and Janae go and see what that is. We will continue but at a slower pace. It might be the others. If it is, shoot a fire arrow in the air. Otherwise return."

They both took off at a run. They disappeared within minutes. Nakobee had the group continue walking, staying close to the rocks of the mountain.

One of the children called out, "Look in the sky."

Everyone looked up and they saw a fire arrow arching through the sky.

Nakobee called out, "It looks like we have caught up with the others."

It did not take long before they were walking among the Leels. Hasina was met by her grandparents. Karl walked up to Nakobee. He stood there grinning.

"I'm glad to see you."

He looked at the others as they walked by and said, "I'm glad to see all of you."

They clasped arms and Karl gave him a hug. It was almost dark, so Nakobee decided they should make camp.

They were sitting around a small fire and Nakobee spoke to Leader Nectar, "I think we should reach the trail tomorrow. Once we find it, we have a long walk up to the cave. Then two days travel through the mountain and five more days before we reach Keele."

Leader Nectar smiled at him. She sat there holding Onex's hand.

"It has been a long trip. So far we have had no issues. Do you think we will continue with our luck?"

"We can only pray that we do. We do not have the numbers to fight off anyone who would attack us."

She stood, and with Onex still holding her hand, they headed off to sleep. Nakobee looked at his men.

"Whose turn is it to take first watch?"

Rae spoke up, "I will take it."

He stood and headed out away from the fires and camp. Hasina looked over at Nakobee.

"I will have Ki and Keia keep an eye out as well. The Leels are great at giving warnings."

She went to find the children.

Chapter Thirty-Three

In the morning as they were getting ready to leave, Karl came running up to Nakobee.

"We have trouble. There is a group of men coming this way. They have one demon and one beast with them."

Nakobee looked in the direction he had pointed.

"How long before they reach us?"

"Within the hour. They are running."

Nakobee turned and started yelling, "Everyone, get moving, we have trouble coming at us. We need to find the trail up the mountain."

Nakobee turned to Karl.

"You and the others take all our arrows and follow us. I'm going ahead to find the trail."

Nakobee looked over at Hasina who was standing with Leader Nectar.

"Get everyone up and keep them moving. I will come back as soon as I can."

He turned and started running. He left his pack where it lay. Hasina picked it up and put it on her back. Then she and Leader Nectar started yelling at everyone to get up and get moving.

Everyone was running. The Leels were up front with the Armels. As they rounded some boulders, they saw Nakobee standing on one. He was waving his arms. As they drew closer they could hear him.

"Over here, the trail is this way."

They reached the turn, and the animals began to head up the mountain path. This slowed them down, as the path was not wide and they had to lead the animals between large boulders.

When the last one was on the trail and heading up, the people followed. Nakobee knew this was the hard part. The enemy could spread out and come at them from either side.

Up on his rock, he called to Hasina, "Hasina."

She turned toward him.

"Bring me my pack."

She ran to him. When she reached the boulder, she removed the pack and raised it up to him. Taking it, he took the bow off and counted his arrows. There were only fifteen left. Two of them were the ones for demons.

Removing all but those, he laid them out. His men found high points and began to get ready.

It was not long before the first wave reached them. Twenty creatures once human, came screaming down on them. Each one was waving a club or spear. Nakobee let his first arrow fly. It hit its target and the creature was dead before it hit the ground. The others began firing their arrows also.

When Nakobee shot his last arrow, he looked around and saw that the others were like him. They had no more arrows. He grabbed the two arrows and jumped down off the boulder. He placed his bow over his shoulder and the quiver on his hip, then drew his sword.

Running forward, his blade cut through first one creature, then another. There was nothing they could do to stop his blade. These things that used to be human, only knew how to fight one way and that was the way the demon was telling them.

The demon could not control each one so he was just having them attack wildly. This helped Nakobee, but it did not help the demon.

Nakobee knew they would lose, there were just too many, and they would soon be over-powered by sheer numbers.

Nakobee saw Janae disappear under a horde of bodies. He started working his way toward him. When he reached where he last saw him, there was nothing.

He heard a loud scream. Looking over he saw Rae being pressed by a group of creatures. Nakobee began fighting his way toward him. As he drew closer, he saw the creature's bodies being chopped to pieces.

Rae was screaming and he was covered in blood. Blood curdling screams came from him. With his two swords in hand, he worked his way through the enemy as if they were just standing there. Nakobee thought Rae had gone insane. With each step Rae took, bodies fell. His blades were moving so fast it was hard to see them until they sliced through a body. Nakobee could not believe what he was seeing. All of a sudden the horde in front of him began to retreat. He was left standing there looking at their backs. Without waiting, Nakobee began gathering good arrows from the dead.

He had only gathered a few when he saw arrows descending. They came flying in, killing those fleeing. Nakobee saw the human horde running back and surrounding the demon. They were covering him, trying to protect him from being hit by the arrows.

Nakobee looked in the direction the arrows from which the arrows came. He saw the reflection of the sun off armor. It was a large group riding toward the demon and its horde. More arrows bombarded the horde of creatures protecting the demon.

Nakobee sheathed his sword and drew his bow. Notching one, he looked for an opening. He saw one and let the arrow fly. It hit a creature that moved before his arrow could hit the demon. The creature fell to the ground dead. Nakobee notched another arrow.

Then the wall of humans collapsed and the demon was gone. The humans began fighting each other. More arrows came flying in, and soon they were all dead.

Nakobee heard a roar. Turning he saw Rae come face to face with a large beast. Nakobee could not believe Rae was just standing there as if it was a normal animal. There was no way he could win in a fight with such a creature.

The beast swung his arm. Rae swung both blades slicing it open. The creature roared and stepped back. Rearing back on two feet, it lunged at Rae. Nakobee let his arrow fly. It hit the beast as it roared and landed on Rae, not moving.

Nakobee ran toward the beast and Rae. When he arrived the beast was dead. The arrow was deep in its neck. Nakobee grabbed the beast to pull it off Rae. He heard a sound behind him. Nakobee spun around pulling his sword. He stood there facing ten elves. They all stopped when they saw his sword.

One was dressed in leather with ornate carvings. The others were dressed in bright silver elfin armor.

The one in leather spoke, "We are here to help. The demon is gone as are the creatures it controlled. We saw the one fighting the beast and came to help. Do you think he has come down from his rage?" he said nodding at the beast on top of Rae.

"Rage? What do you mean?"

The one who spoke looked at Nakobee.

"He had the look of one in a rage. I cannot think of any other reason a sane human would stand face to face with a creature such as that. He is a friend of yours, isn't he?"

"Of course he is my friend. Why would you ask such a thing?"

"Because if he is your friend, I would think you would know how long the rages last."

Nakobee looked at the beast then back at the elf. He was about to speak when Jym came running up.

Nakobee called out, "Jym do you know if Rae enters a rage when he fights?"

Jym looked at him, then the elves. They all looked at him. He could not understand why they were just standing around instead of helping Rae.

"Well do you?" Nakobee stood there staring.

"What, no? At least I don't think Rae goes into a rage. I have never seen him do that."

Nakobee looked at the beast when it began to move. He reached over and grabbed the leg that was moving and raised it. He stood there staring down at Rae, who was looking up, covered in blood, with a confused expression on his face.

"I have no idea how I got under this thing, but are you going to get it off me, or just keep standing there looking at me?"

The elves and Jym hurried over. They raised the leg and body up, as Jym grabbed hold of Rae's arm and pulled him out. Rae stood and looked at them. Then turned and looked down at the beast.

"Where did that thing come from and how did I get under it?"

He saw the arrow, reached for it, and pulled it out. Holding the arrow, he looked at it and turning he stared at Nakobee.

"This is one of your arrows. You killed it?"

"It came at you. You cut its arm, then stood there screaming at it. I did not think you would be able to survive fighting it without help. It fell on you and you drove both your blades into its chest just as my arrow hit it in the neck."

Rae looked down at the beast.

"If I had seen it, I would not have stood there and screamed at it. I would have run. Thank you for saving my life."

Rae handed the arrow to Nakobee. He reached down and pulled his swords out of the beast and wiped them on its fur.

As he walked away he murmured, "I'm covered in blood. I need a bath."

Nakobee turned to the elf.

"I do not think your friend knows he goes into a rage," the elf said.

"I don't think he does either."

They started walking. After a few steps Nakobee looked at the elf.

"Why are you here? And who are you?"

"I'm sorry. In all the confusion I forgot to introduce myself. I'm Galan Gretumal, leader of King Ailluin Leoren's rangers. He has sent us to help Queen Kaila in her war against the demons. We are on our way there now. Do you know where Queen Kaila's land is?"

Nakobee stopped walking and looked at him.

"You are going there to help her and you do not know where she lives?"

"I only know about where it is. Everyone we asked does not know anyone named Queen Kaila or where she lives."

Nakobee just kept staring at him. He raised his arm and wrapped it around the elf's shoulder.

"You are in luck. We are on our way there now. Come with us and I will personally introduce you to her."

Nakobee pulled the elf closer, patted his shoulder, and then let him go.

Gretumal stepped back and nodded his head.

"I will get my men and our things and follow you."

He turned and walked back to his men.

"Gather our men and animals. It seems we have found the way to Queen Kaila's home."

Nakobee and the others left and Galan stood there looking at Nakobee as he walked away.

When Nakobee reached the others he looked around. Everyone was there except Janae. He listened as they stood there talking about how close they came to them all dying.

Jym laughed and told them how they found Rae under one of the beasts he was fighting, and with Nakobee's help, had killed it.

Nakobee spoke, "We lost Janae. I saw him get torn apart. There was nothing I could do. I was too far away."

He looked dejected. They all looked at him.

Karl asked, "Where did he fall? We might be able to gather something and do a burial for him."

Nakobee led them to where he saw their friend fall. They found his sword and a few other items, and what was left of his body. They gathered wood and built a fire. They placed everything but the sword on it. They stood somberly watching as the flames burned.

When the elves arrived, they saw the fire, and understood its meaning. They stopped and waited.

When the fire was out, they headed up the mountain. They reached the others and introduced Gretumal to Leader Nectar.

A couple hours later Nakobee and his group reached the door to the cave. They were too tired to continue to the halfway point inside the mountain, so Nakobee told them they would stop and sleep there.

There was plenty of space for them to make camp. As they sat around the fire, Major Goisch Yorald came walking over.

"First Sword Nakobee, we heard you had a run in with a demon and its horde. I also was told you had to be rescued by these Elves."

Nakobee could tell by his tone what he was trying to do, so he stood and looked over at the Elves.

"If not for Galan Gretumal and his mighty warriors, all of us would be dead. They fought bravely, in the open, and killed everything the demons threw at them."

Nakobee looked at the dwarf, then over at the elves. Then he introduced Gretumal.

"Major Yorald, this is Galan Gretumal, leader of King Ailluin Leoren's famous archer warriors."

Nakobee looking at Major Yorald, asked, "How did you hear about our little fight?"

Major Yorald stood there looking at Gretumal, who just sat there.

Gretumal had heard Nakobee's words. He saw the expression on the dwarf's face, and he was not going to correct Nakobee.

Major Yorald looked at Nakobee.

"It was a great day for you and your men. My scouts saw the fight. They came and told me."

"Then it is a shame the fighting ended before you and your fine men arrived to help. You were sending them to help us weren't you?" Nakobee asked.

Major Yorald said, "Of course I was. We were on our way when another scout told us you had won and were no longer in danger."

"Then we all can be thankful for Gretumal and his men."

Nakobee raised his mug and took a drink. The others around the fire did the same. Major Yorald nodded his head toward Gretumal, then he looked at Nakobee.

"You will be taking everyone with you in the morning?"

"Yes, at first light we will be leaving. It is a long walk, and I'm looking forward to reaching Keele. How is the work coming along in the mountain?"

"I'm glad you asked. If you would be so kind, we have some bags that you can take and give to Queen Kaila."

"I'm sure she will be happy to receive them."

Major Yorald nodded his head and said, "I will have them ready for you at the rest stop. Now if you will excuse me, I have work I must get back to."

He turned and walked away. Nakobee shook his head and poured another drink. They were all going to enjoy themselves for the evening. It had been a hard trip and they needed to relax.

Gretumal sat there looking at Nakobee. He was unsure of this young man. He had not told him he was the brother of Queen Kaila. This Nakobee had stood up for him and his men to the dwarf. This might turn out to be an honorable mission.

He closed his eyes and replayed in his mind, the words King Leoren spoke to him:

"You will go to this Queen Kaila and help fight her war. I have explained to your men that they are no longer under any obligation to you. You are to ask for, and take only those who volunteer to go with you. Those that do not go with you will be spread out to the other divisions.

If you and your men return, you will not be allowed to stay a ranger. You will be given a hero's welcome and a place to live at the far edge of our land where you may live out your life.

If you and your men do not return, we will call out their names in the great hall.

Either way, I will be rid of you. You have two days to gather everything that is yours and the supplies you will need. It is a long way to this Queen Kaila's land. Now go."

He broke from his day dream when he heard his name.

"Gretumal? Are you with us?"

He looked at Nakobee. Everyone was staring at him, even his own men.

"Sorry, I was thinking. What did you say?"

"I was wondering what your title or rank was?" asked Nakobee.

He glanced at his men. They just stared at him waiting for his answer.

"I have no official rank or title. You can just call me Galan or Gretumal. I will answer to either."

Nakobee looked at him, then at those near him. He saw their expressions change. There was something wrong. He would not press now, but he would find out later.

"Well, I will call you General Gretumal. I saw how bravely you and your men fought. To me that is a sign of a great leader."

Nakobee stood and raised his mug, then said, "Cheers to General Gretumal and his brave men. Their timely arrival and their great skills saved all our lives."

Everyone around him including the elves stood, raised their drinks, cheered, and drank.

Rae looked at Jym and said, "I think Nakobee has had too much to drink."

Jym leaned over and whispered, "He is not drinking any of that fermented brew the dwarfs brought over. He is drinking what we are, the fruit drink."

Rae glanced over at Nakobee. Shaking his head, he took another drink. He thought to himself, *This is going to be a long night.*

Chapter Thirty- Four

In the morning they were up and moving through the large doors into the cave. Nakobee was in the lead with the Armels right behind. As usual, the last through were the Leels. They followed the children as they carried their staves with bells. Every few minutes you could hear the bells tinkle. They did this to keep them close.

When they reached the half way point, there was a group of dwarfs waiting for them. Nakobee walked over.

"Greetings, I'm Nakobee. Are those the bags we are to take to Queen Kaila?"

One stepped forward and spoke, "There are twenty bags. Each bag weighs twenty stones. Do you have a way of carrying them?"

Nakobee looked at the bags, reached down and grabbed one and picked it up. He sat it back on the ground. He had no idea gold weighed so much.

"I will be right back."

Walking away he went looking for Leader Nectar. He found her with Onex and Hasina. They were unloading the Armels.

"Leader Nectar, can I ask how much weight these Armels can carry?"

She looked at him, then at the animal next to her.

"They can carry you and a full load with no problem. Do you need to ride?"

"No, I do not need one for that. I need to load twenty bags and each one weighs twenty stones."

"I think they can handle that. Where are these bags?"

"Come with me and I will take you to them."

Nakobee turned and they followed him back to where the two dwarfs were. When they arrived, they found the dwarfs sitting on the bags.

"These are the bags."

Leader Nectar walked over and was about to touch one when the dwarf drew his sword and stood up.

"Do not touch. These belong to Queen Kaila and only First Sword Nakobee may touch them."

Nakobee stepped over and looked at the dwarf.

"She just wants to know how heavy twenty stones feels."

The dwarf looked up at him with a confused expression.

"They do not feel anything, they weigh twenty stones."

"I mean, she wants to know what twenty stones weighs. We do not use stones as a measurement."

The dwarf put the sword away and stepped back. Closing his eyes for a few seconds, he opened them and looked at her.

"Sorry, I forgot. A stone is about six point three eight kilograms. That would make twenty stones equal to about one hundred and twenty seven kilograms"

Leader Nectar looked at Nakobee and said, "A full grown Armel can carry two thousand kilograms. You have twenty bags at twenty seven kilograms each, that is two thousand, five hundred and forty kilograms. It would be better to divide the weight in half and use two Armels. They each would carry one thousand two hundred and seventy kilograms."

Nakobee looked at her.

"Thank you. I'm impressed with how you figured this all out. Now for my next question, do you have two that I can use to carry these bags?"

"Of course. We can rearrange the supplies and bring them to you. You do need it now, correct?"

Nakobee looked at the two dwarfs then at her. He was amazed at how they had figured out the weight and Leader Nectar did the math. He knew they would not want to stay and guard the gold. He needed to take them.

"Yes."

Leader Nectar, Onex, and Hasina left him standing there. The dwarf that had spoken to him walked over and handed him a paper.

"You need to make your mark on this so we can let Major Yorald know you have the gold."

Nakobee took the paper. He could not read all the words, but he could see where it stated there were twenty bags, weighing twenty stones each. He took the stick and wrote his name, and handed it back.

The dwarf glanced at the paper, looked up at Nakobee, then back at the paper.

"This is a strange mark. It looks like you wrote your name? I did not know humans could write?"

Nakobee grinned at him and said, "I do not understand all the words, but I will soon. One day all my people will know how to read and write. We will even learn your words."

The dwarf took the paper and waved his hand, dismissing his men, then walked away.

A little while later, Hasina returned with two Armels. She stopped them next to him.

"I will show you how to handle them and load the bags, so they will not fight you."

"I'm glad. I do not want them to fight me. They might win."

Hasina laughed and they began to load the bags. When they were finished, they stood there looking at the animals.

"You have to take the weight off the same way as you put it on. Do not let one side get too heavy. If you need help in the morning, call me and I will come help you."

"Thank you. If I have any trouble I will ask for your help."

They led the animals to where Nakobee was going to sleep. She helped him remove the sacks. Then she showed him how to feed and water them. When that was finished, she left.

Nakobee sat and ate dried meat. He told the others there was no need for guards, since they were inside the mountain.

Everyone was relaxed and in high spirits. Leader Nectar and her people were looking forward to reaching their new home. She asked Nuka about the land.

Nuka looked at Karl, who nodded his head.

"We are not from Queen Kaila's land. We come from another land. We were sent to Queen Kaila to be sold. Nakobee was not pleased with the way our former Queen had treated us, so he never sent the coins.

However, the land Zolotov is beautiful. There are many different kinds of trees, green rolling hills, a lake so large you cannot see the other side, and it is full of fish. Queen Kaila is building a great wall around the City Keele. There are large buildings where the people live. They have crops planted inside and outside the walls. You will not believe your eyes when you reach the other side of this mountain."

"It sounds wonderful. I'm looking forward to seeing it."

"You will be happy there. Queen Kaila is a great leader. For one so young, she is very wise. I have seen her walking among the people. I have even seen her working alongside them in the fields."

Karl stood, looked at Nuka, and then Leader Nectar.

"We have enjoyed our time with you. If you have no more questions, I think we should get some rest. We still have a long walk before we reach the outside."

Nuka and the others stood and followed Karl.

Chapter Thirty-Five

In the morning, Nakobee loaded the Armels, and stood waiting for the others. When they were ready, he led the way. From the mid-point to the next gate it was all downhill. The grade was not steep, just a slow decline.

They reached the gate, the guards opened it, and stood aside. As they were heading down the mountain, Nakobee saw the trail had been widened, making it easier to travel.

When they reached the bottom, Nakobee led them out into the field of grass. They stopped near the small stream to make camp. The children led the Leels off toward a field of tall grass. Leader Nectar and Onex stood looking out at the landscape.

Onex said, "This is a fruitful land. Our home was never this green. We will have a large orchard and our village will prosper."

She replied, "Yes, this land looks very promising. I hope this war with the demons does not go badly. I'm getting too old for all this walking."

Onex wrapped his arm around her and kissed her forehead.

"Woman, you are not getting old. You are just getting wiser. You know all this walking is not good for us. We should be sitting relaxing with our feet in the running stream over there."

She smiled at him as they walked over and placed their feet in the cool stream.

The sun was beginning to set.

Gretumal led his men off to the side where they set up camp. They unpacked their animals and brushed them down. Then they made a small fire.

Nakobee came walking up to him as he stood near the fire.

"May I have a word with you?"

Gretumal answered, "Of course."

"Walk with me as we talk?"

"Is there something wrong? Have I or my men done something?" asked Gretumal

"You and your men have done nothing wrong. I have not seen men with more honor since I left Rednog. I just wanted to ask you some questions."

Gretumal looked at Nakobee, and asked, "I have not heard of this place called Rednog? Where is it?"

Nakobee looked up and pointed to the sky.

"Somewhere out there."

Gretumal looked up, then over at Nakobee. He was unsure if he was making a joke.

"Up there. You are saying this Rednog is in the sky? I have never heard of a city in the sky."

"Rednog is not a city here on this world, it is another world. My sister and I, along with thirty others from my village lived and trained there for five years. I will explain more after we reach Keele.

I would like to know why you are dressed the way you are. I can tell by the way your men treat you, you are their leader. Yet you do not claim a title or rank. From the way you acted when I asked, I would think you were sent here as punishment."

Gretumal stopped walking. He looked up at the stars. After letting out his breath, he spoke, "I was sent here as punishment. My King is hoping I will be killed in this war. He stripped me of my land, title, and rank.

I was going to be banished, but when he heard that Queen Kaila was asking for help, he said this was a way to get rid of me, and for me to redeem myself.

The men who are with me are all volunteers. All the men under my company wanted to come with me, but King Leoren would not let them. He said only one hundred could go. The rest were spread out among other battalions. They were not happy to be divided up.

They said they would leave and come with me. I told them to stay and protect our land. I left with one hundred men and fifty pack animals. We lost forty men and ten pack animals before finding you."

Nakobee stood there looking at him. He could see Gretumal was ashamed. He would not ask any more questions.

"I do not care to know what caused you to be banished. It does not matter to me. I'm glad you are here. If you and your men had not arrived when you did, we would be dead. When did King Leoren hear about our need for help?"

"We left six months ago. A messenger came with the news three days before we left."

"That is interesting. We were given word that King Bryyra of the forest elves was sending fifty men. We were not told that King Leoren was sending anyone. It does not matter. I'm glad you and your men are here. The Creator put you at the right place and time to save us. As for you, I will still call you General Gretumal. I think your men will do the same."

Gretumal replied, "Please call me Galan."

"I will do so, unless there are others around."

They walked back to camp, Nakobee said good night and left.

Chapter Thirty-Six

In the morning they were moving out. Nakobee heard the children singing, and he smiled as he walked. The children he had rescued had mingled in with Leader Nectar's group. They each found a job they could do and helped wherever they were needed.

Karl came walking up to him.

"Should we send out scouts? Just to make sure the way is safe?"

"Does the children's singing bother you that much?"

Karl looked at Nakobee then over at the children.

"They do not bother me. I'm just worried the singing may alert the enemy."

Nakobee looked at the children.

"You are right. Take whoever you want and scout ahead. We should make it to the stream near the rock outcrop by sundown. Wait for us there."

Karl left and found Nuka and Flan. All three ran out front and disappeared.

The landscape slowly went from rolling grass covered hills, to low and flat grasslands. Off to the right they could still see the mountain. It was becoming rockier with fewer trees.

As the sun began to set, Nakobee saw Nuka standing on a large rock. He waved and Nuka waved back, then jumped down and ran to him.

When he came up to Nakobee, he spoke, "We saw some prints of a large group that crossed the stream a few days ago. They are heading south toward the lake. Are there any villages that way?"

Nakobee looked off in that direction. He knew of no villages that still had people in them.

"There are no villages with anyone living in them."

"Karl is tracking them. He said he will return when he finds out anything."

"We will stop here for the night. You should get some rest."

Nakobee took his Armels and walked over to a large boulder and unpacked them.

Three hours later, Karl and Nuka called out to him, "Nakobee are you still awake?"

"Yes."

They came over and sat next to him. Karl leaned back and let out a deep breath.

"I followed the trail and caught up to those that had come through here. It is a large group of about two hundred. They have six beasts and three demons. I don't know where they are heading other than toward the lake."

"Do you think they are planning another attack on Keele?"

Nakobee answered, "Not with so few, unless there are more coming from another direction. I'm just trying to figure out how they got across the mountain. I know of only the two paths through. The only other way is from the south. If they came that way, why are they here? Why would they follow the mountain?"

"I saw tracks when we first reached the road. I did not think anything of them since this is a large road. I thought more people were using it to reach Keele."

Nakobee nodded his head, then said, "The mountain range is high and too steep to cross over. As far as I know, I have never heard of anyone crossing it, not for another twenty days march south. Then the mountains become lower and there are a few trails that lead across."

"Well, they left the road and that was why I looked at the tracks. I saw the beasts' prints and knew something was wrong. Should we move faster or just keep a better watch?"

"I will talk with Galan and let him know what you have found. Tomorrow, you and Nuka can run out front to scout for us, again. For now, get some food and rest."

They stood and walked away. They did not go far before stopping and sat by the fire, where Rae, Jym, Flan, and Naate were sitting.

Chapter Thirty-Seven

After Karl and Nuka left, Nakobee found Galan. He explained what Karl had discovered and wanted to know Galan's thoughts.

"It would seem they are planning another attack. Like you, I find that strange, since the last time they had more men and were defeated. If you are planning to attack their main force, you will not be able to leave a large contingent behind. They may be planning to attack the city when you leave. You do not have the manpower to protect the city and send an army out," said Galan.

"That is what I was thinking. I was also thinking they found another way to come across the mountains, since we have taken the tunnels back. I will have to ask Sword Master Zale to see if he can somehow find it," Nakobee replied.

"It will take months to search the mountain range. Why not plan how you will attack the main force and how many men you can leave behind?"

"Sword Master Zale has ways of searching that will not take that long. He has seen many battles. I'm sure he will figure out the best way to keep Keele safe. I will let you get some rest. I just wanted to let you know about the new threat."

Nakobee left. Back at his campsite he stretched out on the ground and tried to sleep.

As the sun rose, Nakobee packed the Armels, again, and was looking around. Everyone was up and moving like the days before. They knew what had to be done and they did it without thinking. He was listening for the children who were normally up and singing as they got the animals ready. Then he saw them several hundred feet down the trail.

He went searching to find out who had let them leave. Hasina came up to him as he was asking people.

"They asked me if they could leave. The Leels were getting restless. Karl and Nuka came over and said they would go with them. Since they are your men I thought it was ok. Should I have made them wait?"

"That is alright. I was worried they had gone alone. As long as there are men with them they should be ok. We will be traveling faster today. It normally takes five days to reach Keele from the cave. With all that we have, I'm worried it will take longer. We have made good time, though, so it might only take four days."

"Do not worry. I will get the others moving."

Hasina turned and walked away. Nakobee went back and grabbed the ropes on the Armels and began walking. As he took his first step, Rae, Jym, and the others came walking up. They did not say anything, they just walked along with him.

The next couple of days went smoothly. On day four around noon, they saw the walls of Keele. An hour later, when Nakobee was a hundred feet from the gate, a man came riding out to meet him. It was Lea.

He jumped off the steed and said, "Nakobee, come quickly, there was an attack on Kaila. She is alright. We caught the man before he could do anything. Sword Master Zale and Shaméd are with him now."

Karl took the ropes for the Armels, and said, "Go, we will take it from here."

Nakobee ordered Lea, "Find a place for these people and their animals inside the walls. The little fluffy ones will need plenty of grass. Karl can help you."

Nakobee climbed onto the back of the steed and rode off, leaving Lea there with Karl. He ran the steed as fast as it could go, weaving between people. When he reached Kaila's home, he jumped off and ran straight in.

He saw her sitting at the table and called out, "Are you all right? Did you get hurt? Who was the one who attacked you?"

She smiled and called him over.

"Nakobee, come sit. It is good to see you. How was your trip? Oh wait, Sword Master Zale has kept me up to date on your adventure. So I suppose you do not have to tell me too much. Except maybe, what you think of this woman named Hasina."

Nakobee stood there looking at her. He was unsure of her behavior. He had ridden here at top speed, almost knocking people down just to get here, to find that she just sat there as if nothing had happened.

"What do you mean what do I think of Hasina? I'm worried about what happened to you. We can talk about the people who came back with me later."

She patted his hand and said, "I'm fine. One of the men who was in training with the cleaning crew tried to attack me. As you can see, he was unsuccessful."

"Who stopped him?"

She glared at him and then slowly stood.

"What do you mean by that? Are you implying I need someone to save me? Am I not able to defend myself? Did I not train with you and the others on Rednog?"

Nakobee was taken back by her tone and the manner in which she spoke to him.

"I did not mean you were not capable of taking care of yourself. I just thought one of the guards was here and they had stopped the attacker."

"My guards took what was left of him away, after I pinned him to the ground. Do you wish to see how I took him down?"

She was now standing right in front of him staring up at him. He stepped back at her words.

He smiled at her, and in a low voice said, "You would be unable to take me down."

She grabbed his hand and stepped back. He spun her around as he picked her up in the air, wrapped both arms around her giving her a hug. They both burst out laughing. He put her down and she stepped back, still holding his hand.

Nakobee said, "I'm glad you are ok. Did you send Lea out to tell me about the attack?"

She smiled and said, "Yes, I wanted to talk with you before the others arrived."

Shaking his head Nakobee asked, "Have you heard from Lord Shaméd or Sword Master Zale?"

"They have not sent any word. They will when they learn something. Now tell me about this woman Hasina. She sounds interesting."

"What has Sword Master Zale told you?"

"He only showed me some of what that amulet around your neck showed him. He thinks she might make a good mate for you. Is he right?"

Nakobee let go of her hand.

"Why is everyone trying to find me a mate? I will find one when I'm ready. And that won't be until you have found yours."

She lowered her head and in a low voice said, "If I have found a mate, would that make it easier for you to think about this Hasina?"

Nakobee looked at her as she walked back to her chair and sat.

"Are you saying you have found someone who makes you happy? Who is this person? I want to meet him."

"You know him. You have known him since he was born. I will tell you his name, but only if you promise not to hurt or intimidate him, or chase him away."

"I would never do that."

She laughed, "Did you not think that I have not been watching you? It took me years to figure it out, but you have chased away every boy that ever looked at me since I was five years old."

"That is because you would one day be queen and would need a great warrior by your side. I have been looking for one that would be best for you."

"And have you found one?" she asked.

"There are many warriors among those here. The very best ones are too old. I'm still looking."

"I will be old before you find anyone you think would be a good match for me. That is why I have been searching as well. And I think I have found just the one."

"Does he share the same feelings for you as you do for him?"

She stood and walked away moving her head back and forth.

"I don't know, I have not asked him."

He looked at her as she walked around the room. He went over, pulled out a chair and sat. He was about to speak when Sword Master Zale entered.

He saw Nakobee and smiled as he started talking, "I'm glad you are here. We found out why the man attacked you. He was possessed. It seems he has been possessed for a few weeks. I sent for a Thorn so he can scan everyone here to see if there are any others."

He stopped talking when he saw the look on Nakobee's face, and the way Kaila was standing on the other side of the room.

"Have I interrupted something?"

"She has found someone she would like as a mate. She will not tell me who it is and for that matter she has not even told him."

Sword Master Zale walked over and sat across from him. He looked at Kaila and pointed at the chair. She returned and sat.

"I do not know all your rituals on picking a mate. I'm sure, however, both parties should have feelings for each other. Do you think this man has feelings for you?"

"I believe he does. I just think he will not show me since he is afraid of what Nakobee would do to him."

Sword Master Zale looked at Nakobee, who sat there staring at Kaila.

"Nakobee, is there a reason this man, or any man would be afraid to show their feelings for Kaila?"

"If he is a real warrior, he should not be afraid of me."

"Kaila, has this man seen Nakobee fight?"

"Of course he has. And he knows he could never beat Nakobee if he challenged him."

"Why would he have to challenge Nakobee?"

She looked at him as she answered, "When a man chooses a woman for a mate, he has to pay for her or stand up to her father or a male of her family. There is not a man here that knows Nakobee, who would stand up to him."

"You are a queen. Are you saying if a leader from another tribe came here and wanted you, they would have to offer payment or challenge Nakobee?"

"That is our law. Since as you say, I'm a queen, the payment would be very high."

Sword Master Zale reached down and took the flask off his belt. It was not the water one. He took a long drink and set it on the table. Looking at each of them, he picked the flask up again. Taking another long drink he put it away.

"Here is how you should handle it. Kaila, you need to find out if this man feels about you the same way as you do about him. Nakobee, when he challenges you, you can fight him, just don't kill him, or maybe you can let him win?"

They both looked at him and said at the same time, "Kill him?" They both laughed.

"You are thinking when the man makes his challenge we are to fight to the death? We are not barbaric. He has to swear he would die before letting anything happen to her. And if he did not fulfill that promise, then I would be obligated to kill him and everyone in his family."

"Killing him and every member of his family is not barbaric?" Sword Master asked.

"Of course not. When someone makes a promise they must fulfill it or have a good reason why they could not."

Sword Master Zale reached for his flask as the door opened. Shaméd and Leo walked in at that moment, and

Sword Master saw the expression on Kaila's face when they entered. He put the flask away without taking a drink.

Leo walked over and stood next to Kaila. Shaméd stood at the front of the table.

Nodding at Sword Master Zale, he spoke, "Jrick is here. We have placed him in one of the smaller buildings and have started sending people to him. He believes it will take him two days to scan everyone."

"What about the people I just brought in?"

"He was informed about them and they are included in the timeline."

Sword Master Zale looked over at Nakobee.

"I think we can wait on our little talk for now. We have other things needing our attention at the moment. We will leave and get things settled, you had a rough trip, I would suggest you take a long bath and relax."

He stood and Shaméd followed him out.

Shaméd asked, "Nakobee seemed to be a little upset in there. Is everything alright with him?"

"He is fine, he is just having trouble getting his mind around the fact that Kaila is a grown woman."

"She has told him about the one she loves?"

Sword Master Zale looked at him.

"Do you know who it is?"

"It was not that hard to figure out. Every time Leo walks into the room her heart speeds up and she forgets what is going on."

"I thought that was who it was. Does he have the same feelings for her?"

"He has always had feelings for her. At least that is what I get from his mind. He has never said anything because of what Nakobee did to a young man years ago."

"What did he do and who was the young man? Never mind, I will ask him later."

"You are going to talk with Nakobee?"

"I'm not. I'm going to talk with Leo."

They walked on, talking about the new group and how many warriors Nakobee and Kaila now had.

Chapter Thirty-Eight

The next few days went by quickly. They found two others who were possessed. The demons were dispatched, and the bodies were cared for properly.

Leader Nectar was waiting since her arriving to meet with Queen Kaila. She was getting restless when Nakobee came to her.

"Leader Nectar, I'm sorry to have kept you waiting for so long. Things had been a little mixed up since our return. Queen Kaila would like you, Onex, and Hasina to come tonight for the last meal. Do you accept?"

"Of course we do. I have never met a queen before. Are we required to bring a gift?"

"My sister does not require gifts from people she calls friends. Just come and be hungry. She says she is planning a large feast in your honor."

"We look forward to meeting her."

Nakobee looked around at the place where they had made camp. He pointed to the long two story building a couple hundred feet away.

"I heard you did not want to stay in the building that was offered. May I ask why?'

"It is a very nice place, but too large for me and Onex. There were too many rooms."

Nakobee smiled.

"The building is for all your people. Once things get more settled we will build outside the walls or show you the countryside and you can pick a location for your own village. We will teach you and your people how to make the earth homes. They are strong and will last many years."

"I'm sorry. I misunderstood the man when he said the building was for me. I did not know he meant for all of us. I feel silly."

"There is no reason to feel that way. The place is still yours. Feel free to pick your rooms and have the others do likewise. There is a kitchen in every building."

He stopped talking when he said kitchen. The look on her face had changed.

"A kitchen is the place people prepare meals. Come let me give you a tour of the building. I can explain the rooms to you."

She called out to Onex, "Onex, get Hasina and come with Nakobee and me."

Onex found Hasina and caught up with them as they reached the door to the building.

"We discovered these types of buildings when we were away learning. They are very good to keep those inside warm, when it is cold out, and cool when it is hot. As time goes by, you will understand how it works. I found it hard to believe when it was explained to me. There are two floors. The second floor has twenty rooms. They are each twenty by twenty feet. There are four bunk beds in each room. You can have one or more people in each room. If a married couple moves into a room, the bunks can be arranged to make one larger bed."

Nakobee stood in front of the building and opened the door. They entered and stood in a hallway that was ten feet wide. There were four doors on each side and a large door at the other end. Nakobee walked over to a door.

"These rooms are like the ones upstairs, they are for sleeping."

He opened the door and they stepped in. They saw what looked like tables stacked on top of each other.

"As you can see there are four bunk beds so each room can hold four people. There are cubby holes for storing their things and hooks to hold their weapons.

Now come and I will show you where you will eat your meals."

He stepped out into the hallway. Walking over he opened the door at the end of the hallway. They entered a large room, where they saw two long tables.

Off to their right were wide stairs that led up to the next floor.

"This room is where you and your people will gather to eat. It can hold two hundred people at a time. Those stairs lead up to more rooms like the one I showed you. Now let me show you the kitchen."

They moved forward walking by the long wooden tables. There were long benches next to them and in a few places there were chairs. When they reached the end, they came to a short table that had six chairs on one side.

"This table is where the leader of the house may sit. Of course, you can sit anywhere you please. Follow me now to the kitchen."

He walked behind the small table where two doors ten feet apart were. Each door had a small opening cut into it. He pointed to one.

"This door with the circle and line through it is the door people come out of and into this room. This one here with the arrow, is where you go in. The signs keep people from crashing into each other. On the other side they have the other marking."

He pushed the door with the arrow and it swung open. He entered and they followed. Once inside, Leader

Nectar gasped. She, Onex, and Hasina stood there looking at the room.

There was a rock fireplace with a metal pole inside and a large metal pot for cooking. There were four long tables in the middle of the room and the walls were covered in cubby holes.

Leader Nectar slowly walked around looking at the room. She stopped at a table.

"This place is so strange. What are all these things?"

"When you move in, there will be people who will come and show you how all of this works. It will not take you long to figure it out."

He walked over and stopped in front of a deep rock tub. He reached up and twisted a handle. Water came out.

"This water comes from the large tank outside the building. Each building has its own tank. Near the tanks, are windmills pumping the water up from the river below. There is another room upstairs that has more tubs each with a pipe you turn to let water out.

I know this is a lot for you to understand. You will get accustom to these new ways. Let me show you where you will sleep."

He took them to the back of the room up a set of stairs. These were narrower.

"These stairs, like the ones out front, take you up to the next floor."

He walked up and they were close behind. When they reached the top, he stood to the side.

They stood there looking down a long hallway. There were doors all along both sides. It was like the hallway they saw when they entered, only longer.

"The hallway is wide enough so two men can walk side by side. Each door opens to rooms like the ones I showed you."

Nakobee took a couple of steps and opened a door.

"The rooms below by the main doors are where you should put your guards. This room with the plaque in the door, is where the leader sleeps. It is a little bigger because it has a table where you can do your work. Later you can put your name or anything you like on the plaque."

He stepped in and they followed. Inside the room, they saw a table with a chair near a window. There were cubby holes stacked from floor to ceiling against one wall. A large table that was a foot off the floor was at the far end of the room.

"Why is there a small table over there?" asked Hasina.

"That is the bed. The other rooms had what are called bunkbeds, but this room only has the one. It still needs the mattress. As soon as one is made it will be brought here. I don't think any of the rooms have them yet. Those take a little longer to make. You can use your own bedding for the time being."

"All of this is, it is just so strange. I'm not sure we will get used to it."

"Trust me, when we first saw these things we were scared and unsure. It did not take us long to understand it was nicer. I have one more room to show you. It will not make sense at first but trust me as time goes by you will come to like it."

He left the room and led them down the hallway. When they were halfway he touched a door. On it was a picture of a figure holding a spear. Then he stepped across and touched another door. It had a picture of a figure with a shield.

"This door is for the women. The door with the spear is for men. Both rooms are similar. The one for women is, well after you learn about it, you will understand. For now let me show you the room for the men."

He stepped back and pushed the door. He held it open and they went in. Once inside they saw a room with a long trough and shiny metal on the wall over it. There were five handles coming out of the wall that hung over the troughs. Nakobee reached over and turned a handle. Water came out.

"These are for washing your hands."

He turned the handle back and the water stopped. Then he walked over and stood near another long trough, only this one was on an angle and not as high.

"This is where the men..."

He stopped and looked at Onex, and then the two women. He remembered how he was shown these rooms. Allen and Ted had taken the boys in and Clara had taken the girls in the other.

"I think you can learn about these things later. I will bring others back to explain. Now we can go and you can decide if you want to move your people in."

Nakobee headed for the door, and they followed. When they were outside, Nakobee stood by the building.

"You can also plant food on either side of the building as long as you do not go on to the gravel road."

"What about our trees? Where can we plant them? We were hoping when they are planted it would be where we would be living forever."

Leader Nectar stood there looking at Nakobee.

"If you want, we can take you and a few others out along the lake. We can find a location that you like. Then you can plant your trees and later we can build you your own homes."

"That will be fine. We will go and get ready to meet Queen Kaila. Until then, good day. It was nice of you to show us the building."

Leader Nectar and Onex walked away. Hasina stood there watching them. She looked at Nakobee.

"The building overwhelmed them. I'm sure the children will love all the new things. The old ones will adjust slower."

She looked again at her grandparents as they walked away.

Nakobee smiled at her and spoke, "You and the others have had a great deal to overcome. Take your time to learn what we have to offer. For now live as you want."

She smiled at him and walked away. Nakobee turned and headed for his room to get ready for the dinner.

Chapter Thirty-Nine

There were thirty people in the room when Queen Kaila entered. Kaila was wearing a soft purple and white wrap. There was a wide leather belt around her waist. Her hair was braided and wrapped on top of her head. Everyone turned as she walked in and headed over to the table at the far end of the room. It was on a small platform, so everyone could see her no matter where they sat. She had not wanted it that way. She was told now that she was the Queen, she had to act as one, even if the other Queens had not officially given their blessing. Of course, they were too busy fighting a war for blessings.

However, she did not need their blessing. She had more than enough people to make the claim. Her grandmother, Queen Kailee had sent most of her clan to her, over eight thousand people, mostly old and children fifteen and younger. The only ones still there were Queen Kailee, First Sword Kouly, and five thousand warriors.

Kaila sat and everyone took their seats. The people there were the leaders from each village or household that had come to her city.

She called it a city and not a village, because it was three times larger than any human village currently existing. As far as their history went, there had never been a city this large or with walls as big as the ones encircling this one.

It was time for the guests to come up and introduce themselves to her. One at a time they came, each giving their name and pledging their loyalty. Even the ones from her grandmother's land, who knew when the war was over, they could return to their homes, pledged their loyalty.

When Leader Nectar and Onex along with Hasina stepped forward, Nakobee introduced them. They all wore the typical garb of their tribe. They had a blue sash over their right shoulders to signify their tribal colors.

"I now introduce to you Leader Nectar, First Sword Onex, and their granddaughter, Hasina."

Kaila leaned forward, glancing at Hasina, then over at Leader Nectar.

"I'm glad to meet you. I hope you are settling into your surroundings without too much trouble."

"We are pleased to meet you, Queen Kaila. The building and everything you have given us is beyond what Nakobee offered us. Thank you for your kindness. I want to say that for myself and my people, we pledge our lives to you, not only for what you have given us, but also for saving us."

Leader Nectar bowed after speaking. Queen Kaila turned her attention to Hasina.

"You are more beautiful than I have been told. We should talk later about certain things of interest."

"I'm at your disposal, Queen Kaila."

They stepped down and three elves stepped forward, one dressed in fine leather, the other two in bright silver armor.

Nakobee pointed to them as he spoke, "I now have the pleasure to introduce the men who saved my life. General Galan Gretumal, Captain Xharlion Liadi and Lieutenant Amrynn Beiwynn, of the mountain clan. King Ailluin Leoren sent them to help us and they did, by saving many lives."

Galan visibly flinched when he heard Nakobee call him General. He stood tall and bowed, as did his men when their names were mentioned.

"Gentlemen, I'm so pleased to meet you. I'm also very glad you saved my brother's life. I offer you all a reward. Name it and if it is within my power to give, it shall be given."

Galan spoke, "Queen Kaila, we cannot accept a reward. We saw people in trouble and helped. We are here to serve in your war against our common enemy."

"You may not want a reward now, but maybe later something will come to your mind. If it does, just ask me. As I said, if it is in my power it will be given."

There were five more groups that came forward. When the last one walked away Queen Kaila stood, raised her arms, and spoke, "Let the food be brought out and the feast begin. Everyone enjoy yourselves."

Food was brought and placed on the tables. People began to eat and the talking grew loud. A group of musicians began to play. The music was mostly slow tribal songs.

As the night drew on, people started walking around meeting each other. Queen Kaila saw Hasina standing to the side.

"Leo, would you please go and bring Hasina to me?"

Leo left and a few minutes later returned with her. Hasina stood in front of Queen Kaila and bowed.

"Queen Kaila, you wanted a word with me?"

"Yes, I was wondering what you think of my brother?"

Hasina looked at her not sure what to say. Her face showed fear and uncertainty.

"My Queen, I have not said anything bad about Nakobee. If you have heard something, it is not true."

"Relax, Hasina. I have heard nothing but praise about my brother from your people. I was just wondering, one woman to another, what kind of woman would be attracted to him. Or what type of woman do you think he would be attracted to? Would you have any ideas?"

Hasina blinked her eyes. She blushed darkly.

"I suppose he would want a strong woman, one that would be able to stand by his side in battle or on a hunt. As for what type of woman would be attracted to him, I think every woman who meets him would want him. He is a good looking man and bigger than most. Any woman would be happy to be chosen as his mate."

"I'm glad to hear that. I was worried that a woman would want him because he is my brother. Do you think that might influence anyone?"

"Nakobee would see through them. He is too smart to be fooled by someone like that."

"My brother is smart when it comes to battles, but not so smart when it comes to females. I know, I have watched many girls growing up throw themselves at him.

He would just act as if they were not there. A woman who wanted him would have to be strong and forceful. She would have to show him she cared for him, maybe even take charge and ask him, sort of the way our people did many years ago. Does your clan practice that?"

Hasina contemplated what Kaila was saying. She looked at Leo who stood there with a small smile. Queen Kaila just stood there, her expression unclear. Hasina's mind was racing, and then it all clicked.

"I think I understand your meaning. Yes, there are many clans still practicing that. My grandmother asked my grandfather to be her mate. She told me once when the female asks the male, they are happier."

"I'm glad to hear that. Think on my words and let me know if you think of a good match for my brother. Now I must mingle with the others. It was a pleasure talking with you. I hope later we can talk again."

Hasina bowed as Kaila walked away, Leo by her side. As she turned, Leader Nectar came up to her.

"What was that about? Is there something wrong?"

Hasina smiled at her.

"Grandmother you are always worrying. There is nothing wrong. Queen Kaila was asking me what type of woman I thought her brother would like. Then she asked if I would help find one for him."

Hasina took hold of her grandmother's arm and they walked back to Onex, her mind going over the words she just heard. A little grin crept across her face.

Chapter Forty

A couple of days later, two men came running toward the city. When they reached the gate, they collapsed from exhaustion.

Soldiers came out to give them water. Then through gasping breaths, they gave their report. The Captain of the Guard turned, issuing orders. Within seconds two runners were sent after Nakobee and Queen Kaila.

Nakobee arrived with his sister. They dismounted and stepped over to the two men. They stood looking at them. They were dirty and neither had a weapon.

"What happened?" asked Nakobee.

"There are demons coming. They are coming along the lakeshore, and spread out across the land as far as we could see. Hundreds of those beast creatures were moving among large groups of humans, elves, dwarfs, and trolls."

"How long ago did you see them, and where?" Queen Kaila asked.

"Five days ago. There were ten of us out scouting, when we saw a large cloud of dust. We went to investigate. We saw them and we tried to get closer to see how many there were. We came across a small group of what once were humans. They might have been a scouting party. We fought and killed them, but not before losing five men. Three others were wounded. One died four days ago. The other two could no longer travel; they are hiding up north in the trees. We have been running for three days. We only stopped when we were too tired to go on."

Kaila looked at the men, then at the Captain of the Guard.

"Take them to the doctor. Let their families know they have returned. Nakobee, send out scouts. We need to know how much time we have. I will let Sword Master Zale know what is happening."

She turned to leave as the men were carried away. Nakobee touched her shoulder.

"It will be ok. We have Sword Master Zale and Lord Shaméd with us. You have seen both of them fight,

271

just as I have. Lord Shaméd is a great wizard. These demons do not stand a chance against him."

"I'm glad you have faith in them. All I see is our three thousand warriors against an unknown army. Yes, we have these walls and the bows. But is it going to be enough?"

She turned away, walked back to her animal, and climbing up, she rode away. Nakobee stood there watching her. He had more faith in Shaméd than Sword Master Zale. Sword Master was a great swordsman and leader, but Shaméd was a wizard. A wizard was worth thousands of warriors. He walked to his animal, climbed on and rode off to get scouts.

Kaila sent word to Sword Master Zale. After he arrived, they stood looking down at the table in her meeting room. On it was displayed a miniature of the city, the walls, and the nearby lands. It showed what they had done, and that the walls were completed. They still needed more buildings for all the people.

"I had thought something like this might happen ever since you sent word out asking for men. The first attack was to see how strong you were. They now know about the walls. They are prepared for them, but do not know how many men you have.

I will get with the elves and the dwarfs to figure out where to place them. Kinn and Shaméd have some ideas. They said they would let me know more details when they had them worked out."

Two hours later Sword Master Zale had given her his plans, and she was somewhat reassured.

Nakobee found Karl and his men. They were much older than him, almost twice his age. Even though they were in their prime, he felt obligated to keep them safe, but he knew if he did not pick them for this, they would have complained.

"Karl, you are not to engage them. Just try to see how many and how far away they are. I need all of you back here."

"We understand. We will pack for one day."

They left by way of the north gate so they could use the tree line as cover.

Nakobee began gathering the warriors to place them along the walls. Each group would be stationed as close to their own tribe as possible.

Galan caught up with Nakobee as he was leaving a group of people.

He called out, "Nakobee, may I have a word with you?"

He turned to Galan. The tall elf was dressed for battle. He was wearing his leather armor, his sword on his hip, and shield on his back. The only thing missing were his bow and arrows.

Nakobee greeted him as he approached.

"I was just coming to find you. I see you have heard about the army coming toward us. I suppose you want to know where you and your men will be placed."

"I was going to ask if we could be placed far from the other elves. Would that be alright?"

Nakobee stood there looking at him.

"Is there a problem between the forest elves and the mountain elves?"

Galan shifted his feet. His posture also changed. This was something Nakobee had never seen an elf do.

Galan answered, "They have made it clear they do not want to fight near me or my men."

"Why?"

"As I have told you, I was banished from my land. All the elf clans know about it and the reason for it. They do not want to die near me."

"They are insane. You and your men can stand with me. Come walk with me. I have one more stop, then we can go see Commander Braern Carphyra. I will place him and his elves in the center on the east wall."

They walked on in silence. Nakobee was thinking he might have to ask Galan what he had done after all.

By the end of the day everyone knew their location on the walls. All the animals that were outside were brought in. They began cutting the fields to bring in fodder for them. Two days after finding out about the army they were ready for a siege.

Three hours before sunset, the gates were being closed, and the draw bridges being brought up, when a call was heard.

"Off to the west. They are here."

It was repeated all along the wall.

Those who heard the call, climbed up on the walls to see. What they saw were thousands of bodies moving across the land. The way they moved, it was almost like waves on the lake. The horde swayed back and forth as they walked. The beasts ran around them keeping them moving forward. They ran out front of the horde stopping them three hundred feet from the gorge that surrounded the walls. The gorge was still empty of water. It would be a couple of days before it would be ready to fill.

The horde began collapsing to the ground as if they were turned off, and a demon moved forward.

It was a large blue creature, with what looked like flowing fire running in long lines around its body. On its head were four large horns. The tip on the top right front horn was broken off.

It walked up and stopped at the edge of the gorge. Tilting its head back, it let out a loud earth shaking roar. Then it shook its head, and spoke, "Humans, this wall will do you no good, you cannot hide. Surrender and we will be merciful. We need humans to do our bidding, not like these you see before you. I give you until sunrise tomorrow to give me your answer."

The demon started to turn, then stopped when it heard the reply.

Nakobee yelled out, "We do not need to wait for tomorrow. Our answer to you is leave our lands and you will live. Stay and you will die."

The demon looked up at him, then a sound came roaring out of its mouth. It could only have been a laugh. Its body shook as it made the sound.

"Stupid human, there is no way you can kill a demon. Only the Creator can do that. I give you the chance now. If you think you are so powerful, I stand before you. Strike me down if you dare."

Two arrows flew out hitting the demon in the chest. It screamed in pain as it staggered back. Its hand came to its chest as it tried to brush them away. Two more arrows hit it. There were more screams as it fell to the ground on its knees, then it burst into flames. There was a flash and demon and flames were gone.

Nakobee yelled out, "You see the power we possess. I give you one last warning. Leave and stop this war or we will hunt down every demon and kill all of you."

A roar was heard from the back. The beasts ran among the horde making them stand, and move forward. They slowly stood and moved forward. They tumbled down into the gorge, rolling to the bottom. As more fell, those below stood and made their way to the wall.

At the wall they tried to climb. As more arrived they climbed on top of those before them. Soon there were hundreds climbing on top of each other trying to reach the top.

Those on the walls stood there looking down, not believing what they saw. Then something came out of the horde. There were Trolls carrying ladders.

They climbed into the gorge making their way to the wall. Once there, they placed them against the wall. They stood there holding them as the others began to climb.

Those on the wall began firing their arrows. As bodies fell, more took their place. Soon there were fifteen ladders against the wall, and more were coming. Ladders were being placed all along the wall and the hordes were climbing up.

Sword Master Zale watched. He raised his hand high in the air. After a few seconds, he dropped it. Over the wall large buckets of oil and fire were dumped, covering those below. The bodies fell burning. There were no screams; there couldn't be, as those below were already dead. They had died a long time ago.

There was another roar and the horde slowly began to retreat. Those unable to climb out of the gorge, walked around in circles. A few tripped and fell into fires that were still burning. They never stood back up.

Nakobee was worried. He had not seen or heard from Karl and the others. He stood there looking out across the land. There was no way they could get around such a large force. They were either dead or trapped on the other side.

A man came up stopping next to Nakobee, and spoke, "First Sword Nakobee. There are men on the docks. We think they are the ones you sent out."

Nakobee turned and ran down the wall heading to the docks. When he arrived, he heard the guard talking to the people below.

"I said open the gate and let us in."

"I cannot do that. First Sword Nakobee has given orders they are to be kept closed."

"Then toss down a rope so we can climb up."

"We cannot do that, either."

"Then go get Nakobee. The longer we stay out here the greater the chance we get discovered."

Nakobee stepped to the wall and looked down. He saw Karl and the others standing there looking up.

Nakobee smiled and called out, "I see you found your way home."

Karl looked over at him and grinned.

"It was not easy. It was pure luck that we discovered demons do not like water, and those they control cannot swim. They sink. I think there were twenty of them that died before they stopped coming after us."

Nakobee looked at the man near him.

"Open the small door and let them in."

The man ran off. Nakobee looked back down.

"I'm glad you are back. I see you did not lose anyone."

"You told me not to. I do follow orders, at least those I believe of sound judgment."

Nakobee laughed as the door below opened and Karl and his men entered. Nakobee headed down to greet them.

That night as men stood watch, Kinn and Shaméd walked along the wall casting a spell. It was one that would keep any demons from crossing over.

It worked. Early in the morning hours they heard a scream. As men ran toward the sound, they saw a small demon fleeing. Its body was glowing as it ran. Those watching laughed at the sight.

As word of it spread, morale picked up. There was no longer any doubt they would win. Everywhere there was talk about the arrows that could kill demons. They talked about the elf and wizard who with a wave of their hand could keep demons away.

As the sun rose, they looked out and saw large wooden structures moving toward them. Those on the walls had no idea what they were. But, the men from Rednog knew all too well what they were. Catapults. The demons had made and brought catapults. This was something this world knew nothing about.

Sword Master Zale stood looking out at them. In his mind he knew this world would be changed forever. The demons were holding nothing back. They were bent on bringing these people weapons that could bring a new way of war. Once these people saw and understood the use of catapults, there would be no stopping them. If they were to survive, they would have to join the alliance to keep the peace.

Chapter Forty-One

Just as the sun broke over the horizon, rocks, and bodies came hurtling toward them. Some hit the outside walls, others made it over, crashing into buildings.

Sword Master Zale yelled out orders, "Gather the bodies and burn them."

Then word came that there were demons on the other side of the city. Sword Master Zale called to Shaméd. "Shaméd, we only have a small group over there. Go and help."

Shaméd rose in the air, heading toward the other side. As he went, those below saw him and hid, not sure who he was or what was happening. When he arrived, he saw the dwarfs there fighting. As he lowered himself to the walkway on the wall, he saw the enemy. There were only a couple hundred possessed, two beasts, and one demon that remained out of bow range.

Shaméd waved his hand and an arrow came out of a nearby quiver of arrows. The dwarf who owned it recoiled as the arrow left and floated to Shaméd.

Holding it, he said some words over the arrow. Then he tossed it into the air. It shot up and soon was out of sight. Then they heard a scream. They saw the demon waving its arms in the air. An arrow was piercing its eye. Every time the demon touched the arrow it would scream more. Then suddenly the demon was gone; it just vanished. The horde began to fall to the ground and the beasts began eating them.

The dwarfs began cheering. Shaméd rose into the air and went back to the other side. He dropped down next to Sword Master Zale.

"The threat on the other side has been dealt with. It is a shame we cannot handle those out there the same way."

"I take it you just killed the demon."

"It seemed the best thing to do."

Sword Master Zale nodded his head in agreement.

"We are here to get these people to understand they need our help. Not for them to fear us or grow dependent on us."

"I understand. I also understand there was no way the men there would have survived the attack. What I did made a point to those out there that they face more than just frightened people behind a big wall."

Sword Master Zale looked at him, nodded in agreement, and then faced back toward the enemy.

"If you want to help, can you do something about those catapults?" Shaméd looked at him and said, "Remember what the council said, we are to use as little magic as possible."

"I know what the council said. I also know what Nogar told me. Do whatever you need to do. Well I need you to take out those catapults."

Shaméd grinned and walked away. Reaching the elves, he went to Galan.

"Can you bring your ten best archers?"

Galan looked at the human. He was not the first fair-skinned human he had seen. There were humans that looked like him near his home. This one was different, though. He had seen him before, but never met him. He vibrated with power. He could feel it. He thought he must be the wizard he had heard about.

"All my men are experts with the bow."

"I'm sure there are at least ten even better than the others. Those are the ones I need."

Galan turned and called out ten names. Within minutes there were ten elves standing there.

"Go with this man. He needs your help."

They looked at Shaméd. He had looked them over then without saying a word, turned and walked away. They followed. When they reached a point that was in front of the catapults, Shaméd turned to the elves.

"Spread out along the wall. Two of you per target. Take aim at the catapults, aiming at their base. When you think you are ready, fire your arrows."

They each took out an arrow, aimed, and let it loose. Each one hit where Shaméd wanted. He reached into his satchel and pulled out some strips of cloth.

"Each of you wrap one of these around your arrow. Wrap them tight, try to only leave a little hanging loose."

They took the strips and wrapped them around the arrows. When they were done they stood there looking at him.

"These will fly differently than the first ones. Aim a little higher. I will set each arrow on fire. When I do, shoot at your target. Try to hit as close to your first arrow as you can."

Shaméd tapped an arrow, the cloth burst into flames, the elf pulled back and the arrow flew. As each arrow was lit, the elf shot it. Each one hit its target. When they hit, the flames shot up spreading up across the wooden frame.

There was a roar and the horde came running toward the walls. Those there began shooting. The sky was filled with arrows. The horde kept coming.

Hours later the ground was filled with bodies and the horde was still coming. The men on the walls started calling for more arrows. Sword Master Zale said to Kinn and Shaméd, "We are running out of arrows."

"I could make more," Shaméd said.

Sword Master Zale looked at Shaméd.

"I'm not sure what has gotten into you. Have you been spending more time with Urick?"

"I have increased my time studying with him. Why do you ask?"

"Never mind. More arrows will just make this drag on."

Sword Master Zale was about to say more, when they heard another roar and the horde retreated.

Soon the field was clear, with only dead below. They stood there looking out at the bodies. Hundreds of humans, dwarfs, and troll bodies lay everywhere. The beasts were slowly moving among them, eating the dead.

Sword Master Zale took a bow, notched an arrow and shot the closest beast. It yelped and ran away. Nakobee and Galan came walking up

Nakobee looked at Sword Master Zale and said, "It would seem we have won the day. We will need to make more arrows. Do you think some of us could go out there to retrieve some?"

Shaméd spoke before Sword Master Zale could, "You want to go down there to gather arrows?"

"It would help. We can go out by way of the small doors and collect those closest," Nakobee said.

Sword Master Zale looked at Galan.

"Do you agree with him?"

"I would go with him if he is going out there."

Sword Master Zale looked at Kinn and Shaméd.

"The people on this world are crazy."

He looked back at Nakobee and Galan.

"You do understand those down there are not really dead. They are just not able to move because of the metal in them. Remove it and they start moving again. So no, going out there to gather arrows is not a good idea."

"I might have a way to bring some, if not all the arrows back, and dispose of the bodies," said Shaméd.

Sword Master Zale and the others looked at Shaméd staring over the wall.

"How can you do that?" asked Nakobee.

"I can cast a spell to retrieve the arrows. Once they are up and moving away, I will set fire to the bodies. It should work."

"I know we already went against the council's orders, but we cannot keep using magic. They told me you are not supposed to."

"I believe your words were, "I was told not to let you use too much magic." It would seem I will have to since we are running out of arrows. Or, I can tell Kinn the spell and he can try to perform it."

They looked at Sword Master Zale. Kinn stood there trying not to grin.

Before Sword Master could ask, he spoke, "He could tell me, but doing that type of magic takes time and practice. It would be better if he just did it."

"I hate your memory," Sword Master Zale said. "Ok, do it."

Shaméd looked at Nakobee and Galan.

"Move everyone back to those towers." Shaméd gestured toward the end of the wall. "I will place the arrows on the walkway, between them. Tell your men not to come out, until I'm finished."

The men moved back to the towers.

When the walkway was clear, Shaméd faced out toward the gorge and raised his arms. In a low voice, he began speaking. Below a small cloud was building. It slowly spread out across the bodies. Arrows began to rise up. Within minutes, hundreds of them were on the walkway. When the walkway was covered in arrows, Shaméd clapped his hands. The clouds below burst into flames. The flames were so high and the heat so intense, the people on the wall moved back. In an hour the fire was out. When they looked over the wall, there was nothing but ash.

Sword Master Zale spoke, "This just might scare them. No one on this world has that kind of magic."

There were no more attacks; the horde had moved further away. The beasts were pacing back and forth, roaring threateningly when they came close to each other.

Everyone was talking about what Shaméd had done. Those who had seen it could not stop talking about it.

Hours later, when the moon was high in the sky, those not on watch were asleep. Nakobee was sitting with Galan near a small fire at the base of the wall. Galan's men were asleep. Nakobee tossed a piece of wood on the fire. Sparks flew up.

"It seems unfair. Those we are fighting are not real warriors. Maybe once they were, but not now. None of them have any weapons. They just come at us and we shoot them. Where is the honor in it?"

Galan answered without looking up, "There is no honor in war. There is only death. Later when the fighting is done, those left alive mourn those that died. No, there is no honor in war. Only pain and suffering."

Nakobee looked at him. He could see the pain on his face.

"You have seen war? One like this or worse?"

"I was in a war where elves fought humans. The reason was too stupid to believe. It lasted ten years. Many on both sides died. Then one day a group of humans came forward waving the sign of truce. I, along with two others, met them out on the field.

Their leader said it was over. They and their men would no longer fight. He told us that if we wanted to continue, then we could fight their king. They would bring him out and their King would fight a warrior of our choice. The winner would take all."

"They had a King? I have never heard of humans having a king. What did you do?" asked Nakobee

"We went back and told King Leoren. He sent his chosen warrior out to the field to fight their King."

"Was it a good fight?"

"No, it was not a good fight."

284

"Why? Was their King a weak warrior?"

"Their King was an old man dressed in armor made by dwarfs. It was bought with gold and made to fit him. He hadn't worn it, for many years."

"Then your warrior killed their King and your people won?"

"No, King Leoren's warrior did not kill their King. They stood there face to face and the King begged for his life. He promised to never again invade the land of King Leoren."

"Then your people still won. King Leoren was pleased with the victory?"

"No, he was not pleased."

"Why? If the human King surrendered, he won. Why was he not pleased?"

"Because when he sent me out there, he told me to kill their King no matter what happened and no matter what their King said. But, I could not kill him."

"I understand why killing a man who would not fight and was surrendering, would be a dishonor."

Galan let out a deep breath as he said, "I did not kill him because he surrendered. I did not kill him because he was my grandfather."

Nakobee was taken back by these last words.

"Your grandfather? You are an elf! I thought you said he was human?"

"He was. My mother is his daughter. She is half human, half elf. King Greg had taken a female elf years before. She had given him a male child and a female child. He thought it would bring the humans and elves closer together."

Nakobee sat there looking at Galan. Then it came to him. That explained all the little things he could not understand, and why Galan did not always act like an elf.

"This is why King Leoren banished you."

"King Leoren banished me to get even with his brother, and make him angry."

"How would banishing you anger his brother?"

"His brother is my father. He married King Greg's daughter. When I was born, I had to fight every step to reach the rank I had. It took me years to build trust with my men.

King Leoren smiled when the offer was made that one of his men would face King Greg. That was why he chose me. He wanted to see if I would kill my mother's father."

Nakobee sat there going over what he had heard. Galan was of mixed blood, part elf and part human, and caught between two worlds.

"What happened to King Greg?"

"His men came out and killed him. Then they made his son, my uncle their King."

They sat there in silence. It was broken when screams from the wall were heard.

"They are leaving. They are leaving."

The words were yelled all along the wall. As it spread, people woke up. People thought they were under attack at first. When they found out they were not, they filled the walkways on the walls. They stood looking out as the horde left.

Nakobee and Galan ran to the wall. Sword Master Zale walked up. As he stared at the horde leaving, he grinned.

"It looks like what Shaméd did changed their minds. We can only hope they will go back and tell the others and this war will be over."

Nakobee looked at him and in a low voice said, "You do not really believe this will end, do you?"

"No, I do not. I believe the only way it will end is if we take the fight to them. We are going to have to follow them and fight them in their land."

Nakobee looked at him then at the horde leaving.

"It will take many months to reach their land."

"I know. I have looked at the maps of this world. The home of the demons is on the other side. It will take time and we will have to leave men behind to guard your homes."

He turned and walked away. His mind raced over what could happen on such a long journey.

Chapter Forty-Two

Everyone was around the table talking.

Sword master Zale called out, "I know this sounds crazy. But I'm telling you it will work. We follow the demons and the horde. On the way we attack their outer edge. We know each demon controls around two to three hundred bodies. The count goes down depending how many the beasts eat before being stopped. There are one or two beasts around each group.

We saw ten demons. Yes, they have more men than us. But they do not have weapons. As everyone saw, Shaméd is able to kill from afar. He is not going to do that very often. We do not want the leader of the demons to know just how powerful Shaméd is."

Once again, they all began talking. Sword Master Zale looked over at Kaila and Nakobee. He decided it was time for Kaila to become the official queen over this land. There was no time to wait for the other Queens to give their blessings.

"Ok, everyone please be quiet. There is something we have to do before we make this decision.

They all stopped talking and looked at him.

"We have to make Kaila officially the queen over her land. I know she is supposed to wait for the other Queens to give their blessing, but we cannot wait. She has the people and she has the land. I think we do the ceremony as soon as possible, then we go after the horde. What are your thoughts?"

Everyone started talking at once. No one wanted to wait for the other queens. They decided to do the ceremony that day, or no later than the next.

Sword Master Zale called out, "Then it is settled. Pass the word that Kaila will be made Queen over the Zolotov clan at sunrise tomorrow. As for the other matter we will decide after the ceremony."

Kaila stood there with a surprised expression on her face. She knew this day would come, she just thought her grandmother would be there when it did.

As everyone left the room, Galan walked over to Nakobee and Sword Master Zale.

"My men and I will leave today to follow the horde. We will strike at the edge and kill as many of the beasts and the possessed as we can. If you can spare the arrows that kill demons, we would like to take some with us."

Nakobee looked at Sword Master Zale.

"We cannot let them go. There are only sixty of them. They don't have enough men."

Galan said, "We will not engage the entire horde, only the ones lagging behind. You know this is a good plan. It will be two days before you are ready to leave. By then they will be miles away. They will be too far away for you to do anything but follow them. This way, I can kill some and slow them down."

Sword Master Zale spoke, "Nakobee, you know he is right. They have steeds. They can ride in and out, attacking, and then leave before they can fight back."

"Then I will go with you."

Galan placed his hand on Nakobee's shoulder.

"You must stay here with your sister. It is a great day for her and you. I will gather my men and leave. We do not like sitting around waiting."

Galan smiled as he patted Nakobee's shoulder.

"I will send you as many demon killing arrows as I can." said Zale.

"Thank you."

Nakobee watched as Galan walked away.

"Come, we have things to do before your sister is crowned queen."

Sword Master Zale headed for the door with Nakobee right behind.

Outside, Nakobee saw Leo talking to his brother. Nakobee called to him.

"Leo, a word with you?"

Leo looked at him and Lea walked away. When Leo was close he said, "Is there something I can do for you, Nakobee?"

"There is. I would like to know your feelings for my sister. Before you answer, I know you have always cared for her. I just want to know how much. Would you die for her?"

Leo stood there not sure what to say. He looked at Nakobee then at Sword Master Zale, who stood there watching.

"Yes, I would die for her. Every man and woman from our tribe would die for her."

"I do not care about the others. I want to know about you. Would you face me and claim her? Would you be her First Sword?"

Leo took a step back, he was not sure if Nakobee was going to hit him. How did he find out his feelings for Kaila? He stood straight. He would tell him how he felt, and if Nakobee said he was not worthy then he would still stand by her side as her body guard.

"Yes, I would care for her and take her as my mate. I would be her First Sword or anything she wanted me to be. If I'm not the one you think is worthy then tell me. I will never tell her how I feel."

"You have never told her?"

"Of course not. She is, or will be, our Queen. You are her brother. I would need to come to you first."

Nakobee looked at him then at Sword Master Zale, who nodded his head.

"You will go to her now and tell her how you feel. Ask her if she feels the same. If she does, then I give you my blessing. After she is crowned Queen you will be named First Sword to her."

Leo stood there not sure what to do. Sword Master Zale leaned toward him.

"I think this is where you leave and go find Kaila."

Leo, nodded his head at both of them, turned and walked away. After a few steps, he ran to the building.

"That was a nice move. Making sure your sister has a new First Sword makes it easier for you to leave. When did you figure out he was the one she loved?"

"She has always cared for him. Besides, I saw how she looked at him whenever he entered the room. Now, let's get those arrows."

They headed for the building where Shaméd was. He and Kinn were the only ones on this world who could say the correct words over the arrows.

Chapter Forty-Three

The sun broke over the mountains. Its rays gleamed across the plains and reflected off the lake. It was going to be a beautiful morning and a clear day.

People were standing in front of the building where the ceremony was to take place. There were three steps leading up to a chair in the middle of the platform.

The doors to the building were open. Long red, yellow, blue, and green banners were draped from the top of the building to the stage. These were the colors of the clans belonging to the humans.

On either side of the stage were poles with the same material, only these were the deep purple of the Zolotov tribe.

Ten men, five on each side, were beating drums. A man stepped out wearing a green colored robe. It was Urick. Keeping his two smaller arms covered, he walked out on the stage.

"We come here today to crown the one called Kaila, daughter to Queen Keely. We have all sworn our loyalty to her and her clan. She has met the requirements to become a Queen. Now for all to see, I give you the one called Kaila."

He turned and the drums beat harder and louder. Kaila came walking out in a gown rich in colors of red, blue, and purple. The material was from Rednog. Nogar had sent it to her for this occasion.

When she stood in front of the chair she stopped and looked out at the people. Urick faced them as he raised his hands.

"People of the Clan Zolotov, your new Queen."

He moved aside and Kaila stood there as the people cheered. Tears slowly streamed down her face as she looked out at them. Humans, elves, trolls, and dwarfs, and two ogres were cheering for her.

She raised her hands and the drums stopped.

"People of the clan Zolotov, I, Kaila, daughter of Queen Keely, promise to treat everyone equally. My door is always open. I also promise new and exciting things to come to our land. No longer will humans be without a written language. We will teach our young to write and read. We will teach those with the drive to learn how to build, to build the things you see around you and more. This begins tomorrow with something called a ship. We have canoes, but these ships will be larger. They will hold a hundred people and supplies for just as many.

This is a new beginning for all of us. Each race will benefit from what we are doing. This war with the demons will end. They tried to divide us. But look! We banded together to fight them. We saw through their deceit. We will let them know we are not afraid of them and with the Creator by our side we will chase them back. They openly broke the treaty and we will banish them from our world forever!"

Everyone cheered and Urick walked over. In his hands was something new. He had a thin metal crown. Unlike the other human queens who had a crown of braided colored cloth and twine, Kaila's was made of fine gold and jewels.

It was a gift from Commander Ferdra. He told his King they would not return. The dwarfs were staying to work the mountain for her, and would be part of her clan.

This had made King Daral angry, mostly because of the gold Ferdra told him about. He did not care if his men

292

did not return; they were sent away because he did not like Ferdra to begin with.

Urick held it up so all could see. They stopped cheering and stood there looking at it. As he placed the crown on her head, he stepped back. Turning, he faced them and spoke, "I give you Queen Kaila of the Clan Zolotov."

The cheering broke out and the humans began dancing. After a few minutes, Queen Kaila raised her hands, everyone stopped.

"People, as your new Queen I now choose a new First Sword. My brother Nakobee is stepping down and Leo, son of Lajos, brother of Lea, will be my First Sword and tomorrow he will become my mate."

Leo stepped forward and the cheering erupted again. Leo stood there with a grin on his face.

By noon all the celebration was winding down. Queen Kaila sat in her chair as each person, human, troll, elf, and dwarf came up to meet and pledge their loyalty to her.

Leo stood by her side the whole time. He was dressed in metal armor given to him by Commander Ferdra. It did not quite fit. They told him he had to wear it for a few days, and it would adapt to his body.

The people talked about everything they had heard this day. Most were excited, but some were a little nervous. They had seen so much, and had been through so much, over the past couple of years.

There were some, even trolls, who liked the idea of learning how to build these new homes. As for the ships, the Trolls did not like water so they would just observe.

As the sun began to set, the leaders of each group were back at the long table. Nakobee and Sword Master

Zale stood there waiting for them to settle down. When they did, Nakobee pounded on the table.

"Now that I have your attention, I will be leaving tonight. I will catch up with General Galan and his men. Sword Master Zale will lead the rest of you in a few days."

Sword Master Zale looked around, then pointed at the map spread out before them.

"We have explained all this to Queen Kaila. She agrees with the plan. The dwarfs, along with half the humans, will stay here. We know it means cutting our force in half, but it makes the most sense. Kinn will also be staying, as will the humans from Rednog who were brought to work on the city. We will have one thousand warriors from Rednog joining us in two days.

Each of you who are going will pack whatever you think you will need. We will bring fifteen wagons loaded with supplies. As Nakobee already said, he is leaving to catch up with General Galan. They hope to cause trouble for the demons heading back home.

We know it is a long march to the demon homeland. If the ship or ships get built in time, they will come and pick us up. If not they will be there to bring us home. Any questions?"

There were a lot. Nakobee left after the third one. He found Kaila, now Queen Kaila, with Leo in her throne room. They were sitting at the table off to the side of the room.

"Sister, I wanted to let you know I'm leaving."

He walked over and she stood and gave him a hug.

"You be careful. I do not want to lose you."

"I will be fine. Shaméd has said the war will be long, but he has confidence we will win."

"I'm sure Lord Shaméd will live. I do not think there is anything on this world that could kill him. He has lived for almost two thousand years. I will remind him he is to protect you."

"I do not need protecting."

Nakobee stepped over to face Leo.

"I have given you the most precious thing in my life. Take care of her."

"I have told you I would die for her, and it is true."

"I do not want you to die for her; I want you to live for her. All others coming against her can die. You both must live."

Nakobee reached out and grabbing Leo's arm, pulled him close, and hugged him. They had been friends since childhood. Without another word Nakobee let him go, turned, and left.

He found his steed waiting for him outside the building. Climbing into the saddle he rode off.

Nakobee caught up with Galan the following night. As he unpacked his animal and was brushing it down, Galan came over.

"How was the ceremony?"

"It was beyond what I thought it would be. She stood there and gave her speech and I was proud. I could saw our mother standing there."

"I'm glad. We have had fun. We killed a beast and twenty of what once were dwarfs. Those were the easiest, since they do not walk fast. We burned them when the horde was out of sight."

"That was how I found you, I followed the smoke. Once I smelled it, I searched for your tracks."

Galan nodded his head as he spoke, "I was thinking the fire might be a problem. But then those we are chasing are not the brightest. The demons do seem to be in a hurry. We saw some disappear, then later return. When they leave, it is a feast for the beasts. Without being under control, the horde begins to wander off. The beasts chase them, eating as many as they can. If the demons keep leaving, the beasts will do our work for us."

"I wonder why they are leaving, and where they are going."

"I don't know. Tomorrow, you can see what happens if anymore leave."

They talked a little longer as they sat near a small fire.

In the morning they ate a cold breakfast. After saddling their animals, they rode onward. After three hours they caught up to the horde. The trail was not difficult to follow. The land where they walked was devastated and there were leftover body parts scattered along the way.

Galan waved four of his men back. They took the pack animals and headed for a group of trees off to the right. Then he waved half to go left. The rest went with him straight ahead. Nakobee went with the group to the left.

The land before them was open because of the hoard. What few trees there were, were now shattered and lay on the ground. The thicker tree line was to the right.

If they had been chasing a normal army, they would have been seen a long time ago. These were possessed beings that could not think for themselves. They rode slowly so as not to attract the attention of the beasts.

When they were a couple hundred feet away, Galan kicked his animal. Bow in hand, he notched an arrow then let it fly when he found a target. Each of his men did the same. Each arrow hit a target and a possessed being fell. After a few arrows, a beast came running at them. Galan and his men retreated. The beast was catching up, when Nakobee and the others came up behind it. Galan and his men turned and faced the beast as they surrounded it. Fifteen arrows and the beast lay dead.

They rode off into the trees to wait. As night fell, they went back and gathered the dead. They built a fire and burned the bodies. They left the beast on the ground. After collecting their arrows and keeping those not broken, they went back to the trees and made camp.

The next day they rode out. By noon, they found what was left of the horde. Bodies were scattered everywhere. Three beasts were off to the side, they appeared to be asleep.

They stopped and stared at the sight before them. Nakobee dismounted and with sword in hand, crept closer to the three beasts. He touched one. It did not move. Looking into its eyes, and then searching the body, he stood straight.

"It is dead. Its throat was slit."

Galan and the others dismounted. They found the other two beasts were also dead, their throats slit.

"Why would they do this?" asked Nakobee.

"I think the demons did not want to walk all the way back."

Nakobee kept walking. He saw movement to the right and headed for it. There was something lying on the ground, hurt. At first, Nakobee thought it was another beast. When he got closer, he saw it was not, but a large animal of some kind. It did not move as he came closer. Nakobee pointed at it.

"Look, it is bleeding."

He walked up and stood there looking at it. It was half the size of the beasts. It was bleeding and appeared to be still alive. Nakobee crept closer. The animal moved its head. As it did, it made strange sounds.

Nakobee put his sword away and walked up to the animal. It stopped moving, either from being too tired or from not caring. Nakobee reached out and patted it on the head. The animal closed its eyes and seemed to relax.

Turning around, he headed back to his steed. Taking his canteen off the saddle, he went back to the animal. It moved its long nose and Nakobee poured water into its mouth.

He heard Galan call out, "What are you doing?"

"I don't know. I just felt it needed some water so I gave it some."

"Kill it," Galan said as he walked over.

"I'm not going to kill it. Look at it; it is not like the others. It is smaller and there are no scales. I have never seen one that looks like this with the horde. I do not think it is a beast. I think it is some sort of large animal."

"A beast is a beast. It is here among the hoard, so it must be with them," Galan said.

Nakobee looked at the animal's wound. The back leg looked as if it had been bitten. He saw it was not very deep. He looked the beast over trying to find other wounds. He found one on its back. This one was deeper and he could see it was a bite.

Chapter Forty-Four

Nakobee went back to his steed. Taking his pack off, he returned to the small beast.

Nakobee looked at Galan.

"I'm going to see if I can help it. Take your men and make sure the others are dead, then burn their bodies."

Galan shook his head and left, and Nakobee started cleaning the wounds. The deep ones, he stitched closed. The animal laid there, eyes closed, not moving.

When he was finished, Nakobee stood, patted it and went and sat in front of its face.

"What are you? Why are you here?"

The animal opened its eyes and just stared at him. Nakobee could see that it meant him no harm. He had never seen anything like it.

Galan came riding up, climbed off and stood next to him. He looked at the animal, then at Nakobee.

"It has been three hours. Will it live?"

"I do not know. Have you ever seen anything like it?"

Galan walked around the animal then came back and stopped next to Nakobee.

"I have heard of animals similar to this one, but I have never seen them."

Nakobee looked at him, then the animal.

"Look at its head. The nose is so long and its ears? Have you ever seen an animal with ears that large?"

Galan stood there, staring at the animal.

"I have never been away from my homeland. Coming here is the farthest I have ever been. I have never seen anything like it."

"The skin is so wrinkled. It has very little hair." Nakobee ran his hand over the body.

"I still think you should have killed it."

Nakobee looked at his steed. After removing his things, he looked at Galan, and said, "I will camp here tonight. Can you take him with you? Bring him back in the morning?"

Galan took the rope and walked to his steed. After climbing up, he looked at Nakobee.

"Are you sure you want to stay here?"

"I will be fine. See you in the morning."

Nakobee turned back to the animal and spread out his bedroll. He ran his hand slowly across its side.

"You are a strange one. I do not understand why I helped you. You must have cast a spell on me."

The night was filled with sounds of scavengers snuffling around. They were sniffing at the fire, trying to pull the bodies out of it. Others were eating the dead beasts.

It made sleeping difficult for Nakobee. He would awaken whenever a scavenger came too close.

In the middle of the night he built a pit and gathered wood and grass to burn. It kept most of the scavengers away. The brave ones that came too close, felt his sword, and a couple left with an arrow in their sides.

In the morning Nakobee woke to a horn blowing. Standing, he saw Galan and the others riding toward him. They rode frantically waving their arms. Turning around, Nakobee saw seven large beasts a few feet away on the other side of the small beast. They looked like the one on the ground. Two were about the same size, but the other five were twice as large.

Slowly he stepped back. One of the beasts came closer to the one on the ground. It ran its long nose over it. Then it raised its nose into the air, and a strange sound came out. Nakobee reached for his sword. It was not there. He looked and saw it near his bedroll.

There was a movement to his right. Turning, he crouched down, and then he saw Shaméd.

Shaméd, without looking at Nakobee, walked over and patted the nose of the large beast standing over the one on the ground.

Shaméd spoke to it, "Hello there big girl. Is this your baby? Let's take a closer look to see if there is anything more we can do to help it."

He moved closer to the one on the ground. Shaméd spoke as he bent down to look at the wounds.

Over his shoulder he called to Nakobee, "Can you stop Galan and the others from charging at us?"

As he laid his hand on the animal, he said, "They don't mean you any harm."

Nakobee turned and ran toward Galan. He waved his arms. Galan and his men rode up and stopped next to him. They sat on their steeds looking at Shaméd.

"How did he get here?" asked Galan.

"Shaméd is a wizard, remember?"

They watched as Shaméd took things out of his pouches. He spread what looked like ointment over the wounds. When he was finished, he called to Nakobee.

"You can come over now."

Nakobee walked over and looked at the wounds. They were healed. The ones he had stitched were fading. No trace of any of the wounds could be seen.

"How did you? Never mind. Will it be alright? I think it cast a spell on me. I don't know what came over me. I just felt that I needed to help it. I don't understand why."

"You helped it because it needed help. The evil beasts attacked it, and these came as soon as they could. They want me to tell you thank you for helping their young one. They have not seen many two legged ones that would have helped."

"You can understand them?" asked Nakobee

"I talked with them in mind speech. I have always been able to talk to animals. These are very smart, gentle and wise creatures."

The one on the ground began to rock back and forth. After a few times, it was up on its feet. Shaméd patted its long nose.

"It wants to thank you as well. I told her your name. Hers is Little One. Of course, that will change when she gets bigger and becomes an adult."

"She is not full grown?"

"Look at her parents."

Nakobee looked up and saw they were indeed bigger. The one to the right had two long teeth sticking out of its mouth.

"I see what you mean. Tell her I'm glad I was able to help."

The little beast moved closer to Nakobee. She rubbed his arm with her nose, sniffing him as she did. Nakobee never moved. When she was done, she walked over to her parents, and they all walked away in the direction Nakobee and the others had come.

"I told them it would be safe for them to go that way, and they would find plenty of food. I said I would see them in a couple of days."

As they left, Nakobee looked at Shaméd.

"How did you know to come?"

Shaméd stood next to him and smiled.

"Word was sent that you found a, I have never heard what they are called on this world. Each world has different names. One world calls them the land whales. They are a gentle animal, unless provoked. They make great companions and work animals.

As for why I'm here, I was told you found it, and it was hurt and you were helping it. Now that it is better, I will leave. I will inform the others that the horde is dead and the demons have returned home."

Shaméd took a step and disappeared. Galan and the others gasped.

"How did he... never mind he is a wizard," Galan said.

Nakobee packed his things and got on his steed and they rode on slowly. They reached a river two days later and made camp. Nakobee said they would wait for the others there.

Chapter Forty-Five

Sword Master Zale and his group caught up with Nakobee three days later. Over the next six months, they traveled across rolling hills, through swamps, and a large forest that took days to travel through.

After leaving the forest, they began walking out across a savanna with high grass and no trees. Over the next five days the grass slowly disappeared, also. On noon of the fifth day, the grass completely disappeared and they stood looking out across a desert.

Sword Master Zale signaled for them to halt and called for a meeting.

"We need to determine how big this desert is. We will camp here until we learn more. Tell everyone to take it easy with the water."

Everyone went to make camp and Sword Master Zale called Shaméd over.

"Go to the Mirror Gate room and see how big this desert is. See if there is water, or if we are going to have to do something special."

Shaméd closed his eyes; a minute later he took a step and disappeared.

Two hours later when Shaméd returned, he appeared next to Sword Master Zale and Nakobee.

Pointing at the desert, he said, "It goes on for miles. There is only one good way to continue, and that is to head east. After a three day march we will reach the ocean. We can travel along it to the hills. We cross them and it will be a few more days to reach the demon's main camp."

"They would not have come that way. It would be too close to water. They had to have come across this desert. How did they cross it with all those people?"

Shaméd looked back out at the wasteland.

"I checked a year back and this land was all covered with trees and animals. As the demons crossed, everything died."

"There should still be some signs of vegetation. How did it all vanish so fast?"

"We do not know. I left Reklan and Ted looking into that. They said they would let me know as soon as they figured it out."

"If the demons caused this, why did it not happen everywhere they went?" asked Nakobee.

"That is another question I asked. Another was why did it spread as far as it has. It goes from the ocean to the river. That is a three day march in both directions. It makes no sense."

"Three days to the ocean?"

"Yes, three days, and it stops a few hundred feet from the water. It is the same near the river."

There was movement behind Shaméd. He turned as Ted appeared.

"We know what happened. Or at least the Thorns think they do."

"What did they say?"

"The demons drained all the life from the plants and animals here. They did it so fast we did not see it. We slowed the images down and that was when we saw it. Two demons with their hands in the air caused all of this. As they walked, death spread behind them. Tyriq saw a spectrum of light not seen with human eyes. It was like a swirling vortex that he said came up from the plants and animals and went into the demon's hands. Then it spread out across the horde and beasts."

"That must be why they killed the horde. They could not sustain them any longer," Sword Master Zale said.

"What about the group Nakobee found? Are they still there?"

"No. They left and are now at the demon's main camp. They arrived two days ago. They have tents set up at the base of a hill. Before you ask, we saw Jon. He is kept in a tent with other prisoners. Reklan was going to step through to get him. Nogar said it would be too dangerous because of the demons being so close.

We saw on top of the hill a large chair and I mean a large chair. Whatever or whoever sits in it, must be a hundred feet tall."

"Ted, thank you, and thank Tyriq, as well."

Ted nodded and took a step and was gone.

Galan walked up as he disappeared.

"Can all of you do that?"

Shaméd looked at him and answered, "Only when the Mirror is aligned and we ask for a doorway."

"That is too bad. You would think it would be a good way to move an army from place to place."

Shaméd looked at Sword Master Zale, who looked back and smiled.

"That indeed would be a good thing to be able to do," Sword master Zale said.

"Since we are staying here, do you mind if my men and I do a little scouting?"

"That would be a great idea. What direction are you going, east?

Galan looked at the three of them and grinned.

"Would you like us to go east to make sure it is clear?"

"Yes. I would like you to go east."

Galan turned and headed for his men. They watched as Galan and his men rode off; sixty bright shiny figures, with their leader in leather in front.

Nakobee was a little worried. He hoped nothing would happen to them. Galan was a man who wanted to prove himself. He thought dying was the only way to redeem himself in the eyes of his King.

Nakobee thought it would be a shame for a man like him to die. He looked at Shaméd as they were walking.

"Lord Shaméd, may I ask you a question?"

"Of course, you want to know how we can help Galan."

Nakobee was not even upset he had read his mind.

"Yes. You have met him and I think you know what happened to him was wrong. How can we show him that his death would be a waste?"

"We have to show him that his living will be beneficial to everyone."

"How?"

"As you could see by his request to leave, he is not one to sit around. He wants to belong to something important. Like you, he wants his life to matter. You have spent your whole life making sure your sister would be queen. You wanted the right man to stand with her. You have done that, and now you are going into battle to make sure the people on this world can live without being controlled by demons. Once that is completed, what will you do? What will Galan do? I do not know what you will do when this is over. But, whatever you decide to do, it will keep you going. He needs something like that to keep him going to make him want to live, also."

They walked on in silence, Nakobee thinking on Shaméd's words. He was right, his whole life was to protect his sister and make sure she became queen after their mother. Now that he had done that, what was he going to do?

Chapter Forty-Six

In the morning they headed east. Galan had not returned or sent any word. They stayed near the edge of the desert traveling between it and the grass land. As the sun began to set, they saw riders. Six of Galan's men came riding up. They stopped next to Sword Master Zale and Nakobee.

"Greetings from Galan. He has sent us to let you know there is a small oasis a short distance from here. You should reach it an hour after sunset. He has started some fires to guide you."

"Tell him we thank him for the news."

They turned and rode back the way they came. Nakobee sent word through the convoy they would not be stopping until after sunset.

And hour and a half after sundown, they saw a glow and a shadow of a man on top of a sand dune. It was Galan standing there waiting.

As they came he called out, "I was worried you might pass this place. We almost did. It was just luck that one of my men rode up to this hill. He saw the oasis and we checked it out. It has lots of water and trees. The fruit on them is not too bad either."

He walked with them. The troops slowly spread out. They were all tired from the long day's march. Sword Master Zale looked at the place. It was indeed an oasis. There were fifty or more trees with a large pond in the center. He saw a small stream flowing off toward the grasslands.

Shaméd walked up to Sword Master Zale.

"I agree we should stay here for a day. It is only another day's march to the ocean. Once there, we will have plenty of water to look at, but not much to drink."

"I hate when you read my mind," Zale said.

"I know, and that is why I do it."

Shaméd grinned as he walked toward the water.

They stayed the next day resting up, then bright and early the morning after they were up and heading east. They arrived at the ocean by nightfall.

The five day trip along the shoreline was made better by the cool breeze coming off the water each day. On the morning of the sixth day, they moved off toward the hills. Three days later, Galan and his men rode up.

"You need to make camp. There is a large horde just over the next hill."

"How large is it?" asked Nakobee.

"There are maybe twice as many as we have here. We could not get a good count of the possessed. There are five demons and ten beasts."

Sword Master moved off to the side. Nakobee and Galan watched, wondering what he was doing. It did not take long. Men began appearing a few feet away. They were all dressed in blue clothing with metal armor, shields, spears and swords.

Soon there were three hundred humans after which large green men appeared; a hundred of them wearing similar clothing and armor to the humans. Afterward, came two hundred elves, dressed in elfin armor. Their armor was bright gold in color with blue cloaks tossed over their right shoulders. They, like those before them, carried a shield, sword, and spear. When the last one stepped through, Sword Master Zale approached them.

"Greetings. I'm glad to see all of you."

A leader from each race stepped forward. Galan sat there on his steed, staring. He was amazed at the sight. They had told him that their fifteen hundred men would not face the demons alone. He had no idea what or who the green ones were, but he knew they would be a formidable foe. Each one was twice as large as any one man, maybe even twice as large as Nakobee.

Sword Master Zale called everyone over. When Nakobee, Shaméd, Galan and the others were all there, he pointed at the three next to him.

"I would like to introduce Goran. He is the leader of the ogres. This is Galan Urikrana, leader of the golden elves of Ryland. And this is Taylan, I should say, General Taylan. He has led many men into battles on many different worlds.

Again, I'm glad you are all here. As each of you know, we have a horde over those hills. I can only assume they are there to stop us. General Taylan, do you have any plans?"

"I'm here to follow your orders. I will do so as long as your strategies remain wise."

He sneered at Zale.

Zale replied, "Of course, you will let me know if and when I do make any unwise decisions?"

"Of course," General Taylan answered.

"Then I suppose I should take a look at what we are facing. I do not want to make bad choices. You can make camp and when I return we can all talk."

Sword Master Zale walked away. The three leaders headed back to their troops. Each group spread out to set up their camps.

The others stood there looking at Sword Master Zale's back as he walked toward the hills. Nakobee looked at Shaméd.

"Is there something going on between this General Taylan and Sword Master Zale?"

The others came close to hear the response. Shaméd looked at them, then turned and watched as Zale walked up the hill. Once he reached it, he stood there bold as could be, hands on his hips, looking down at the horde.

"Yes, there is. A long time ago, Sword Master Zale told General Taylan a battle plan he proposed was unwise. Taylan told Zale when he was the leader, he could make the plans. Until then he was to shut up and follow orders."

"What happened? Was Sword Master Zale right? Was the plan bad?" asked Galan.

"The plan was not completely bad, it was working. But Taylan did not stick to it. He became too sure of himself. He made changes causing the death of half his men. More would have died if not for the arrival of King Nogar and the other dragons.

They arrived and the battle went from a disaster to a victory. Of course, Zale and Taylan had words when it was over. They have not been the best of friends ever since. I just wonder why Nogar sent him."

Shaméd walked away as the others looked up at Sword Master Zale. That night Sword Master Zale had the leaders in his tent.

Galan walked over and stood next to Galan Urikrana.

"I would like to introduce myself. I'm Galan Gretumal."

Urikrana turned and looked at Galan and smiled.

"You are General Galan Gretumal of the mountain clan. Your King is Ailluin Leoren, correct?"

"Yes, King Leoren is the king of the Mountain Clan."

Urikrana looked at Galan, and asked, "But he is not your King? Is it because of what happened? Before you say anything, no one told me. I saw it in your mind. You were thinking about it as you came over. Be assured I'm pleased with how you handled the situation. I'm sorry your King did not feel the same. There is nothing for you to be ashamed about. We are all friends here. I'm glad we share names. Now come let us get closer to the conversation, so we do not miss anything."

Galan followed him to the table. He was glad to know another elf felt he did nothing wrong and he did not think him dishonorable for not following his King's orders.

As they came closer Sword Master Zale was explaining his plan. General Taylan stabbed the map with his knife.

"This plan sounds similar to a plan of mine."

Sword master Zale looked at General Taylan.

"That would be because it is based on the one you made on world ENDOH749."

"The very one you said was bad?"

"I never said your strategy was bad. If you had made the changes I suggested, it would have been better."

General Taylan glared at Sword Master Zale.

"So, my plan, with your changes, makes it a better plan. I cannot wait to see how this plays out. Go ahead show us the rest of your great plan."

Taylan stood straight as he glowered. The others around the table stood there watching, unsure what was happening. Only Shaméd knew, the side of his mouth pulled up in a slight grin.

The next hour Sword Master Zale explained where each group would be placed for the attack. When he gave the command, he would lead the charge, then each group would attack at their given time.

They went over the plan five times emphasizing a different step each time. The last time, Sword Master stood straight and looked at each of them.

"If there are no more questions, then I suggest we all try to get some sleep. It will be a difficult day tomorrow."

Everyone left except Shaméd, Nakobee, and Sword Master Zale.

Zale looked at Shaméd and Nakobee who were looking at the map.

Nakobee, without looking up asked, "Do you think we can do it?"

"Yes, as long as General Taylan does not decide to get even with me and hold his men back."

Nakobee looked at him, a puzzled expression on his face.

"He would cause the deaths of so many just to get even?"

"I don't know. He was very angry with me when I told him his plan needed some changes. Later, I realized I should have said it when we were alone. He might have accepted the changes. I asked Nogar why he was chosen to lead the humans. He said it was the council's decision, not his."

Shaméd looked at Zale as he spoke, "I will keep an eye on him. If it looks as if he will not follow through I will intervene."

"Then it is time for both of you to get some sleep. Shaméd, I know I'm wasting my breath on you. You hardly ever sleep. You should try, though. Tomorrow's battle will be larger than any you have ever been in. You will need to be ready for whatever happens."

"Do not worry, I will be ready." Shaméd said

Nakobee and Shaméd left. Outside, Shaméd went left to his tent and Nakobee kept walking to where he placed his bedroll. Nakobee saw Jym and Rae as he walked by. They had set their tents close to Shaméd's tent. Nakobee was camped with the men who came with him from Keele.

As he sat on his bedroll, he felt calm. Somehow he thought he would be nervous. He sat thinking was Jon still alive? He could not think of any reason for him to be thinking about Jon. Why he thought about him was strange; he did not even like him. Jon had made him angry, and in doing so, caused him to be taken off guard duty. No one had ever made him that angry.

Rae and Jym both said it was what Jon liked to do. They called it pushing buttons. They were used to his ways. They liked him and were worried about him. Nakobee liked Rae and Jym, so he would help get Jon back for them.

Chapter Forty-Seven

In the morning, Sword Master Zale walked up and once again stood on the hill looking out at the Horde. His army came up before dawn and was stretched out along the ridge. They were outnumbered three to one. His men knew this and yet they were ready to give their lives to save all those they left behind.

The council on Rednog had said they would match man for man whatever Nakobee and this world could gather. It was a shame they could only gather fifteen hundred warriors for this battle.

Nogar had argued for more, but was only granted the six hundred. The reason the council only sent those was because Sellax pressured the council. He said one ogre was worth three humans, and one elf was worth two humans. He said that sending those six hundred was like sending one thousand and that was more than these people deserved.

Zale told him it would be more than enough. He knew that with Shaméd with them, their odds increased in his favor. By how much, depended on how and what Shaméd decided to bring to the war.

In a low voice Zale said, "The boy has learned a great deal of magic. He has also studied the word of the One. With all that knowledge, I'm sure he can figure out more ways to beat these demons. He was the one who figured out how to kill them. Whatever he did to the arrows worked. He said that it would either kill them, or drive them back to their own realm, and it did."

It was time. The horde was beginning to advance. Zale was hoping they would do this. He did not want his men out on the flat plain to face the enemy.

The ground was open and there was very little life anywhere in the demon's land. Since entering it they had not seen a tree, only brown grass and brown shrubs.

Once the horde reached the bottom of the hill, it began charging up. It was eerie to Zale to see a large army running at you and yet hear no sound coming from them. Only the beasts running with them made noise. Their growls were a loud piercing scream.

Zale looked at the men around him. He saw fear on their faces. The humans on this world had fought each other, but they never had a defense for fighting the demons or those controlled by them until now.

Demons had never openly attacked; they would stay hidden in the background, pressuring others to wage war. This time it was different. Once they were found out, they had nothing to lose, so they came at them with all they had.

News had reached him that there was open fighting in each of the race's lands. That was another reason they only had fifteen hundred. The rulers did not want their lands left defenseless.

When the horde reached the right spot, Zale raised then dropped his arm. Archers raised their bows in unison, and then let their arrows fly. Each archer drew and shot five arrows, one after the other, toward the horde. The sky was filled, blacking out the sun over the horde.

The arrows continued arching up, and when they came down, bodies fell. Even the beasts were hit, but not all those hit, died. They screamed and threw themselves to the ground to break the arrows off.

When the arrows stopped, below them lay about a thousand in the dirt. Zale saw three beasts not moving; the rest were running back. However, what was left of the horde was still slowly moving forward. Zale raised his hand again. This time the archers fired three arrow volleys before stopping.

More than half the horde now lay dead on the hill. Those still alive or moving were still coming up. Zale raised both hands. The archers put their bows away and drew their swords.

When the horde was close, hand-to-hand fighting began. The horde was no match against their swords. The only way his men fell was when the horde over ran them. It happened more than Zale liked.

Zale yelled a command, and men started building walls with their shields as others retrieved their bows and began firing more arrows. Zale blew once on his horn and Galan and his men rode out with their swords and spears.

An hour later what was left of the horde was retreating. Zale blew twice on the horn, the men on the hill slowly advanced. Galan and his men moved off to the side.

As the foot soldiers moved forward, they killed those too slow to get away. As Zale and his army reached the middle of the valley, what was left of the horde began dropping to the ground, dead. Zale blew a long blast on his horn and his men came to a halt. His medics ran out and started taking care of the injured warriors.

Zale, Nakobee, and Shaméd kept walking. Slowly they made their way to the top of the next hill. It stretched off in both directions as far as the eye could see. Looking forward, they saw another mountain range. Both were barren of life. Between the two mountains was a valley with a small river running through it.

They watched the beasts and the demons they had been fighting, running away. They watched as the demons blinked away as they came close to the small river. The beasts just ran through the river then up to a large corral where a demon stood.

They looked at the encampment. It was massive. There were thousands of bodies, tents, and corrals with beasts in them. Like Ted had told them, there in the center of the hill sat a chair, and it was huge.

Zale imagined the size of the demon who sat in it. It had to be larger than Nogar in his dragon form.

As they stood there watching, they saw soldiers coming out of the tents. They were elves, wearing armor, each one carrying shields, swords, and spears. Next they saw the dwarfs. Like the elves, they wore armor and carried swords and shields.

At each tent there was movement. They watched as trolls began coming out, each one of them with clubs in their hands. Then, they saw humans exiting tents carrying spears and shields. Each group numbered in the hundreds.

"It looks like we found the demon's real army," Nakobee commented.

"Yes, I would say the next battle will be more challenging. We should head back and let the others know."

Zale turned and headed back. Nakobee took another look before following.

Shaméd stood there staring at the army. He was trying to read a mind, any mind. He could get nothing. The minds he felt were thinking one thing: kill, destroy, hate, and death. Over and over it was repeated. The hatred was so strong, he could feel it building in the minds of those coming out of the tents. Humans, dwarfs, elves and trolls alike; each one coming out and heading toward them had the same thought: Kill!

He turned and walked back to the others.

As Zale walked down the hill, he stopped when he reached the middle. He looked out at the death spread out in front of him. He saw that they had killed a thousand of the horde and five beasts.

Zale knew he had to get his men to the top of this hill. Blowing his horn, his men gathered up their gear and began climbing the hill. Once there, they spread out and stood facing the enemy. He looked at Shaméd.

"You need to burn those bodies. Can you do it without our help?"

"Yes, it will not take long. I will do what I did at the wall. We might need the arrows."

Shaméd walked toward the dead, his hands raised. As he walked arrows and bodies filled the air.

Zale called for the archers to get ready. They watched as the enemy walked across the river straight for them.

Zale raised his arm, and as the enemy started up the hill, he dropped it. Arrows flew, but unlike before, most of the arrows bounced off the armor. The enemy kept advancing. It was not long before the enemy reached their line of defense.

The fighting was fevered. Shields and swords clashed. As the army was pushed back, Zale blew three short blasts on his horn. General Taylan and his men rushed in from the left.

The enemy was trapped between the two armies. It did not take long before the demon's army began to collapse. Some were running away and General Taylan and his men chased after them, killing them as they fled. Zale saw them crossing the river, going deeper into the enemy's territory.

The signal for retreat was two long blasts. Zale had to do it twice, before General Taylan called to his men. They stopped and returned back across the river.

The battle had lasted over an hour and there were many wounded and dead. Zale ordered them taken care of. When the wounded were moved back out of harm's way, Zale blew the horn, and what was left of his army slowly moved forward.

As they reached the river, the demons again sent out their army, this time with hundreds of beasts.

Suddenly there was a fireball screaming through the air. It crashed among the men on Zale's right, exploding, causing bodies to fly everywhere.

Then they saw another and where it came from. A demon, he was the largest one they had seen yet, standing off to the side on top of the hill. As his hands twisted and turned, he conjured up, then tossed balls of fire. His body was red and black and covered in scales. There were six large horns on his head.

Zale and his men kept going. As they entered the river, hundreds of soldiers, beasts, and small demons came charging toward them. As Zale and his men came out of the water, they had very little time to react.

Nakobee entered the water when suddenly he was hit by a fireball. It slammed into his chest with a force so hard, it picked him up and tossed him into the air, then slammed him down on the bank of the river.

Shaméd saw him land and ran over. He grabbed Nakobee by the arm, dragging him into the water. Another ball of fire came toward them, but Shaméd pushed Nakobee under the water and covered him with his body. The ball of fire came crashing down hitting him in the back. It slammed them down, but only bounced off the dragon skin he wore. Shaméd placed his hands on Nakobee's wound. The fireball had hit Nakobee in the chest. The amulet Nakobee wore, along with the metal chain, was fused into his flesh.

There was movement to Shaméd's right and Kinn appeared.

"Take him to Doctor T at once." Shaméd yelled.

Kinn picked Nakobee up, tossing him over his shoulder, took a step, and disappeared. Those around saw it and when Shaméd stood, they followed him toward the enemy.

Shaméd began making and tossing his own fireballs, but his were white. When the white fireballs hit the demons, they shrieked and began to disappear.

Shaméd hurriedly tossed fireballs at the enemy's army, smashing into them, and tossing them into the air, killing them. The demon army began to fall back.

As they came up the hill toward the large demon, Shaméd began creating a fireball. As he walked he rolled it around in his hands. It kept growing until it was too large to stay between them, and it floated up into the air.

When it was twice the size of him, Shaméd pitched it like a ball. It erupted on the demon, and with a loud scream it was gone. The other demons disappeared as well. The battle was all but won. They only had to stop the ones controlled by hate and kill the beasts.

General Taylan and his men handled what the men were calling the "hate" filled. Shaméd and Galan, along with the other elves, fought the beasts.

When the fighting was over, the dead belonging to the horde were piled together. Several pits were dug and their bodies placed in them. Wood and other burnable materials were placed on top. A fire was started on top of that.

Rae and Jym went searching for Jon. They found him on the other side of the demon's camp, far from the fighting and sitting near a fire, eating. His hair was a mess. He was covered in dirt and dried blood. What little clothing he had on would scarcely pass for rags.

They walked up, and Rae looked down and said, "You do know there was a battle going on, right?"

Jon looked up and grinned.

"Hi, I was wondering when you guys would show up. You should try this. It has a great flavor, but a funny aftertaste, but still, it's not bad."

He held out a large bone with burnt flesh.

Rae and Jym both grimaced and waved it away.

"No thanks. How did you get away?" Jym asked.

"There was this crazy old elf who was trying to read my mind. He wanted to get information from me. I kept telling him I did not know anything. The others wanted to kill me, but he kept telling them no. He said I was hiding something and if it killed him, he was going to find out what it was."

"Where is he?" Jym said as he bent down to Jon.

"Back in that tent over there."

Jon turned, pointing to a burning tent.

"I left him sitting on the ground babbling to himself. He started screaming and tossing things, and he sort of forgot about me. He was yelling to someone to get out of his head. I think he went even crazier.

I heard the fighting and knew you guys were coming, so I just left. I saw this fire and the food, and I was hungry. They did not feed me very much. I figured I would wait here for you."

Jym looked up at Rae, then back at Jon. Jym reached out and took the meat from him.

"Come on. We have better food back at camp."

Jon stood and Jym tossed the meat into the fire. They led Jon away. By the time they reached their camp, the wounded were being taken back to Keele by way of the Mirror Gate.

Nogar, in his human form, was talking with Zale, Shaméd, and Thom. Rae looked at Jym.

"He should go and see Doctor T. Take him and I will meet up with you as soon as I can."

Jym led Jon over to where the wounded were being led through the gate. Rae walked over to Zale, Nogar, and Shaméd. As he approached, he heard Thom talking.

"The fighting has stopped all across the world. I do not think the demons will return. We have looked everywhere on this world, and we have not seen any signs of them."

Nogar looked at each man, then focused on Zale.

"Then all that needs to be done is for these men to return to their homes. I leave that to you. When they have returned, you and the rest of our people will return to Rednog. I think Queen Kaila can finish building her city, and whatever else needs to be done."

"Maybe we could stay just a little longer to help?"

"There is no need. She will have plenty to do. Queen Kailee will need Queen Kaila to help rebuild her land, or pass it to her. And of course she will also have to deal with Quoin, and figure out what to do with Queen Liseran. You should tell her the best option is for her to take over Queen Liseran's land and her people. You should tell her to treat Queen Liseran as her younger sister. This will help heal any wounds among her people. There might be a few who would like to see the royal line restored, even if there is no chance of it happening. Now I will return and let the council know your plans. Finish what needs to be done here, and then come home."

Nogar turned and disappeared.

Zale looked at Shaméd and Thom. Then he saw Rae standing there.

Zale looked at them and said, "Well you heard him. We have a lot to do, so we better get to it. Thom, will you keep us updated on Nakobee's health?"

"Yes. As soon as I return I will find out if there is anything new. I will send you news as soon as I can."

Thom left them standing there. He walked over to where people were stepping through the Mirror Gate.

"We are not just going to leave Queen Kaila here to figure out how to rebuild this world, are we?" Rae said.

"Of course we are. Nogar gave me orders. What I heard him tell us, was to take care of what needs to be done here. That is just what we are going to do. Now what can we do to make sure she has a smooth transition in taking care of this Quoin?"

Zale smiled. Rae and Shaméd grinned as all three walked to Zale's tent.

Chapter Forty-Eight

Nakobee woke to pressure on his chest, as if something or someone was pressing down on it. He looked down and saw it wrapped in bandages.

He looked around and discovered he was in a room. There were several wounded people in beds around him.

A nurse saw he was awake, walked over and asked, "Good to see you are awake. Are you feeling any pain?"

"No pain, it just feels tight here." he said, as he pointed at his chest.

"That is to be expected. You were hit by a fireball, and were badly burned. Doctor T will be here soon to talk with you. He will tell you everything."

"Is the battle over? Where are Sword Master Zale and Lord Shaméd?"

"As far as I know, they are both still on your world. Master Kinn brought you here. He went back when we told him you were stable. Would you like something to drink?"

"Yes, thank you," Nakobee said.

She left and returned a few minutes later with a glass of water. She helped him sit up and handed it to him. Nakobee took a sip, and then set it on the table next to his bed.

He fell asleep, but woke up later and the lights were out. He looked around. He saw someone sitting in a chair at the end of his bed. At first he thought it was Shaméd, but then he realized it was King Nogar. He tried to sit up.

"King Nogar, forgive me. I did not know you were here."

Nogar stood and stepped closer, placing his hand on his shoulder.

"Stay down. I'm only here to see how you are doing. I was told you would have a full recovery and be able to return home in a couple of days."

Nakobee grunted as he said, "I'm glad to hear that. I have not been told anything."

"That is because you have been sleeping for the last four days. Your body took a beating and had a lot of healing to do."

Nakobee reacted to the words by trying to sit up again, but failed when Nogar pressed him back down.

Nakobee lay there looking up at Nogar.

"I have been here four days? What has happened on my world? I need to return and help with the war."

"The war is over. You won. Zale and Shaméd are making arrangements for your sister to take over your grandmother's land and the land of Queen Liseran."

"Has something happened to Queen Kailee?"

"Nothing bad. She was hurt and many of her warriors killed. Queen Kailee has returned to her village. I have sent people there to help. Now, if you are feeling up to it, I have a question to ask?"

"Of course, ask whatever you want."

"When you are back on your feet and have gone home to finish what you need to do, would you be interested in returning here to help build a group that would work between your world and mine? We have been trying to get your world to join our coalition, as you know. You would be a great asset in making that happen."

Nakobee lay there thinking. He had given up his right as First Sword. There really was no reason for him to stay there.

"Yes, I would like to help. I will return and help my sister, then come back here. I know she will do everything in her power to get the other leaders to join the alliance."

"Good. Now you get some more rest and we will talk when you return."

Nogar patted Nakobee's shoulder and walked out of the room. No one had awakened during the whole conversation. Nakobee closed his eyes and smiled. He was glad to know they had won.

Chapter Nine

Four weeks later, Nakobee was sitting in a chair talking with Doctor T.

The doctor stood there staring down at him.

"You do understand what I have told you? I didn't remove the stone when you arrived, because of the damage to your body. Now that you have recovered, I can remove it and heal the scars."

"Yes, I understood everything you told me. As I have said, I don't want it removed."

Doctor T looked at him. He didn't understand humans very well, and this one was worse than most.

Leaning forward, he said, "I understand that you want to return to your world. That is fine, but if you will let me, I can remove the stone and heal the scars. You will have to stay in a stasis chamber for at least two weeks. We can do it when you return, since you do not want to do it now."

"I understand what you have told me, and I have said the stone can stay where it is. Now if you have no more to say, I need to leave and go back to my world."

Doctor T pointed to the door. Nakobee stood and walked out. When he reached the Mirror Gate room, Shaméd was there waiting.

"You are looking better every time I see you. The scar on your chest will be a symbol of honor. Every time your people see you, they will ask about the battle and how you fought in the demon war."

"That is what I'm worried about. I do not remember much once I was hit by the fireball."

"It does not matter. Your people will look at you and think there stands a man who was hit by a demon's fireball, a man who is still alive. A man even a demon cannot kill."

Nakobee looked at Shaméd, smiled and said, "Maybe I should have you with me to tell the tale. You tell it so well."

They both laughed.

Reklan called out, "It is ready."

They looked at the Mirror and saw Queen Kaila's throne room. They walked over and per Nakobee's wishes, Shaméd stepped through first.

When Nakobee stepped through, he was surprised by the cheering. He turned and saw his sister and about twenty others standing there.

Shaméd stood next to him smiling.

"They knew you would not want anyone to make a fuss over you, so only a few are here to welcome you. The others are outside waiting."

Kaila came over and hugged him. When she was done she stepped back and spoke, "People, I give you the returning hero of the demon war, my brother, Nakobee."

Everyone began cheering again. Nakobee raised his hands.

"Stop. I'm not a hero. I did nothing more than any other warrior who was there. The real heroes are the ones who gave their lives so we would be free."

They came over one at a time to tell him how glad they were that he was back. When Galan came over, he took Nakobee's arm in one hand and placed his other on his shoulder.

"Your friends helped me return my men who had fallen to our homeland. King Leoren was surprised about my return and that of my men.

When I appeared out of nowhere, his soldiers came running. They stopped when my men appeared behind me carrying our fallen warriors. Then Galan Urikrana and his men came. They were helping with the rest of my men.

Urikrana stood before King Leoren and told him of the battle and how brave his men were. Then he said, since he had banished such a brave and noble warrior, that King Kivessin Ianthyra, of the golden elves, on the world of Ryland, his King was welcoming me, my men, and their families to his family. King Leoren just sat there staring at me and my men. I had told my father this before so as not to surprise him, as did my men with their families."

"What did King Leoren say?" asked Nakobee.

"He said nothing. When the ceremony was over, I asked my father if he wanted to return with me to this land, go to the world of Ryland, or stay there. He, along with several others, came here. We are going to stay and help you and your sister build your land and unite it with King Nogar's world and that of Ryland."

"Your men? What did they do?"

"My men, as well as their families, joined me. Even those that were spread out among the other battalions, came. It didn't make King Leoren happy, but he could say nothing, as the offer to me was also given to all my men. A total of two thousand warriors and their families came back with us.

You will even be more surprised to hear that Rujin and his men are staying. They asked Commander Ferdra if they could help work in the mountains. He agreed and they left yesterday to go there. It would seem that your sister now has a queendom with all the races, living and working together. This is something no one has ever been able to accomplish. Your land is now one of the strongest and largest on this world."

Nakobee was pleased to hear this news.

Galan, still holding Nakobee's arm, said, "The demons thought to pit us against each other and drive us further apart. What they did instead, was unite all the races. We are stronger together than apart."

"Did everyone return by way of the Mirror?" asked Nakobee.

"No. We were heading back and when we reached the ocean we saw a large ship flying the Zolotov flag. We went to the shore and there were small boats there. Lea was there with men. They came to bring us all back, including the wagons. The ship is large. It took us almost six months to reach the demon's land and only four weeks to return. These large ships will increase the wealth of your sister's land even more."

"I'm glad it was completed in time."

Nakobee talked with a few more people before going outside where more people were waiting. It was late when he was finally able to go to his room and sleep.

In the morning, he met with his sister and Leo as they ate. He stood at the end of the table.

"I hope you do not mind my interrupting you? I have some things I need to talk to you about, and did not want to wait to be announced."

"You are always welcome and you never need to ask to see me. What do you wish to talk about?"

"I was asked to go and live on Rednog to help build a better relationship between our worlds. Before I do that, I would like to visit Queen Kailee and Kouly. Then I would like to take some men and go through our land to make sure the people are safe and everything is coming together."

"That is a good plan. I'm planning to leave tomorrow to speak with Queen Liseran."

Nakobee had heard she was going to do this. He just didn't think she was going to do it so soon.

"Are you going to force her to give you Quoin?"

"I'm going to confront them and explain to her what he did. If she is as unfit as Lieutenant Lepton has told us, then we will force her out and take over her land. I'm sure most, if not all of her people will agree, once they know what Quoin did."

"I'm sure most already know. As for Lepton, I don't think he is a Lieutenant in her army any longer. I gave him that rank in our army. He will be stationed on the other side of the lake. We are building a small city there. Captain Lea will be in charge and make sure everything goes as planned."

"I'm glad to hear that Lea is now a Captain. I'm sure he will be happy building the city. He has always liked building things. As for your going to see Queen Liseran, I will go with you. Since you are leaving tomorrow, I will leave today to go visit Queen Kailee and Kouly. Then I will meet up with you in a day or so."

"You can call her grandmother when we are together. I'm sure Leo will not tell anyone," Kaila smiled at Nakobee as she spoke.

"It is a habit. Only you were allowed to call her grandmother. The one time I did, mother corrected me. I have never done it since."

Kaila shook her head. She had forgotten about the day when Nakobee had said grandmother. Their mother had slapped and scolded him, and told him to never call her that again. She was young and did not understand; she still didn't. She decided long before this that many of the old ways needed to be changed. This memory only confirmed that she had a lot to do.

"If you don't mind, I would like Galan to travel with me, unless you have other plans for him and his men?" continued Nakobee.

"I have none. I was going to ask you where best to use them. This will give you more time with him to help us figure that out."

"Then I will find him and we will leave as soon as we are ready."

Nakobee bowed his head and left. He went and found Galan. Galan quickly gathered his men. He told Nakobee he would get him a steed to ride. Nakobee only had to gather his supplies and weapons. Within an hour, they were heading for the cave.

Chapter Fifty

They arrived at his grandmother's village and when Nakobee saw what was left of it, his heart broke. Almost every home was gone, burned to ashes. There were people working on building new homes.

Five warriors watched as they came riding up. They saw that these men wore robes with the purple color belonging to the Zolotov clan. The group was formidable. There were sixty-one of them including Nakobee.

As Nakobee and the others rode in, a warrior stepped forward and called out, "Halt! Who are you and what do you want here?"

"I'm Nakobee, grandson to Kouly. I'm here to see him and Queen Kailee. Can you let them know that I'm here?"

The man stepped closer and looked up at Nakobee. When he saw the scar on his chest and the imbedded stone, he turned and called out, "Go get First Sword Kouly, and let Queen Kailee know that Nakobee is here to see her."

Another man ran off as Nakobee sat there and waited. The man who had spoken, looked up.

"We heard about the battle where you were hurt. I see the wound on your chest. You must have killed many to have won such a great wound. We also heard you were no longer First Sword to Queen Kaila. Why did you step down? Was it because of the wound?"

Nakobee would not have answered him, but he recognized the old man. He was an old friend of Kouly's. He had heard the stories about how the two of them would wander the land in search of adventure.

"I stepped down because I left to fight the demons. When we made Kaila Queen, she took another First Sword. As for the scar, it was from a demon's fireball. It is the worst wound I received from the war."

First Sword Kouly came walking up. When he was close, he called out, "Nakobee, it is good to see you."

Nakobee climbed down and Kouly gave him a hug.

Nakobee said, "I'm glad to see you are well. Your new scars tell of your great battles!"

Kouly smiled at him as he answered, "These are from simple battles. They are nothing compared to the ones we have heard about yours. Come, we can go see your grandmother. She will be happy to see you."

"I need to first find a place where my men can rest."

Kouly looked up at those still on their steeds. When he saw they were elves, he looked at Nakobee, then back at them.

"You travel with elves?"

"These are fine warriors. They fought by my side. There are no finer warriors I would ride with. Queen Kaila has given them equal rights and they are now people of Zolotov."

Kouly looked at them and nodded his head. He looked at the old man next to him.

"Take them to the river. Let them set up camp and bring them anything they need."

The old man waved at them and walked toward the river. Galan reached over and took the reins of Nakobee's steed and followed the old man.

Kouly led Nakobee to one of the huts that had been rebuilt. They went inside. Nakobee saw Queen Kailee sitting on a blanket, propped up by pillows.

Kouly called out when he saw Kailee.

"Look, Nakobee is here. Come sit close so we can all talk and be heard."

Nakobee entered, and four feet from Queen Kailee, he knelt to one knee. With his head bowed he spoke, "Queen Kailee, I thank the Creator you are well and I pray that the Creator gives you a long and healthy life."

He looked up when he was done speaking. He saw a smile on her face. He had never seen her smile like that before.

"Nakobee, son of my only daughter, Keely, I welcome you and I'm very glad to hear you lived after being hit by the demon's fireball."

Nakobee looked from her to Kouly.

"I was unaware so many had heard of my wound. It was only a few days ago that it happened."

"You forget, Sword Master Zale came here and explained what happened. He told us you would be in their hospital for at least two weeks. We know how bad the wound was. Your grandfather and I were very glad they acted so fast to save your life."

Unsure how to react to her words, he looked at Kouly, then back at her.

"I'm glad you both are doing well. Is there anything I or my men can do for you?"

"For me, there is nothing that you can do. For my people, yes there is. We lost over half of my warriors and every village is destroyed. If there is any way you can send people to help rebuild, I would be forever in your debt."

"I will contact some people as soon as I leave here. We will help all that we can," Nakobee said.

"I was hoping you would say that. I sent word to all those still alive to stop working on their villages and come here. When they arrive, I will inform them that I'm stepping down as their Queen and placing Queen Kaila as their new Queen. All this land, and what few people are remaining, will be hers."

Nakobee looked at Kouly. He saw the look in his eyes, the fear that his wife was dying.

"Queen Kailee, I'm sure the Creator will give you strength and you will grow strong, again."

"Nakobee, my boy, you do not have to call me Queen. Why have you never called me Grandmother?"

Now he was confused. He saw in her face what his own mother would have looked like if she had lived. Everyone said they were like sisters instead of mother and daughter.

"Queen Keely told me it was disrespectful for me to call you grandmother."

"My daughter was one for the old rules. That must have been the reason why you never gave me a hug or came near me. I thought you were trying to be a man like your father. He was the type of man who did not like to hug. If I had known, I would have told you to disobey her. I'm sorry for all those years you kept your distance. I think it is time for you to give your grandmother a hug. Not too hard, I'm old, after all."

She laughed as she put out her arms out toward him. He stood there unsure what to do. Kouly waved at him and he stepped forward. Bending down to his knees, he wrapped his arms around her body as her arms wrapped around him. She felt so frail. He tried to let go after a few seconds, but she would not let him go. Finally, she patted his shoulders and let go. He stood and stepped back. She looked up at him smiling.

"You are indeed your father's son. I remember giving him a hug, once. It was the only one he let me give him. Your shoulders are as broad as his."

Nakobee's mind was racing. He was confused about what he was experiencing. Emotions and feelings battled within him. He had never felt this before. His mind came back when he heard his name.

"Nakobee, are you all right? Is the wound bothering you? Do you need to rest?" Queen Kailee called out, "Bring some wine and water for Nakobee."

He saw the concern on her face and smiled.

"Grandmother, I'm fine. I was just overcome by everything that has happened."

An old man and a young woman entered. The old man was carrying a jug of wine and a jug of water. The young girl had a tray with three cups.

They placed it before Queen Kailee and poured wine in each cup. Kouly picked them up and handed one to her, the other to Nakobee.

"To family, the one thing that binds us together."

Nakobee took a long drink, then Kouly told him to sit. He did and they talked for the next two hours. They stopped when he saw Queen Kailee was getting tired.

"Grandmother, I must take my leave, I have men waiting for me. Tomorrow we have an early start. We are meeting Queen Kaila as she makes her way to meet with Queen Liseran."

"Is she going to demand the head of her First Sword? He was a major factor in all of this. I cannot believe a Queen would sit by and let even her First Sword cause so much pain to her people."

Nakobee stood.

"I'm sure Queen Kaila has plans for him. Now I must leave. I thank you for your time and I will be praying to the Creator for your health."

Nakobee gave a bow to her, then turned and left. Outside, he stopped, took a deep breath and let it out slowly. His mind had already come to a decision. As he walked, he placed his hand over the wound covering the stone. He was not sure it if still worked, even though Doctor T had said it would.

"Sword Master Zale, I need to talk with you."

He said it twice and headed for Galan and his men. When he reached the shore, Zale was there talking with Galan and the others.

Galan looked at him and called out, "Nakobee, looked who appeared out of thin air."

Nakobee looked at Zale, who sat there holding a drink. Zale stood, took a long drink emptying the cup, and handed it to Galan.

"If you will excuse us, there is something I need to discuss with Nakobee."

He began walking away and Nakobee looked at his back and then followed him. When they were far enough away, Zale stopped and looked at Nakobee.

"I talked with Nogar. He took your demands to the council and they all have agreed to them."

Nakobee looked at him confused.

He asked, "What demands? I have made no demands?"

"Yes, you did. You told them to me. I took them to Nogar. He in turn told the council if they wanted you and this world, they would have to do what you demanded. They have agreed. So it is done. You have nothing to worry about."

"What do you mean I have nothing to worry about? I have no idea what you are talking about."

Zale, frowning at him said, "Your grandmother, Queen Kailee. She and your grandfather will be taken to Rednog and examined. Everything that can be done will be done. They will stay and live on Rednog for as long as they live. There will be people sent here to help build homes for her people. It will not be as big as Keele, but it will be strong and safe.

Since Queen Kaila is now the Queen of over three quarters of the humans on this world, she stands a better chance of convincing those on this world to join the alliance. That was what you told me, wasn't it?"

"When? I have not talked with you in days."

"Yes, you did. When you left the meeting with Queen Kailee. You talked with me then."

"I…"

Sword Master looked at him and spoke slowly, "Yes, you did. You contacted me by way of the AM-U-LET. You know, the one embedded in your chest. The one that records everything around you. Even now, as we speak, it is recording."

Nakobee looked at Zale. Zale was nodding his head toward his chest. Then Nakobee understood. Zale had seen and heard everything that had happened. Zale knew what he was going to ask, so he went and talked with Nogar. Nogar went to the council and told them they had to give Nakobee what he demanded, even though he had not demanded anything. And what they had agreed to was beyond what he was going to ask. All of it took maybe a couple of days, but to him on this world, only minutes had passed.

Nakobee stood straighter, placing his hands on his hips, he looked at Zale.

"I'm glad they agreed. Thank King Nogar for his help, and tell him I will be back on Rednog in a few days. I still have the matter with Quoin to take care of."

"He knows and understands. Now if there are no more demands, I must go. There are still some things I have to get started."

Before Nakobee could say anything, Zale turned and disappeared. He walked back to the fire and Galan.

In the morning he walked over and saw Kailee and Kouly. They were standing in front of their hut.

"Good morning, Queen Kailee and First Sword Kouly. I'm glad to see you both. As I said yesterday, I need to leave and catch up with Queen Kaila. It is a long ride, so the earlier we start the better."

"We are sad to see you leave. But we know what it takes to build a strong land."

"Yes, there is a lot to do and treaties to be made. I have made arrangements for people to come and help rebuild your village. They will be here soon, so do not worry."

As he spoke, people and material began to appear off in the distance. Kouly pointed and they all turned to see what he was pointing at.

"It looks as if your people are arriving already."

"So it would seem. They will be coming to take you both for an examination on Rednog, also.

Now I must leave. I will see both of you soon. Take care and may the Creator keep you both safe."

"You as well Nakobee. Take care."

Queen Kailee leaned on her husband's shoulder. Nakobee climbed up on his steed and waved. Then he turned and led the others away.

Chapter Fifty-One

Six days later, they met up with Queen Kaila and her group. There were three hundred men with her: fifty dwarfs, fifty elves, and two hundred humans. They were all in armor, even the humans. They each wore the colors of the tribe Zolotov: purple and green.

There were ten wagons at the end of the group. Nakobee found his sister riding out front with Leo, her First Sword, and four riders behind them. Nakobee saw her and smiled. She rode tall and proud.

As he rode up, he greeted her, "Hello Queen Kaila. I see you are getting used to riding."

She smiled.

"It does take some getting used to."

"I know. I hurt for two days when I first rode one. How are you holding up?"

"They made me a special saddle. It has extra padding. Maybe they can do that for you?"

She grinned at him.

"That will not be necessary, I'm fine now."

"How was your visit with grandmother and grandfather?"

"It went very well thank you. We hugged and we talked for a couple of hours. Grandmother is not feeling very well. She told me to let you know that she is giving you her land and people."

"Master Zale informed me of her decision. He also said you demanded they be taken to Rednog and looked after."

He started to speak but stopped when she held up her hand.

"I told him it was a good thing, because I would have demanded the same."

"Yes, I'm sure you would have."

They rode on talking about what was happening in Keele and the improvements to Ondo. They made camp two hours before sundown.

Early in the morning there was a commotion. Everyone was on their feet with their weapons drawn.

Galan walked up to Nakobee and Queen Kaila.

"We found a group of people. They were trying to go around us. They are being brought in so you can speak with them."

A few minutes later, a ragtag group of men, women, and children were brought in. When they saw Nakobee, they threw themselves to the ground.

They were yelling and screaming, "Don't kill us, please don't kill us."

Queen Kaila looked at them, then Nakobee. She dismounted. Her face showed her confusion.

"I think you scared them. What did you do?"

"I have done nothing to them, I have never been here."

Galan reached down and grabbed the arm of a young man. When he was up on his feet, he looked at Galan and screamed louder.

Galan shook him and yelled at him, "Shut up. Why are you screaming?

"Please do not kill me."

He was shaking and tears streamed down his face.

Galan looked at him and asked, "Why are you people so scared?"

"First Sword Quoin said you were coming to kill all of us. He told everyone to prepare for war. We were running away so you would not kill us."

Galan looked at Nakobee. He rolled his eyes. Queen Kaila walked over to the man. She placed her hand on his shoulder.

"We are not here to harm any of you. We were coming here to see if Queen Liseran is ok. Can you tell me if your Queen is well?"

He looked at her, then at Nakobee.

"He will not kill me?"

"My brother will not harm you. Why would you think that?"

"Because a demon came and told First Sword Quoin and everyone in the village that he survived a fireball from the fire demon. The demon said it meant he was unable to be killed by any human. Then the demon told us he was coming to kill us for working with the demons."

"They told you Nakobee was coming here to kill you?" asked Queen Kaila.

"The demon did not give his name. They said they did not know it. We would know him because of how large he is and the scar on his chest."

As the man spoke, he pointed at Nakobee.

Everyone looked at Nakobee. Galan burst out laughing. Everyone turned and looked at him.

Queen Kaila looked at him confused. She had never heard of an elf laughing.

She asked him, "Why is this funny?"

"Because Nakobee has become a legend. You have become even more powerful because of Quoin and the demon."

Galan looked at Nakobee and said, "I wonder why he told them you were coming. You did not even know, did you?"

"I had not decided until after I returned. I told Leo and Kaila I would meet them after I saw our grandparents."

Galan looked at Leo and Kaila and tilted his head. He stood there thinking. There was a movement next to Queen Kaila. One of the human warriors came charging at her.

Galan yelled, "Look out."

The man lunged at Queen Kaila. Leo grabbed her and pulled her back, and spun her around with his back to the attacker. The man's knife drove deep into Leo's back. All three fell to the ground with Leo on top of Kaila.

Nakobee ran forward but before he could grab the man, he had stabbed Leo four more times.

Taking hold of the man's neck with one hand, Nakobee raised him up into the air and smacked the man's wrist. There was a loud snapping sound, and the knife fell away. Then Nakobee reached out to grab the man's leg. He raised him above his head and brought him down across his knee, breaking his back.

Galan lifted Leo off of Kaila. The people that saw what Nakobee had done, dropped to their knees and stared.

Nakobee tossed the dead body to the ground. Turning, he looked at Galan, then his sister who was holding Leo in her arms, crying.

Galan walked over to Nakobee and whispered, "Be careful, we need to see if there are any more hidden among our men."

Nakobee took a deep breath. As he slowly let it out he said, "I will contact Sword Master Zale. He can send a Thorn. We will find any others who have been turned."

Nakobee walked over to Kaila. He reached down and took her hand.

"We will put him in the tent. Do you still want to continue?"

She looked up and in a low voice said, "I want this Quoin killed. I do not care how you do it, I just want him dead."

She slowly stood and walked back to her tent. As she walked she spoke so everyone could hear her.

"We leave in an hour. Feed these people and send them on their way."

Everyone began moving at once. Galan took the people and led them to the cook fires. The cook was already getting food ready.

The camp was in a big uproar. Men were running around packing. Sword Master Zale showed up with two men, and Jrick. The two men picked up Leo and followed Sword Master Zale back through the Mirror Gate. Nakobee just sat there staring. Jrick walked around the warriors. He read each of their minds. He found two more that were infected by a demon.

Jrick nodded his head at Galan, and said, "There are no more." Then taking a step, he disappeared.

Galan took them away and killed them. Their armor was placed in a wagon.

When they were ready to leave, Kaila sat on her steed and as always rode out front, the only difference was that Galan and nine elves rode with her.

It took three days to reach Fendal. As they approached, they saw people running from the fields to the village. Warriors were standing out front.

They stopped two hundred feet from the small wooden wall that surrounded the village. Queen Kaila sat there staring at the men behind it.

She rose up in her stirrups and called out, "I wish to speak with First Sword Quoin. I'm Queen Kaila. Bring him to me, now."

The tone in her voice said she was not going to wait long. A man ran away. A few minutes later, a man dressed in metal armor came walking up, stopping next to the wall. He stood there looking out at her.

"I do not know any Queen Kaila. What do you want?" he yelled.

"You do not know me yet, but you fear my brother. I'm here because you made a deal with the demons. They lost, and now we are here to see that you pay for your crimes. If Queen Liseran and her people surrender you to us, then she and her people will come to no harm. If she does not, then every man, woman, and child behind those walls will be ripped apart and fed to the wild beasts. Have I made myself clear?"

The man laughed as he answered, "I still do not know you or your brother. We are not afraid of your little army. We outnumber you three to one."

She raised her hand and Nakobee dismounted. He placed his cloak across his steed. He walked, only stopping when he stood ten feet from the wall. Nakobee drew his sword and pointed it at Quoin.

"I challenge you, First Sword Quoin, to a one on one battle. Come out here and face me. If you win, Queen Kaila will take her men and leave. She will promise never to return. If I win, however, then this land will become hers to do with as she sees fit. Do you accept my challenge?"

Quoin looked out at him, then he saw the scar. So did his men. Within minutes everyone in the village, all one thousand men, women, and children knew who stood out there.

Quoin looked at his men and yelled, "Kill him."

No one moved. They stood there looking at Nakobee then at Quoin. Before he could do anything, they dropped their weapons and ran.

Quoin grabbed a spear, then threw it at Nakobee. The spear dug into the dirt a few feet from Nakobee.

Nakobee slowly walked forward. Quoin moved back. When Nakobee reached the wall, he reached out and grabbed a fence post. Then he pulled and all the muscles in his arm and back bulged. The post came out of the ground. The poles around it fell, leaving a gaping hole in the wall. Nakobee stepped through.

"Face me. Who knows? You might win. If not, at least you will die like a warrior."

"I cannot kill you. The demon said no human could kill you."

"Then you should at least die fighting," Nakobee said as he took another step.

Quoin took two scuttling steps back for every one Nakobee took forward. When Quoin took another step he bumped into his men. They were standing there in a line, keeping him from going any further.

One man called out to Nakobee, "You said if you fight him and win, this land will belong to Queen Kaila. Will you and your Queen kill us?"

"Our quarrel is with him. He has mistreated you and Queen Liseran for years. He will pay for everything he has done. So to answer your question, when I win, no harm will come to any of you as long as you do not help him or interfere with our fight and swear loyalty to Queen Kaila."

"Then we will stand here as is the custom. The two of you will fight within the circle of honor."

The men slowly moved out creating a large circle around them.

"Now you must face me. Should I tell you what I did to your brother?"

Quoin looked at him, in a low voice he said, "You killed my brother?"

"I captured him and after he proved to me that he was a brave warrior, Queen Kaila gave him his own village. He is a better man than you."

Quoin roared as he jumped forward swinging his blade. Nakobee blocked it, shoving him away. Quoin regained his footing. He stood there glaring at Nakobee. His face grew darker and he began to mumble under his breath.

Quoin swung again, Nakobee blocked it. Each time Quoin lunged or came after Nakobee, he would block it and just stand there.

Nakobee looked at Quoin and asked, "You wear the armor of an elf. Where did you steal it?"

"I did not steal it. It was given to me by the demon Gull."

"Then when I find him, I will kill him, too."

Quoin charged and for the next few minutes their blades clashed. Nakobee blocked each swing. He could see Quoin was getting tired.

Quoin lunged at Nakobee, again. He blocked him, and as Quoin moved by Nakobee reached out, grabbed him by the neck, and tossed him to the side.

When Quoin stood he was even more livid. He once more started mumbling. As he circled Nakobee, his mumbling grew louder. The dirt began to swirl around them. Nakobee's skin began tingling. Then the dirt became thicker. All at once, it shot up into his eyes.

Nakobee raised his arm to brush it away. Quoin lunged, but Nakobee blocked the blade but not the knife in Quoin's hand. The knife sliced Nakobee's arm. Nakobee brought his sword back and the blade sliced between the armor on Quoin's arm. Blood shot out from the wound. Quoin stepped back, dropping his sword and grabbing his arm. Nakobee, with his eyes closed, drove his blade into Quoin's neck. He felt it enter and he pulled it back. Quoin fell to the ground dead.

The men of the village moved back. They had no weapons to drop, as they had already dropped them when they ran. One by one they knelt down.

There was a sound behind Nakobee and he turned to face it. His eyes were hurting from the sand.

"It is me. Let me clear the dirt out of your eyes."

Galan poured water over his eyes.

Queen Kaila walked over to the men. Six elf warriors were by her side.

"Take me to Queen Liseran."

One man stood and led her and the six elves to the hut where their Queen was waiting. When Queen Kaila entered, she saw their queen sitting on a rug. She was playing with dolls. All of her anger faded.

"Good day, Queen Liseran. I'm Queen Kaila. May I play with you and your dolls?"

Liseran looked up, her face showed confusion at this strange woman who stood there. After hearing Kaila say she wanted to play, she shook her head yes.

"Yes, come and play. Quoin never lets anyone play with me."

When Kaila sat down next to her she asked, "Would you like to come live with me?"

"I don't think Quoin will let me."

"You do not have to fear him any longer. He went away and will no longer hurt you or your people."

Queen Liseran sat there smiling at her, as she held her doll close to her chest.

"I would like to go live with you."

"Then it is settled, you will come live with me. We will leave as soon as we make sure your people have enough food to last the winter."

The next day, Queen Kaila surrounded by elves, stood in front of the people. The people had gathered there and were waiting to hear their fate.

"All of you now belong to the Zolotov clan. I'm your new Queen. Liseran will be coming to live with me. She will not be harmed and she will live a long life. Any of you can come see her. For now, all of you must rebuild your homes. Do not worry about tariffs at this time. I will return one day to ask you for them when you've regained your wealth and made your land prosperous again.

I leave you five bags of gold, one for each village. You will send men out to give each village theirs. I will know if you do not do as I ask. I require loyalty and devotion to a greater cause. Do not disappoint me."

Queen Kaila left three days later. They had discovered all the gold Quoin had collected in his hut. It was packed in two wagons and they headed home. The first night while they camped, Kaila called Nakobee to her.

"Will you become my First Sword again?"

"No, I'm leaving. There are good men here. I know you will not find one that you love as you did Leo, but you will find someone. Whoever you pick as your First Sword, let him know he will not be your mate. After some time, you may find someone you care for. Then you can take him for your mate."

"Do you know of anyone who would make a good First Sword?" asked Kaila.

"Talk with Galan. He is half human. He would give his life for you and our land. I trust him."

"I will think about it. When will you leave?"

"I'm leaving now."

"Then I will say goodbye."

She stood and they hugged. The air swirled and Shaméd stood there.

"Are you ready?"

Queen Kaila turned to Shaméd.

"Remember your promise."

Shaméd nodded his head at her. Nakobee was unsure of what that was about. He turned and gave his sister a kiss, then stepped over next to Shaméd. They both took a step and disappeared.

Made in the USA
Middletown, DE
09 September 2023

37719871R00208